Missed Periods

A Novel

Denise Horner Mitnick

iUniverse, Inc.
Bloomington

Missed Periods
A Novel

Cover design and author photo by Emily Mitnick

iUniverse books may be ordered through booksellers or by contacting:

iUniverse
1663 Liberty Drive
Bloomington, IN 47403
www.iuniverse.com
1-800-Authors (1-800-288-4677)

ISBN: 978-1-4502-9502-4 (sc)
ISBN: 978-1-4502-9503-1 (hc)
ISBN: 978-1-4502-9504-8 (e)

Library of Congress Control Number: 2011901926

Printed in the United States of America

iUniverse rev. date: 07/11/2011

For Stephen, Emily, and Lizzie
My loves

Acknowledgments

This book has had many inspirations and iterations. I wish to thank my muses, encouragers, and those whose lives provided the proverbial grist for the mill.

I am forever indebted to my husband and best friend, Stephen. He urged me to continue when I wasn't sure "the girls" had anything worthwhile to say. He knew there was more to the story than whining and, in fact, there was a lot more. We are true partners in the possible, and I still cannot believe, even after all these years, that we found each other in this great big world.

My daughters, Emily and Lizzie, are just the best of it all for me. I am amused, amazed, and perennially entertained by them. Each has grown into a beautiful woman, full of dreams and goals to make the world a better place. Their unending energy and devotion to their respective crafts inspire me to believe the world is truly a better place for women today than it was yesterday and, thanks to them, it will be even grander tomorrow.

My parents, siblings, and friends have all patiently waited for a book to emerge. I hope it meets their expectations, as they deserve a great story. I want to offer a special thanks to my mom, who endured endless hours of phone conversations when I was up to my eyeballs in alligators. She always believed this day would come.

Finally, thank you to the many women who earned a place in history as they struggled and toiled to find a collective voice that made equality seem simple, work and home congruous, and feminism, in all its guises, worthwhile.

Denise Horner Mitnick
Philadelphia, PA
June 2010

Chapter One

Charlotte was awakened by the first crack of light that seeped through the plantation shutters in her bedroom. She rolled over to look at the clock but couldn't see the digital numbers because of the clutter on Charles's nightstand. The hum of his snoring machine muffled any noise she would make as she found her way to their bathroom in the filtered dawn light of the bedroom suite. Her outstretched arm felt the footboard's post. Shuffling along to the other end of the king-sized bed, she turned and reached for the armoire that housed the media center. Around the corner would be the open bathroom door. She carefully pulled the heavy door behind her, quietly turned the knob so it didn't make any noise upon shutting, and flipped the light switch. She winced at the reflection of bright lights in the mirror that ran the length of the elongated marble double-vanity. She brushed her teeth, barely running the water above a drip—spit and rinse. She splashed cold water on her face and dabbed it dry with the hand towel she'd placed by her side of the vanity. She ran her fingers through her hair, scowling at the persistent tangles. She'd wait to use one of the downstairs toilets so as to not awaken Charles.

Charlotte turned off the bathroom lights and reversed her path through the dark bedroom like a night stalker. This time she felt her way to the solid wood double doors, which led to the upstairs hall that overlooked the entrance hall on the first floor. She grabbed her silk robe from the chaise lounge in the corner near the doors, where she had deposited it the night before. Charles turned. She halted. The humming machine resumed, and Charlotte made her quiet exit.

"Ah, coffee and quiet," she whispered as she glided down the grand wood-carved staircase to the center hall. The smell of freshly brewed coffee permeated the air, and she followed its aroma, flipping light switches on her path to the kitchen. She made a stop in the center hall powder room, noting the dusty gilded light fixture on her way out. She threw the paper hand towel that was emblazoned with a gold-embossed *W* for Wentworth in the kitchen trash compactor. She stretched, taking a deep sniff of the coffee.

How sweet of Charles to preset the coffeemaker, she thought, pouring her first cup of the day and taking a long sip. *His coffee is so good!* Situated to the right of the coffeemaker on the black granite countertop was a small television. She turned it on, adjusting the volume to low and clicking the remote to one of the early newscasts. The news became background noise as she turned to face the work island in the center of the huge kitchen.

The island resembled an old workbench and had been made from rafters of a demolished mid-nineteenth-century barn. The top surface was finished with the same black granite as the rest of the designer kitchen. Big pots and baskets filled the shelf just above the floor level, and drawers just under the granite top housed ladles, knives, and other tools for a serious cook. The island was also home to Charlotte's miniature orchids, which were planted in an antique feeding trough in the center of the island. Charlotte took a few sips of the black coffee and poked her well-manicured finger into the soil. "Perfect! Not too dry, not wet," she said, satisfied she'd figured out just the right amount of watering necessary.

Each morning after checking her orchids, Charlotte would inspect her property. She enjoyed this morning ritual and valued the time as a way to clear her head and prepare for her day. On this morning, she retrieved her periwinkle quilted jacket from the coat closet near the kitchen—the springtime air was nippy at this hour of the morning, and she was still wearing her nightgown and silk robe as she slipped out of the side door after turning the house alarm off.

The sun had not quite fully risen and the moon lingered in the retreating night sky, adding a hint of mystery to her morning meandering. Crocuses were giving way to daffodils, which would soon be followed by forsythia. Charlotte crouched down to inspect what she thought was a small plant peering through a pile of winter debris. She moved some of the decaying leaves and dirt, smiling to find the nascent plant beginning its thrust through the soil. She wiped her dirty hands on the already soiled jacket and continued sipping her now-lukewarm coffee.

As she walked the rear half of her private acre lot, she heard the distant drone of cars on their early commute from Penn Valley into Philadelphia. She sat in an Adirondack chair at the foot of an old maple tree, where she had a view of her favorite gardens. She leaned her head back and scanned the top of the old maple, its pregnant leaf buds awaiting the first hot day to burst into spring. She heard some chirping birds, which were probably looking for worms. Charlotte giggled at the playful scampering of several squirrels that had emerged from their long winter hibernation; one had its cheeks full of nuts.

She pulled the blue jacket tighter around her neck and shivered from the morning chill. Picking up her damp silk robe, she started toward the side door. She had just closed the gate to the rear yard when a truck pulled into the driveway, with its headlights shining directly into her eyes.

"Darn it, the driveway gate was left open!" she said aloud, turning quickly to retreat into the rear yard. She ran along the flagstone path, gathering up her long robe in her arm, revealing her long, lean legs. She stumbled up the large stone steps that framed a garden on either side of the rear terrace—clogs were not made for running—and pounded on the glass French doors.

"Charles! Charles!" She could hear men's voices and the rattling of what sounded like a ladder being moved. "I think the painters are here!" she yelled. She tried the handle, knowing the door was most likely still locked from the night before. She saw Charles's salt-and-pepper hair through the window. "Hurry," she reprimanded as she pounded on the door for effect.

"What's all the fuss, Charlotte?" he asked as he unlocked the door and let her in. "It's only the painters, here to do some touch-up from the winter storm damage. You can't be this panicked over the painters, can you?" He kissed her on her head as she looked around to see where the painters had erected their ladder. "They're starting in the front. That's where most of the peeling is," he reassured her, sensing her discomfort.

"Oh, my goodness, I was so startled! And look at me! I'm in my pajamas, I have no makeup on, and I'm wearing this ridiculous get-up," she said, out of breath. "Did you forget to close the driveway gate again, Charles? Gosh, you know how I relish my privacy. I hate when people just enter the property without being buzzed in."

Charles rolled his eyes and began his morning espresso ritual, which included grinding fresh beans. The volume on the television had been adjusted to accommodate the espresso machine.

"Do you mind if I turn this off?" Charlotte asked. With his back to her, focusing on his espresso production, he didn't answer. "Charles," she raised her voice over the cacophony. "Are you watching this?" Still, he didn't answer. She turned it off, and the grinding came to a halt.

"I was watching that," he said. "Why'd you turn it off?" Charles moved to turn the television on again. The bottom rungs of the painters' ladder were visible through the dining room window. Charlotte moved quickly to close the door joining the two rooms. It swung back and forth a few times until it settled into place, not quite aligned with the door jam.

"Do you think we could talk instead of having that thing on?" Charlotte asked in an annoyed tone. "Isn't it enough that I sleep listening to your snoring machine humming, and all day long I hear your fax machine, phones, and e-mail reminders? I mean, really, do you think we could actually just visit over our coffees one morning? Like this morning? And possibly with no noise?"

Charles ignored her as he examined the thin layer of foam at the top of his cup of espresso.

"Charles, I am talking to you! You are so arrogant! I have no idea how you function or why people take to you. You must not treat everyone else like you treat me. I guess I have to pretend I'm a real estate deal. You know, it's not funny how I tell people you wouldn't notice me even if I set myself on fire!"

Charles took a sip from his espresso and sighed as he looked up at her. "The television was on when I came downstairs, like every morning. I turned it up so I could hear it while I made my espresso, like every morning." He took another sip from the tiny cup. "I make a damn good espresso." He sighed again and then said, "Charlotte, please stop with the setting-yourself-on-fire comment. It's really getting old. Why are you in such a crappy mood today? What could I have possibly done in the twenty-two minutes I've been awake?" he asked, glancing at the wall clock.

"You just don't get it, do you? I was outside, having my quiet time—peace and quiet. And then I was startled because, despite what you think you said, you didn't tell me the painters were coming, or I wouldn't have been outside in my pajamas. And what the heck are they doing here at seven o'clock in the morning?"

"They are working hard, and I'd hardly call that"—he pointed to her silk robe—"pajamas." He used his finger to wipe the inside of the espresso cup, then licked his finger.

"Stop that!" yelled Charlotte. "You are so uncouth. How can you maintain such a successful business when you behave this way? Do you lick your cup when you go out with your investors?" She took a deep breath. "Gosh, Charles, you really got my morning off to a chaotic start! You know, you could at least have said you're sorry."

"For what? What should I say I'm sorry about? You need to calm down," said Charles.

Their sixteen-year-old daughter, Betsy, came bouncing into the kitchen. "God, you guys. Can we have one morning when you're not fighting?" she whined.

"*We* aren't fighting," said Charles. "Your mother is yelling at me again. That's not fighting."

Charlotte ignored his comment and instead turned her attention to Betsy. "Nice outfit," she said sarcastically. "Where is all the new stuff I bought you for your birthday?"

"This is it, Mom. You *did* buy me this. What's wrong? I don't get it. You buy me the stuff. We fight when you buy it, but you buy it anyway. What? So you can pick on me? I mean, if you don't want me to dress in hippie clothes, then why do you buy them for me?" She opened the kitchen drawer to take out a power bar.

"That's not enough for breakfast, Betsy. Don't you have a calculus test this morning? You need protein," Charlotte said in a concerned voice.

"This *is* protein," Betsy said, shaking the power bar at Charlotte. "God, I can't even choose the right breakfast. Is there anything I do that's right by you? You know what? Don't answer that because I don't care." Then, walking toward the center hall, she yelled loudly, "Dad! We're going to be late! Let's go!"

"Betsy, I wish you'd tuck that shirt into the skirt. It just looks so sloppy, and the cami isn't outerwear. I bought it for you to wear under lightweight blouses, not as a top. I'm not negotiating. Button the blouse, at the very least. And where are your shoes? Sneakers are for jeans or sports, not skirts."

"Stop it, Mom! Just stop it! Why can't you be like Emily Wilmet's mom? She doesn't constantly pick on Emily, and she even let her pierce her nose. Her mom is a doctor, too. She actually does something all day besides think up ways to torture her kids."

"Well, I'm sorry you think all I do is think of ways to torture you and your brothers."

"Not your beloved Elliot or James," Betsy said. "Just me. You just like to torture me, probably because I'm the only one besides Dad who's still at home."

Charlotte continued, "Well, whoever you think I set out to torture from all my *boredom*, I actually have a lot going on. I serve on the board of the Art Museum, I manage the administrative part of Daddy's business, I help out my friend who happens to be our senator, and I run our lives, yours included. Laundry, gardening, bills, travel, college stuff, holiday planning—all of it is my deal!"

"Puh-lease! You have people for your people," said Betsy, "like those guys out there today. And, by the way, how about a heads-up when freaky-looking old men are going to be peering through my window first thing in the morning!" Betsy threw away the power bar wrapper and stepped into the center hall, "*Dad!* Let's go."

Charlotte took two steps toward her. "I didn't schedule the painters."

Betsy rolled her eyes.

"Quiet down, Betsy. I'm coming," Charles said firmly as he adjusted his tie.

"Dad, we are always late. I'm never going to get parking privileges if I'm late every day."

"You'll be fine. You are not late *every* day," answered Charles. "And besides, whoever said anything about taking the car to school once you get your license?" He went to make a second cup of espresso.

"Charles, you don't have time," said Charlotte. Betsy started toward the garage, where she would assume the relished role of every sixteen-year-old: driver. Charlotte called after her, "I'll be picking you up in the Suburban after school, so no driving home today. I have an appointment, and I need my car."

Betsy turned and scowled. "That car is a gas-guzzler and you shouldn't be driving it. Why don't you get rid of the damn thing?" She looked out the side door to be sure the painters' truck wasn't blocking the garage.

Charles shoved a piece of a power bar in his mouth and shrugged at Betsy's comment. He grabbed his jacket and Betsy's backpack, which she'd left on the floor in her enthusiasm to drive.

"I'm with Betsy on this one," said Charles, "but not for the same reasons. I just don't think your car suits your image." He kissed Charlotte on the head. "Someone with thoroughbred legs like yours ought to be swinging them out of a sleek sedan like a Jag or a Mercedes. Not a clunky Suburban." She frowned. "I mean it, Charlotte. Pearls, blazers, and button-down collars don't jibe with a Suburban. Nor do pressed khakis, for that matter," he added. "You have so much power in that conservative, sleek look of yours." He came back for a quick kiss. "God, you are one gorgeous woman!"

"I don't want power in my looks. I want power in my brain and my actions," she said as he juggled the backpack and his briefcase while trying to finish eating the power bar.

"Think about it—the whole image thing," he suggested, making his way to the garage.

"I have nothing that implies 'thoroughbred' in me," she insisted. "I'm a simple girl from the country."

He laughed, putting down his briefcase to look for his keys. "Yeah, real simple—that's what comes to mind when people think of you! I'm taking you for some test drives. Then you'll be convinced."

Betsy honked the horn. "Dad, let's go!"

"Does she have the motor running with the garage door closed?" yelled Charlotte as she hurried down the hallway to see for herself.

"I'll handle this," said Charles firmly. "You need to stop picking on her, Charlotte. She's sixteen, and she's not like our sons. Let go of some of this petty stuff!" The door slipped out of his cluttered hands, and it shut in her face.

"That's not petty!" she yelled through the door, locking it from the inside. She heard the garage door open. She looked down at the morning paper, which the painters or Charles had left on the side door stoop. She opened the door, quickly grabbing the paper. The front page photo was an image of her college friend, Jennifer Holmes Bartlett. The caption read "Senator Visiting Philly Neighborhoods Today."

Chapter Two

Charlotte was running late, as usual. She had a standing appointment at the hair salon every Thursday but was never on time, even though the salon was minutes from her house. She crossed the art deco style bridge that connected the suburbs to the city, and turned right onto Main Street in Manayunk, a Philadelphia neighborhood. The car rumbled over the partially exposed cobblestones, and Charlotte was reminded of the city's history.

"Don't even think of pulling out," she muttered as she passed a parked car whose driver was leaning into his side-view mirror, waiting for a chance to pull into traffic. She came to the first traffic light and stopped as a group of women crossed the street. It was the end of the business lunch hour, and these women apparently were in no hurry to return to their offices. They looked at her oncoming Suburban as if they weren't sure it was actually going to stop. Charlotte sat up high in the big SUV and realized how intimidating the car could appear to pedestrians. She smiled a reassuring smile, letting the women know she saw them. They continued their banter with each other as they crossed in front of her. A straggler who was part of the group came running out of the restaurant directly behind the women and shouted, "Wait! I got them!" She was waving her glasses, and as the five women all turned to look at their friend, the light changed to green, and the impatient driver behind Charlotte honked his horn. But she motioned to the women, indicating she would wait for them to cross before moving her rig.

Charlotte took notice of other passersby as she carefully navigated the old, narrow street. There were young women pushing strollers, parents toting babies in snugglies, and friends walking arm in arm. Business people of all ages walked with a greater urgency, some talking on cell phones or checking their messages and e-mails. College students, taking a break from classes, were lined up at the local coffee shops and hamburger stops. Many people were hanging out in stores and cafes, but it was the middle-aged women to whom Charlotte gave the most notice.

"Gosh, what was *she* thinking when she got dressed this morning?" Charlotte said aloud about a jolly-looking woman wearing a long, nubby, knit skirt and an oversized sweater. *The old trying-to-camouflage-her-chubby-middle-section trick*, she thought. The woman was walking with another fifty-something gal, and they were eating soft pretzels as they talked. By contrast, the friend was wearing leather pants and spiked-heeled boots. Her makeup was dramatic, and her poncho added to her I-am-not-growing-old-gracefully image.

"Wow, she needs a mirror!" Charlotte said, as if she was actually talking to someone. She adjusted her gray flannel trousers, which were creeping up in the crotch as she drove, and looked down for a moment at her cordovan alligator loafers, admiring her good taste. She was so busy people-watching she almost missed the valet parking area at the salon. She turned sharply to slip into the designated area, where there were more cars than usual.

"Hello, miss," the valet greeted her.

She handed him her keys, thinking that he looked silly in a white shirt and tie with baggy pants and grease-covered workman's boots. She waited for the ticket. "Looks busy today," she observed. She reached over to the passenger seat to grab her camel-hair coat and matching alligator pocketbook, adjusted her pearls, and draped the coat over her arm.

"Yeah, the senator, you know," the valet answered.

"No, I don't know. Which senator? At the café?" asked Charlotte, remembering the daily newspaper's front-page photo.

"No, upstairs," he said, pointing to the salon a few storefronts away. "I don't know her name, but her helpers told me no cars are allowed to stay here in this spot until she's gone. My partner better come back soon," he said, motioning to the line of cars.

"She? Then for sure it is Senator Holmes Bartlett. She's a friend of mine! I didn't know she was going to be here today."

"Yeah, man. It's in the paper and everything. My boss told me to wear this stupid tie today. I think it's a big deal, you know." He moved to the rear of the car to jot down the license plate on the ticket. "Cool car, man. I would love to have one of these, but my wife would kill me. Too much gas, but man, I got four kids, you know. It'd be so cool." He handed Charlotte the ticket. "You must be rich, or somethin', havin' a car like this and knowin' the senator and all."

Charlotte smiled an uncomfortable smile and took the ticket stub. "I'll be about three hours," she said as she tucked the receipt in an outer pocket of her handbag. She bent over to check her smile in the car's mirror and looked at her men's-style watch. She'd be a little late, but she loved getting an espresso and croissant before her appointment. It was her weekly routine.

Charlotte's hair had remained within a predictable pattern of light auburn in the fall and spring, a deeper shade of red with hints of burgundy in the winter, and a summertime let-the-sun-take-care-of-the-bleaching look during June, July, and August. Her style always went from hair that was long enough to pull into a tight knot at the nape of her neck to a bob that fell just above the shoulder. Jerome, the slight-built French hair designer and salon's proprietor, had new ideas, but Charlotte never wanted to experiment with her hair. Her hair was a sure thing in her life. It was always straight, no matter what the weather provided in surprises. And she knew how to work with what she had. No styling products were required; no brushes or gels. Just wash, dry, and wear. She was the master of her own universe. She looked at herself in every storefront window she passed, running her fingers through her hair.

The ATM was in a corner of her favorite neighborhood café, where she stopped every week before her hair appointment. Yet she cocked her head and looked around, as if there was a reasonable expectation it might not be there. She took out four hundred dollars and tucked the crisp bills in the zipper compartment of her bag, holding on to a twenty for her order. Two hundred dollars would cover the cut and color, which left the rest for spending money.

She waited patiently in line until the mom with two small children in front of her collected her drinks and snacks and moved the stroller out of the way. A patron's dog had been resting but saw the toddler and barked. The baby cried, and the hassled mom shoved a cookie at the child.

"Been there, done that, got the T-shirt," said Charlotte, trying to ease the woman's frustration. The dog's master reprimanded the dog. Charlotte stepped up to the counter.

"Hi, I'll have a plain croissant and a double espresso with zest, please." She smiled, looking right through the barista at a blackboard behind him, which described the lunch offerings.

"For here or to go?" he asked.

"For here," she said. "New menu today?"

"Oh, yeah, we wanted to do something a little different, because the senator is in the neighborhood and … well, whatever. We just thought we'd mix it up."

"I'll have to try something else one of these weeks. I always get the same thing." He handed Charlotte her order and she paid him. "Good luck with the new menu, and I hope the senator stops in." She smiled.

The barista wiped the counter and asked the next person in line for her order.

The café was crowded, but Charlotte spotted a couple getting up from a table near the door, and she moved quickly to secure the spot. As she skimmed the patrons, she noticed how young and energetic the crowd seemed; how very European she felt—a crowded café, youthful energy coupled with the smell of freshly ground coffee beans, scarves being wrapped and unwrapped as people sat or got up to leave, the din of conversation just below the treble of the music.

She looked at her watch again. It was just one o'clock. There was plenty of time to call Charles; Jerome was always late anyway. She wondered if Jennifer was in the salon. She took out her cell phone and pressed "C" for Charles, utilizing the phone's speed-dial option.

"Hello?" echoed his deep voice. There was feedback in the line.

"Hi. Could you do me a favor and check the paper for something? I left it on the table near the door to the garage. I think Jennifer might be in the salon today and … well, do you mind checking?" *How convenient that Charles works out of a home office*, she thought.

"Wait a minute. I have to get off this call first," he answered.

"Oh, never mind," she said, somewhat disappointed. "I'm sorry. I just thought if you weren't too busy, I'd like to know, but that's okay." But she was already on hold.

"Okay, I'm back," he said. "Let me see. I have the paper right here on my desk." He was quiet for a few moments. "She looks great in this photo. Did she lose weight?"

"I don't know. I haven't seen her in a while, as you know. I hope I don't run into her. I wonder if she knows."

"Charlotte, nobody knows because you haven't told anyone but Suky. And besides, what difference would it make? Jennifer is a dear friend."

"Suky has no discretion. I never should have said anything. What if I want to work for Jennifer? Even if I don't want to work for her, what if I want to use her for a reference? God, why did I tell Suky?" Charles cleared his throat, but she cut him off abruptly before he could say anything. "I don't want to talk about it anymore."

"I found nothing about her itinerary, Charlotte. But it does say 'Charlotte Gibbons Wentworth, married to real estate entrepreneur,

Charles Wentworth, is the luckiest girl in the world because she is adored, beautiful, and brilliant.'"

Charlotte blushed, even though no one could hear Charles's sappy remarks.

"See you later, darling," he said. "Enjoy your afternoon. I'm going to make some calls about cars I think you should look at."

"I don't want—" The connection went dead before she could finish. She looked at her watch: a few more minutes before she'd go. She couldn't get thoughts of Suky and whether or not she'd betrayed her confidence out of her head. She just didn't want to get into anything with Jennifer today. And after all, Suky lived in New York, so it was unlikely they'd see each other.

Her closest friends resembled a social strata patchwork. Suky, a college remnant who was still single and had no tolerance for her married friends' distractions with real life, spent her days running a thrift shop. Her job was fitting, as she was preoccupied with her past to the point of being perennially stuck in the seventies. She reviewed events of her college days as if she were twenty-two instead of fifty-three. She irritated most of her friends to the point of abandonment, but Charlotte loved her creativity and ability to find beauty in other people's giveaways.

Charlotte's good friend and college roommate, Jennifer Holmes Bartlett, was a beloved United States senator, representing Pennsylvania. Her life in the political arena permitted little time for anything else, so she was skilled at bringing the personal into the job. Many of her friends served as advisors, fund-raisers, and spot fillers at requisite rubber-chicken dinners.

Then there were those friends who fell between the leftover hippie, Suky, and the consummate professional, Jennifer. Charlotte's buddies from her consulting days, who still worked at museums and galleries, were among her most balanced friends. They had a sense of discipline because of the many moving parts in their respective lives. Managing a balance between work and real life was a necessity.

And she had a few friends who, like herself, had worked early into their motherhood experience but then chose the stay-at-home mom route and were now trying to reinvent themselves in midlife.

Charlotte had distanced herself from many of her inner circle, and they didn't actively pursue her either. Perhaps it was a sign of the times—or most likely it was a sign of changes that were occurring in their respective lives. Their bodies were betraying their ages; their marriages were under intense evaluation and scrutiny; their parents were aging exponentially; and their kids were leaving the nests.

All this was enough for Charlotte but additionally, she was dealing with the work/family conundrum which, by age fifty-four, felt like taking a dive out of a plane with the realization she'd chosen the wrong parachute. Whichever parachute Charlotte chose, work or family (or what seemed like a half-baked combination), it was seemingly the wrong one, and she felt as if she was about to crash. And the way she knew her parachute was the wrong one was the feeling in the pit of her stomach every time she met someone who had chosen the *right* parachute. There was the perky stay-at-home mom model, who could throw a dinner party using organic meat and locally grown vegetables, host a book club that was the envy of the neighborhood, and refinish antiques that she'd collected from her travels with her husband and children. Contrast her with the successful career-woman model, equally as threatening in her confidence as she described her recent four-country tour in Africa, where she conducted research on empowerment through microbanking for the World Bank. That's when Charlotte felt that social isolation seemed the only viable solution to maintaining any dignity. *Let people write their own damn script for my life while I'm figuring out a workable plan, or at least an explanation for my sorry malaise.* And that was pretty much where Charlotte's head was lately—in isolation—except for her weekly visits to Jerome.

Her shiny Suburban went zipping by the café window as the valet took it to the parking area. She loved her car and admired the valet's adroitness behind the wheel.

Charles never thought the Suburban suited Charlotte's image, especially not in a silver metallic finish. It glittered like an iridescent seashell on a sunny day. To many who knew Charlotte, her taste in fine art and her superb aesthetic sensibilities didn't blend with the silver metallic, ding-covered SUV. Recently Charles's insidious method of persuasion was creeping into Charlotte's awareness. She was sure she didn't want a sedan but hated listening to his unrelenting harangues, and she could feel one brewing. Perhaps she'd just give in and go on for a few test drives. Like most people, some aspects of Charlotte's personality seemed inconsistent. The car presented one of those incongruities.

Another of Charlotte's quirky characteristics—in addition to the car and her eclectic collection of friends—was her passion for tending her gardens, even though it meant having dirt under her nails from mid-March through the first frost.

"I don't know why you don't pay that gardener of yours to move those plants around, Charlotte," said her mother on a recent visit from the assisted living facility where her parents lived. "You're getting older you know. You're no spring chicken anymore. If I'd had your money all those years ago when I tended the house and gardens, believe you me, I'd have paid someone."

"I like knowing where every plant is, Mom. And I like planning the colors when I move things and thin stuff out. Plus, I enjoy the time I spend in the garden. I think while I'm digging. It's good exercise too, with all the bending and lifting and hauling."

"Well, you could at least wear gloves so your hands don't get so beat up," her mother continued.

"Mom, are you upset about something else? Because I know you love gardens, and Daddy was a gardener. That's where I learned my love of the earth."

"Oh, rubbish. He wasn't a gardener! I did all the work. He planned the thing and went to the farms and gathered the plants with you and your brother, but I maintained it all," her mother said defensively.

"Well, I'm sorry. I didn't remember that part, Mom. I remember the fun of watching the vegetables grow, and then we'd eat them. That seemed magical to me as a kid."

"I hope you kids have lots of good memories, because I feel like my chances of having new experiences and any more good memories are over. I feel like all it is now is waiting around for other people to include me in their fun and *their* memory making."

Charlotte thought she saw a tear. "Mom, I don't know what it's like to be in my eighties, but I'm really glad you're here with me today and that you want to come visit and be a part of our lives." She hugged her mom.

Her mother had missed Charlotte's tenderness. "And you know, Charlotte," she said, "I can't really get in and out of that crazy jalopy of yours. Why don't you pick me up in one of your cars instead of that truck?"

Charlotte reflected on that afternoon with her mother, and she hoped she'd have the chance to resolve issues with Betsy before necessary conversations became repressed and hardened into their relationship. Charlotte held her hand out, inspecting her nails for dirt. Maybe she'd have a paraffin wax treatment before she left the salon.

The woman with the small children was talking to the toddler, and the two men at the table next to them commented on how cute the children were. The young man with the dog was sitting with a friend, and they were deep in conversation, with the dog asleep at their feet. Someone who Charlotte recognized as a stylist from the upstairs salon entered and engaged a group of women sitting a few tables away from Charlotte.

"Hello, Sylvia," the stylist said.

"Hi, sweetie," Sylvia responded. "Is it crazy up there? My friends and I are here for the event with the senator."

"The senator won't be here for a while. I think she had some other stops first, but we are really excited." The stylist smiled. "Are you having any services today or just having lunch?"

"I'm having a mani/pedi," said Sylvia, "and my friends are having facials after lunch."

"That's great. Have a super time. I heard the senator is really nice. Well, see you all later, ladies." The stylist moved to the counter to order.

Charlotte smiled at the women, catching the eye of the two facing her. "Hi. What's the event upstairs?"

"Oh, Senator Holmes Bartlett has asked a group of women-owned small businesses to join her for lunch," answered one woman.

"Oh," said Charlotte. "I volunteer for her, and I hadn't heard about this, but now I know why I wasn't invited." She laughed awkwardly. "I don't have a business … at least, not anymore."

"Yeah, well, it's hard. We're probably a bit older than you, and we didn't start our businesses until our kids were in high school," one of the women said.

Charlotte smiled. "It is hard. Oh, well. Nice chatting," she said, grabbing her coat and bag. She thought is best not to mention that she and these women were probably contemporaries. It would just make her feel worse about her lack of productivity. She scanned the café as she was leaving and realized she was the only person sitting alone.

She looked at her watch. One-ten. She'd better run—not to be too late, just late enough to let Jerome feel she wasn't too desperate for his capable hands. She threw away the remnants of the croissant and the to-go espresso cup. She held the door for a group of young girls who weren't paying attention.

"You're welcome," Charlotte said to the last girl in the group.

"Oh, yeah, thanks," the girl said, the sarcasm being lost on her.

Charlotte checked her teeth in the reflection of the elevator doors in the lobby of the building where the second-floor salon was located. Then she ran up the stairs instead of using the elevator. She hung her coat in the small coatroom at the top of the steps, and tied her Ferragamo scarf around her pocketbook handles. She admired herself in the mirror before leaving the coatroom. *The scarf is a nice touch on the pocketbook*, she thought as she moved toward the salon reception area.

Yvette, the tall bleached blonde at the front desk, begrudgingly adjusted Charlotte's appointment to reflect her habitual tardiness. Jerome, the salon proprietor and only stylist Charlotte allowed to cut, color, or blow-dry her hair, was unaware that Charlotte's appointment was at one o'clock and not one fifteen. Each week, Yvette hoped Charlotte would show a scintilla of humility for her rudeness, but an apology was not forthcoming.

The salon was rarely crowded at midday. Charlotte hoped she wouldn't run into anyone she knew, especially the senator. She had become antisocial, a behavior she'd developed in midlife as her insecurities became more prominent.

"Hey, I understand the senator is going to be here today. What time?" she asked Yvette.

"I thought you'd know since she's your buddy," Yvette answered. "She'll be here while you're here, I'm sure. She's having a fund-raiser." Yvette forced politeness, asking, "How come you're not going?"

Jerome entered from the other room. His slender frame made his hands seem even larger than they were. "Hello, Charlotte! How are *you*?" he asked in his thick French accent. "What we are doing today?" He ran his fingers through her hair, tossing his head back so his long bangs wouldn't be in his eyes. Charlotte loved the whole experience. "Did you color your hair, Charlotte? It is not my color, yes?"

"No way, Jerome! Are you kidding? I would never color my own hair. My friend from college did that once and her hair turned to straw, not to mention that the color looked like it came out of a box of Crayolas." Jerome looked puzzled. She explained, "Crayolas. Crayons. Kids use them to make pictures in school."

"Oh. Yes, yes, yes. I know. What did you say? Craylas?"

Charlotte was amused. This was the most interaction she'd had all week. "Cray-oh-la. Crayola. But really, Jerome, it's just that I missed a few appointments because I thought I'd start to let my hair go gray—"

"*What?*" he shouted. "Are you crazy?" He ran his fingers through her hair again and walked toward the wash area. He continued reprimanding her, "You are nuts, Charlotte. You are too beautiful to have gray hair. Too old, it will make you look."

She followed Jerome to the heart of the salon, never noticing Yvette's annoyance with her. The receptionist flicked her blond tresses behind her shoulder and clicked her manicured nails on the desk. Her receptionist partner, Bobbi, muttered, "The customer is always right," and laughed. The two girls looked like bookends behind the counter, the two bleached blondes. But Yvette pointed out that Charlotte was always late, and of all days, today was the fund-raiser for Senator Jennifer Holmes Bartlett. They had appointments booked with every stylist, manicurist, and spa employee. Yet Jerome never said anything to Charlotte. Yvette was steaming mad. Bobbi reminded her how long Charlotte had been coming to the salon and all the people she had referred to Tres Belle.

"Who gives a crap?" barked Yvette, shoving a fresh mint in her mouth. "They all stopped coming over the years, thankfully. They're all as snooty as she is! Every week I put up with her attitude. She never even comes over to the desk. She expects me to go around to the seating area to welcome her and ask if she wants anything, and act like I'm okay with her being late. She's so bitchy! She acts like she's really somebody!"

Bobbi responded, "She is somebody, Yvette. When Jennifer Holmes Bartlett started coming here, it was because Charlotte brought her here. She *is* very well connected, and she was very helpful to Jerome when the salon first opened. She brought in a ton of customers. She is the best tipper this salon has, *and* she comes almost every week. So, I remind you, she is 'somebody.'"

Charlotte was too engrossed in conversation with Jerome to notice the salon's energy. Every chair was filled. Every sink was bustling with hands, hair, and shampoo. Dryers were humming, scissors clicking.

"So what are you thinking, Charlotte?" Jerome knew he would most likely not be cutting her hair today, just color touch-up, wash, and blow-dry. "I want you should get rid of the gray, huh? It's necessary," he said with authority.

"You make it sound like a done deal. Color the gray, then, Jerome. What color?" she asked, as if she had no say. They continued talking hair and color, and Charlotte was still oblivious to the activity in the salon and Jerome's distraction with it all.

Bobbi from the front desk approached Jerome and whispered something to him. He nodded. Donald, who was a senior stylist in the chair across from Jerome's station, interrupted him with a question. And so it went.

Charlotte continued talking to Jerome as if she had his full attention. "So Jerome, you can't believe the idiotic thing my husband wants me to do. You know I drive a huge car, right?" He nodded. She went on, "And I love it, but my husband thinks I should be driving something fancier. Well, frankly, anything would be fancier to him. He hates the car. Even my mother hates it. She calls it a truck or a jalopy, something like that. But anyway, my husband is setting up appointments for me to test drive sedans. I am so mad!"

"So what do you care what he thinks you should drive? You aren't one person. He drives what he wants, no?" Now she nodded. "So should you!" Then he added, "Continue, lovely Charlotte." He tossed his head back again, as if he had a twitch. His tight jeans outlined his lean frame.

She continued explaining her dilemma. Charlotte had been through enough trial-and-error to understand what worked for her and what didn't. This was her third Chevy Suburban. The car was an authentic reminder of good elements of her past—happy days hauling artwork to and from clients' offices, or three baby seats in the middle row, two cocker spaniels in the third row, and ten bags of groceries in the rear hatch. All were signs of a busyness that now seemed elusive. The Suburban driving experience was familiar, and as a woman in her early fifties, where changes were happening all too often, familiarity and predictability meant more than she could adequately describe to

Charles. "I don't know, Jerome. Maybe he's right. My kid thinks it's a gas guzzler, and it really is. Maybe I'm just being stubborn. He's been talking about this for a while, now. He doesn't think it suits my image, of all things."

Jerome seemed confused, "I don't understand you, Charlotte. You are so beautiful and smart. You are married to a sweet man who loves you, no? You have wonderful children. Why you are having—what do you call them—self-doubts?"

She shrugged. Charlotte knew she wasn't an art consultant anymore. And she had only a little over a year remaining as the mom of a school-aged kid. She didn't want to be a charity moll, and she didn't want to be a social doyenne. Charlotte needed time and space to figure out the details of her life, and meanwhile, time was passing too quickly. Her graying hairline and waning libido were constant reminders of her midlife status. Charles didn't seem to be having the same issues regarding midlife. His career was robust, and he was set in his daily routines. He had mastered his life's rhythm and walked to his own drumbeat. There was very little to shake his world—that is, except for Charlotte's unrest.

Jerome said, "So you can get what you want, no? Beautiful women always do. They just don't know it, and they make themselves *craaaazy* in the meantime. You see what I mean? Just do what you want to do, Charlotte. So, so simple it is." He sighed.

Charlotte responded, "Oh, Jerome, if only that were true!"

"It is true, Charlotte. Look at my business. Women only want to be beautiful. That's it. Simple, no?"

"No, I don't think that's all women want, Jerome! They want everything men want and more. They want to be beautiful, smart, good wives and mothers, successful business people—"

"Charlotte? Oh my goodness!" a familiar voice interrupted her. Charlotte gasped when the diminutive Jennifer Holmes Bartlett leaned in for a better look. "How are you? I wasn't sure if I'd run into you today! I hope you aren't upset that I forget to mention this little event when we saw each other last." Charlotte noticed Jen was wearing her signature low-heeled pumps, a Ferragamo scarf, and pearls. Her perfectly coiffed, short wavy hair added to her polished, professional image. She had just enough gray to give her a sense of maturity but not appear haggardly.

"Don't think about it," said Charlotte. She stood, moving the coloring foils out of her eyes. "Jen, you look great! Charles saw your picture in the paper this morning and asked if you had lost weight. You've become a real star, girlfriend!" Charlotte grabbed Jennifer's hands.

Jennifer blushed. "Stop, you're embarrassing me. So, what are you up to besides harassing people with your feminism lectures and volunteering for me like crazy?" Both women laughed. She let go of Charlotte's hands. "I mean it. Every time I'm in my downtown headquarters, you're there. You are so sweet to help out so much. And I'm such a jerk for not hanging out with you when you're there. You know, it's so hard for me. I hope you understand that I try not to show favoritism to my buddies who help out. I am so lucky to have so many volunteers. I guess I've been a lousy friend, though. I have no idea what's going on in your life, even though I appreciate you from a distance."

Jennifer's assistant seemed annoyed, looking at her watch several times. Jerome took the opportunity to shake hands with the senator and offer his hospitality again. Cell phones all around were ringing.

Charlotte responded, "Stop it! Don't even give it another thought. I love working in your headquarters. You're doing great stuff, Jen. You know I love you. We'll get together one of these days." She rolled her eyes.

Jennifer said, "Make me feel worse that you're so nice about it!"

Charlotte continued, "Anyway, I'm still moseying around with the work issue. I'm thinking of getting back into the art world. You know, aside from my kids and Charles, of course, art is my passion. I'm pretty much stuck in the same spot I've been in for the last ten years. You know, Jen. I don't move very quickly!"

"How about Charles? What's he up to? I was just looking at old photos the other day, trying to find a good picture to motivate me to get back in shape, and I found some shots from your wedding. Remember how nervous we all were? You moved quickly then—it was so fast. None of us even knew you were serious." Jennifer shook her head from side to side. "But you knew. You just knew. You were the first of all of us to get married. How long has it been?"

"We just celebrated our twenty-fifth."

Jennifer gasped, and her assistant interrupted, "Senator, we are on a tight schedule."

Jennifer rolled her eyes. "I'm sorry, Charlotte." She looked at her watch. "I have to run, but how about if we get together for a serious chat? I can really use all the help I can get, and you are always so creative. I think about calling whenever I see you in the office and then … well, you know what happens. Life happens! Anyway, it's been too long since we've hung out. Just hung out! Too long. Too long." Charlotte must have looked surprised at Jennifer's show of regret over their drifting friendship. "Really, Charlotte, I mean it. You are just the person I need right now."

Before Charlotte could catch herself, she said, "Yeah, yeah, I'm still a Democrat and my Rolodex is too! I might even know some well-heeled Independents, Jen!"

Jennifer waved her hand in the air, indicating her comment was nonsense, but Charlotte knew it was true. Jen was no fool. Charlotte's Rolodex was very impressive. She reached in her bag for a card and handed it to Jerome's assistant. "Please give this to the senator's assistant."

A minute later Jennifer leaned over the balcony from the second floor and called down to Charlotte, "I'm going to call this time—really, I am." Charlotte couldn't hear above the whine of the blow-dryers, but she was relieved that it had gone well with Jennifer. Clearly, the senator really *didn't* know anything about what was going on in Charlotte's life.

Jerome explained the fund-raiser agenda to Charlotte, who decided to stick with the same hairstyle. They talked about Charlotte's college days, when she and Jennifer—then just "Holmes"—were roommates.

She explained that she had worked for every one of Jen's campaigns throughout the years, as a trusted aide, chief schlep, phone-crew organizer, or head of whatever Jennifer deemed necessary. How life had changed for both of them! Now, Jen would likely be taking a run for the presidency in two years. At least, that's what the pundits were saying.

Seated in two of the drying chairs across the salon from where Charlotte was situated were Charlotte's neighbors, Ginny Arena and Mimmi Biddle. Charlotte hadn't noticed them—or anyone else for that matter—but they noticed her and were trying to read her lips. Ginny, a modern-day town crier, had already made several well-placed calls to the local Main Line paper. Then she called her husband, Joe, to share the news of Holmes Bartlett's salon visit.

"Put that phone away, Ginny! People are starting to look at us," said Mimmi.

"Just a second," said Ginny.

One patron asked, "Who was that the senator spoke to?"

Ginny piped in, "She's a friend of ours."

Mimmi's eyebrows arched.

Ginny, annoyed, said, "Well, she used to be." Then after a pregnant pause, "We should look her up again. I used to like her."

Jerome accompanied Charlotte to the wash area again to remove the foils and check the color.

"Beautiful, beautiful, Charlotte. You look young, so young again!" exclaimed Jerome.

"Oh, Jerome, you are as blind as my husband. And you know what? I like it. I'm going to capitalize on that and skip the test drives. I love my car. I don't care if the damn car is politically correct or not. After all, I'm not a senator!"

Chapter Three

Ginny jumped off the train at the Wynnewood stop.

"Paper, paper, come and get your morning paper!" yelled the old man hunched over a bench stacked with Philadelphia daily newspapers. "Read all about it in the *Daily News*!" He jingled the change in his dirty red apron pocket.

"Hey, Chas," Ginny said, handing over her change. "Did you see the picture in the paper today of the senator? I saw her in the hair salon in Manayunk a few days ago. She's much better looking in person."

"Gimme a break, Ginny. She ain't pretty. Come on. Now you—you're a doll. You're something worth lookin' at, with that beautiful head of blonde curls!"

"Really, Chas, she's cute," Ginny insisted as she walked toward her office in the Wynnewood Shopping Center, curls bouncing with each step.

"Shut up! I'm gonna be sick," he yelled jokingly. "Paper, paper, come and get your morning paper." His voice trailed off as her pace increased. She had a lot to do today, with her daughter's school meeting and showing the Betts's estate.

Ginny had lived in several of the Main Line's provincial neighborhoods for her entire life. The Main Line, a collection of small suburban Philadelphia towns, was eponymously named for the train line that ran through Philadelphia's western suburbs. The Main Line train line was built during the nineteenth century to accommodate wealthy Philadelphians who wanted an easier commute to their country retreats than by horse and carriage. This train, along with its sister line, the Chestnut Hill Local, which developed on the east side of the Schuylkill River, were still in operation, even after almost two hundred years.

Ginny grew up in Narberth and had been riding the train from the time she could remember. She was the third stop on the Main Line run. She attended Lower Merion High School in Wynnewood, went to Villanova University, and settled in Penn Valley right after she married her childhood sweetheart, Joe. She worked in the Wynnewood office of a small, family-owned real estate business after her college graduation and continued to be one of their most successful agents. Ginny seemed to know everyone, everywhere she went. She was the unofficial neighborhood greeter when a family moved in.

"Hi, I'm Ginny Arena. I live around the corner," she'd said to the new neighbor, Meredith Baldwin, who moved next door to her friend Kate Hahn. Then, shaking her hand, she continued. "I've lived in this neighborhood my whole life, and I know everything there is to know, so if I can help, I'm at 600 Hagys Ford. And I'm a realtor too—not that you'll be moving anytime soon." Meredith's toddler peeked around her mother's legs to catch a glimpse of a basket of cookies that Ginny had made. "Well, hello there, cutie pie," said Ginny.

And so it went with everyone new to the neighborhood. She'd offer a firm handshake, which belied the recipient's expectation of such a small-framed woman. The neighborly basket of cookies or muffins she'd bake complemented her tough-as-nails ability to collect valuable information. She was not to be trifled with in matters of neighborhood trivia and could gather information as well as any gumshoe and disseminate it like a Hollywood gossip writer. She had the inside scoop on neighboring families, schools, dry cleaners, grocery stores, and specialty items. Those families she liked were given the name of the best deli. If she really liked them, the wife might even be invited to join Ginny's walking group.

"Meredith, you should talk to your new neighbor, Kate Hahn," Ginny suggested. "She's a real sweetheart, and we walk in a group together. You're more than welcome to join us. Kate can fill you in on the details of when and where we meet."

"Thanks, that's so nice, but I work," said Meredith.

"Well, so do I," answered Ginny without hesitation. "But how's a girl supposed to keep her figure if she doesn't make time to exercise? We've been walking and talking since 1983, way before it became trendy. We've planned thousands of meals, critiqued hundreds of movies, helped prepare a lot of funeral luncheons, and saved at least two marriages. Not to mention, we warded off osteoarthritis in the process! But you have a few years before you need to worry about that. Welcome to the neighborhood—and think about walking with us. We could use some younger blood in the group. It keeps us on our toes." Ginny had a quintessential salesperson's personality, and no one could resist her magnetism—except, that is, for Charlotte Gibbons Wentworth.

There was curiosity surrounding Charlotte and her husband, Charles, when they bought a house in the neighborhood. Charlotte had already made a name for herself among the Main Line's elite, procuring art from the world's greatest collections for their personal portfolios. It was at the urging of Charles's work mentor, Phillip Rothschild, that they looked at his sister's estate. Mr. Rothschild was a Philadelphia icon whose sister's husband had recently passed away. She was moving to the venerable White Oaks retirement community, a *Who's Who* among the Philadelphia affluent and often referred to as God's country club.

Charlotte fell in love with the property at the end of Fairview Road, and Phillip Rothschild couldn't have been more pleased, as he thought Charlotte was exactly the kind of wife his junior partner should have. Mr. Rothschild felt all his partners should have beautiful, culturally adept wives, but few fit the bill as well as Charlotte.

He encouraged Charles to stay with the corporate real estate investment firm but sensed his influence was waning. His founding partner had heard through the proverbial grapevine that Charles was looking around at investment properties on his own, something strictly prohibited by his employment contract. They didn't take action against Charles, however, because Mr. Rothschild needed his skills. And Charlotte's allure was great for business. Hoping to convince Charlotte it was in her best interest to have Charles gainfully employed at the firm, Mr. Rothschild offered to show his sister's estate personally.

"I knew I'd love this place, but we can't afford it," said Charlotte as she preceded Mr. Rothschild up the hand-carved-wood staircase. "It's not simply that it's large, Mr. Rothschild, but—and I mean no disrespect to your sister—the house needs work. The kitchen, the bathrooms, the wood floors—it's a lot." She was taken aback when Mr. Rothschild hinted that he would make sure they could afford the property, including its updating and maintenance, if Charlotte would secure Charles's position at his firm for several more years.

At first, she wasn't sure she heard him correctly. "I'm not sure I understand, Mr. Rothschild. This house must need a few hundred thousand to get it up-to-date. And that doesn't begin to cover the outside."

He winked at her and admired her lean figure, eyeing her quickly up and down. Charlotte took a step back and pulled her khaki trench coat around her.

"My dear, as your very capable husband will tell you, if the price is right, you might just have the money you need for the inside work. And when you see the outside, you will understand why I want this house to go to someone who appreciates the arts. But let's continue our tour and then we'll chat."

Although the place needed lots of tender loving care, Charlotte could picture herself living there, along with her three young children and her handsome husband. She just couldn't picture an income that could pay for it all.

"You know, Charles is very valuable to our company, Charlotte," Mr. Rothschild said, "and we'd be willing to offer him a more senior position that would carry with it a hefty bonus—one that would amply cover your costs here. But I need a guarantee of at least five years. At least. And if you are on board, I'm sure you have more power to convince your husband than I—or a big bonus, for that matter." His toothy smile seemed even broader in his wrinkled, sunken-cheeked face.

Outside, formal gardens transitioned into overgrown English cottage gardens. Although it was the beginning of spring, Charlotte could see remnants of hydrangeas, phlox, daylilies, and foxglove. Daffodils were popping up in the grass. The statuary from the former owner's travels was magnificent.

Mr. Rothschild sent Charlotte ahead while he stayed on the flagstone patio just outside the kitchen, smoking a fat cigar. He watched her take it all in.

Minutes later, when she'd finished perusing the property, she asked, "Are the bronzes included? Two are obvious copies—good copies but copies. Some look as if they could be original. The piece in the very back looks Native American—the symbolism is rich." She turned to look at it again, as if assessing its authenticity. "I guess you've had the originals removed—I noticed bare spots."

He nodded.

"This was a nasty trick, bringing me here, sir," she joked. "I will talk to Charles, but the trick may be on you, Mr. Rothschild, because I *love* this place. And my husband likes to please me. But be warned—he drives a very hard bargain." She winked as she walked past him, showing just enough leg to entice the old man.

The moving trucks were barely out of the driveway on the Wentworths' move-in day before Ginny appeared at their large mahogany front door.

"Hi! I'm Ginny Arena, and I've lived in this area my entire life ..." The speech was the same for every household. Charlotte was gracious and accepted the cookies, but she didn't offer her new neighbor a tour of the house. She also declined the opportunity to walk with the group.

"Thank you so much, Ginny. How kind of you, and these cookies look delicious. My kids will devour them, I'm sure."

Ginny walked away, disappointed she couldn't get a peek at the estate. She was surprised that Charlotte wore pearls on moving day.

Ten years had passed since Charlotte and Charles moved to Fairview Road and much had changed in the eclectic neighborhood. The old gaslights were converted to electric; the county put in sidewalks; and the old Gilbert estate, once owned by a member of the Rothschild family, had been lovingly restored by none other than Charlotte and Charles Wentworth. Much of the estate had been sold off prior to their ownership and many of the neighboring houses were built on those parcels. The original house and cottage were left on one acre.

Ginny's walking group had also changed over the years. Neighbors came and went, but the core group—Ginny Arena, Mimmi Biddle, Marianna Silver, and Kate Hahn—were still walking. When their children were younger, Kate had asked Charlotte if she was interested in walking with them; after all, their daughters knew each other in elementary school. But then Charlotte's daughter moved on to an independent school, and the women's lives didn't seem to intersect. Charlotte kept more and more to herself, and Kate got tired of asking.

Charles had left Mr. Rothschild's firm after his five-year contract and created a business of successful real estate projects, which he liked to describe as "below the radar." He managed to earn enough to support both the property and Charlotte's expensive tastes.

He worked out of their home and was often the unlucky recipient of Charlotte's annoyance as she observed the walkers from behind her silk damask living room draperies. They were finally at a point in their lives where Charles could predict Charlotte's behavior. She'd walk her gardens in the early hours of the morning, before he or Betsy was awake. She'd have coffee and read the papers. Then she'd walk her house, looking for unattended details that she'd add to the never-ending list for household staff.

Charles thought she'd been more spirited since her recent encounter with Jennifer Holmes Bartlett. His office was directly adjacent to the living room, and he often left the doors open so as to not feel closed in while working in the mahogany-paneled room.

"Charles, look. There they go. That chubby one really annoys me. She has that fat dog with her and neither one ever seems thinner. Why does she bother?" She moved away from the living room draperies, adjusting their pleats.

"Maybe they're walking for something else, Charlotte. Maybe it's not about being thin." He continued typing on his laptop computer, his arms resting on his middle-aged paunch.

"Then why don't they just sit at a café or at someone's kitchen table? Why wear those hideous outfits and fritter away the day? Why aren't they volunteering or working? Think about it. They get up, see their kids off to school, throw on sweat pants and those polyester jackets, and walk for an hour. Sometimes it's longer, because I've seen them stop and stand in front of Ginny Arena's house. Now, it's noon and what have they accomplished? Nothing. That is the answer. Absolutely nothing." Charlotte rearranged coffee table books and knick-knacks on the wall shelf. Charles grunted an acknowledgment.

"The housekeeper really needs a personal tour of our house with instructions on how things should be placed. Doesn't it drive you crazy that we pay her all that money, and she doesn't put things back where they belong? Okay, I don't expect her to have a sense of aesthetics, but doesn't she know we're fussy?" She sighed heavily and frowned at her husband. "Charles, are you listening?"

"Barely, Charlotte, I'm trying to work here. Why are you so wrapped up in these women?"

"I'm not wrapped up in anything, Charles. And besides, I wasn't talking about the walkers, I was talking about—"

The doorbell rang. Charlotte stretched her neck and could see from the corner of one of the living room windows that it was the walkers. She slid down the corner wall, behind the voluminous draperies so as to not be noticed if they were peering in. When no one answered immediately, Ginny used the lion's head knocker. *Clang, clang, clang.* The fat dog barked.

Charles stood up from his desk. "Charlotte, are you getting that? What are you doing on the floor?" Annoyed and exasperated, he shook his head and walked through the living room toward the door.

She whispered, "It's the walkers."

He hesitated, half turning to look at her. "I don't believe I've met them. Are they the new folks across the street? You know, we should get to know our neighbors. We've been here ten years, and I still don't know anyone. It's weird." *Clang. Clang. Clang. Buzz. Buzz.* "Really, Charlotte, get up!"

Charlotte didn't want to talk to them, and she waved at Charles, indicating that he shouldn't answer the door. Her attempt to get his attention went unnoticed, as he had his back to her and was reaching for the doorknob. She stood, catching a glimpse of herself in the parlor mirror. She poofed the back of her newly colored hair. *Jerome really did a great job with the color the other day*, she thought. She checked her teeth for food particles.

Charles was a bit surprised to see that "the walkers" were not, as he had assumed, "the Walkers."

Ginny didn't wait to be greeted. She chimed right in, "We came by to congratulate Charlotte." She held up the week's edition of the *Main Line Times*, with an article about Jennifer Holmes Bartlett and a fuzzy picture of her in the salon with Charlotte.

Charlotte made her entrance. Gracefully extending her manicured hand, she said, "Hi, Ginny … Kate. So good to see you both. I see you've brought a committee with you." Charlotte had mastered the condescending smile: a cocked head, lips just ever-so-slightly turned up at the corners, arched eyebrows—and silence. After giving the group a quick once-over she reached out to the others. "I'm Charlotte Gibbons Wentworth and this is my husband, Charles. I don't believe we've met."

Charles smiled, nodding, and then excused himself with a wave and a "Good day, ladies." He shuffled back to his office on the other side of the living room, sliding the heavy pocket-doors shut behind him.

Ginny expressed her congratulations, waving the newspaper. Charlotte grabbed it out of her hand. A bit startled, Ginny took Charlotte's aggression as a sign of engagement and asked if Charlotte wanted to join them for a walk. Her vanity overcame her insecurities and surprising herself, she stepped out of her vestibule, pulling the door behind her, leaving her comfort zone.

"Do you want to change? We'll wait," Ginny said.

"No, I can walk in these shoes just fine. I'll just go a few blocks with you gals."

Kate arched her eyebrows as Mimmi eyed Charlotte's leather pointed-toe oxfords.

"Well, you sure make us look like a bunch of schleps!" said Marianna. "Here we are in our jogging suits and sneakers, and you're looking so professional in your crisp blouse and trousers."

"Let's not forget the pearls," added Ginny.

"Ladies, as I said, I'm only going a couple of blocks with you. And this is a real growth experience for me—I'm not even wearing lipstick."

Kate rolled her eyes, and Mimmi almost started to laugh. Ginny was babbling about something as Charlotte continued skimming the paper.

"I can't believe someone took my picture without asking my permission. Isn't that against the law? I mean, I'm in foils, for goodness sake," said Charlotte, removing her bifocals and letting them dangle over her pearls from a hand-beaded chain.

Mimmi blurted out, "It was Ginny. Ginny took the picture with her new cell phone."

Ginny looked as if she wanted to clobber Mimmi but offered an excuse instead. "I was trying to get a shot of the senator, you know. I didn't realize you were in the photo until I saw today's paper."

Charlotte wasn't sure she believed that, but she was happy to be seen with such a high-profile person. Perhaps this was what she was missing—the action. She used to love the action of her work life, and in this small town, this little incident was a big event. Seeing Jennifer in the salon had occupied her thoughts and conversations with Betsy and Charles for the past week.

"I am really ready to go back to work, you know, Charles," she had said just the night before at dinner. "Maybe if I get the chance to meet with Jen, she'll have some ideas about the art business, or better, maybe she'll have a little something for me at her headquarters. You know, for pay."

"Why a 'little' something?" he asked. "After all, your art consulting business before we had kids wasn't little, Charlotte."

"God, can I be excused?" asked Betsy. "This is so boring."

"I'm really excited to see Senator Holmes Bartlett again," snapped Charlotte.

"Yeah, well, she was probably just being polite, Mom. Why would she want you to work with her? You're just a stay-at-home mom who hasn't worked in a bajillion years," Betsy snorted, getting up to leave the room. Charlotte couldn't respond because she was frozen with hurt.

"I believe in you, Charlotte," Charles said quickly. "At the very least, you'll have a nice lunch or coffee and catch up with Jennifer. But you should definitely think about trading in your car now. You can't be seen driving that thing, Charlotte."

Charlotte scowled. "Gosh, Charles, you don't get it! I'm not driving a sedan. I like this car, and that's that! I mean, it's got room, I sit up high, the mirrors are huge, and it's even got a rear windshield wiper!"

Ginny's initiative to get Charlotte walking with the group came at a perfect time and was just the push Charlotte needed. As the women walked, Charlotte started telling them about her relationship with the senator. To her surprise, she was having a good time.

"Can I just ask you a question about your outfit, Charlotte?" asked Ginny. "Do you always dress like this, because I don't even look that together when I go to church!"

"Yeah," said Kate. "I picture dressing like you someday when I work again." Then she seemed to consider what she'd said. "Oh, did you come from work? What do you do?"

"No, no, I didn't come from work. Oh, the dreaded 'W' word. I dress like this because I don't know how else to dress. This has been a uniform for me forever, unless I'm in my garden. Maybe it is a leftover from my work days, though, Kate." They walked by a beautiful rock garden; a woman was cleaning it up. "Don't you just love working in your garden?" Charlotte asked. "Even though it's at times rigorous, I find myself so much more relaxed afterwards. It's transformative." The neighbor agreed, and they chatted for a few minutes about plants and how long they'd both been gardening and where to get the best deal on annuals. Charlotte leaned over to take a closer look at what was sprouting through the mulch, holding her glasses so they didn't dangle off the chain.

Meanwhile, the other women had walked to the next house, where they stopped and talked among themselves until Charlotte finished chatting and caught up with them. Mimmi looked at her Timex watch tucked under the sleeve of her pink velour jogging suit. "I've got to get going, or I won't make it to the market and back in time for the school bus. Crap, I have another coffee stain on these pants."

"Yeah, I've got to get going too," said Kate, adjusting her designer sunglasses that had slid down her sweaty nose. Her glossy dark hair reflected the sunlight. "It was really good to see you again, Charlotte. We have to catch up on our girls. Well, actually, on all of our kids. Your boys must be married by now."

"Oh, no, but they are grown up, for sure."

Ginny handed Charlotte the paper and said, "Here, you keep it." Then she asked Charlotte to join them the next day, and Charlotte agreed she would. She thought perhaps being with other women and getting some exercise might help her out of a midlife slump.

When she returned home Charlotte showed Charles the local paper's picture of her with the senator. "I look like an alien in those foils. And it doesn't help that I tower over Jennifer either. Now I know why I don't buy the *Main Line Times*. Ugh. But how cool is it that I'm photographed with her! My gal, Jen—she really is something, huh?" She put the paper down and looked at her husband. "I have to figure out how to tell her what's going on with me, Charles."

No words were necessary. They embraced.

Chapter Four

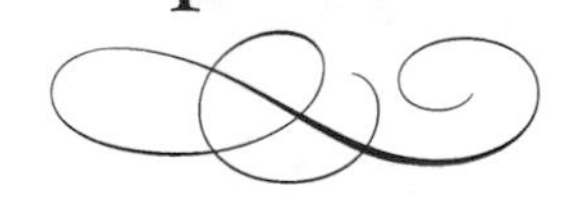

Charlotte was late to meet the walkers. Giving driving lessons was not her strongest parenting skill, but sixteen-year-old Betsy had the ambition of every newly minted driver, which meant as much road time as possible. Betsy wanted to meet the required number of hours behind the wheel so she could obtain her Pennsylvania junior driver's license. Charles had been invited to play golf at Winged Foot in Westchester County, New York, by a banker with whom he did business. That left Charlotte to fill his role as morning driving teacher on the ride to school, but Charlotte would rather tolerate Betsy's pouting than to stomach her driving. So she bribed her with a stop at Starbucks instead, and they had a muffin and coffee. Charlotte was unsure of herself these days, and Betsy, like most sixteen-year-old girls, was a roller coaster of insecurities, so mother and daughter made a poor match. But they managed well enough to get Betsy to school with her self-esteem intact so that she could muddle through her day as a high school junior. Charlotte had averted Betsy's usual feistiness with a Starbucks's blueberry muffin.

Charlotte drove back to her neighborhood, looking at the other houses. She loved architecture, and her neighborhood's eclectic collection offered her aesthetic sensibilities a real boost. Even the smaller houses were distinctive. Her favorite houses were the very old styles, like the house owned by her new walking friend, Kate Hahn. The old design features, like slate roofs, copper gutters and downspouts, and clapboard siding added character that newer houses lacked.

The walkers had already left for their usual two-mile morning jaunt, but Charlotte was hoping to catch up with them. She could see Mimmi's dog in the distance and found the women standing at the end of the next block. Charlotte drove up next to them, window down, preparing to back into a parking spot across the street.

"Sorry I wasn't ready this morning!" she shouted as she parked the car with two wheels on the curb. "I had to take Betsy to school." Jumping out, she locked the doors. She surprised herself with her own excitement over having caught up with them. She ran across the street, where they were still standing. "I took her to Starbucks as a trade for driving. I hate that she's driving. It was so different with the boys. They were so much better at the whole thing." She bent over to retie her hiking shoes, tucking her auburn hair behind her ears. She looked up because no one had responded; they were just standing still. The beagle barked.

"Your window is down, Charlotte," Ginny said.

"Oh, it's okay, I'm sure. Okay. All set," she said as she finished tying her shoe. The group was unusually quiet. She repeated herself, "Again, I'm really sorry I'm late, but I had the whole Betsy thing, and then I must have been behind every senior citizen on her way to bingo." Flustered, she continued, "But I made it; I'm here. And look, new walking shorts and shoes." She stuck out one leg as if they couldn't notice otherwise. Still, it was quiet. She was anxious, thinking perhaps she'd broken some walking protocol.

Marianna, who had been standing behind Mimmi, gestured toward Mimmi. She cocked her head and raised eyebrows, hoping that Charlotte would pay closer attention. But before she could successfully manage to inform Charlotte of what was happening, Charlotte blurted out, "Oh, Mimmi. Sam is peeing on the hostas."

Mimmi was quick to respond. "Charlotte, I don't give a crap if he's peeing on the neighbor!" Charlotte was flabbergasted. Mimmi turned to face Charlotte and stepped closer to her. "My husband," she yelled, pointing her finger into her own chest, "wants to move out, and he thinks he's in love with a girl he met in the park. Imagine that, Charlotte Gibbons Wentworth!"

Charlotte gasped, covering her mouth and started to shake a bit. She wasn't sure if her response was because Mimmi was crying or because of what she was saying. Mimmi continued yelling as the women stood in place across from Charlotte's poorly parked car.

"I'm almost forty-five. I thought I was married for life. I've never worked outside of my home. I went to college and got married the summer I graduated from Bryn Mawr. Yes. I am one of their failures. You know their infamous quote: 'Our only failures only marry.' My two teenagers have no idea what I'm going through. All they care about is whether they'll have to change schools or if they can still have friends at the house." She took a few steps back, tugging on the chubby beagle's leash. Charlotte noticed a blue plastic bag hanging from the pocket of Mimmi's mauve stretch workout pants. Charlotte couldn't decide if Mimmi's socks were mismatched or dirty. Pointing and screaming at all of the women, Mimmi continued. "And none of you can possibly know what I'm going through either. What would you know, Charlotte?" She wiped her nose on the sleeve of her well-worn Penn sweatshirt. "Your husband is never more than three inches away from you all day. Or you, Ginny, what could you know about infidelity? Joe is so sweet. He does the goddamn laundry! Or you, Kate. What do you know about cheating husbands? Douglas probably still brings you flowers like when you were dating." She took a deep breath. Sam continued sniffing around in the flower bed.

Marianna moved toward Mimmi to hug her, but Mimmi stepped back, almost tripping over Sam. Her heavy chest bounced as she stumbled. "Don't play psychologist with me, Marianna. You think you know everything about everyone else's life. You sit all day long, prying into the most personal stuff that makes up a life. So do you ever examine your own relationships? Do you? Do *you* worry? Do you ever let personal fear enter your thoughts?"

Marianna nervously felt her earrings to be sure they hadn't fallen out. She wanted to respond but understood that Mimmi was venting. She continued listening.

Mimmi moved her attack back to Charlotte. "Graham thinks you're gorgeous, Charlotte. Imagine if your husband thought *I* was gorgeous." Charlotte was feeling very uncomfortable and wanted to say something, but Mimmi didn't give her a chance. "Maybe if I looked like you, Graham wouldn't need to screw some park-bench bimbo!"

Ginny laughed out loud. "Come on, Mimmi. Really? A *park-bench bimbo*?"

"Do not laugh at me! This is real." She became hysterical. She began blubbering. Charlotte moved closer, but Mimmi barked, "Get away from me! You don't have any idea how lucky you are, Charlotte. If your rich husband flips out and has a midlife crisis, deciding to run off with a girl half his age, you can at least live in the same house and assure your children that their perfect little world won't collapse. But my world *is* collapsing because I don't have a *rich* husband, and I can't guarantee my kids anything right now. Do you get it? So, I don't care about the neighbor's hostas or where my dog's peeing."

"Well, that's good because he's now taking a crap in the pachysandra," said Charlotte, spinning around on one heel toward her car and struggling to control her shaking.

Ginny chimed in, "Look, Charlotte, Mimmi didn't mean to make you the target of her anger. Come on. Let's get walking here, girls. Charlotte, don't leave! Come walk with us. It's just a bad day here for Mimmi." Ginny turned and addressed Mimmi. "Mimmi, sweetie. We are here for you. But take this rage and go yell at the jerk you married, not us!" She grabbed Mimmi's dog's leash from her and scolded him, "Sam, your mother has enough issues right now. Behave yourself!" Then she turned to the group. "Let's walk it off, girls. Screw Graham! What was he thinking? Really! Why do they all think with their you-know-whats?"

They started walking briskly, following Ginny's lead. "By the way," Ginny said to Charlotte, "We don't *all* think your husband is perfect. We don't think anyone is perfect, honey, not to worry! Not even you!"

Have they talked about me behind my back? Charlotte wondered. *What is happening?* She knew there was a reason she hated these women's groups. Women could be so catty. Mean-spirited and catty, just waiting for you to misstep to claw your eyes out. But what was her misstep? They'd sought her out. She was content to sit at home and plan an art business. It hadn't been her idea to join them; it was theirs! Now, they were turning on her. *And how dare Mimmi say something about a rich husband,* she thought.

"No, my life isn't perfect," she snapped back, although her voice was quivering. "You are right about that! My life can be difficult at times. I just don't talk about it to everyone. Actually, I don't talk about it to anyone. I don't talk about anything with anyone. Ever. Not even with Charles. That's how perfect my life *isn't.* I don't talk about *things* with my own husband!" She directed her next words at Mimmi. "Why are you so mad at me? Did I hurt your feelings? Have I offended you? Am I that unaware?" She swallowed hard.

Marianna, nervous and stifling her psychologist's urge to answer Charlotte, roughed up her short-cropped graying hair. Her dangly ankh earrings swung back and forth. *Of course Mimmi is mad at Charlotte,* thought Marianna. *Mimmi is mad at everyone who has a seemingly healthy marriage. And she is mad at every young woman who is a stand-in for the park-bench bimbo, as she distastefully described the woman Graham pursued.* She shook her head as she contemplated these thoughts.

They were walking at a pretty fast clip. Ginny rubbed Mimmi's back as Mimmi described how mad she was at Graham. The other women offered support where necessary.

"Why didn't I ever question his damn perennial tan or those Tuesday and Thursday tennis dates? He was probably running around then! But he's so fit and trim; I thought he must be working out! It must be the tennis! He still can fit into his college clothes, after all. He wears that buckskin jacket that I always loved in college—and those worn-out Frye boots. Agh!" She was sobbing again. Ginny continued rubbing her back as they walked. Mimmi wiped her arm across her face. "Oh, I'm so stupid!"

"Stop it! You aren't stupid. You got married and, for goodness sake, we all believe our husbands are faithful. That's part of the deal, Mimmi. It's not you," said Charlotte.

Mimmi had no idea what had happened after she married Graham. He became consumed with belonging to the right clubs and being seen at the right restaurants. He chastised her about her weight gain during her pregnancy with Will. She never lost the extra fifteen pounds after he was born, and eighteen months later, she became pregnant with their daughter, Meg. Mimmi could count the number of times she and Graham had had sex since Meg's birth and none of those times was in the last two years. It wasn't the extra twenty-five pounds she lugged around with her that turned her husband off to intimacy, she admitted. "It's probably my fault. I really lost interest in how I look and in working outside of the house. Life just got so complicated once the kids came along. What did I do that was so wrong? Wasn't it hard for you guys too, once kids came?" she asked.

Kate didn't want to get involved in this private marriage stuff. She twitched her cute button nose. "Mimmi, maybe it's a passing thing with Graham," she said, her nose twitching again. Her dark hair turned up on her shoulders, making a flip that bounced and gave her an extra perkiness. She was tall, like Charlotte but not as thin. And also, like Charlotte, she wore coordinated outfits for walking, although Kate's were more casual, usually sports gear, in black to camouflage the residual effect of four pregnancies. "My sister and brother-in-law toughed out a marital situation," Kate said, using two fingers on each hand to make air-quotation marks when she said *situation*. "That was about four years ago, and my sister says she's happy she hung in." They had walked two blocks already and were about to cross onto Righter's Mill Road when they heard commotion behind them.

"Oh, geez, this doesn't look good," Ginny said. "Let's walk faster."

"What's the matter?" asked Charlotte.

"Just walk faster," responded Ginny. Mimmi started crying again. "Get it together, Mimmi," scolded Ginny. "That lady is coming after us!"

"Who is *that lady* and what does she want with us?" Charlotte asked worriedly. "Why is she yelling?"

"That's the woman whose house we were just standing in front of. You know, the hosta-bed lady is coming after us, and she is a witch."

Kate looked like she had seen a ghost. "I can't walk any faster. You know, for all the walking we do, we should be in better shape! Crap, my foot is killing me."

Marianna's short hair was stuck to her head from nervously running her hands across her head. "This is supposed to be fun and meanwhile, I'm so stressed-out here," whimpered Marianna. "Look, she's got company following behind her!" She picked up her pace. "Crap, I'm not up for a confrontation with a bunch of old ladies!"

"This is ridiculous!" exclaimed Charlotte, coming to a complete halt and bending over with her hands on her skinny thighs. "That old lady's not going to intimidate me or my friends!" She took a deep breath and turned to face the woman, who had slowed down and stopped yelling. Charlotte started toward her.

"You're looking confrontational," Marianna advised.

"This isn't a good idea, Charlotte. Do you know who that is?" Ginny called after her.

But Charlotte was angry. As she came within earshot of the old woman, she asked, "Are you okay? Were you calling us? Do you need something?" She hoped to disarm the woman and her old friends.

"Oh, you bet I was calling you, missy," the woman responded, waving a bag of something that Charlotte assumed was dog poop. They were now standing about fifteen feet apart. Charlotte's walking buddies were approaching her from behind when the woman started yelling again. Her white-haired companions had their arms crossed in front of them, like schoolyard bullies. The woman held up the plastic bag and began swinging it back and forth, like a metronome. With her other hand, she wagged her finger at Mimmi and said, "I cannot believe you let your dog pee and poop in my garden! Have you no dignity? I take care of my property. I pay people to weed and trim regularly. I walk my property two times daily. It is my pride and joy! I do not want to ever see you or your fat dog near my house again, or I will call the police!"

Charlotte stepped closer and raised her voice, surprising even herself. "I'd shake your hand, but it seems it's not a good idea today. I'm Charlotte Gibbons Wentworth, and I live two blocks in *that* direction." She pointed, indicating she lived in the wealthy area of the neighborhood. "My friend is having a crisis, and her dog's messing on your property is unfortunate but not tantamount to an assault or property damage. It seems you took care of cleaning up the mess and, under normal circumstances, Mimmi would have done the same. Do you see the plastic bag she has hanging out of her pants pocket? You should try a different approach. You know you can catch more bees with honey than with vinegar!"

"Well, I'm having a crisis too!" yelled the old woman.

Charlotte stepped even closer to old curmudgeon. "That's quite enough. You have no idea what my friend is carrying around with her. Suffice it to say it is like an entire valise filled with what you, ma'am, have in that little bag! Now I mean business. Enough for today! It's dog crap, not nuclear waste!" The woman started swinging the bag, but Charlotte turned to her friends and said, "Let's go, girls."

As they walked away, Ginny said, "Do you know who that was?"

Charlotte said, "I don't care if it's the president's mother!"

"Well," Ginny said, "she's not quite of that stature, but she's close. She is the wife of the governor's chief counsel."

"Then all the more reason for her to watch her p's and q's. Who does she think she is?" She turned to Mimmi, who, in all of the excitement, forgot for the moment that she was in the midst of a horrible mess. "I hope I have redeemed myself," Charlotte said, "because I never want to have to do that again. And I feel like that horrible smell is stuck up my nostrils! Ugh! What was that woman thinking?"

"My God Almighty," Ginny said, "we haven't had a day like this since the early 1990s, when that lady in the corner house off of Hagys Ford and Righter's Mill—"

"The lady with the amazing garden," Marianna interrupted.

"Yeah, that's the one," said Ginny. "She caught her husband with the babysitter. Her reaction was so interesting."

Mimmi asked, "Am I going to be the neighborhood entertainment for decades? This is getting worse than I expected."

Charlotte was walking faster and faster. Marianna, who didn't walk as regularly as the rest of the group because of her work schedule, was getting out of breath.

"Really," said Mimmi, "I still can't believe that old lady with the bag of dog poop."

"Oh, Lord, Mimmi. That was three blocks ago!" Ginny barked. "The old lady's history. It's like your husband. Is he history or not? I think, like Kate's sister, it's your call. Let go, let God. Keep him or not. The old lady goes, the husband goes. Whatever."

"Stop it! *Whatever*? That's mean-spirited!" Mimmi cried.

"You have to decide to step it up, Mimmi. Either kick him out, or kick him in the ass, but you have to do something," said Kate. "You can't just cry. How long ago did you find out?"

"You know what? It doesn't matter how long ago she found out, ladies. Mimmi decided to tell us today, and we should just let this day be about Mimmi," Marianna reprimanded.

"Okay, okay. Cool it, Marianna," said Kate, swinging her dark hair and twitching her nose again.

"Mimmi," said Charlotte as she grabbed her new friend's hand, "I don't know what you're going to do with your bastard husband right now, but I suspect it's not as easy as Kate or Ginny would have you believe. But I do know one thing for sure and that is this: I'm with you on the subject of that old, annoying lady! She really offended me too! She had that nothing-ever-bad-happens-to-me attitude. How could she have missed that we are all clearly in distress?"

Mimmi wasn't sure how to respond; only ten minutes earlier she was screaming at Charlotte and now they were practically good friends. Having reached the halfway mark of their walk, Ginny directed the group to turn around. Marianna wanted to walk farther, so she and Kate continued. Kate wanted to see the house with the magnificent garden around the corner.

Before the group said their good-byes, Marianna offered up a juicy tidbit. "The guy who cheated and his wife still live there. So don't point or anything," she advised.

Mimmi couldn't believe what she'd heard. "What did you say? They survived his cheating with the babysitter? Oh, that can't be true. It must be neighborhood lore." She pointed to Kate and Marianna. "I'm going with you two. I want to see the house." Then she coaxed Ginny and Charlotte. "Come on, come with us."

Charlotte indicated that she was moving toward home. She was emotionally spent. But Ginny, who never wanted to miss anything, wanted to go too, so she, Kate, and Mimmi continued walking with Marianna. Charlotte directed her thoughts elsewhere. She waved absently over her shoulder as she walked toward her car. The others were busy gossiping and didn't notice.

When Charlotte reached her car, she found the bag of dog poop looped through the handle of the driver's side door. She ripped it off and sent the smelly lump hurling through the air. Charlotte heard a thump and realized the bag had hit the old woman's house. As she was feeling around in her pockets for her keys, she heard the woman yelling. Charlotte jumped into her Suburban and closed the open window. As she passed the old woman's driveway, she saw her waving her arms franticly as she spoke with her posse.

Charlotte hoped the woman had learned her lesson and that she wouldn't hassle her neighbors over such nonsense anymore. *Oh, my gosh, is that a siren? Could that woman have called the police?* she wondered. She checked her rearview mirror and decided not to leave her car parked in the driveway when she returned home.

She could barely fit her lean frame between the garage wall and the side of her huge car as she nervously pushed the button to close the garage door. It occurred to her as she was turning off the house alarm that the old bat had probably jotted down her license plate number.

"Charlotte Gibbons Wentworth," she told herself, "you'd better get that impulsive temper of yours in check!"

Chapter Five

Mimmi had no idea what to do. Her husband was in the midst of an affair, believing he had met the woman of his dreams. Her children were furious with her, which made no sense to Mimmi. She didn't have the courage to tell anyone but the walking group about her domestic situation. Not even her sisters were aware of Graham's indiscretion. They continued living together because she was too embarrassed to make his affair public. She convinced herself that his behavior was a phase, and they'd work through it. She naively believed the affair was over when she discovered the tiny lace panties in a pocket of his trousers.

But one man's indiscretion is another man's fantasy. The walkers talked to their husbands about the sordid details of Graham's affair. Joe Arena tuned out much of Ginny's storytelling, but this was better than *Penthouse* Forum. As they stood in their kitchen, preparing dinner together and awaiting their daughter Anna's return from after school sports, Ginny had Joe's full attention.

"Wait a minute, Gin, I wanna grab a beer from the outside fridge, but I gotta hear this story. I can't believe that wimp had an affair!" He hung his blue blazer with the real estate company's logo patch in the coat closet and rolled up the sleeves of his yellow oxford-cloth shirt, exposing his muscular forearms. He wiped his hand across his balding head, forcing the few sun-streaked tufts left to spike up and give him the appearance of more hair.

"Get some potatoes out of that bin near the refrigerator, Joe. Anna loves those roasted potatoes I make," she said.

"Yeah, okay, potatoes. Got it." Joe moved quickly, eagerly awaiting the titillating story. Returning to the kitchen, he dumped the potatoes, which he had carried in a makeshift shirttail pouch, into a bowl and then opened his beer.

"God, look at the mess you made all over that shirt," Ginny admonished but only half-heartedly, because she was distracted by his toned stomach. He was in great shape for a guy about to turn fifty.

"Let it go, Gin. Finish telling the Graham and Mimmi stuff. You got my undivided attention here."

"Have. You *have* my undivided attention," she corrected. She continued the story as she peeled the potatoes, letting the skins collect in the sink. Joe sat at the kitchen table.

"Mimmi said this girl of Graham's is only twenty-five. Can you imagine, Joe? Twenty-five! He's old enough to be her father. She lives in town, and Graham met her in Rittenhouse Square on his lunch hour. They were sitting on a bench together, and he had the nerve to tell Mimmi the girl's blouse was unbuttoned, exposing one of her breasts. Apparently, she wasn't wearing a bra. She bent over to get something out of her bag and Graham told Mimmi he couldn't contain himself. They talked. She invited him to her place for a drink after work that night. He went. Like an idiot, he went to her freakin' apartment. What did he think would happen? Did he think they'd have good conversation? Of course not; he had bad intentions. Then, the worst of it, Joe. Oh, my God, I'd have to kill you if you ever did anything like this to me. He told Mimmi that when he got there, this bimbo met him at the door, wearing a kimono, which she let drop to the floor. And yup, you guessed it. She was stark-ass naked, Joe. Graham reminded Mimmi that he'd been a virgin when they married, and he'd never seen another woman naked, except in movies. He went on and on about it. Mimmi just screamed at him, crying and crying for him to stop. It's cruel, Joe, downright mean. Isn't it, Joe?" She waited for a response, but Joe just took a big gulp of his beer and ran his hand over his head again. "Joe?"

"Yeah, yeah, I'm listening. Believe me, I'm listening, Gin." He stood up and walked to the sink. He leaned his hip against the counter next to Ginny and rested his arm on the countertop. "Come on, Ginny. You really believe this story? Like a gorgeous babe is going to walk up to that Casper Milquetoast and, like, come on to him?" Then Joe leaned in and grabbed his wife of twenty-two years and said, "Now, if it was me, you'd believe it, right?" He nibbled on her neck.

She brushed him off and went back to peeling potatoes. "Stop, Joe! This is Mimmi we're talking about here! It's awful, what happened. And you're getting turned on. Are you kidding me?"

He didn't stop his advances. He put the beer down and stood behind her with his arms over her shoulders. Her tiny frame looked even smaller next to his wide shoulders. He still looked like the football player she'd fallen in love with in high school. She giggled. She was getting turned on herself.

"You'd be turned on if it was me, right?" Joe persisted. "You know it, huh? Big-shouldered, tanned stud like your old man, here, huh?" He turned her toward him and planted a wet kiss over her entire mouth. She let the potato peeler drop to the tiled floor. He kicked it out of the way.

She slightly resisted his advances. "Joe, what the hell's got into you? Anna might be home soon." She looked around her kitchen to check windows and doors, although no one could easily see them in the rear of their house.

"How soon?" he asked, continuing his amorous touch. "We gotta have time, because I'm gonna explode right here. I need your hot body, Ginny Arena. Three minutes." She continued gently resisting. "Don't make me beg." He unzipped his pants and put his hand up her shirt, and he placed her hand on his manhood. "I love your big ones," he moaned.

Ginny couldn't believe herself. She was having sex right in their kitchen. He was wrong, though. He only needed a minute.

Around the corner at Marianna's house, Aaron Silver was listening to a variation on the theme of cheating. They had been having wine in the living room, reading the papers, when Marianna broached the subject.

"So guess what happened on our walk today?" she teased. He peered above the *New York Times*, adjusting his horn-rimmed bifocals to show interest. She proceeded to tell him about Mimmi and Graham's dilemma. "It was stressful, watching her make herself vulnerable like that. And it's always difficult to hear about a marriage in demise, don't you agree?"

"Of course, of course. I'm sorry your walk wasn't fun today. You usually enjoy the gals' company," he said, still glancing at his newspaper, which he held off to one side.

"Well," Marianna continued, "I told Mimmi about the couple with the gorgeous gardens. Do you remember, Aaron? The husband had an affair with the babysitter."

"No, no. I don't recall that story at all. It seems I would. Who would be so stupid as to fool around with a kid? And why did you tell her about that?" he asked curiously.

"Mimmi was feeling so bad about her circumstances, so I thought it would help her to know that couples can survive affairs, even ones so blatantly wrong as an adult and a teen."

"She was a teenager?" he asked in disbelief. He put the paper down and took off his glasses. He readjusted his sensible shoes on the ottoman and unbuttoned his navy-blue cardigan sweater. His almost completely white hair made him look older than his early sixties.

"Your blue eyes are sparkling," she commented. "Do I have your attention, Dr. Silver?"

"You always have my attention, Madam Dr. Silver," he answered.

"The couple still lives at Hagys Ford and Righter's Mill Roads. The babysitter apparently was a Lolita. Rumor had it that the guy would drive the babysitter home and tell his wife he was talking to her parents. You know, explaining why it took so long. After all, the girl only lived a couple of blocks away. But there wasn't any talking going on. The wife, suspecting something was amiss, left her kids home asleep in their beds while she coasted her car into place across the street from the babysitter's house, strategically situated behind some kind of tall bushes. She watched her husband and the girl grope and kiss and do all kinds of seamy stuff. When the guy finally got out of the car, he adjusted himself, if you get my drift. The wife had the weirdest reaction, though. She apparently found it stimulating and began touching herself."

Aaron couldn't resist. "Masturbating, Marianna. Adults call it masturbating, not touching one's self."

"Yes, Aaron, I know what it's called." She rolled her eyes. "So, yes, the wife began *masturbating* right there in her car. The owner of the house where she was parked called the police. When the police car's headlights shined in her car window, she was at a loss to explain to the officer why she was wildly digging around in her own crotch. She told him she had dropped a bag of candy in her lap and was feeling around for the pieces. The officer asked her to get out of the car. At that very moment, her husband's car pulled out of the babysitter's driveway, and he saw his wife engaged with the officer. Can you believe this story?" Aaron had flipped the paper over on the side table and was reaching for his glasses. "Aaron, are you listening?"

"I'm fully engaged, Marianna. I'm actually quite intrigued. Have I ever met these people?" he asked, standing to refill her wine glass. He poured another for himself and rested his glass on the baby grand piano, leaning on it like a bar as he faced his wife.

"Yes. I'll tell you who they are in a minute," she answered. "Listen to the end of the story. The guilty husband assumed the officer had been called because they were on to his antics with the babysitter, and he started out with 'It's not what you think, Officer.' The cop said, 'Who are you?' Stunned, because he assumed his wife had already explained his affair with the girl, he said, 'She's older than she looks.' Thoroughly disgusted, the officer said, 'Listen, lady, I don't know who this kook is,' and she interrupted and explained that it was her husband. The cop said, 'I'm going to arrest your wife for indecent exposure unless you have a good explanation as to why she was wiggling around and steaming up the car here, having her own little party at one o'clock in the morning.' The guy was so relieved it wasn't about his affair with the babysitter that he said he wasn't sure what his wife was up to but offered she had been acting strange lately, and he suspected it was due to hormones. He promised to keep a closer eye on her if the officer would just let her go home with him. The husband was driving some kind of fancy sports car that the officer thought was sweet or something. They talked cars for a minute. The husband, being aware he'd just received a huge break, slipped the officer a crisp fifty-dollar bill. The officer agreed to let the woman go home, and the couple apparently learned their lesson."

Aaron looked perplexed. "Why was she masturbating? Would you find it stimulating if I was fooling around with a kid—one of Jeremy's girlfriends, for example?"

She responded, without missing a beat, in her best psychologist's voice, "Have you thought about fooling around with one of Jeremy's girlfriends?"

"Don't do this, Marianna. It can only end poorly," Aaron warned.

"Maybe not," she quipped. "I've thought about you with a younger woman. Your white hair, neatly groomed beard, your professorial demeanor—it is all such a turn-on for younger women. Kind of like a Freud thing, the big daddy of them all. Come on, Aaron, all those late nights marking papers. Really? Just papers? No taut-skinned coeds to counsel?" She stood now too, and was very close to him, running her fingers around the edge of her wine glass.

He became aroused, thinking of the myriad of opportunities that had presented themselves over the years. University campuses were a breeding ground for indiscretion, but Aaron never succumbed to the temptation. He met his bride when she was finishing her PhD in psychology and fell madly in love during a heated debate about sexism.

She confidently convinced him that chivalry was sexist and that her arms were capable of opening her own doors. He reprogrammed his behavior to reflect her beliefs. He adored her then, and over the years, he grew more deeply in love. Their sex life wasn't as active as it once was, but Aaron attributed that to his age. He was almost sixty-three. It wasn't that he didn't desire her, but he was just a slower start than he was twenty-five years ago. But this discussion was working its magic on him.

"Really, Marianna, it's always been you, darling. The young ones come into my office. They employ their best feminine wiles, and I think of you—your confidence, your mind, your supple body, your experience, your commitment to our family. You are it, my darling. You were then, and you are now."

"When you met the *masturbating woman*, you commented on how little makeup and pretense she had."

Aaron wanted more talk about their relationship. "Oh, Marianna, I don't care about this odd couple. I care that we have survived all this nonsense and are still so intrigued by one another. Doesn't that mean anything?" He looked at her with the crooked smile she had come to understand as his effort at flirtation.

She smiled. "But you are attracted to other women. I've seen it." She wouldn't quit.

"Of course. I'm old, not dead. But you and I have a history. We know the nuances. I know you have a bump on the nape of your neck and that you have a heart-shaped mole on your inner thigh. I know your right breast is slightly bigger than your left. I know your favorite poet is Emily Dickinson and that your favorite movie is *Moonstruck*." He paused, hoping this would be enough. She just looked at him. He continued. "I know your favorite philosophers are Sartre and Anais Nin. I know your favorite food is osso bucco. I know you lost your virginity as an undergrad with your advisor."

She stood as close to Aaron as she could. Because he was short and she tall, they were almost eyeball to eyeball when she kissed him gently on his neck. Marianna wouldn't give up with her teasing. "I introduced you years ago, when Jeremy was still going to the playground. She's the only woman who ever made me feel jealous." She paused for a moment, as if she was digging deep into the recesses of her mind; then, she went on. "She's a redhead. I almost cried because I knew you were attracted to her, and you told me I was ridiculous. Then I asked why you changed our commuting route to include driving past her house."

Aaron lit up, although he tried to disguise his recollection of the beautiful redhead. Admittedly, he did love seeing the redhead in cut-off denim shorts. What legs! "Oh, yes, yes, yes. And then I met her husband—very disappointing man. Not as self-assured as she. Yes, I do remember. Wow. That's the couple? She was gorgeous."

Marianna knew she'd piqued his interest. "And I know who the babysitter was too." She leaned in closer. "She was also a real looker."

"She must have been quite a looker for the husband to risk losing that redhead!" He thought of what the girl must have been like. "You are a tease," he scolded playfully. "Who was the babysitter?"

"A former student of yours."

"Of mine? You're sure? Why is it just coming up now? Why not then, Marianna? You are fabricating this as you go along." He waved her off and shook his head from side to side. "Forget this nonsense! You don't know the babysitter!" He walked back to his reading chair, reaching for his glasses that he'd left on the side table.

She approached him from behind and said again, "I do know who the babysitter was and yes, she was once a student of yours." He pivoted to look at her. She gently rubbed his groin through his pants. "Oh, yes, I do, sir. Oh, yes, I do!" She giggled uncontrollably.

He wanted to hear more. "Tell me more, you storyteller, you. I know you're making this up, and in a strange way that makes it more titillating." He was becoming aroused as she continued her tease.

"Maybe I was afraid to tell you because I … I don't know why."

He threw his head back, laughing. Marianna hated that gesture. She felt it was condescending. She stopped her game, but he continued.

"You are talking to a psychiatrist, and you are a psychologist. Do you expect me to believe that you think this conversation is coincidental, or that you don't know every detail, or the why and the how, or the why now? Really, Marianna!" The thrown-back head was definitely a condescending gesture.

"Okay. I thought you'd have a vicarious interest in the babysitter because of her connection to the redhead. I knew you were attracted to the redhead. The babysitter would be an easy path to getting to know the redhead. It's not logical, I know. But I'd never seen you have such an obvious attraction to another woman. I didn't want to take any chances." She moved away, running her hands through her short shocks of gray hair.

He put his glasses back on the table and started toward her again. Then he spoke more loudly. "That's my girl. I knew you were aware. That really turns me on. Come, come. Let's do reminisce." His hands were all over his lovely bride—his brilliant, beautiful bride.

She slightly resisted his touch but turned around to face him. Her glaring green eyes didn't intimidate him. "What's the first thing that comes to mind, Professor?" She simultaneously brushed him off and retrieved her almost-empty glass of wine from the piano. She tipped the glass upside down over her opened mouth, then returned it to the piano. She brushed against him. "I love reminiscing," she whispered in his ear. She wrapped her leg around the back of his thigh and held on to him. He braced himself on the piano. He was in amazing shape. She could feel the result of years of working out in his strong shoulders. "Mmm. You smell so good. I love your musk," she said. He pushed her backward while caressing her and kissing her neck. He held on to her leg that was still loosely wrapped around his. They stumbled into the reading chair where they continued their game.

"And you are so provocative, Dr. Silver," he said, kissing her hard.

"Or is it—" she started, but he interrupted her with a *shush*, and he continued to kiss and caress her until they heard a car door close in the driveway.

Marianna quickly jumped up and moved to the couch on the other side of the room. She fluffed her short-cropped hair and giggled like a school girl. Aaron had already smoothed his sweater, which had become twisted. He was adjusting his reading glasses and resumed reading the paper as Jeremy unlocked the door.

"Hey. What's up, Dad?" he said as he dropped his backpack and gym bag in the entrance hall. "Oh, hey, Mom. I didn't see you there." Marianna stood and approached him for an after-school kiss. "What's for dinner? I am starving!" Then to Aaron, "Dad, you should have seen me today. I was awesome in practice."

"That's great, son. What was your time?" Aaron asked.

"Two seconds better than yesterday!"

Their banter went back and forth, and Marianna was relieved that Jeremy didn't seem to know anything had been transpiring between his parents.

Charlotte, meanwhile, sat in her living room, thinking about the day's events over a glass of Merlot, while classical music played softly in the background. Any one incident would have sufficed to make her day interesting, but together, the events amounted to overload. She picked up the glass and swirled the wine, slurping in a big gulp. A cordial breakfast with Betsy; Mimmi's revealing of her sad marital circumstances; the crazy old lady with the bag of dog poop; and then the weird story about the cheating husband and his publicly masturbating wife was all too much for her. She pushed off her velvet monogrammed house shoes and tilted her head back into the chair's headrest as she replayed the day. She'd have plenty of time to do some reminiscing of her own: Charles wouldn't be home until much later from his New York golf outing, and Betsy was rehearsing for the school play and wouldn't be home for several hours.

Maybe I should be more concerned about my marriage, she thought, glancing at their wedding portrait on the bookshelf next to her chair. *After all, Charles is handsome and financially successful. He'd be a good catch for anyone*, she thought, fearing he might be tiring of her midlife ailments. She reached for a more current photo of Charles that was on the same shelf as the wedding portrait. She had recently put his photo in an antique silver frame, a frame that complemented his salt-and-pepper hair. "You are still a good catch for me, Charles Wentworth," she said, hugging the photo to her chest. She took another sip of wine, still hugging the photo. The music was coming to a crescendo. Charlotte put the glass on a small drum table next to the green velvet chair and put the photo back on the shelf.

"I'm exhausted," she said, yawning and stretching her arms. She dozed off, dreaming of her handsome groom and eagerly awaiting his return so she could share the adventures of her day.

Charlotte was startled from her dreamy state by the slamming of the front door.

"Mom, I'm home."

"Hi, sweetie, how was rehearsal?" Charlotte yawned and fussed with her hair, then got up and walked toward Betsy.

"Just waking up?" Betsy asked sarcastically.

"Yeah, you know, Daddy's not coming home until late tonight, and I thought I'd chill out here with a glass of wine and listen to some music." Charlotte hesitated saying more, not wanting to ruin what had been a good morning between them. "I really enjoyed our morning together, Betsy. I wish they could all be like it was this morning." She kissed her daughter tenderly on the cheek. Betsy arched an eyebrow and smirked. "I did like it," Charlotte reinforced.

"Actually, Daddy is coming home earlier tonight. He texted me while I was at the play and said he'd try to reach you but you didn't answer. Apparently, the golf outing ended earlier than he'd thought it would, so he wanted to come home. He said he'd call when he got off the turnpike."

Charlotte had ducked into the powder room to catch another glimpse of herself, even though she had just glanced in the living room mirror.

Betsy, who had gone to the kitchen, was calling, "*Mommmm*! I thought after your breast surgery they told you to dump caffeine and alcohol. Did you drink all this wine tonight? And I know you are a caffeine nut. Come on. What would you do if I ran or something after I had mono. You could get cancer again, Mom. It's just stupid, you know."

Charlotte cupped her left breast. Just hearing the word cancer made her cringe. She'd dodged the bullet two years ago, enduring six weeks of radiation but not needing chemo after a lumpectomy. Betsy was right; she should be taking extraordinary measures to take better care of herself—she was at risk now that she'd had cancer. She closed her eyes, shaking her head. *No, no, no.* She was one of the lucky ones, and still the ordeal had left her scarred and scared and often paralyzed emotionally.

"I've cut back on my social drinking, Betsy, but I really do enjoy an occasional glass of wine," Charlotte said, joining her daughter in the kitchen. "You make a good point, though, sweetie, and I'm going to take it as a sign that underneath all that rough and tumble girl of mine, you really care about me." She smiled. "How's calc going?" Betsy rolled her eyes as she grazed through the leftovers with the refrigerator door open.

Charlotte was thrilled to see Charles, who returned shortly after Betsy had left the kitchen with a tray of junk food, leftover veal stew and rice, and the requisite teen drink, Red Bull. Charles used the powder room, leaving the door ajar and yelling to Charlotte, who was filling two glasses with filtered water from the refrigerator's door.

"I had a great game today. Man, I hit the ball like I was thirty again," he joked. "No, really, I was hitting them long and straight today.

And that course is one special golf club! Wow! It was almost worth having to golf with that pompous ass, Kennett Deans." He raised his voice so Charlotte could hear over the flushing toilet and the tap water he ran to wash his hands. He splashed water on his face and sighed. "God, that guy just gets to me. Every hole, he had to comment, like he was a pro or something. But you know what, sweetie?" He looked around for a hand towel to dry his face. "I'm probably going to be in on the parcel near New Hope that I told you about. Kennett is locked in with the zoning guys and for whatever reason, the guy likes me." He put the towel back. Charlotte was standing in the center hall with the two glasses of water. "Oh, I didn't realize you were right there," he commented. "So anyway, that was my golf day. Did I kiss you yet?" he asked as he pecked her cheek. "I'm fried." He took the glass and started upstairs. "So, how was your day?"

Charlotte followed him, turning off light switches as she made her way upstairs. "My day was interesting," answered Charlotte. She shut the big doors behind her. "I had a great morning with Betsy, and I actually think the good energy from our Starbucks distraction-from-driving experience spilled over into our conversation after school." She placed the water on her bedside table and moved to the dressing room adjacent to the bedroom, where Charles was already undressing. They stepped into their respective walk-in closets simultaneously. Charlotte reached for a silk embroidered T-shirt and slipped it over her head. Then she stepped into the matching swingy-cropped bottoms. They exchanged smiles and some garbled niceties while brushing their teeth and gargling. Charlotte was removing her wedding rings, which she left on her night table, as Charles sat on the bed.

"Ah," Charles sighed as he plopped himself onto the down comforter.

"No, no, no," she reprimanded. "Not on the comforter!" He grumbled and stood up as she removed the bedcover, placing it on the nearby chaise. He wasted no time getting comfortable under the lightweight blanket and crisp sheets.

Charlotte opened the double door to the center hall and yelled a good-night to Betsy, whose suite was down the long hallway and around a corner. She heard a muffled response, which she assumed was Betsy's indication she had heard Charlotte. She shut the door and turned off the lights. Situating herself next to Charles, she used the cover of darkness to broach an uncomfortable subject.

"Have you ever cheated on me, Charles?" There was quiet, except for a neighbor's barking dog. Charlotte felt like she could hear her heart pounding. "Ever? Did you ever touch or kiss or anything with anyone else?"

Charles rolled over, facing her, although it was tough to see anything. "What in the hell happened today? Why would you ask me this ridiculous question? Why would I cheat on you? I hate these inquisitions. I fucking hate it." He rolled back to his side of the bed and covered his head with a pillow.

She persisted, raising her voice. "I'm serious. Have you ever done anything that even resembles cheating—touching, kissing, drinks, even ... like a date?"

He grumbled through the pillow and then threw it off his head to the other side of the room. "No! Why are you badgering me with this crap again? I have never cheated on you, and I never will. I might leave you someday because you can drive me nuts. And believe me when I tell you this, Charlotte. If I ever leave you, it will be because of this insecure behavior. I fucking detest this!"

She didn't give up. Clearing her throat, she continued. "Well, I'm sure Graham Biddle didn't plan on cheating. It just happened. And now their whole family is going to come undone, just like that."

Charles fumbled for the light on his nightstand, knocking over the water glass he'd placed there. "Goddamn it, Charlotte! Now look what you've made me do. Is it possible I could have just had a great day and fallen asleep without this nonsense?" He clicked on the switch, and Charlotte scrunched her face. She had just gotten used to the dark. He continued yelling as he got up for a towel to soak up the water. "Their life didn't come unraveled *just like that*," he said, mocking her. "Come on, Charlotte. You're smarter than that. And I am not Graham Biddle. I don't know him, but I can tell you he's an ass." He returned with a towel and began wiping up the mess. "Married people shouldn't cheat. Period. It's that simple. And I resent being lumped together with asses like him."

She got up and picked up the empty glass that was on its side on the rug. "I don't know. Maybe it's the breast scare again. I mean, God, what will we do if I have cancer again?" She welled up. "I mean, it was two years of shit—finding the lump, getting evaluated, second opinions, surgery, depression, and all the waiting. In some ways I feel like we're still waiting. Oh God, the waiting! I feel so guilty saying it like this because I caught a break, but I don't want to go through it again."

"I was there too, Charlotte. We all were there—Elliot, James, and Betsy, too. But come on. What does that have to do with this crazy shit you pulled tonight?" He went for another towel to clean up the rug.

She felt as empty as the glass she held. She just stood watching him.

"Look, Charlotte, a recall for testing isn't a death sentence. Wait to see what happens. I can certainly get that you're scared, but look at you. You still have your life, your health, your breast, for godssake. That's way more than a lot of women wind up with."

She wiped her eyes with a tissue from the decorative tissue box holder on her nightstand. She blew her nose and got up to throw the tissue in the bathroom can. Charles looked at the wall clock, wondering if he'd be able to go to sleep soon.

Charlotte returned from the bathroom. "I want us to make it, and I want more out of life."

"You sound depressed again, Charlotte. You were doing so well. I don't understand how someone in the neighborhood that you barely know can have marital trouble and that causes you to come unglued."

"There's so much more, Charles. I mean, being organized around you and your work stuff all these years has taken its toll on me." She got back in their bed and continued, "I'm embarrassed for myself. I've let myself go, intellectually and professionally. I can barely hold my own at cocktail parties."

"We haven't been to a cocktail party in so long."

"Oh, come on, Charles! I'm pouring my heart out and all you can add is the cocktail bit? Do you ever have feelings about us? You are such a—"

"Let me finish, please. I really want to tell you this. I very much want you to know that I know there is something wrong here. I'm sure it's been hard with the breast cancer scare. But you're not alone. I'm here for you. You have friends that care, but they don't even know. You blew them off. You shut them out. How can you wonder why you're lonely?" He struggled to find the next words. "I know it's not all you or all about the breast situation, this loneliness and insecurity you feel. I know there is a component to it that has to do with where we are in midlife—both of us, individually and probably together, too." She rolled her eyes, and he scolded, "Don't minimize what it's like for me, Charlotte."

"Let me tell you what it's like, Charles; how it feels, okay? Then you tell me if you really get me," she said. "I feel like I died along the way, and I can't even tell you when or how it happened. I'm not alive. Not even during what used to be happy events for me." She blew her nose. "You work. You make deals. You have a purpose. What is my purpose? Making a castle for you and the kids? Entertaining stuffy business associates?" She was crying now. "Where is that young vibrant girl? I loved her! She was full of promise. She was brilliant and beautiful. She wanted to have a career. She wanted a large family." Her voice grew louder. "I wanted it all, Charles. Just like you! I wanted big things for myself, just like you. Not the same things but big. I wanted a gallery or to be a college professor. I wanted to be the beautiful hostess in a silk dress who sat around a table drinking fine wines and discussing the future of the world with intellectuals and artists and people who gave a crap about the stuff that interests me!"

"Charlotte … Charlotte … you are still that girl. Time is still ticking, and you have lots of it left to live. Go open that art gallery. Go be that professor. Stop giving lectures where you don't feel it matters."

"That's what you say now, but twenty years ago you couldn't find your way out of a brown paper bag without me, and I helped you, at the cost of my own work life. And look at me. I hate myself! I've become one of those women that I hated in college. I've smiled behind the scenes at too many *Charles* events. When is it my turn? When can I use the resources for me? And now this …" she cupped her small breasts in her hands.

"Look, Charlotte. Don't use this retest as another excuse. No one is stopping you. Go get what you want for yourself. I still see that vibrant girl. You can still have what you want. It's not too late." He sighed, then yawned. "I'm here, Charlotte. There's no need to be lonely. I'm here and I'm not going anywhere, but we can't keep rehashing the past; it's over—your mistakes, my mistakes; why you're where you are; how I became successful; why the boys grew up to be such great men; why, why, why. It's a vicious cycle. Forget about where you were. Here you are, and here I am. Go get what you want."

She fell back onto her pillows. He gently brushed her cheek. He then felt her left breast, leaning in and kissing it through the silk T-shirt.

"I love your body and your mind. I love all of you. Just love yourself, Charlotte." He moved to his side of the bed and got settled under his covers. He was asleep almost as fast as his head hit the pillow.

"I love you," she whispered.

Chapter Six

"Thanksgiving arrives on the fourth Thursday of November each year," Charlotte began as the walkers set out on this early November morning. "Yet each year I am surprised by how family dysfunction, which tags along as an unexpected guest, is so highlighted." She'd hit a chord with her friends, and the walkers all started chattering at once, discussing the messiness of the holidays and why that came as a surprise. After all, if the past was a predictor of the future, then most likely this Thanksgiving would bring disappointment, anger, and frustration.

"Gosh, doesn't this Thanksgiving stuff get old?" asked Charlotte. "Here we are, the first week in November, and I'm already stressed."

"What do you mean?" asked Kate as she stopped to adjust her new Ugg boots. Kate, like Charlotte, liked her walking outfits to be coordinated. Her shoulder-length hair was pulled up in a fashionable clip, creating a floppy ponytail that complemented the rest of her sporty look: slate-gray spandex pants and mock turtleneck top. Her white quilted vest was a sharp contrast to her shiny dark hair. "I love Thanksgiving. I mean, I don't love the extended-family hassles, like who can come, where we'll have it, or lately, the kids' resistance. Now that they are older, they want to stay local to be near their friends. But overall, it's fun to be with the whole family, whoever shows up. I love that Doug isn't thinking about work, and we all pitch in to help cook and clean up. The refrigerator-grazing the next day is fun, too, even if we all overeat. I don't even mind having company. The only thing I don't like is traveling if we go to my in-laws' place in Connecticut. The traffic is always horrendous."

"So how can you say you love Thanksgiving if you have all those annoyances?" Charlotte asked.

Kate adjusted her hair clip before answering. "I don't know. I just tune out the noise, and I love having the bonding time with Doug and the kids." She unzipped the white vest and pulled up the waistband of her workout pants. The spandex workout outfit revealed a middle-aged figure. She'd stopped working out regularly and walking was the only exercise she engaged in anymore, yet still she carried herself confidently.

Charlotte described her irritation over her sons' dilemmas. Elliot and James were in their twenties now, and she was agitated by the notion that a guy should spend the holidays with his girl's family. "Wait until your kids are romantically involved," said Charlotte. "Your son will be expected to go with his girl's family. I don't know who made that rule, but it certainly wasn't my boys. I can hear the angst when James talks about having to spend the holiday with his girlfriend's pedestrian family."

Kate cringed. Marianna, trying to divert Charlotte from what she suspected was a sore subject for her, said, "Wow, look at that! Aren't these leaves incredible? I love living where the seasons change. I would hate living in Florida or California or someplace where it's virtually the same climate all the time."

"Yeah, but do you rake your own leaves? That's a pain in the neck," said Ginny. "And forget Anna helping. Joe and I can hardly get her to make her bed, let alone clean up the yard."

"I know, it's hard to get the kids to help with anything,". said Marianna. She didn't want Charlotte to talk about Thanksgiving anymore. "All Jeremy cares about right now is driving." She rubbed the sides of her head, fluffing her very short locks until the hair in some spots stood straight out.

"What's with you and the rubbing the hair all the time?" Ginny asked brusquely. "You look like a damn hamster—they're always grooming themselves. Really, you drive me nuts with that."

Marianna giggled nervously. Mimmi, who had been quiet, giggled too.

"It's a nervous habit," said Marianna, looking a bit embarrassed. "I drive my husband crazy too. I'm working on it."

"What are you nervous about?" asked Ginny, not letting it go.

"You are harsh," Charlotte reprimanded Ginny. "Look at the leaves on that lawn," she said, pointing to a Tudor-style house with burnt-orange shutters. She'd let go of the discussion about her sons.

"That's the Wilkes's house. I noticed they've been painting and fixing up. I wonder if they're thinking of selling, now that they're empty-nesters," Ginny wondered.

Charlotte couldn't imagine selling her house after Betsy left for college next year.

"Hey, Team Fairview, could we slow down?" gasped Kate. "This cold air is getting to me." She coughed to emphasize her point.

"Oh, I love that we have a name. Team Fairview! We should have T-shirts made," exclaimed Mimmi.

Charlotte quelled that notion before it had a chance to materialize. "Oh, my sweeties, I don't wear logo shirts. They make me look—"

"Pedestrian?" Kate blurted out, then turned beet red.

"No, not *pedestrian*. It's just simply that T-shirts are unflattering on almost everyone! We are not wearing them and parading through this neighborhood. We'll be the laughing stock of the Main Line!" declared Charlotte.

Kate rolled her eyes. Mimmi pulled the zipper on her ski jacket so as to not reveal that she was wearing her kids' high school logo T-shirt.

"I'm going to head home," said Kate.

"No, don't go. I'm sorry," said Charlotte.

"It's not anything to do with you guys," Kate said. "I'm meeting with a guy who is looking for a creative director for his home-product wholesale business." She shrugged. "Maybe this will be the thing. You have to throw a lot of stuff against the wall and hope something sticks."

"Or you make a plan," said Ginny. "Whatever. See you. Good luck, Kate."

"What was that about?" asked Charlotte after Kate walked away. "She seemed a little abrupt."

Ginny explained that Kate had looked at many business opportunities and talked about them endlessly, but she'd only focused on the obvious benefits of each opportunity. Then, when they didn't work out because she hadn't fully vetted them, she was disappointed. "It's been a way of life with her since we met her. She has very little idea of what it is she's looking for, and I think she needs to be more selective. She looks for ideas, projects, companies for sale—you name it—all the time. She's ridiculous. Anyway, forget about it. She'll either find something, or she won't. In the meantime, we can just be supportive." Turning to Charlotte, Ginny asked, "So, what did you do last year for Thanksgiving? Do you have a tradition?"

Charlotte sighed.

"That's a big sigh," Ginny said.

"I was recovering from breast surgery last year," Charlotte blurted out. "A lumpectomy. My brother's family came to our house with my parents, and they all cooked. My kids didn't even think of going anywhere else." She ran her hands over her sweater, smoothing it to reveal her small chest, as if to reassure them she still had both breasts.

"Jesus," said Ginny. "I had no idea. I usually know all that stuff. Are you out of the woods? That must have been scary."

"Don't feel like you have to talk about it right now," said Marianna. "I know it takes time to open up about these things. The important thing is that you are here and walking, and you look fantastic."

"No, it's okay. I never told anyone, except one old friend and my family. I felt really awkward. I didn't want any attention. And I was afraid everyone would be asking for details about my breast, the tests, results of tests, my prognosis, my marriage. I felt like everything would become fair game. I've seen it with other women. I don't know how they deal with the lack of privacy! I just didn't want to be all about what wasn't working instead of what was. But the irony is that nothing worked, because I convinced myself it was going to be awful, so it was. It was really awful. The whole issue still is really awful. I was really depressed and my marriage and family life has had to bear the brunt of it. I worry …" She welled up. "See, this is why I can't share this stuff." Tears streamed down her face.

"This is exactly why you should share this stuff," Ginny said convincingly. The group stopped walking, and Marianna reached for Charlotte's hand.

"No, no. Don't feel sorry for me. Please, don't do that. Let's keep walking. Here's the skinny, and then I can't talk about it anymore, not right now: I had a malignant lump removed. It was very, very tiny and completely contained. It was found during a routine mammogram. I couldn't even feel it, even when I knew it was there. I had some radiation, didn't have any terrible side effects, and I have my breast. It looks a little dented." The women laughed. "But I have these horrible tests all the time, and I just got called back for a suspicious-looking something, and I'm terrified."

"Well, of course, you're terrified," said Marianna. "You had cancer. Anyone of us would be feeling the same way. Charlotte, sharing this burden with other people, especially your friends, is important. It is your body, but it isn't just your burden. It belongs to all of us. Each and every one of us lives with the terror each time we have a mammogram or hear about another diagnosis. And we will fight with you, girlfriend, just like you would fight for any one of us." She hesitated. Then jokingly, she added, "You would fight for us, wouldn't you?"

"Thanks, but let's not talk about it right now. I'll let you know what's happening next, but I'm going to fall apart here." Charlotte blew her nose on a tissue she had stuffed in her spandex pants pocket. The women walked in silence for a minute, which seemed like ten.

Marianna felt like the Thanksgiving subject couldn't be worse than cancer so she began talking about her Thanksgiving cooking concerns. She was in a full panic about planning a menu and preparing food for guests. She was considering having dinner catered, but Aaron really wanted to fry a turkey this year.

"I am married to the only Jewish man who wants to fry a turkey! He is convinced it is unique, and he's been researching techniques and brining recipes. I don't want to quell his enthusiasm, but frying turkeys isn't his idea—it's all the rage. There are articles about it in every newspaper and cooking magazine."

"Are they healthy?" asked Mimmi. "I can't even imagine an entire turkey fried." She turned up her nose for effect.

"Of course; it'll be organic."

The women broke into hearty laughs at the notion that the turkey's organic origins mitigated the unhealthy aspect of frying it.

Mimmi pointed out that they were walking by the old lady's house, and she wasn't up for any confrontations. The group had avoided that end of the street since the memorable day when Charlotte confronted the stalwart Mrs. Jaimeson.

"Good call, Mimmi! I certainly would like to forget that day! Can you believe I had to talk my way out of being arrested because of that stodgy old bat?" said Charlotte. "Oh, that would really push me over the edge today!"

They reminisced about how Charlotte's flinging the bag of dog poop set off a string of unfortunate events, not the least of which was being questioned by a group of local officers after she got home.

"God," said Mimmi, "you were almost arrested by that cop! If he hadn't recognized you as the woman who served up the best Christmas cookies in the neighborhood when he came collecting door-to-door for that retirement fund, you'd probably have been arrested! Imagine that!"

"Well, thank goodness my mother had delivered her Christmas ration of cookies to the Wentworth household, or I would have been screwed!" exclaimed Charlotte. "He was really cute, that burly officer. I remembered him right away. Charles used to make jokes about how I had a thing for him. I sort of did. He had the most beautiful smile."

"Yeah, Charlotte, I'm sure it was his smile that turned you on," Marianna teased. "I can tell you one thing: I sure wasn't looking at his smile when he came by my house collecting donations. He's what you call real eye candy!"

The women walked around a huge pile of leaves waiting to be cleaned up by the township. The big truck with a vacuum-cleaner-like attachment could be heard as it sucked up piles of leaves throughout the neighborhood.

"Oh, is that what you sophisticated ladies call it? Eye candy?" asked Ginny. "Where I come from we call the likes of Officer McMillan—"

"Please bite your tongue!" Mimmi broke in before Ginny could do more damage. "I can only imagine what you call him." All eyes turned to Mimmi at once. "What? Why are you looking at me?"

Marianna asked if Graham had actually moved out yet.

Mimmi was a bit defensive. "Yes, I told you we finally told my parents a few weeks ago. I was hoping everyone else just knew by now."

"We aren't sitting in judgment," said Marianna. "But I think we're wondering if you are ready to see anyone yet."

Ginny took over without subtleties, as usual. "You should go out with Officer McMillan, Mimmi. He is so hot. He isn't married. I know."

"How do you know?" Mimmi asked.

"Aha! See? You are interested!" Ginny shouted excitedly. "*How do I know*?" she mimicked. "How do I know anything? It's my job to know what the hell goes on here in River City!"

"River City?" Mimmi was confused.

"From *The Music Man*." Ginny sang a few lines. "The show?" She waited for a glimmer of recognition but none flickered in Mimmi's eyes. "Never mind. Just think about it. Not the show. Officer McMillan.

I can arrange it. I sold his mother's house last year. His first name is Sean."

"I'll think about it," Mimmi said reluctantly.

"That's great, Mimmi!" said Charlotte.

"It's a good time for you to just do it," said Marianna. "It'll be a real boost to your ego. And, by the way, you look great, Mimmi. Have you lost weight?"

"I have been working out at that LA Fitness in Bala Cynwyd. I've been using the bike and the elliptical machine. I can tell I've lost a few LBs because my clothes are a little loose."

"They have a pool there too, don't they?" asked Charlotte. "I thought about joining there because I really need to work out regularly. It's not as much for weight as it is for toning and …" She hesitated.

"What? What were you going to say?" asked Mimmi.

"Well, it'd be good for me to keep my mind off of my health issue. I was really ready to go back to work and then this, and now all I do is … wait. I don't even know what I'm waiting for. I certainly don't want bad news, but it's as if I expect that." Charlotte sighed again.

The women had changed course in their walk to avoid Mrs. Jaimeson's house, and the talk returned to Thanksgiving, as they felt they had exhausted the conversation with Mimmi's marital situation and Charlotte's bomb about her breast cancer.

"Listen, honey, we are all with you. The best thing you did for yourself was start walking with us. We are strong, and we can get through anything," Ginny said confidently. "Let's talk about this Thanksgiving stuff again because I'm curious about what everybody does. I'll tell you about the Arenas, okay?" Ginny was excited about seeing her sisters and brothers and their respective kids. She described the upcoming scene. "I've been celebrating Thanksgiving the same way since I can remember. We get together with my entire extended family. Everybody brings something, and we go to my mom's house, even though our house is a lot bigger and can better accommodate everyone comfortably. It's just out of the question to change venues—no one even asks if it is a possibility.

"I make the cannoli every year. I am so tired just thinking of how many I have to make this year. I never have enough, and every year there seems to be a bigger crowd at my mom's. I love it, though. All my aunts and uncles, cousins, and their kids are there. It's a scene I cherish from my childhood, and it's remained virtually unchanged, except my dad's gone."

"How can you be so skinny and be such a great Italian cook?" asked Marianna. "Are you about a size four?"

Without missing a beat, Ginny said, "Two. I'm a size two. I don't know. Maybe it's my father's genes. He was so skinny! My mother was always feeding him, and he was like a toothpick!"

Even though Mimmi had lost some weight, she was self-conscious about being a bit chubby. She tugged at the jacket that hung at her widest point over her hips. Mimmi's silence about her holiday plans was like the eight-hundred-pound gorilla walking along side of them. But no one had the courage to ask her what she was doing, for fear of inciting a meltdown.

"Well, here we are, Team Fairview," said Marianna as they arrived at her driveway. "Wish me luck with the whole cooking thing." They all started hugging and air kissing.

"I'm going to my brother and sister-in-law's this year," Mimmi awkwardly blurted out. "With the kids; I'm taking the kids." She waited for a reaction. They all stopped and turned, as if waiting for more information.

Marianna spoke first. "I am so glad, Mimmi. You sound up for that. Are you?"

"I am. I'm ready to move forward. I feel like I've been royally screwed, but then I realized, oh, right, he's royally screwing someone else!" The women all giggled nervously, and Mimmi tugged on the hem of her jacket again. "I am so mad and sad," Mimmi said with a quivering voice. "I just want to put the whole mess behind me and move forward, whatever that means. I don't know. I don't have a picture of what moving forward means, but I know I can't stay stuck here in my sensible shoes. I'm buying new kinds of clothes: heels, dresses, and sexy things. And nail polish and lipstick. I told you I even joined a damn health club!"

"You *are* looking great, Mimmi," said Ginny. "I noticed you have new walking shoes. Very hip, Mimmi."

Mimmi wasn't done. "Maybe I am ready to date. I'm lonely; I know that." She wiped a few tears and then assured the women she was okay.

Marianna didn't feel like they could leave on this note. "Well, then we'll start collecting numbers for you, girlfriend! Way to go!"

Ginny chimed in, "I already made a contribution. What about Sean McMillan? Really."

Mimmi started walking toward her house around the corner. "I'm done. I just want you all to know where my head's at."

"Okay, then," Charlotte called after her. "We got it, Mimmi. And we're on your team." Mimmi turned and gave her a crooked smile. "Okay? We are all on your team," Charlotte reiterated. She turned to the other ladies, who were standing in Marianna's driveway. "See you all next week. Good luck with all your plans, and happy turkey day to all!"

The women took separate paths to their respective homes, with Mimmi just slightly ahead of them.

The women hadn't met for a walk since the first week in November. The weather had been brutally cold, and an early snow had covered the streets the week before the holiday. But it was the Tuesday after Thanksgiving and everyone had much to tell, so despite the freezing-cold air, they got together for a walk.

Ginny and Mimmi lived close to each other and not far from Kate's house, so they each walked to Kate's place; she was waiting at the end of her driveway.

"You look so cute in that hat," said Mimmi.

"Actually, I'm thinking my ears are a little cold." Ginny tugged her cap closer around her ears. "Is Marianna coming today? When I called to see if she wanted to walk, she said the holiday season was a super-busy time for her. You know people get depressed and sad for all kinds of reasons around the holidays." Kate's wide-eyed look told Ginny that she might have said the wrong thing in front of Mimmi. When she tried to recover, she made it worse. "I don't know how that girl does it. You know, I'd want to kill myself, listening to other peoples' problems all day long. I'd tell them to go home and get a life!"

"Well, thankfully, Marianna doesn't do that, Ginny," said Kate. "I bet she's really good at what she does. She's a really kind person." Kate turned to Mimmi. "Was Will home much over Thanksgiving, or was he busy catching up with high school friends?"

"Oh, he was home just enough to make the house a mess," Mimmi answered. "He actually brought home a guy who lives on his floor who's from India. Having someone around who had never celebrated Thanksgiving was fun for all of us. The kids enjoyed explaining the custom and our traditions to him, and he was really into it. I think GW has been great for Will. He's thinking about majoring in international studies, which is one of the university's strongest majors."

They stopped walking to look for oncoming traffic before crossing the busy intersection at Conshohocken State Road and Centennial.

The last leaves were hanging on the trees, but most had fallen and collected along the street gutters, which made walking a challenge. The air was cold enough that they could see their breath, and it was crisp enough to keep the walkers moving at a fast clip.

"Oh, look," Ginny said, pointing out a tree that had snapped in half in a nearby yard. "That's happened since we last walked. We are so lucky to have these big, old, beautiful trees, but man, when they go, they can do real damage if they hit the house."

"We have several old trees on our property, but I'm taking them down in the spring," said Kate. "Douglas and I are doing a huge landscaping project."

"Isn't that going to interfere with your finding just the right business to buy, missy?" Ginny asked. "You have to stop sabotaging yourself!"

Kate's mouth dropped open, and she stopped in her tracks. "I am not going to sabotage myself. I can do both: work and have a landscaping project. This business is different!" Ginny let it go.

Marianna was running a little late and had agreed to meet the walkers at Charlotte's house. She was waving to the group, and Kate was grateful because she wanted to bite Ginny's head off for making the remark about her landscaping project. Charlotte's gate at the end of the drive was open, so they meandered onto her property.

"Hi, girls!" yelled Charlotte, jogging to the end of her walkway to meet them. Her auburn hair shined in the sunlight. Her crocheted headband covered her ears, and the large gold hoop earrings hugged her neck. She was wearing shiny, navy-blue spandex and her new hiking boots, along with oversized socks that she rolled over the tops of the boots. Her fisherman's knit sweater complemented the head band.

"Hello, gorgeous," said Ginny. "Did you go shopping over Thanksgiving? New?" She tugged at the sweater.

"No, I've had this forever, but I love it." She looked at everyone. "I'm so glad we are walking today. I really need the exercise. And I can't wait to hear about everyone's holiday."

Mimmi commented on the beautiful pumpkins and gourds that were beautifully placed in urns along Charlotte's driveway. The chrysanthemums were in fall hues of rust, gold, and burgundy, and they served as a centerpiece in each urn. "Did you fill the planters yourself?" asked Mimmi, pointing to the urns.

"No, my gardener has the formula down. He knows exactly what I like each season of the year. But I did this." She stepped over the thick, black decorative chain that hung between posts, meant to indicate to would-be trespassers to stay off the lawn. The other walkers followed her. There in her side yard, leading to the rear of her property, she had covered the arbor in dried hydrangea and highlighted it with winterberries. The red berries attracted the birds that hadn't yet left on their migration to warmer climates, and the arbor looked like a Currier and Ives holiday card.

"Charlotte, it is beautiful!" exclaimed Kate. "Did you take photos of it?"

"You are so talented," Mimmi joined in, admiring Charlotte's creativity.

"Stop, ladies. You're embarrassing me," said Charlotte. "It's just my nervous energy."

Kate arched her eyebrows. "Something you want to tell us?"

"Really, it's nothing," Charlotte responded.

"Okay, then, let's get on with our walk, and Martha Stewart, here," Ginny teased, nodding toward Charlotte, "can lead the way in telling and sharing the tales of Thanksgiving." The women moved across the lawn to the long driveway and then out to the street. "You know you have the nicest house in the neighborhood, Charlotte, right?"

"I feel very blessed," said Charlotte, blushing.

Thanksgiving had left a tangled web of feelings in its wake. Kate was the first to speak. She flipped her dark hair over her right shoulder and adjusted her sunglasses. "Our Thanksgiving was great this year. Emma brought home two girlfriends from her pledge class—you know, her sorority at college. They were adorable. Bess and Rachel, being a typical high school freshman and junior, were fascinated with Emma's friends, and Jake was free of the usual pressure from his older sisters. It's tough being thirteen and the only boy. Doug and I talked about what was different this year, other than Emma's friends. Over the past few years our extended families have become so demanding that it's virtually impossible to please them, so we don't even try. The noise is still there, but we're happy doing our own thing. And it's become hard, with

Emma in college now and Rachel in her junior year of high school and beginning to think of herself as not having to participate in every family event. There are too many moving parts; too many people to please."

"Kate, sounds like your holiday came off without a hitch," Charlotte said.

"That's great," commented Mimmi.

"Hey, Mimmi, how did it go with Will home?" asked Charlotte. "That can be rough sometimes, that freshman first-time-home visit."

Mimmi repeated the story she had already shared with Kate and Ginny.

"Okay, so how was your Thanksgiving, Ginny?" asked Charlotte.

"We all we went to my mother's house, as planned," said Ginny, "and it was the usual cast of thousands. Joe says it's like a Cecil B. DeMille film. I come from a large family, and I'm the youngest one. But as I told you a few weeks ago, I love it!" They walked around a parked car. Ginny looked back to be sure no cars were coming as they edged out into the street.

"Oh, Ginny, what happened with your nephew who's dating that black girl?" asked Kate. "Did he bring her?"

"African American, Kate," Marianna reprimanded. "Not black."

"Please, You have no idea," said Ginny. "The poor girl—forget whether she's African American or black. She's not Italian, and that's the problem with my family. She is adorable in every way—smart, beautiful, poised. But why he would bring her to Mother's house with such a bunch of narrow-minded idiots is beyond me. My Anna and her boyfriend talked to her. My sister Ro and her family were sweet. But the rest of them! Please, they'd rather have their toenails pulled out. It was tense. The only good news for the kid is that my family's insane. I think she was in shock and didn't even notice the freakin' nut-jobs they are."

"Whose son is dating her?" Mimmi asked.

"My brother Tony's son, Tony Junior."

"They call him Tony Junior?" Mimmi continued.

"Clearly, you are not Italian," Ginny snapped. "Anyway, I think between my mother's sisters and their extended families and my dad's family, who still come, out of sympathy for my mom—"

"How long's your dad been gone?" Charlotte asked.

"Twenty years." Everyone laughed, including Ginny. She was different from her extended family and yet they were her people. She fully and proudly claimed them as her own.

"Doug's family is a little like that," said Kate. "Maybe it's just the nature of large families—you know, more things to go wrong."

"Or maybe it's the nature of ethnic families," piped in Marianna. "Are you ready for my story?" The group paused to look for cars as they crossed Hagys Ford Road. Marianna continued, a little out of breath. "Aaron's wacky brother from Washington called to say he couldn't come because his ten-year-old Labrador retriever was hemorrhaging, and they'd probably have to put him down." The walkers grimaced or moaned. "We love our dog too," Marianna continued. "And maybe we overthink things—"

"Not you and Aaron, Marianna," Kate broke in. "You would never overthink anything. Really, a psychiatrist and a social psychologist?"

"Don't make fun," Marianna said, looking a bit hurt. Everyone laughed anyway. "Okay, but come on. He had train tickets for the whole family. The kids were excited to see their cousins. Put the damn dog in a kennel and be done with it. Or one of them could have stayed home, and the other one come with the kids. It is a holiday, after all."

"What did Aaron say?" asked Kate.

"Well, that's where it gets complicated. He tried using the shrink stuff. *I know the dog is like a son to you. It must be so difficult. I'm so sorry you have to say good-bye to your loyal old friend. He has been a good companion to you, Mariel, and the children.* It didn't work, so in shrink-speak, 'he acted out,' and then I got pissed, and then Jeremy weighed in."

"God, I'm worn out just listening," said Mimmi. "Did the dog live?"

Marianna rolled her eyes. "Well, apparently. But they spent four thousand dollars to keep him alive. He's ten freaking years old! My God, you have no idea how nuts these people are! The dog has a titanium hip, he's had an ACL done, and he's had a bunch of surgeries because he grows these weird tumors. It's not like they don't have children, and this dog is a substitute child or something. They are so eccentric, it's unbelievable." She paused for a bit as they crossed another street. "So in the midst of regrouping, we kept getting Licorice Silver updates." She mimicked her brother-in-law, "*Licorice is so amazing. I think he's doing a bit better. We went to visit him today*. Blah, blah, blah, blah, blah! Really, you could puke."

"Oh, my God, that is the cutest name for a Lab!" said Mimmi, tugging on the hem of her new North Face coat. It covered her torso from neck to knees in down-quilted comfort and style. She chose brown to complement her strawberry-blonde hair.

Marianna continued, "And then they came anyway, on Sunday, for the day. By Sunday, I had had it with everyone. I didn't want more company. We wound up having Jeremy's friend's family, the Bronsteins, because the mom had bronchitis, and they'd canceled their plans to go to New York. They were going to be alone, and I thought we were going to be alone, so I invited them. No good deed goes unpunished! I had such a houseful; by Sunday night, I was ready for the loony bin!"

"Aww, but the dog lived," said Mimmi, ever the cock-eyed optimist.

"Yes, Mimmi, the dog lived," Marianna sighed.

Kate rolled her eyes. "Everybody has their craziness around holidays," she interjected. "How about those people who tell you how many people they had for dinner, like it's meaningful? It drives me crazy. My sister-in-law, who uses paper plates, was bragging that she had forty people. Who cares? I swear she drags people in from the street just to make her numbers bigger. It's like a sales meeting instead of a family dinner. You know, everyone reports on their very best experiences for the year that's passed. They eat a lot, and then, when they get bored, they start to drink."

"That does sound like a sales meeting," said Charlotte. "You know, going along with the sales meeting theme, I heard Jennifer Holmes Bartlett went to the islands with the whole extended family and stayed at the Ritz-Carlton. They have a large family. I think the article said there were sixty-two of them. There's been a second marriage for one of her in-laws or something. I think that's why there are so many of them."

Kate chimed in, "A second marriage. It sounds like a joint venture—sixty-two people. My God, we have four kids, and I can't imagine it ever getting that large. Bigger is definitely better in some circumstances, but sixty-two people for dinner is ridiculous."

Charlotte nodded as she continued with the story of her former college roommate. "Jennifer's mother thought it'd be great, since there's always someone who can't travel too far. She thought if they picked a fun family spot and everyone traveled about the same distance, more family could come."

Ginny commented that she had read about the story in the *Philadelphia Inquirer* in a special section on how local people were celebrating the holiday.

Kate piped in, "I think it's so cool that your college roommate is a senator. Were you guys really close in school? I mean, I know you were roommates, but a lot of people aren't close with their college homies." She explained that *homies* was an expression for people you live with. "As in h-o-m-e," Kate said. "Homies."

"Thanks for that explanation," said Ginny. "I was a little lost there for a minute."

"Just wait till Anna starts college," said Kate. "You'll get a whole new education."

Charlotte cocked her head and bit her bottom lip ever so slightly, as if Kate's question required a lot of thought. "Was I close with Jen in school?" she repeated. "We were. She was always really interested in the greater good. I always felt so inadequate around her, because I was an art history major, and I used to think, *Wow, here's somebody who's majoring in public policy, who's an activist and a straight-A student. She's actually doing stuff already. She's not waiting until after college to start her life. This is her life.* Yeah, we were close in a lot of ways, and I always looked up to her. I still do. She's one of those amazing women who can simply focus on the task at hand and the rest seems to just take care of itself. I mean, she's doing big, big things. And ladies, she is the real deal. She has always believed in service. I love her. I am so proud to call her my friend."

Marianna added her opinion. "Well, I think people know when they're young if they have a calling to service, like rabbis and ministers, or doctors."

Charlotte mentioned how much she adored Jennifer, but at times, Jennifer was just another reminder of the life Charlotte had let drift away; that many people from Charlotte's past had accomplished big goals and expected the same of her. Yet when she'd bumped into the senator at the hair salon, Jennifer made her feel like it was old times. They *did* have wonderful times together—like the time Jennifer ran for student body president, and they worked around the clock for days, silk-screening T-shirts with her name and potential office on the front, and her platform printed on the back. Jennifer conscripted someone in the art department to work pro bono for her cause. From that time through her first senate run, Charlotte was part of Holmes Bartlett's A-team.

"What the heck happened to me, ladies?" Charlotte wondered aloud. "I was very close with Jennifer for so many years. I did so many big things for her, for businesses I was involved with, for charity causes. What happened to me?"

Everyone in the group made light, joking responses, because they saw Charlotte as the most accomplished of all of them. They didn't know she felt as unraveled as each of them did.

"Charles happened to you. Your three kids happened to you. Being a working mom happened to you," Kate said.

Ginny added, "Aging parents, moving, what else?" She threw her arms up. "It all happened. Life happened to all of us, didn't it?" Then she jokingly added, "Shit happened!" She put her arm around Charlotte as the group walked in silence.

To everyone's relief, Marianna changed the subject. "So what did you do for the holidays, Charlotte? Did your boys come home? Betsy must love the action."

Charlotte sighed. "Well, Elliot came home with his girlfriend, Zoe, whom I adore. James flew in Tuesday night but spent Thanksgiving with his girlfriend and her family in Bridgeport, Connecticut. Do I need to tell you anything else? Bridgeport, Connecticut." She sighed again before continuing. "I can't say the girl has anything objectionable about her, but she's simply not comfortable."

"Maybe it's you," Ginny suggested. "You are pretty judgmental about her and her family, after all."

"Maybe it's that, or maybe it's that she really isn't right for James," Charlotte answered defensively. "Anyway, aside from that, we had a great holiday." She glanced over at Mimmi. "So, what did you do for the holidays? Did you and Graham resolve the kid-sharing issue?" She adjusted her headband, adding, "I didn't know if we should ask. Did you wind up going to your brother and sister-in-law's?"

"Yeah, I'm sorry, honey," said Ginny. "How was it? Musta been awful!"

Mimmi took a deep breath and blurted, "I met someone!"

The group collectively stopped walking. Kate started to well up. Marianna's mouth was agape.

"Like … a guy?" Ginny asked. When the group looked at Ginny like she was out of line, she offered a lame retort, "Like, she met a guy to *date*—that kinda thing."

Charlotte glared at Ginny. "Nice, Ginny," she snorted. "What other kind of guy would Mimmi be interested in? Of course, she means a guy to date." She turned to Mimmi. "Tell us!"

"I didn't know if it was too early to mention it," said Mimmi. "I don't want people to talk, you know. I like him. He's my sister-in-law's cousin, and he's been divorced for five years. No kids. He owns a painting company. He's a rugged, outdoors sort—not at all like Graham. Who knows? He asked for my number and asked if it was okay to call. We'll see what happens."

"Mimmi, he'll call," Charlotte said matter-of-factly.

"Oh, he already called. I should have said that more clearly. Yes, he called, and we went out."

Everyone was stunned. "Oh, my God, is he cute?" asked Marianna.

"No," Ginny teased. "He's ugly. That's why she told him he could call and that's why she went out with him!" She turned to Mimmi. "How cute? Like cute enough to fix your sister up with, or cute enough that you close your eyes when you're doing the dirty and think of him?"

Charlotte, the consummate protector, said, "Have you no filters? Who talks like that?"

The truth was they were all flustered with Mimmi's news, but it set off a flurry of activity and a new dynamic among the walkers. Mimmi was concerned that her children now had to navigate two families during the holidays—two sets of grandparents; two sets of aunts, uncles, and cousins; and two parents with their new *friends*. Mimmi had a lot of anger about the situation. She wanted predictable holidays. She never thought she'd get divorced, but it seemed like she was on her way. They now had a legal separation, which Mimmi's sister's husband had arranged. He felt protective of Mimmi and found a high-powered attorney to represent her.

"The guy wants me to meet his family," Mimmi told them. "We've only seen each other once since I met him, and I think it's too soon."

Ginny didn't blink before she responded, "Then just say you're not ready. Do you really think he cares? It's you he wants. And remember, girlfriend, *you* have all the power."

Mimmi looked puzzled. If she had all the power, why was her husband sleeping with a girl young enough to be his daughter?

"What's his name?" Kate asked. "And where does he live?"

"His name is Gregory Ott. He's so sweet." Mimmi hesitated a bit and then said, "He brought me flowers and wine. I met a couple of his friends—nice people. He's never met the kids. I'm not into that. I'm not even sure I want to continue dating him. I'm a wreck. Maybe I'll just take a break over the holidays. I don't know. I'm just scared. I can't imagine sleeping with anyone but Graham."

Charlotte said, "What would be wrong with that? Are you remembering how you wound up in this situation? You're allowed, Mimmi. You are a grown woman, and I'm sure you have desires for Gregory, or you wouldn't have agreed to see him. You should think about this. If you like the guy at all, Mimmi, this might be just what you need."

The women discussed that Mimmi wanted Graham back. She wanted her life back to normal. She wanted to put up the Christmas tree together with the kids and not worry about if she should buy gifts for her in-laws or buy gifts for Graham from the kids. She wanted to put on flannel pajamas on Christmas Eve after church and open gifts by candlelight, with carols playing in the background. She wanted to smell Graham's musk. She wanted to close her eyes … and have the nightmare end.

"Have you lost more weight, Mimmi?" asked Kate.

"I told you guys I joined a health club. I've been working out like it's my job! It's so neat. I have a personal trainer who tells me what to do. All I do is show up and do the work. I think I might weigh a little bit less, because my clothes are all loose."

Charlotte commented that she thought Mimmi looked great. Mimmi admitted that she had been paying attention to her style more than she had in years. She'd changed her hair color a bit, toning down the gray and highlighting her strawberry blonde streaks. She bought a few new clothes and was wearing lipstick. Charlotte thought Mimmi had an extra bounce in her step, too. All were hopeful signs for a woman who had been on the brink of disaster several months earlier.

Chapter Seven

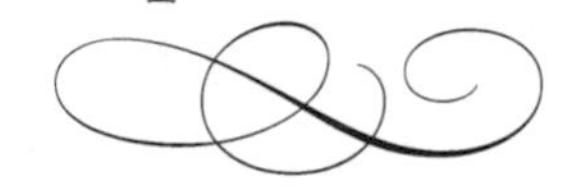

The walkers took a break in mid-December because of their hectic holiday schedules; they planned to resume their activities after the first of the year. January's weather, however, wasn't cooperative, as it was unusually snowy. The Philadelphia region was served up snow that was measured in feet and had lingering freezing temperatures. That double punch from Mother Nature kept many people housebound, including the walkers. By February, they were missing each other and their regular jaunts around the neighborhood. Charlotte complained to Charles that an occasional chance meeting or run-in at the supermarket with one of her new friends was a sore substitute for real time together. So, at his urging, Charlotte planned a dinner party for her new friends and their spouses. Of course, she would tell Mimmi to invite a friend. Charlotte hoped Mimmi was still seeing Greg Ott, the fellow she had met at Thanksgiving.

She wanted to be sure for Mimmi's sake, however, that the timing wasn't around Valentine's Day, so it wouldn't be awkward. Charlotte didn't want to be insensitive.

She walked around her house imagining the party. She'd need to replace the tired orchids and prune the ficus trees. The candles would be a vibrant shade of chartreuse, and she'd use green orchids with their delicate pink centers. Green, a portent of spring, would certainly be a fitting theme, since each of the women was beginning a rebirth at her own midlife junction. Charlotte loved theme parties.

As she wandered around her house with a party planner's eye, she was reminded how lucky she was.

"Having fun, darling?" asked Charles as he walked by Charlotte on his way from his office to the kitchen. "I can tell you're thinking and scheming for the party."

"I am thinking about the party, Charles. That's why, in the past, our parties have come off without a hitch. Planning is the key." She followed him into the kitchen, grabbed one of her favorite Italian hand-painted mugs out of a cupboard, and filled it to the brim.

"Mmm, still good," she commented. Charles smiled, knowing it was meant as a compliment for his fine barista skills. "How could I feel lonely or sorry for myself?" she asked. "I have to be the luckiest girl in the world!" Charles waited, unsure if it was a rhetorical question. "You're right, Charles. I still have my life. I still have a breast." She ran one hand over her silk blouse as if to reassure herself that her breast was still there. "And it's not just the health issue that makes me lucky, although if that had gone differently, the rest would be moot."

Charles waited for his espresso maker to heat up. "I'm in agreement with that. I feel like we dodged a bullet together, and we need to remind ourselves often." He leaned with his back to the counter, facing Charlotte, with his arms crossed. He knew she had thoughts to unload.

She took a sip of the hour-old coffee and straightened her creamer collection on the old mahogany hutch situated in the corner of the kitchen. It had been her grandmother's hutch, and Charlotte often used it for coffee service when they entertained.

The buzzer dinged, indicating the espresso maker had reached the proper temperature for brewing. Charles turned away from Charlotte but told her, "I'm still listening."

"Well, I can't help but wonder what my grandparents would think if they had lived long enough to see me in this big life." She moved a tall porcelain creamer with gilded banding on the top rim from the rear to a more visible position on the hutch. "This was probably the most valuable thing my dad's mother ever owned."

"You're waxing sentimental, Charlotte Wentworth," Charles said. He'd turned his head just to the side so she could hear him above the brewing sound.

"Charlotte *Gibbons* Wentworth, sir; don't you forget that," she corrected.

Charlotte had opportunities that her grandparents couldn't have imagined and a lifestyle her parents believed was reserved for the privileged class. Life had changed in America for many of Charlotte's generation, where grandchildren were the first in an extended family to attend college. For some families, educated girls continued in careers, where they were the first women in a family to hold managerial positions. But for Charlotte, it was more than changing demographics. She dreamed big, and her ambitions didn't betray her. She took risks and sacrificed when others were dating, traveling, and just not working as hard as she. She worked long hours in the art business: first galleries, then an auction house and, finally, as a private curator. She went to school in the evenings to earn an MBA. And it all paid off. She was on the fast track.

That was, until she committed herself to family life.

Charles finished making his espresso and started back to his office. "Charlotte, come join me for a mid-morning coffee break. Come sit in my office for a bit. The sun is so warm through the French doors. Come on," he coaxed.

She poured more coffee for herself and joined him. She fluffed pillows on his herringbone-tweed settee before sitting down. Charles had already positioned a marble coaster for her coffee mug on a side table. "I know that I have this big life, and it certainly comes with many, many privileges that I never dreamed of, like the art, the European vacations, this mansion, the kids' fabulous educations, and my jewelry. Goodness, I don't even wear half of it. You know the list. It goes on and on."

"But?" Charles knew it was coming.

She put the coffee down and hugged one of the small sofa pillows to her torso. Charles was sitting on the other side of the room in his large leather desk chair. He glanced at his computer screen and then up at her.

"*But* I don't know if my life is substantively richer than my grandparents' or my parents' lives. I mean, all this striving and hard work—for what? The kids leave, the husband still works hard at his craft, the parents still grow old, and like my mother, I'm carrying the load of family life."

Charles sighed. "I can't get into this now, Charlotte, but I can tell you that your life is substantively richer than your parents' and grandparents' lives. Lord Almighty, are you thinking clearly?" Charles asked in an annoyed tone. "Your father drove a bus, for godssake, and your mother cleaned and clipped coupons. Come on, Charlotte."

"Yeah, but look at how my career has had to take a backseat to yours. Yet you get to be a father. And really, I was a better wage-earner than you. It's only because I have ovaries and a uterus that I am where I am—just like my mother and her mother before her." Charlotte was revving up, but Charles's phone rang.

"Well, this went well," he sniped as she stood to leave.

She pulled the heavy pocket door shut as she left his office, shutting out the sunlight and Charles in one quick, mad tug.

During her children's early years, Charlotte was busy with many meaningful activities. She volunteered at their schools, teaching art history and inspiring a passion for learning through her palpable interest in academic life. She threw great craft parties, designed sets for the school plays, and organized play dates to museums and historic venues that were the envy of every parent in the neighborhood.

When her children attended middle school, she instilled a sense of duty to volunteerism and created a network of service sites for the students to give back to their community. And although full-time parenting was a conscious decision, she felt underappreciated and defensive about her choice. She often found herself beginning the requisite cocktail party introduction with "Before kids, I was an art curator …" Now that Betsy was a junior in high school, she felt an unspoken judgment that she should be *doing* something with her life. Yet there seemed to be a paradox: women of her generation who chose to work full time were often tagged as negligent parents, and women like Charlotte, who chose part-time work and, ultimately, full-time parenting, were most likely seen as uninspired and ordinary.

As she walked through the living room and center hall to their grand kitchen, echoes of dart-like, judgmental comments filled her head: "Well, of course you volunteer at your kids' schools. Aren't you a dear? I could never do that. I'd have to glue them all to their seats!" Or the condescending "How can you stand being home all day with kids? I'd lose my mind?" And the most hurtful: "What will you tell your daughter when *she* only wants to stay home with kids?"

Charlotte thought how each of those comments was true, and yet they bothered her because none was a complete representation of her. She chose a combination of parenting and work and tried to siphon the most important parts of each experience and craft a modern family portrait. After all, no one asked Charles how children impacted his career or personal agenda. And they did. How could they not? Men never got asked ridiculous questions after a baby arrived on the scene: *Don't you feel terrible leaving him with a stranger? Doesn't it just rip your heart out when you have to leave her sobbing at the front door? How are you sure the nanny is capable?*

Charlotte thought the worst offenders were the women who worked full time or *their* mothers. She guessed that they, like most women in her generation, had reservations about whatever choice was made, but those women couldn't justify admitting that this dual-working parent situation was an experiment, and no one knew how it would turn out. Charlotte's cousin Marguerite called them the "business bitches." Once, Marguerite was flying somewhere, and the woman sitting next to her was seemingly aghast that Marguerite was reading *People* magazine. The woman, a tightly wound, suited-up version of femininity, was all about her laptop, screen glare, and spreadsheets. No niceties were exchanged, but when the woman finally took a break and closed her computer, Marguerite asked her if she'd like the magazine. She later jokingly told Charlotte that the woman was paralyzed. No words came out of her mouth.

"You'd think I'd handed her pornography. Business bitch!" And the phrase stuck.

Charlotte was experiencing a telltale sign that her full-time at-home gig should end—and it wasn't a telegram from the Business Bitches Association; it was her unrest. While she was still uncomfortable with the perceived judgment of people regarding her stay-at-home choice, she'd finally mastered that rhythm. Yet as time wore on—at least by the time Betsy came along—the busyness turned to tedium, and the seeds of unrest were blooming.

While Charlotte was preparing for the dinner party and reflecting on her past, Mimmi was avoiding looking back. She was focusing on the future: a job, dating, and trying to get Graham out of her thoughts. Mimmi mixed up her life. She enrolled in Weight Watchers and continued regular visits to the local health club she had recently joined. The club had a youthful energy, with pulsing, loud music. There were, however, people of all ages in attendance, so she didn't feel uncomfortable. The personal trainer assigned to new members was sensitive to Mimmi's apparent lack of experience in a gym, and she carefully demonstrated how the machines worked, setting the weights, seat heights, and other variables for Mimmi's particular goals and strength. Mimmi kept an exercise log, a journal with pertinent information, so she could eventually workout unassisted. She was pleased with her quick results and hoped someone other than the walkers would notice—and not just anyone other than the walkers; she wanted Graham to notice.

She still loved him.

She also loved letting her mind wander as the endorphins kicked in from cycling. She pictured herself in an office somewhere as she pushed the bike to 120 rpm. That level made her chest feel tight, but she was sure it wasn't the increased speed on the bike. An office implied a degree of expertise in something, and the only thing Mimmi felt like she was an expert in was baking. She loved cookies and, aside from Charlotte's mother, made the best Christmas cookies in the neighborhood. Graham used to say that's why he married her—for her baking skills. Her meringue melts with little chocolate morsels in the center were legendary. Mimmi didn't want to dwell on her insecurities. *Forget an office,* she thought. She could more easily picture herself working in a local pastry shop. A dessert shop! That would be perfect. She was, after all, a great cook, and cakes and sweet delectables were her forte. The pastry shop idea was less daunting.

The buzzer on the bike went off. No wonder she was exhausted: fifty minutes had passed! She slid off the bike, barely able to stand. Her wobbly knees took hold like a colt's first upright. She lifted her baggy T-shirt and wiped the dripping sweat from her face and neck. She made a note to herself to bring a small towel, like the other regulars in the gym. She shuffled to the paper-towel dispenser, grabbing more than an adequate amount required to clean away her sweaty imprint. She squirted so much disinfectant on the bike's seat and back that the young woman on the next bicycle coughed. Mimmi smiled awkwardly, her way of acknowledging the intrusion of her cleanliness obsession. She continued wiping the bike seat and the controls, then the handles. She also made a note to get some type of music device, so she could tune out the horrible selections the club played. The pulsing bass reminded her of her kids' annoying music.

As she headed for the door, discarding the paper towels along the way, she removed the clip that held her strawberry blonde curly tresses in a sloppy yet sexy updo of sorts. Shaking her hair out made her a bit lightheaded. She held on to the door handle a bit longer to regain her equilibrium. She was exhilarated with the idea of working and having her own money. This new goal fueled her newfound energy.

She didn't notice Gregory Ott squinting from the other side of the gym to see if it was really Mimmi leaving.

Kate was sipping a cup of Sumatra in Starbucks while sifting through the latest *Maine Cottage* furniture catalog. She was planning a re-do in the master bedroom of the beach house, which was tired after ten years, four kids, and two sandy dogs. She loved the shrimp color for the bed, and she'd complement it with a striped awning fabric somewhere in the room—pillows, a comforter, or valances.

Kate needed a project. The kids consumed her. Emma, in her freshman year at Tufts, called several times a week obsessed with grades, sororities, and finding a boyfriend. Rachel, in her junior year of high school, was beginning the college search process—PSATs, SATs, SAT IIs, and lacrosse were all-consuming. Bess was a freshman and worried that her acne was too severe and that she'd never get asked to the prom. Jake was thirteen and dreamed about cars, food, and football—he was easy.

It was almost three thirty and time to pick up Jake, take him to guitar lessons, swing back to pick up Bess, wait for her at the dermatologist, and then return to pick up Jake, and take them home. It would be five thirty, and then she'd start dinner. Rachel would complain about emptying the dishwasher, Jake would wonder aloud why someone else couldn't feed the dogs, and Bess would talk about why every girl in her school had a boyfriend except for her. Doug would report about his day at the office, ask the kids about their days while gobbling his dinner, and wink to let her know he noticed her. He and Kate would retire to the living room, while the kids argued as they cleaned up after dinner, and he'd dose off before she got into any heavy conversation. Kate would pour herself a glass of red wine and daydream about the shrimp-colored bed for the beach house. One of the kids would present a crisis for the next day. They'd problem solve, and then Kate would dole out kisses on the forehead. By the time she went to bed after tucking everyone in, turning off lights, and reminding Rachel that her brain needed rest to thrive, Doug would be snoring, and the eleven o'clock news would be finishing.

Kate was bored and in desperate need of a jump-start for the second half of her life.

Ginny was reviewing Anna's list of colleges. As a junior in high school, it seemed all Joe, Ginny, and Anna talked about was who was thinking of applying to which college and what strategies would work. Anna was an honor student at a private Catholic girls school and dreamed of a coed college. She played the piano, was president of her class, and ran track. Yet her counselor wasn't sure she'd get into Georgetown, her first choice.

Anna was relaying details of a meeting she had earlier in the day with the new college counselor, Mrs. D'Angelo. "She thinks it's a reach."

Joe piped in, "What the hell's a reach? What is she talking about? Probably some big donor's kid has her eye on Georgetown, and they don't think Georgetown will accept more than one kid from the Academy." He looked for support from Ginny and then barked, "You could say something here, Ginny. You know what I'm saying is true, right?"

"Joe, let's just try to be real about this. If Mrs. D'Angelo says it's a reach, it probably is, and we ought to help Anna look for other schools too. Remember that meeting we went to? You paying attention to what I'm saying here?" She put her hands on her hips and tapped her foot. "Remember? They said most kids aren't getting into their first-choice schools. The demographics are dramatically different than they were ten years ago."

"Yeah, well, what did I send my Anna there for, huh? Demographics? Twenty-five thousand a year so I can hear about demographics? I don't think so, Ginny. As a matter of fact, I know so! My daughter's going where she wants to go. I'm telling you that."

And that's how the conversations surrounding Anna's college search and applications had transpired for months. In between college tantrums, Joe managed to talk about the residential real estate market and how hot it was. Ginny was great at balancing work with home. She felt that work really added to her ability to be better at everything she did, and Ginny Arena did a lot!

Ginny was the top producer in her office, because her focus was on larger estates. She knew almost everyone and was very skilled at pricing properties to sell. Her listings didn't last long on the market because she knew how to create a sense of urgency. Her assistant, Marie Myers, worked six days a week to keep up with Ginny's paperwork, and Ginny kept Marie motivated with quarterly bonuses.

Ginny also ran the auction at Anna's school each spring. The antique auction was anticipated by every vendor in the Greater Philadelphia region. It was a wonderful atmosphere in which to mingle with parents and other people from the community, and there was something for everyone. No one went home empty-handed. There were trinkets, furniture, bric-a-brac, rugs, and artwork. Each year, Ginny mixed it up a bit by changing the music and food. She was a natural marketer and enjoyed the accolades afterward.

At Marianna's house, there was hustle and bustle surrounding the preparations for Jeremy's sixteenth birthday. Most of her friends' daughters celebrated their sixteenth birthday with traditional Sweet Sixteen parties. Marianna prodded Jeremy for party ideas that would excite him, but Jeremy just wanted his driver's permit. But that wasn't enough for Marianna. She consulted Aaron, who felt it should be Jeremy's choice. Since Jeremy couldn't decide, Marianna made the decision—a car-themed party.

The invitations, which Marianna made herself, were mailed to his classmates and a few neighborhood friends. Marianna had his picture juxtaposed into the driver's seat of a Ferrari. Below the picture it read,

"Ladies and gentlemen ... Start your engines." Jeremy was so excited when he saw the invitation that the remaining party details flowed from his enthusiasm. Aaron made a few CD mixes for the event, many of which included songs about cars. The songs were mostly oldies, but the kids knew them all. The tablecloth and napkins she selected were bordered in a black-and-white racing flag motif. The drinks table would be draped in a Ferrari flag, and Marianna and Aaron chose Corvette, Audi, Porsche, and BMW flags to decorate the center hall.

Marianna planned entertainment that included a jukebox, a photo booth, and a fortune teller. Jeremy and Aaron had fun deciding names for specialty drinks, like Audacious Audi, Powered-Up Porsche, and Corvette Cooler.

The most difficult aspect of the party-planning was the adult list. Grandparents were out—Aaron's parents were gone, and Marianna's parents lived in Arizona. Aunts, uncles, and cousins simply amounted to too many people. So Marianna and Aaron decided the only adults invited should have a relationship with Jeremy. That meant parents of some of his close friends and Marianna's new buddies, the walkers. Aaron didn't want to invite any of his colleagues, but he did decide his research assistant and her husband should be on the list.

Marianna was very excited about the party—sometimes, she thought, more than Jeremy, who was preoccupied with practicing driving in their long driveway. Planning was a nice distraction from her work, which often overpowered her personal life. She took her clients' issues seriously and while much of her work was routine, it was the few challenging cases that kept her from a peaceful night's sleep, trying to weave the threads of information about each into a meaningful diagnosis and, ultimately, a prescription for healing. Nothing was more exhilarating than leading a patient to a place of sustained productivity and normalcy.

Chapter Eight

Charlotte sat in the window seat of the nail salon with her hands and feet under the dryers. The young woman sitting in the chair next to her was newly pregnant. Her voice was like a tape loop, repeating every five minutes. She was on her cell phone the entire time that Charlotte had been sitting there. "Fourteen weeks. I feel better now, but in the beginning it was horrible. I'm hoping to continue working after the baby comes."

Charlotte counted five pregnant women passersby that morning. She went to the post office afterward and then to the market. She lost count. They were everywhere. The human race would surely not become extinct this year! Although it was only sixteen years since her last baby was born, Charlotte felt like it was a lifetime ago. On the ride home from the market, she thought about her pregnancy with Elliot, her oldest child and her toughest pregnancy. She was working as a corporate collections coordinator for an international art gallery. Her pregnancy was planned but not well. She hadn't counted on being sick from the third week until she finished her sixth month. Charlotte actually lost weight during the first trimester. Charles had wanted her to quit her job, but she couldn't imagine giving up her work. She planned to continue working after the baby came, albeit on a reduced schedule. She had built a large, satisfied client list that included big names, such as Drexel

Burnham, Arthur Andersen, Price Waterhouse, Schneider, Harrison & Segal, and Morgan, Lewis & Bockius.

Charlotte was a superstar in her field. She knew better than any art consultant in Philadelphia how to match a client's space, budget, and taste with a portfolio before the funding expired. She had a reputation for excellence, which landed the artists she represented on the walls of every prestigious firm in the City of Brotherly Love. It also landed them in the personal collections of the CEOs occupying each of the respective firm's corner offices. Old Main Line Philadelphia parlors and center halls were filling with contemporary artists alongside the old masters, which had been handed down through the generations. Her Rolodex was the envy of every sales organization, wanting access to the likes of Biddles, Longstreths, and Clothiers. But Charlotte remained shy and insecure. She wondered why she couldn't overcome her roots. There wasn't anything untoward or embarrassing about her humble beginnings; she was living the American dream.

Charles Wentworth had occupied a corner office, but he too was uncomfortable in his own skin. He had hated the image that was required of him. He had worn the requisite finely tailored suits, custom shirts, and European shoes. He'd carried an expensive briefcase, and he hadn't worn jewelry, although a wedding ring would have been acceptable, even desirable, by the firm's partners. At the age of thirty-two, he had been expected to be in a serious relationship. He just hadn't met anyone—that was, until Charlotte Gibbons walked into his office.

Charlotte was wearing a simple gray suit with a crisply starched white shirt, and a simple strand of pearls tucked neatly below the collar. The only flash of color was in the photographed art she had displayed in her portfolio file. Her voice was soothing, and Charles couldn't keep his attention on the content, focusing instead on the cadence. His secretary was deeply interested in the art and so, when prompted by Charlotte to select some of the art that he wanted brought into his office for approval, he deftly deferred to Ms. Whiting for her "impeccable taste and style." But to Charles's great disappointment, his quick pass off to a subordinate gave the signal that Charlotte was dismissed, and the meeting came to an abrupt end.

Charles schemed for the next weeks, as the collection was assembled, as to how he could get alone time to discuss the art with Charlotte—that is, alone time that wouldn't betray his attraction to her. He had no idea what it was about her that had captured him. He remembered every detail of the day, from the moment she walked down the long corridor toward his office. Her legs were like those of a thoroughbred horse. She was tall and thin but not too thin. Her eyes were like deep pools of chocolate. Her hair was … He couldn't remember her hair color. *What color was her hair?* He started to sweat. How could he not notice her hair color? He remembered almost everything else. Why not the hair? He closed his eyes and leaned back in his burgundy leather chair. He asked Ms. Whiting to hold his calls, because he was so deeply focused on remembering the details of that morning.

That was how he recalled the story to Charlotte a few years later. Her memory was that he ultimately purchased a collection of black-and-white photographs of significant American historical events, including the National Women's Party's march in the late 1880s. He was more interested in the subject matter than the artists, which appealed to Charlotte. She had met so many self-impressed executives who would ask her which artist had the most likelihood of increasing in value. She quickly fell in love with Charles's authenticity. If only that were enough to keep their flame going.

The question she struggled with these days was her own authenticity. She missed the early years of her marriage when, after settling in, they had had their first child. Although her pregnancy was difficult, the rest of her life was like a storybook. She regained her beautiful figure. Elliot was a gorgeous baby with light brown curly hair, who smiled and cooed and slept through the night by eight weeks. He was an angel, and Charles was enamored of him.

Charlotte hired a live-in nanny and returned to working, but she missed being with the baby. Charles's career, as timing would have it, had taken off soon after his engagement to Charlotte, so they thought it wise to have Charlotte transition to stay-at-home mom. She started her own company, working twenty to thirty hours a week. Life was perfect. She felt she had the best of both worlds. She became pregnant with their second child, also a son, when Elliot was just a year old. James, too, was easy, and Charlotte worked fewer hours, so as to spend as much time with the children as possible.

Charles was putting in more and more time at work, yet despite his success at building a class A office-building portfolio, his firm closed. The financial markets crashed, along with related industries, such as commercial real estate. Charles was devastated, and he no longer had a six-figure salary and matching bonus—all this and a third child on the way!

Charles couldn't bear the thought of being out of work, and he became severely depressed. Consistent with his authentic behavior, he plummeted rapidly. He couldn't find meaning in his family life or make sense of his professional life, despite a recession that crossed all social and economic barriers.

Charlotte worked hard, but many companies were hit by a poor economy, and the first part of their budgets to go was the buying of art. The couple looked at each other over leftovers one night and wondered if a divorce wasn't easier than tearing each other apart over mistakes of living too high, not saving for a rainy day, or even questioning whether they were well suited to one another. Add to the mix two toddlers and no money for extras, like a nanny or housekeeper, and it was evident their fairy-tale life was falling apart.

Charlotte's frustration grew as quickly as her belly. Cleaning toilets and emptying the dishwasher two times daily replaced the glamour of eating lunch at her twice-weekly reserved table at the Four Seasons. Stunning suits and beautiful pocketbooks were supplanted by oversized

T-shirts and jeans with elastic waistbands. Playing cheerleader to a morose husband was her chief activity besides toilet training.

Betsy Gibbons Wentworth came as a breath of fresh air to an otherwise stale, tiring lifestyle. Charlotte had an uneventful delivery, and Betsy's birth seemed to shake Charles out of his depression. He spent a great deal of time nurturing all of their children. They went for walks, visited the zoo, and played at the local park for hours. When Betsy was three months old and the Wentworth's bank account seemed to be at the half-empty mark, Charlotte proposed a whimsical solution for refreshment and a change of pace.

"Charles," she spoke softly, so as to not wake napping Betsy, "I've been thinking. Why don't we have an adventure? We've survived the worst of this recession. We are so blessed to have these three wonderful babies. Let's take off! Let's sell everything we have and buy a Winnebago. We'll travel across America and write about downward mobility." The baby stirred. Charlotte lifted her top and offered Betsy a full breast.

Charles, thinking she was joking, started singing, "Home, home on the range. Where the deer ..." He stopped singing abruptly and asked, "Have you lost your mind? We're ready to kill each other in a four-thousand-square-foot house. How can we have fun in a Winnebago with three babies and no money?"

"I'm serious, Charles. We need an adventure. We need a change of pace. You know, you're not the only one who isn't working here. I'm depressed, too. Of course, I love my kids, but I want to work at my craft in the same way that you want to work at yours. I am a person here, Charles. This isn't all about you!" The baby started to cry. "I'm sorry, Muffin-girl." The baby smiled up at her. "Yeah, tell Daddy who wants to go for a Winnebago trip? Huh?"

The trip would not materialize, but Charlotte's idea scared Charles enough to go job hunting.

She pulled her sparkly silver Suburban into the garage and popped open the rear hatch. Charles met her at the door to help with the groceries.

"Wow. A big haul today, huh?"

She held the door with one foot and struggled with two bags. "Yup, remember we're having that dinner party this weekend for the walkers? I'm really excited for you to get to know them." He held the garage door to the rear hall for her as they carried the bags into the kitchen.

"It should be nice. Have you met their husbands?" Charles asked as he placed the three bags on the island.

"Watch the orchids," she cautioned.

"I know, I know. I'm not going to bump your precious orchids."

"Let's see … I've met Joe Arena. He's nice. I met Doug Hahn. He's really handsome." She unloaded a bag of frozen food into the freezer, saying, "I haven't met Marianna's husband. I know he's older than Marianna, but I don't know by how much. And of course Mimmi's husband won't be there. He'll be boffing bimbos, I guess."

"Boffing bimbos. Sounds like a porn movie," Charles said. "What's with that situation? I haven't heard you talk about it much." He opened the pantry and put away canned goods as they talked.

"I don't know the situation," Charlotte said. "If you cheated, I certainly wouldn't be out walking with the neighbors or going to a health club. I'd be in therapy and be organizing my financial life, like getting a job or something. I really can't figure out Mimmi. You'll have to take notice and see what you think. She almost seems relieved, in a weird way. I really don't think she's all that sad, Charles. I really don't." She continued unloading the frozen food.

"I think it's odd that she isn't mad," Charles observed. "Wouldn't you be really pissed off if I started—what did you call it? Boffing bimbos?" Charles laughed.

"Don't laugh, Charles!"

"I can't help it. Why do we think of all bimbos as blonde with huge boobs? Maybe there are …" He didn't finish his sentence. No sooner did he realize she was holding a bag of frozen vegetables than she heaved it at him with all her might.

"When you're in a hole, stop digging!" Then she laughed. "You didn't think I'd throw it, did you? Don't get too comfortable, Charles. I've been thinking a lot, and not about my big house. I've been thinking about how it's important to mix it up. Life needs to get mixed up. Don't ever think you know me so well that you are surprised by frozen vegetables flying through the air!"

He rubbed his head and walked away. "That was mean, Charlotte."

"No! Talking about bimbos and big boobs is mean, Charles. You're mean in a different way. At least with me, you see it coming right at you, between the eyes. I never see your kind of mean coming at me. I just feel it down to my core."

He stopped in the rear hall before retrieving the rest of the groceries and called back to her. "If my talking about bimbos is mean, you need your head examined!"

Charlotte responded, "It *is* mean, and not for the reasons you think. What is the equivalent of a male bimbo? Why is it that the women with whom men cheat are bimbos, but the men … well, what are they?" She pounded the food into the freezer and slammed the door to make her point. "It's all this condescension that women have gotten used to that makes me feel like a second-class citizen. Really, Charles, maybe the woman just wanted sex, and she acted upon it. After all, I don't think she was getting much more than that from Graham. He could barely afford to keep Mimmi, who isn't exactly demanding materially, you know. You have such antiquated views on women," she continued yelling. "You know you have a daughter, and your sons will be choosing wives soon. You should get with it, Charles. Maybe you should be more supportive around here and lead by example."

Charles rolled his eyes and went into the garage for the groceries.

Chapter Nine

Charlotte eyed each flower arrangement carefully, pushing any uncooperative blooms into their proper places. Walking through the rest of the house, she checked the powder room for extra toilet paper and decorative disposable hand towels. She fluffed sofa pillows and straightened lampshades. Knick-knacks were lined up on shelves like attentive sentries, and the table was reviewed for any noticeable flaws. Her art collection was exquisite, and she couldn't wait to show off her house to her new friends. She was also excited to show off her new friends to the other guests, who were mostly Charles's work associates.

"Mom, do I need to wear a tie?" Elliot yelled from upstairs. Charlotte and Charles included Elliot and his girlfriend, Zoe, because one of Charles's guests asked if he could bring his twenty-four-year-old daughter in lieu of his wife, who had a work-related conflict. Since Elliot and Zoe were already planning to come to town for a visit that weekend, their company seemed an easy complement to George Welsh's daughter. Charles and Charlotte were always proud to include their children. Betsy was having a sleepover at a friend's house and was delighted to have escaped the rigor of an adult cocktail party.

"No tie, Elliot," shouted Charlotte.

The walkers were equally excited. They had been a group for many years, but it took Charlotte, their newest addition, to bring them to this point of socializing. Husbands were invited too. The husbands knew about each other, although none had actually talked to any other. Joe Arena was the exception because, like his wife, he was a get-to-know-you kind of person. He made it his business to know everyone in the neighborhood, so he was acquainted with the other husbands, as well as their wives.

Charlotte was confident her party would be successful. She had hosted so many dinners over the years that this one would be routine for her. Plan, shop, cook, call the serving staff, and show up. It was that easy.

The first guests to arrive were Ginny and Joe Arena. Ginny wore a navy-blue pinstripe pantsuit and a coordinating scarf; Joe a blue blazer, khakis, and rep tie. They brought a box of hand-dipped chocolates from a local gourmet chocolate shop, and Ginny handed it to Charlotte.

"Oh, thank you," Charlotte said. Then turning to one of the servers, she said quietly, "Could you put this on a dish and set it out in the family room, please?"

"Certainly, Mrs. Wentworth," said the server as he smiled at Ginny and Joe.

Ginny's eyes were all over, taking in the art, the fabrics, pillows, rugs, and flowers. She stepped into the living room.

"Well, if you ever decide to put this place on the market, it would surely fetch top dollar," she commented, as a typical realtor. Charles felt uncomfortable, as he always did when guests commented on Charlotte's impeccable taste and ability to make beauty in their world. She had the Midas touch; that much was certain. That Midas touch led to great success when she was in the art world.

Charlotte responded, "Well, I'm not going anywhere! This is it." Then she added, "Right, Charles?" He arched his eyebrows.

The doorbell rang again. Charles excused himself, leaving Charlotte to talk about her beautiful decorations and art with the Arenas. He pulled the door wide open and announced the arrival of Aaron and Marianna Silver, as well as Kate and Douglas Hahn. They had already introduced themselves in the driveway.

"Come in and join us for a drink," said Charles, welcoming the new guests into the center hall and taking their coats, which he handed to the evening's hired help. One of the staff took drink orders, while a server passed Asian pork steamed rice balls, which Charlotte had made a few weeks ago.

"Let's get out of the draft," said Charles, motioning the Silvers and the Hahns into the living room. Joe extended his hand as he reintroduced himself to the newly arrived party guests.

"I love that pants suit," Kate said to Ginny. "You're so tiny, you can wear pants. I look like a hippo in pants. They just accentuate my *wide* hips." The women all laughed at her exaggeration.

"And Marianna, lipstick? Is that lipstick you're wearing?" asked Ginny.

"I am wearing lipstick," she answered. She refrained from rubbing her hair and giggled nervously instead. "Aaron said he wasn't sure if he liked it."

"I said no such thing," Aaron interrupted. "I said I wasn't used to it. That's different than saying I don't like lipstick."

"Okay, okay. Whatever." Marianna pointed to the painting over the mantle. "This is something, isn't it?" she said, commenting on the massive piece of fluid colors. It looked as if someone had spilled gallons of paint, and the canvas had been tilted and moved in many different directions.

As the server passed out drinks, the guests admired other works of art, antiques, the piano, and Charlotte's unmatched ability to make the eye bounce from one vignette to the next.

Kate was in awe of the flowers. "Charlotte, where did you get the flowers? They are magnificent!"

Charlotte responded, "That little shop in Manayunk; you know, the one between the Italian luncheonette and the jeans shop."

"You're kidding. I thought you were going to say Florabundance in town," Kate responded. She leaned in for a sniff. "Look at these, Ginny."

The two women wandered through the house while the men chatted over hors d'oeuvres. Charlotte checked in on the kitchen help. She glanced at her watch, hoping Mimmi would arrive soon. She had timed the entrée to serve at eight, and it was now seven thirty. She grabbed a glass of sparkling water on her way out of the kitchen. Charlotte never drank alcohol when she entertained. Details were too important to her to ruin an evening over a drink or two. She joined the men in the living room after catching another glimpse of herself in the oversized hall mirror. Her off-the-shoulder peach wool dress showed off her beautiful shoulders and pale skin. The color brought out the natural red highlights in her hair.

Aaron lit up. "Now, Charlotte, I didn't know you were an art consultant. Charles tells of a very impressive client list."

Charlotte was modest. "Well, Aaron, he's my biggest fan, but that was many years ago."

Charles took the opportunity to brag. "Although she was an amazing art consultant, Charlotte is making quite a name for herself in the local camp for Jennifer Holmes Bartlett. Her chief of staff called here a few nights ago and asked if Charlotte would consider becoming a paid employee of the campaign. Maybe run something for the senator here in good old Pennsyl-vain-i-a." He put his arm around Charlotte. "I'm so proud of her. She's a regular Renaissance woman."

The other walkers wandered back in the room. Kate spoke up. "You must be talking about Charlotte. You *are* a Renaissance woman. Goodness, I wish I had one-tenth of your talent." She came over and gave Charlotte a kiss. "Your house is stunning." Charlotte was relieved to distract her guests from the Holmes Bartlett conversation and welcomed Kate's compliment.

God, she thought, *my husband has no sense of appropriate behavior!* She hadn't even decided if she was going to meet with the senator, and here he was blabbing about it. *Do I need to give him a precise list of dos and don'ts with everything?* she thought.

Doug said, "Charlotte, you should skip working for Holmes Bartlett and start a decorating business with Katie. You two could make a killing here on the Main Line."

Charlotte cringed, but Joe joined in, "Yeah, and Ginny and I will fix you up with all the right clients." He winked. Charlotte was embarrassed that the cat was out of the proverbial bag with her offer from Senator Holmes Bartlett. The walkers looked curiously at her, but the doorbell rang, and she was able to dodge the conversation as she excused herself. Still, she wasn't sure she'd be able to avoid the conversation for the remainder of the evening. She'd have to quash the idea quickly and do damage control. She wasn't sure she should be taking the liberty of talking about it anyway. She scowled at Charles as he went for the door. "I'll get it," she said in a tone he understood meant *back off.*

Charlotte opened the door and the walkers, who were gathered in the adjacent room, quickly turned their attention to Mimmi and her date. Charlotte's foray into politics was pushed aside.

Mimmi announced herself as she stepped over the threshold, "Hi, everyone. This is Graham. He's my escort for tonight."

While everyone stared, Charles's blueblood upbringing forced the situation from awkward to cordial. "Come in. Come in," he greeted them. He took the bottle of wine that Graham was holding out and handed it to the help. "Mimmi, I'm so glad to see you. What can I get the two of you?" Then, turning to Graham, he asked, "Are you a bourbon drinker? I have an unopened bottle of Booker's that I'd like to crack."

The girls all ran to the kitchen, while the men headed in the opposite direction to Charles's office and the bar.

"Don't make any judgments," Mimmi shrieked, while closing her eyes and holding up her hand, as if to keep them at bay. It didn't work.

Charlotte half-frowned. "You couldn't warn me? I was almost rude!"

"Are you mad that I brought him? Ladies?" She scanned their faces. Kate couldn't make good eye contact. "Kate, are *you* mad?"

"It's not my party."

Mimmi shot back, "What kind of an answer is that?" She turned to Charlotte, who had started to busy herself with adorning salad dishes with an herb bouquet. "Well, it is *your* party, Charlotte."

The doorbell rang again. "It must be some of Charles's associates," Charlotte said, relieved she could scoot out of the room. She moved quickly to help greet them, and on her way out of the kitchen she put her hand on Mimmi's shoulder. "Mimmi, I am delighted you are here, and if you want Graham to be here, I am sure it is okay with everyone else." She cocked her head slightly. "But like Kate, Marianna, and Ginny, I *am* a bit surprised. I think that's the best description of how I feel—surprised." As if to examine her own thoughts to be sure that surprise was her only feeling, she said it again. "Yes, I am surprised." The swinging door from the kitchen was ajar when she turned to her friends and said, "Ladies, are we one good-looking group of women, or what? Kate that color is stunning on you, and Marianna, why do you not wear makeup all the time?" She left to join Charles at the door.

"She already told us we were gorgeous," laughed Ginny to the others as she hugged Mimmi.

The kitchen help went on being invisible, until the door swung open, and Joe Arena asked where everyone was, startling a helper who dropped a tray of hand-rolled sausages and a collection of gourmet mustards.

"Joe, you scared her," reprimanded Ginny. The rest of the kitchen help had the mess cleaned up before anyone could react. Ginny led everyone else out of the kitchen, and they laughed and giggled as if nothing at all was unusual.

Joe shrugged and said, "You can dress a guy up, but you can't make him a gentleman."

"Oh, stop feeling sorry for yourself," Ginny shot back. "Give me a kiss, you big galoot!"

Charles's friends and business associates mixed well with Charlotte's friends. The conversation was all about a new painting over the fireplace in which the artist had used a medium that caused the paint to bubble in certain spots, giving the huge canvas a sense of being in motion. The paint looked three-dimensional in places, and it inspired unique commentary from its novice viewers.

"I think it looks like a volcano," said George Welsh, one of Charles's investors.

"Oh, Daddy," responded his daughter, "abstract art isn't always supposed to look like something real. That's the whole point. We can enjoy it in unique ways."

"You see what we get?" he said jokingly. "We pay for our kids to get educated so they can make us look like idiots!" His daughter blushed.

Charlotte came to her rescue. "Well, George, she's right. This is simply a study in color and fluidity. I was drawn to its vibrancy. And also, it gives us pause to reflect on how life is fluid and mercurial."

Charles grabbed his friend and cohort by the elbow and said, "Let's get seated quickly, before Charlotte decides to make us look even less cultured than we are, George."

Dinner was served buffet-style, except for the first course and the salad. Charlotte asked everyone to sit where they were comfortable. She found a casual seating arrangement had always worked well in the past, relaxing the guests, which in turn, elicited better vibes during dinner. There was only one exception that Charlotte could recall—she and Charles had hosted a dinner party many years ago for Charles's colleagues, where the guest of honor was the chairman of the board of the largest law firm in Washington DC. His third wife, a woman half his age and someone whom every man at the party fancied, sat next to the first and only wife of an elderly, wealthy patron of the Philadelphia Museum of Art. When the older woman asked a guest seated across the table whether he was enjoying the breast—referring to a lovely breast of veal—the chairman's third wife threw a glass of wine in the elderly woman's face.

"I paid a lot of money for these, honey!" she cried, cupping her huge fake meal tickets. "And they have served me better than this asshole," she added, pointing to the waiter who was ogling the specimens. Charlotte giggled to herself, remembering the incident, hoping there would be no repeats tonight.

As fate would have it, Graham sat between Charlotte and George Welsh's daughter, Susan. The girl, who was helped by Mother Nature in all the right places, was very animated, and her chest bounced with every gesticulation, of which there were many. Charlotte couldn't help noticing Mimmi's intense glaring at Graham. She hoped there wouldn't be a scene. *What is it about some men and breasts?* she thought. Maybe those who were weaned too early were emotionally scarred and seeking to return to a place of nurturance and comfort.

Dinner went exceptionally well, given the addition of Graham to the menu. He was affable and caught on that Mimmi was not happy about his location at the table. After all, it was a pick-your-own seat option. He made up for it by talking about his kids and making conversation with Mimmi, who was seated diagonally across the table from him. That was enough to assure her she'd made the right decision to bring him to her friend's party. It was also helpful that Elliot and Zoe were attending the party and making the other young guest feel comfortable.

The twentysomethings—Elliot, Zoe, and Susan Welsh—were a nice addition to the event, and Charlotte reminded herself to take note of the interesting conversations that resulted. Susan Welsh was particularly interested in linguistics and had recently accepted an internship at Children's Hospital, studying the effects of teaching sign language to cognitively impaired babies. Mimmi was interested to learn how the young woman came to the connection of sign language as a linguistics major in college. And then there was the topic of alcohol poisoning, which was at an all-time high on college campuses.

"Well, one of my suitemates had such an issue, and we reported her," said Zoe. "When we couldn't reason with her, and we tired of cleaning up her messes and staying up to be sure she didn't lapse into a coma, I called my dad. He said we had a social and moral responsibility to get her help; that the issue was a health issue, and we were not equipped to handle her."

"Yeah, well, the sad thing is," said Charles, "some people still don't see alcoholism as a disease. And while your suitemate may not have been an alcoholic, she probably has a predisposition."

"We heard that when the school intervened and put her into a program, her mother wanted to get a lawyer," said Zoe.

"There you go," said Joe. "Parents are always looking to cover their own asses—pardon me, ladies."

"Joe!" reprimanded Ginny.

"I'm sorry, but it makes me mad," he justified. "That's why we always pushed Anna to play sports. Don't you think that kids that play sports are less inclined to get into trouble?"

George Welsh cited a litany of professional athletes who were busted for crimes, but Ginny and Joe weighed in on the efficacy of sports and the role it played in healthy societies, bringing together people of otherwise disparate social strata and intellectual interests. There wasn't a lull in the conversation all night.

When the last guests had left and Charlotte was directing the help to hurry along the cleanup, Charles had plenty to say about the evening. Their usual interaction post-dinner party wasn't much different, but it had been a long time since the invited guests were Charlotte's invitees.

Charles went to the living room and kicked off his shoes, sitting in Charlotte's favorite green velvet chair. He had poured himself a hefty glass of Booker's bourbon over ice. Charlotte stood at the bar in his office, contemplating a drink, but couldn't decide.

"Mom, Zoe and I are going up to the third floor. We're pooped." Elliot leaned in for a kiss, and Charlotte gave him a hug. "Nice job tonight, Mom and Dad," he added. Zoe was already standing on the third step, ready to go upstairs.

"Thank you for including me, Mr. and Mrs. Wentworth," said Zoe. "Susan Welsh is really nice. I can totally see getting together with her again."

"You are very welcome. I'm glad you both had fun. Good-night. We'll see you in the morning. I'm sure Betsy will want to see you both when she comes home from her sleepover tomorrow. Sweet dreams," said Charlotte. She poured a glass of Montepulciano, her favorite red wine.

"Good-night, son. Zoe, you're a sweetheart. Good-night," said Charles. Zoe blushed and put her head down bashfully, as she and Elliot retreated to his suite on the third floor. Charles raised his glass to his wife. "Well, Charlotte, once again you outdid yourself. Everything was delightful. Just a lovely event, darling. And I was so proud of Elliot and Zoe, weren't you? George's daughter seems like a nice kid too. Your new friends, our neighbors, are an interesting bunch."

"That doesn't sound like a resounding endorsement," she responded defensively.

"You're right. I'm sorry. I really did have a great time. I'm trying to figure it all out, though." He took a sip of his drink, then said, "Don't take it the wrong way. I'm so glad we had company tonight, and your presentation was spectacular, as usual. It's just that our usual dinner guests are, for the most part, more predictable."

Charlotte plopped into the deep sofa, splashing some of her red wine on a silk pillow. "Crap, look what I did," she whimpered. She stood, grabbing the soiled pillow.

"Forget about the damn pillow," Charles implored. "Please stay! I really want to visit with you. I'm tired, and I want to be with you."

She sighed and wiped the splash with a cocktail napkin. She threw it back on the sofa and sat again, this time more carefully.

"Kate is so much prettier than I remembered," said Charles, pleased that Charlotte sat down. "Is it just that she fussed with herself? I guess maybe I've only ever seen her from a distance, and she's usually in workout clothes. Doug—or Douglas, whichever it is—is fascinating.

He's had quite a career. And Aaron and Marianna, what is their relationship about?"

Charlotte flashed back to herself as a young bride, hosting one of their first parties as husband and wife. Charles had worn a pair of gray flannel pants and a burgundy cashmere sweater, with cordovan crocodile loafers and his dark horned-rimmed glasses. Charlotte remembered that her hair had been pulled in a tight bun at the nape of her neck, and her signature pearls adorned her perfectly taut neck, accenting her chiseled chin and jawbone. She'd worn a coordinating cashmere sweater and dress. Their guests were clients of Charlotte's, and Charles worked hard to make a great impression. How time had changed the dynamic of their relationship! Now it was Charlotte who worked at impressing Charles—not his clients, just Charles. He was talking, she realized. "I'm sorry, Charles. What did you say?"

"I asked if this evening was as you expected it to be?"

"I was just thinking of our first dinner party," Charlotte answered, "and I could remember everything. You wore those crocodile loafers that we bought in Brazil in 1980. Forget the dinner party. Remember how stupid we were coming through customs with those damn shoes?"

"Forget customs. Do you remember how sick we both got?" he recalled. "You almost broke up with me after that trip. I never thought you'd marry me, and I'd contemplated asking you to marry me on the trip."

"Did you have a ring?"

"No. I thought it'd be romantic to buy one there—a memento," he said.

"Oh, my goodness, my ring isn't from that trip is it?" she asked with trepidation.

Just then a Louis Armstrong song came on the CD player, and he offered his hand, inviting her to dance. She accepted. They twirled around their living room as if it were a ballroom.

"The ring is my grandmother's, silly. Can't you tell it's old? She gave it to me before she died. She said, 'Charles, I know you are going to find a very special woman someday, and she should have a part of our family history. I want you to have this and know that your grandfather and I were lovers and best friends. That's the only way marriage works, dear.' And I took it, thinking, 'Well, those are big shoes to fill.'"

Charlotte was touched. "How is it that I never found out this was your grandmother's ring? Your mother never said anything, nor did your dad. Which grandmother was it? Why did you never tell me that?"

"I thought you'd think I was cheap or something. So, I'm not sure why I'm telling you tonight … but Charlotte?"

"Yeah?"

"I loved her more than anyone in the world. I swear that's why it took me so long to find a wife. I thought, whoever wears this ring is going to have to fill my grandmother's shoes. And, my darling Charlotte, you are the one and only. You are everything in the world to me." He collected himself. "Tonight was so special in so many ways. But most important, I feel like I've got my Charlotte back from wherever you've been." He kissed her deeply.

She was overwhelmed by his expression of affection.

Elliot came downstairs to retrieve Zoe's overnight bag from the hall closet and caught sight of his father, eyes closed, and his mother snuggled into his neck. He sat on the top step and watched them dance, wondering if he could ever love Zoe as much as his father loved his mother.

Chapter Ten

Mimmi was trying to enjoy her new lifestyle. She got up earlier, stayed up later, watched television shows of her choosing, and was able to make unilateral decisions about the kids' daily lives. She loved her new energy for fitness, even though her friends thought she was obsessed. She had lost fifteen pounds after a few months of spinning classes, and she felt like a new woman. For the first time in her entire adult life, she was considering the workplace. Her kids were adjusting well enough to the new family arrangements and, overall, life was okay for Mimmi. Being a divorced woman with two almost-grown children wasn't even close to her life's plan, yet it seemed that was where she was headed.

Mimmi had suffered through the first weeks after the panties-in-the-pocket event, hoping Graham was simply having a midlife crisis. They continued living together for the sake of the kids, and Mimmi was sure he'd come to his senses. Graham wanted to leave from the outset, but his guilt persuaded him to comply with Mimmi's wishes.

"I need some time to figure this stuff out, Mimmi," he'd told her. "It might take a while, and if you want to file for divorce, I'll understand."

"You'll understand? Understand what? I am married to you, Graham. Do *you* understand?" And he packed a couple of suitcases and left.

Mimmi didn't cry. She didn't get mad. She didn't ask her children how they felt. She simply went about the business of living her life. But life wasn't the same. She felt like she was on an interminable vacation. The kids weren't around. Graham wasn't around. And she had more leisure time than she could manage. Her friends talked about their weekends in terms of what they did with their husbands. The world was set up for couples. She felt alone but in an anticipatory way, as if Graham would return from a long business trip. Something didn't feel permanent about the experience. The constant reminders of Graham and the life they'd built added to her camouflaged grief.

She dismissed these uncomfortable ideas about her circumstances as quickly as they entered her mind and instead, focused on happier thoughts—like the dinners she and Graham had once a week under the guise of talking about the kids and financial matters during this separation. But Mimmi thought of these meetings as dating. She looked forward to seeing Graham. She'd carefully plan what she would wear and where they'd eat. She and Graham sometimes giggled and laughed, and often, they'd tend to parenting issues or pick up Meg from a friend's house or an after-school activity. Mimmi was able to compartmentalize the time she had with Graham from the part of his life she wondered about when they weren't together.

She'd been reading about mindfulness. Charlotte had given her a book on the subject, which Charlotte said was helping her through her own midlife slump. Mimmi wasn't certain what Charlotte could be blue about; actually, she thought Charlotte's circumstances enviable. Charlotte had an adoring husband and three healthy kids. Her house looked like it was plucked from an *Architectural Digest* layout. Friends, dinner parties, black-tie fund-raisers, and a college roommate who'd become a United States senator—all this, and she had a fabulous figure and great sense of style. What was there to be in a blue funk over?

Mimmi, however, felt justified in her malaise. Will was a freshman at George Washington University and rarely around anymore. Meg, at fifteen, was on a hormonal roller coaster, and Graham was sowing his wild oats. Mimmi hadn't worked since college, and her parents were utterly disgusted with her situation, blaming Mimmi for not working harder at making her marriage work. Money was just as complicated as before Graham left, so at least that struggle didn't bring any new angst to her life. But there was the new anxiety of wondering whether Graham would continue depositing his paychecks into their joint bank account. Her old friends weren't involved enough in her life for her to let them in on her circumstances.

But her walking friends helped her from becoming a mess, and now, she was working on staying in the moment. And at this moment, she was more fit than ever and had renewed excitement about her friends. She did worry about how all of the changes would affect her kids, though, especially Meg. After all, her brother had left for college, her father lived in an apartment, and her mother was a workout nut who'd stopped doing domestic chores. There never seemed to be food in the house, and Meg never seemed to have clean underwear anymore.

"Let me introduce you to the washing machine, Meg," said Mimmi. But although she taught her daughter how to use the washing machine, Meg found another option: staying at her father's girlfriend's apartment, where his girlfriend did the laundry. Graham pampered Meg, and she thought his girlfriend was really cool—she talked to Meg about school, friends, clothing, and MTV.

Mimmi felt betrayed by Meg as well as Graham but didn't talk to her about it. They had bigger issues to tackle, like Meg's staying involved in school sports, working hard in her classes, preparing for college, and maintaining healthy friendships. Mimmi had hoped the visiting-Graham novelty would wear off with her daughter, like most novelties with any fifteen-year-old girl. Mimmi was, however, grateful for time alone. She had gone directly from her parents' house to being married to Graham, so she had never spent time on her own. This was a newfound luxury. No sooner would the time seem lonely, than Meg would return home to remind her that she was still a mom; that she hadn't dreamed up her previous life.

Mimmi felt conflicted about Meg's relationship with Graham. She was relieved that Graham spent additional time with Meg, yet she felt betrayed by him all over again. It was good for Meg to feel Graham hadn't abandoned her, but Mimmi felt as if she needed to compete for her daughter's affection. Meg seemed genuinely happy when she planned her visits and was equally perky when she returned.

Mimmi continued to focus on being in the moment and the positive aspects of her new life—time for herself and shared parenting responsibilities with the kids. She and Graham were only several months into the new arrangement, so her friends advised her to give the situation more time to work out all the rough spots.

Mimmi accumulated Bed Bath & Beyond coupons with a passion that the walkers couldn't understand. "Hi, everyone. I'm sorry to ask again but any more coupons? I'm going tomorrow to get Will's college stuff. He's so excited to be joining a fraternity, and he needs a bunch of new things. I figure it's a good time now, because they're having their big winter sale. So with the coupons and everything, I should be able to get some real deals." The women stared at her. She laughed nervously and continued. "Will couldn't care less about this room stuff. Boys are like that, though." Then, turning to Charlotte, she looked for validation. "Right, Charlotte? You have boys in college. Well, one still in college, but you've been through this already."

"My boys couldn't care less if I put daisy sheets on their beds and lined their drawers with lavender-scented paper. They only care if they have money, jeans, and a few T-shirts. They don't wear shoes until November; until then, it's flip-flops," she responded dryly. "Didn't you just go crazy getting him outfitted for college? Are you sure you should be doing this? I mean, is Graham paying for all of this stuff?" Charlotte wanted to ask about Graham's attendance at her dinner party, but she let it go.

Mimmi smiled. This was her self-appointed job. She had just been fired from her job as "wife of twenty years," so "project manager of fraternity-bound kid" felt safer, even though she hadn't been officially hired for the position. "Don't worry about it, ladies. Everything is cool." She hesitated and then, as if she was creating a script as she went along, she continued clumsily, "That's why I brought Graham to the party. We spent the weekend together. Well, not *together* but together as co-parents, to work out all the kid stuff and money and … well, you can imagine."

Charlotte thought, *Yeah, I can imagine!*

But the weekend for Will's scheduled move into the fraternity house would be another disappointment for Mimmi. He was home for the weekend and staying with Mimmi, although he had previously asked Graham to return with him to college without Mimmi in tow, because she was more overbearing than usual. Graham told him that could present additional problems with Mimmi, so they agreed to a caravan of sorts. Mimmi wasn't keen on driving to Washington DC by herself, but she complied, at the risk of being shut out entirely. She felt, however, as if she were losing ground in all her important relationships. As they headed off after a tense morning of loading her station wagon and Graham's old Bavaria, Mimmi nervously shadowed Graham.

Will kept looking in his side-view mirror. He was ready to burst. "Look at her, Dad! She's so close, we might as well put her on a tow hitch. She's probably trying to read our lips! What is wrong with her? How did you put up with her all these years? She's suffocating me." Will heaved a deep sigh. "Listen, Dad. I know you're in a bad spot with Mom and all, but you gotta keep her away, or I swear I'll transfer to a California school or something. She's visited me three times already! I mean it. She's driving me nuts. Why the hell does she need to come to see me so much? It's not like I'm in a show or playing sports or something like that. I could at least get that. I mean, when she comes to DC, I feel like, what the hell do I do with her? She treats me like I'm four. She better not act smothering today. God, my fraternity brothers will think I'm a pussy!"

"Don't talk about your mother like that, Will," Graham admonished. "She's given her life for you and your sister. This family change has been difficult for her. Don't make it any harder. And besides, you're out. Meg has to bear the brunt of her attentiveness now." Will didn't respond, so Graham added, "I mean it. Shape up. You have to help me out here."

Will glared at his father in disbelief. "Are you trying to make me feel bad? For real?" He looked out the window and then turned back. His father was still cruising along Lancaster Avenue, headed for Route 476 South. Will raised his voice a bit. "You fuckin' cheat on her, shack up with your girlfriend—who, by the way, is closer to me in age than she is to you—and you're trying to say I need to take it easy? You think I need to take care of her? You fuckin' married her, dude! And you cheated on her. You fucked somebody else!"

Graham's face turned bright red. He tightened his jaw, which made his neck veins protrude. "Watch your tongue, young man! And I am not a dude. I am your father!"

"Then why don't you act like one? You didn't ask me if it was okay. You didn't even explain yourself. It's just over. Our whole life like it used to be is over. Over! And yeah, Meg will have to bear the brunt of it." Then, without thinking, Will added insult to injury, yelling, "Maybe she'll find a sugar daddy, just like your girlfriend did!"

Without thinking, Graham swung out his right arm with full force; the back of his hand hit Will's mouth. Will's teeth ripped open Graham's hand, and Graham jerked the steering wheel, simultaneously pushing on the brakes.

Mimmi's station wagon slammed into the rear of Graham's BMW and, in the only passion she had felt in twenty years, she screamed, "*Sh-i-i-it!*"

A distant car slowed down but didn't stop when it passed the accident scene. Two cars on the other side of the road stopped and pulled over. Within seconds, Graham and Will jumped out and limped over to Mimmi's car. She couldn't move her right leg, and her forehead was bleeding badly. The police arrived within minutes, and an approaching ambulance siren could be heard.

"Mimmi, I'm so sorry. Tell me you're going to be okay. I'm such a loser!" cried Graham. "God, are you okay? Please tell me you're okay.

I love you, Mimmi. Please tell me you're okay!" Graham was beside himself with fear. He couldn't believe his feelings for Mimmi. He really did love her. He really wanted her. He hated the family's being estranged too. He'd never forgive himself if she was badly injured.

"Shit, Graham! What the hell happened?" She touched her forehead gingerly, then looked at the blood on her fingers. "Get me a rag or something for my head." She saw that his hand was bleeding, and he was limping. "Is Will okay?" she asked, and then she yelled, "Will! Will, come over here! Are you okay?"

Will was talking to the police officer, so Graham said, "He's banged up a little in his face. He hit the windshield but not hard. Maybe knocked his teeth a bit but nothing too bad. There was something in the road. I swerved." He couldn't look at his son, who had just approached his mother's car but continued with the lie as means of an explanation. "I think it was a dog or something. I'm so sorry, Mimmi. And you too, Will. He looked up. "I'm so sorry, son. I've really screwed up again."

Will didn't look at his father. "Mom, you look horrible. Do you hurt anywhere?"

"Yeah, my head is killing me, and my knee hurts. I can't move it." She looked at her son. "Is everything a mess in the cars? How are we going to get you moved in today?"

"Mom, you're nuts. We can't."

The police approached Graham and were talking to him when another car pulled up behind them.

"Mimmi, is that you?" It was Joe Arena. "Jesus, is that Graham's car you hit? Is everyone okay?" He moved into the street and directed cars around him. A police officer approached him and asked him to get out of the road.

"I'm helping my friends here," Joe protested.

"Well, help them over there." The cop motioned to the side of the road. An ambulance arrived, and a medic ran over to Mimmi's car. She was worried about her son, however, more than herself.

"Did you look at my son? He's on his way to college. He's got to get there today. It's important." She waited for a response. "Ouch! My leg is killing me. Damn it! I asked you if you've examined my son."

"Yes, ma'am. He's fine; just a couple of bumps and bruises."

Mimmi yelled. "Joe! Are you here?"

"Yeah. Yeah. I'm right here, Mim. What do you want? I already called Ginny, and she and the girls are on their way."

"I want my husband to get this mess cleaned up, and I want my son to get to college, as planned." The emergency worker walked away, saying he'd return shortly. "Is Will's stuff a mess, or can we get him to his school with it by the end of the day?"

"Whatever you guys want, Mimmi."

Graham was still talking to the police, and Will had joined his father.

"Get my son over here, Joe. Please."

Joe yelled, "Will!" He motioned for him to come close. Will ran, which Mimmi took as an encouraging sign. She winced. The pain was really getting to her.

"Well, I guess he's okay," Joe said in a reassuring tone. "Look at him run."

Mimmi forced a smile.

"What, Mom? You okay?"

"Yes. I'm going to be fine, as soon as they fix this damn leg of mine. I want you to go to school. Daddy and I will work this mess out. Take out what you absolutely need, and call Aunt Lil and tell her what happened. Make sure you tell her Daddy and I are okay, and then maybe she and Uncle Bill can get you down to DC."

Joe Arena overheard the conversation and offered to drive Will to school. "It's no problem, really, Mimmi. Wouldn't you do the same for me?" Then jokingly, he added, "You better say yeah, or else."

Mimmi graciously accepted, but Will was reluctant. Mimmi convinced him, "Really, I'm okay, and if Mr. Arena wants to help, it's better than Aunt Lil. Don't you think? Imagine her and Uncle Bill trying to organize your room! Really, you should let him help you out."

"But Mom, what about you and Dad?"

"We're fine. You hear me still being bossy, don't you? Just get that face cleaned up. What happened to you anyway? It looks like you really hit hard."

"I hit the window. Don't worry about me." He didn't want to add to his mother's worries by letting her know the truth—his father had slapped him and lost control of the car. The medics had returned to help Mimmi out of the car. They had a stretcher. Will thanked Joe Arena as they walked toward his dad's car to begin assessing which belongings were salvageable. Will had tears in his eyes.

"Thank you so much, Mr. Arena. This is so nice of you, really. I can't thank you enough."

"Like I said to your mom, Will, wouldn't you do the same for us?" He looked across the street to see Ginny and Charlotte. "Look. You see? I told you they were on their way!"

After looking both ways, they came running across the street. Graham intercepted them as they tried to talk to Mimmi. The EMTs didn't want any interruptions as they got Mimmi out of the car.

"You couldn't have found a more convenient place to have an accident—around the corner from the police station and minutes from the hospital," said Ginny. "Is Mimmi okay? I see Will looking around at his belongings, of course. What else would an eighteen-year-old be concerned about?"

"Mimmi wants to get Will to school, Gin," said Joe.

"No problem; we'll get him there." Then, turning to Graham, she said, "I assume you're going with her."

"Of course, of course. And listen, my sister and her husband can take Will—"

"Mimmi wants us to do it," said Ginny, cutting Graham off. "Let's give her a break, huh? Let's just do it Mimmi's way." Charlotte had already begun assessing what had to be ditched and what could be reloaded into her Suburban.

"How are you, Mimmi?" Charlotte asked nervously.

"My leg is killing me but other than that, a little headache. No big deal. I want to get my kid to school, Charlotte." She looked so frail, lying on the stretcher, with the neck brace and her legs strapped in place.

Within ten minutes, both Mimmi and the belongings were loaded in their respective vehicles, good-byes were said, and Graham and Mimmi were en route to Lankenau Hospital. Ginny and Charlotte were on their way to GW to take Will to his first day as a frat boy, and Joe was supervising the loading of the damaged cars onto the flatbed tow truck.

Mimmi spent the next weeks learning to navigate with a cast and getting used to having Graham around again. He decided it was important to take care of Mimmi, although she was sure she could manage with her friends and Meg helping. Perhaps it was Graham's guilt for causing the accident that convinced him to stay; maybe it was the realization that he loved Mimmi despite their lackluster relationship. Whatever his reasons, he stayed. Mimmi assumed he had told his girlfriend it was over. He came home with the suitcases he'd left with. She felt an unusual sense of empowerment, given her weakened physical condition.

He went to work as usual, ran errands, and chauffeured Meg to and from sports practices and extracurricular activities. Cooking was relegated to reheating food delivered by friends, and there was plenty of that to go around. He talked to Will frequently to be sure he was settling into frat life as easily as he had settled into his first semester at college. He waited on Mimmi as much as possible. He was, from all appearances, trying to earn her trust.

She relegated him to the guest room and considered herself generous to have allowed him back home. He was given a new key (she'd had the locks changed), but there was a reserve that Mimmi never had with him before. She wouldn't bathe or use the toilet when he was in the room. She never dressed in his presence. And, for some phone calls, she requested privacy. Kisses were infrequent. He did manage a few intimate overnights in her bed but on Mimmi's terms. Graham found the uncertainty titillating.

She kept her excitement to herself. She was delighted to have Graham shower her with so much attention. The day she was to visit her doctor for her six-week follow-up, Graham insisted he should go with her.

She struggled to navigate the doctor's waiting room. Mimmi was annoyed that she was still in a wheelchair—her leg was supported but almost at a right angle to the rest of her body—and her patience with being immobile had worn thin.

Graham was checking in at the front desk as a nurse came out and called, "Mimmi Biddle?" The nurse indicated Mimmi should follow her. "How are you today, Mimmi?" asked the nurse, barely turning her head to look at her. "You seem to have figured out the wheelchair pretty well. Soon it'll be crutches, and before you know it, you'll be back to normal."

Mimmi wished that could be true in so many ways. The nurse held the door to the examination room open and then followed Mimmi in; Graham knocked on the door shortly afterward, having finished at the front desk.

The young nurse opened the door and exclaimed, "Oh, my God! What are you doing here?" The nurse looked at Mimmi and then at Graham. "Oh … is this your sister?"

Mimmi cocked her head and scrunched her face, while Graham averted her glare.

Graham cleared his throat. "Uh, no. This is my wife."

Mimmi's heart sank. *Is this the other woman?* she wondered.

"Your wife? Weren't you just at Heather's party on Saturday night? Does Heather know you are married?"

Mimmi had all she could take. "Excuse me! Remember me, the patient?" The nurse just looked at Mimmi and then back at Graham, shaking her head. Graham stuttered, but Mimmi shut him down before he could form the words. "Get out of here!" she shouted at him. "I mean all the way out! Don't even wait for me, you idiot!" The doctor walked in before Graham could stutter a few explanatory syllables. Mimmi said, "Save it for Jesus!"

"Mimmi, I really need to explain," he said.

"Move on, Graham. Just move on!" She turned her weepy attention to the doctor. "Hello, Dr. Bennett. I'm Mimmi Biddle, and that ass who just walked out the door is my husband, who's been having an affair with your nurse's friend, Heather."

Dr. Bennett raised his eyebrows questioningly. "Well, that's more than I expected after lunch, but do tell me why you're here … uhh …" He flipped over the file nervously, looking for her name, which he'd forgotten in the chaos that had just occurred. Mimmi felt invisible and unimportant, even to her doctor.

She had reached her breaking point of invisibility. No one would ever again discount her, her feelings, her ideas, or her presence. She would tolerate none of it any longer. She had paid her dues and her debt to society with Graham. She'd married for life, but it seemed he married for no good reason at all.

She wanted the house, the cars (after they were repaired), and any investments. And the kids—she wanted the kids. After all, she'd given birth to them. She'd nursed them and had gotten up in the middle of the night when they cried. She'd gone to every game or play or presentation they had. They should have always been *her* kids. He wasn't even a good father. He was an okay wage-earner. *What did I see in him?* she wondered.

As she struggled to check out at the front desk, she looked down at her now cast-free leg. It was pale and wrinkly, but she was able to bend it, which was encouraging.

"Did Dr. Bennett give you the prescription for physical therapy?" asked the office manager from over the counter. The woman could see Mimmi was struggling with her pocketbook and the file, so she came around the high counter into the waiting room. Mimmi couldn't make eye contact with her because she felt sure Heather's nurse friend had already spread the word of her husband's infidelity. She couldn't look at the few people in the waiting room for fear she'd recognize someone and start to cry. She felt fragile again.

After settling business matters with the doctor's staff, the office manager asked her if she wanted assistance to her car. Mimmi simply asked for her to hold the door as she wheeled herself out. She called Charlotte from just outside the office, barely able to keep her composure.

"Where's Graham?" asked Charlotte. Mimmi's sniffling told it all. "Did he leave you there?" Mimmi was muffling a cry. "Okay," Charlotte continued, understanding something else had gone wrong for poor Mimmi, and she wasn't able to talk about it. "I'll be there in ten minutes. I'm leaving now."

Mimmi began wheeling herself faster and faster toward the elevator. She pushed the down button and the doors opened quickly. She pressed L and wheeled herself to the curbside quickly. Her mind was racing as fast as her chair. An elderly couple glared at Mimmi as they moved out of her path.

"Slow down, sister," an orderly joked as he pushed a woman connected to an IV pole. Mimmi was oblivious.

How could he have gone to Heather's party on Saturday night? He went to the pharmacy and the market and rented a few movies. That ass! How could he have lied again?

A young man held the outside door for her. She waited for Charlotte and hoped she didn't see anyone she knew. Her head was spinning.

Had he ever gone to one of Will's games? Or ever seen Meg toss a lacrosse ball? She couldn't remember his being at the school. He was probably running around with his secretary. He was always strange at those company functions she was required to attend—the Christmas party, the summer barbeque at the boss's house, the annual sales awards dinner.

"Mimmi?" It was Charlotte trying to get her attention. "Mimmi! Mimmi! I'm here!" Mimmi turned and swallowed hard to hold back tears. Charlotte hugged her. "Oh, sweetie."

Mimmi's tears let loose, as she motioned to Charlotte to get her out of the public space. When they reached the parking garage, she blubbered and cried aloud, oblivious to cars going up and down the ramps and doors opening and closing around her.

"What was I thinking? I *hate* him. Why is this happening? It's not fair, Charlotte. It's not fair. He blew it! I thought we both wanted the same thing, and he lied and cheated! I've been such a fool!"

"I know. I know it must feel that way. But you are not a fool. You are a kind, sensitive person. He took advantage of you. He wanted it both ways. He wanted a kind, quiet, sweet person who is a great mom by day and who turns into a stripper at night! I'm sorry, Mimmi. I really am so sorry." Charlotte helped Mimmi into the front of her Suburban and then folded the wheelchair and put it in the rear hatch. Charlotte was feeling nauseated from the smell of the hospital, which seemed to permeate the garage air.

Mimmi cried and cried and cried. She never made it home at all that evening. Charlotte called the other walkers, who once again came to Mimmi's rescue. They each pitched in with the kids, the house, Graham, and of course, Mimmi. Ginny Arena called her friend who was an internist. She came to Charlotte's house and, after assessing Mimmi's condition, suggested she take a sedative so she could sleep off some of her emotional pain. Mimmi agreed only after she could see Meg and talk to Will. Charlotte talked her out of that idea.

"You're not in any shape for your kids to see you or talk to you, Mimmi. Come on, now. This is hard enough on them. We'll tell Meg it was hard getting the cast off, and you decided to sleep here. And Will doesn't know what's happening, and that's just as well." Mimmi agreed to Charlotte's plan and took the sedative. She slept until one o'clock the next afternoon.

Joe Arena went to coax Graham to move out again. Ginny said it'd be best if there were no signs of him left when Mimmi returned home. When he knocked on the door, Graham looked like he had been crying.

"Hey, Joe. What can I do for you?"

"Well, I thought I'd ask *you* that question. I understand that things got ugly today with Mimmi and I was wondering what I could do here. You okay?"

Graham welled up, and Joe gently reached in and put a hand on Graham's shoulder. Graham mustered up an explanation of sorts. "She's been really distant since she started the change, and I strayed. But I love her and the kids." He broke down. "I love the kids. I can't live without them, Joe. I can't see them whenever a judge thinks I should see them. They are as much mine as they are hers. I love them for sure. And my seeing the girl on Saturday night was simply to end it, once and for all."

Joe hesitated, wondering if he wanted to get into the thick of it with Graham. So he took a middle road. "These situations are always bad, you know. Lots of shit happens—good, bad, really bad; it's just sucky. Then there just isn't enough emotional capital left in the marriage when something really big and bad happens, and poof! It's over! Years and years—and poof! It's over, buddy, just done. Nobody really gets it when it's over. And maybe it's not really over for you. It might not be over. Maybe you just need a break from each other." Joe peered into the house. "Where's Meg?"

Graham answered in a voice that sounded like it would crack. "She's at her friend Alicia's. I told her what Charlotte told me to say—that the cast was tough coming off and Charlotte was helping her with the pain." Graham looked at Joe with such a helpless face that Joe actually felt sorry for him for a minute.

"All I mean is that you need to decide if you can't live without her," Joe advised. "Then you got an answer. But right now, I'm thinking you might not be so sure. So take a break. You know what? Mimmi needs a break right now. You should give her that much, right?"

Graham cried, "I don't know where to go, Joe. This is my fuckin' house. I don't know where to go. I can't go back to Heather, and I can't afford an apartment. I don't want an apartment."

"Graham, I don't know what to tell you, bud, but you should have thought of that when you decided to stick the old pen in the community inkwell. It's a little late for sentimentality." He sighed and shook his head. "So listen, I'm supposed to tell you Mimmi doesn't want you here when she comes home tomorrow. Okay?"

"No! No! It's not okay!"

"Okay. Then I'm going to leave." Joe hesitated for a moment, then let go of the screen door he'd been holding open. He turned back before Graham shut the storm door.

"And Graham, one more thing: it sounds like you really fucked up with Mimmi. I've been married for twenty-five years to Ginny, and there have been plenty of bimbos available. But I never would have fucked over my wife. So stop feeling so fuckin' sorry for yourself, because you know what? That's how the judge is going to see it—that you're a selfish son of a bitch. So start thinking of your kids. That's what you've got left. Later."

Chapter Eleven

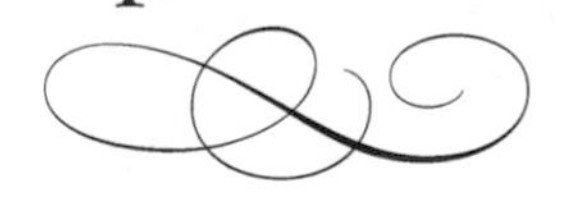

Charlotte was eager to become involved in something outside of her own family, although there was always something to be done in family life—and it was seemingly all important. If it wasn't immediate family life that was a distraction from reentering the workforce, it was an issue with extended family. Lately, her new friends and their respective needs preoccupied her.

Kate had been suffering from severe indigestion and pains under her rib cage, which she suspected was an uncooperative gallbladder. Her family doctor had recommended ultrasounds over the past few years, so she had a diagnosis of gallbladder disease and knew the symptoms well—all part of the midlife malaise she was experiencing. She and Douglas were at their Jersey Shore beach house for a quiet weekend without the kids when she was stricken with the most severe attack yet. They'd been packing to return home Sunday morning, right after a breakfast of eggs and sausage.

"I feel yucky," said Kate, while washing dishes in the tiny kitchen of their Cape Cod-style house. She turned off the water and put the sponge down, grabbing the butcher block countertop to brace herself against the sharp, piercing pain.

"Yucky? Are you four? What does 'yucky' feel like?" inquired Douglas, shutting the sky-blue bead-board cupboard door after drying the last glass. They enjoyed a simple lifestyle at their beach house, although today, not having a dishwasher seemed imprudent.

"It's my gallbladder. I'm pretty sure. Only this time I feel like I'm having a heart attack."

"We shouldn't mess around with this, Kate! All the popular literature says heart attacks are now the number-one killer of women."

"Douglas, who's messing around?" she asked. "I want to go home. We should be close to better hospitals. And nice going with the number-one-killer—*agghh*! Oh, my *God*!" she yelled, gasping for breath. She hunched over and grabbed the back of the red spindled dining chair for stability. She tried to take a deep breath. She couldn't. "Burp me," she managed to say, grimacing.

Douglas burped her. It was something he'd gotten used to. She belched like a drunken sailor again and again.

"I'm calling your doctor," he announced.

"Ahh. That feels better. Douglas, it's my gallbladder. Let's go home, and I'll call Dr. Akers in the morning, unless this gets worse. It's Sunday anyway. She's probably not on call."

He drained the sink, leaving the rest of the dirty dishes, and ran upstairs to retrieve their overnight bag. "Let's go!" he yelled.

She was hunched over the weathered pine dining table, where each of her children had carved his or her name, along with other creative designs. "I'm nauseated. This is a new symptom. Get a puke bag for the road," she demanded.

The hour-and-fifteen-minute ride home was quiet, except for Kate's belching. Douglas was concerned, feeling that perhaps he should take charge and call Kate's internist.

"If it were me, Kate, you'd be calling the doctor for me. I'm calling Dr. Akers now."

She nodded in agreement. The road was quiet on this spring Sunday morning, so he could safely use his phone while driving. Her symptoms were not subsiding as with prior episodes. Dr. Akers called back within minutes and spoke to Kate. The doctor agreed that the symptoms sounded like gallbladder, but she sent Kate directly to the hospital for an ultrasound. Douglas called his parents, who were at the house with the kids, to apprise them of their changed plans. Kate was admitted to the hospital and scheduled for surgery the next morning.

The surgery went well and Kate left the hospital with a Band-Aid on her belly button and a mild painkiller. She used a step stool to get into bed and fell in and out of sleep for the next two days. That was, until she became so constipated that she felt like her belly button would burst and her insides would come pouring out. She called Ginny, who arrived with Charlotte, Mimmi, and an entire apothecary of stool softeners, laxatives, and enemas.

"Ladies, am I ever glad to see you. She's a mess," said Douglas as he shut the door and motioned for them to follow him upstairs to their bedroom. Charlotte had never been inside Kate's clapboard-sided house and was taking in her friend's country-style decorating.

"What a charming home you have, Doug," said Charlotte. "Oh, these black-and-white portraits of the kids are beautiful."

"Kate shot them but had them professionally developed. Yeah, they were taken a while ago, as you can tell," said Douglas.

"Gosh, I cannot believe the wallpaper matches the balloon shades. Your wife is very talented," Charlotte added.

"Don't I know that," Douglas said, turning his head to acknowledge the compliment. "She can take stuff she finds in people's trash and turn it into a work of art."

When they reached the top of the stairs, there was Kate, looking miserable in bed, propped up with five pillows. The step stool told the story.

"Look who's here, Kit-Kat," Douglas said using her favorite pet name. "Mimmi, how are you doing with the crutches? You seem pretty agile," he said as he ushered the ladies into the bedroom.

"I get around great, given that I have virtually no upper-body strength. The crutches are my workout," Mimmi replied.

Ginny spilled the contents of the pharmacy bag on their bed, "Well, girl, if this doesn't clean you out, you need Roto-Rooter."

Charlotte was peering above her bifocals, reviewing the benefits of each, explaining the fastest relief would come from the enema. Ginny was blabbing about the beautiful floral arrangements Kate had received from well-wishers.

"I've never had an enema before," Kate said. Douglas took that as his exit cue. She continued, "Is that the little waxy-looking stick you put up your butt?"

Charlotte was looking at the boxes. "I don't think so, sweetie."

Ginny said, "Let me see that." She pulled the box out of Charlotte's hand, and Charlotte scowled. "Oh no," said Ginny. "This is a bag of water, basically, that you shoot up your butt and, boom, like an explosion, everything comes flying out!"

Charlotte shuddered. "Ginny! That's not helpful!"

"Well, that's what happens."

Kate was still looking puzzled, so Charlotte explained the unpleasant details.

Ginny continued, "You've never had an enema?"

"No, Ginny, and frankly, although I could cry because I'm so uncomfortable, I have no idea how I'll be able to bend and reach to put this nozzle up there."

"Well, what about your husband? Can't he do it?" Ginny was going from bad to worse.

Kate yelled, "No! My husband can't do that!"

Douglas was standing a bit down the hallway, eavesdropping. He thought he'd weigh in. "Kate, we should call the surgeon. She might not think this is a good idea."

"Douglas, I need to crap! I don't care what Dr. Taft thinks, or Dr. Akers, or *you*!"

Ginny yelled back, "Oh, for the love of God, I'll do it!" She grabbed the package out of Charlotte's hand. Kate started crying. Mimmi still hadn't said anything.

"No one is putting anything up my butt! No one! Got it?" She crawled to the side of her bed and slid down the side of the mattress onto the step stool and then stood. The girls watched her. "Give me that thing," she said gruffly to Ginny. Then, turning to Mimmi, she said, "Read the directions to me and stand outside the bathroom door in case I pass out or something. You're the only one with any sense here right now."

Mimmi looked as if she'd seen a ghost, but she followed Kate into the bathroom just off the bedroom. Charlotte took her bifocals off and pushed Ginny, who wanted to stay, out the door and into the hallway.

"We'll be right out here, girls. Just yell if you need us, okay?" said Charlotte. "Get going," she said to a resistant Ginny. She pulled the bedroom door shut.

Mimmi read the instructions carefully aloud, while Kate leaned on her sink for support.

"If self-administering, kneel on all fours. Lower your torso onto the floor and raise your hips so your body is at a forty-five degree angle. While hips are raised, reach behind and insert the enema."

Kate started to cry. "Okay, I got it. Pull the door and just stand there, please. I know it's awkward, but—"

Mimmi was already out the door. Charlotte, meanwhile, gave Ginny a fierce look and whispered angrily, "Great. I guess we're lumped together now—two obnoxious, insensitive cohorts."

"I'm sorry. I don't have good filters," answered Ginny.

"Good filters? You have no filters, Ginny. For godssake, the girl just had major surgery, and she's on the floor with her ass in the air, shooting a bottle of water up there, and you offered to be there when explosive crap comes flying out. You think that is having bad filters? Read my lips. You have *no* filters. You need to count to ten before you open your mouth."

Kate yelled from the bathroom that it was working. Mimmi was standing guard like a sentinel. Douglas was having bourbon over ice in the family room.

The next couple of weeks were rough going for Kate, and she couldn't lift anything over five pounds. Mimmi was very helpful with groceries. She went to the grocery store daily since her accident recovery; she couldn't manage a lot of weight either but certainly more than five pounds. Helping Kate took her mind off her life's issues, and she loved driving the motorized cart in the grocery store.

Ginny and Marianna walked Kate's dogs when they went on their walks. Charlotte sent books and magazines and stopped by for interesting conversation. Kate and Douglas were very grateful for the help.

Kate mended in a few short weeks, although driving was still off limits, as was lifting more than five pounds. But Charlotte could again focus on herself, guilt-free, and returned to perusing the newspapers for jobs. Nothing was interesting—that is, until she saw an unusual ad seeking a person with many of her skills.

Charlotte had many ideas for work, most of which included consulting in the art world, but so far, they were just ideas. Charlotte blamed her stalled career on Charles, for his lack of support, yet she wasn't able to articulate just how a supportive mate could have made a difference. More important, she couldn't articulate what a supportive mate would do or say *presently* that could make a difference. Instead, Charlotte isolated herself more and more from the very people who could help her return to the robust career she had left behind. She feared they would judge her harshly, perhaps because she did so herself.

"Hello, my gorgeous wife." Charles gently pecked her on the cheek as he passed by her on his way to his home office. She was peering out the window in the kitchen. "Checking out your garden?" He hadn't noticed the tears. When she didn't respond to either the kiss or his words, he persisted, this time paying closer attention. "What's going on, Charlotte?"

She turned around, exposing her mascara-streaked face. "Nothing's going on, Charles, absolutely nothing."

He stepped in closer for a hug. "Sweetheart, what is wrong?" He held her. She wasn't receptive. "Charlotte, did something happen? Did Betsy give you trouble again this morning?"

She hesitated, thinking perhaps she should avoid a confrontation, but he wasn't going to let her be dishonest. His concern was as palpable as her pain. Charles fell short in many ways, but she could overlook most of his shortcomings because of his profound interest in her. He simply lacked the skills to attend to her neediness. Charlotte hadn't realized that her happiness wasn't Charles's project but solely her own. She pushed back so she could focus on him, literally. Presbyopia had set in, a harbinger of midlife.

"Where are my glasses?" she moved away from him, toward the junk drawer where she usually had several cheap readers stashed away.

"Don't you like that chain I bought you?" Charles asked. "You really ought to wear it. You're always looking for one of ten pair of glasses, Charlotte."

"I ought to do a lot of things I don't do, and I feel like something other than my glasses is missing. Like I'm supposed to be somewhere or I missed a deadline or something. I wake up that way and I go to bed that way, and the rest in between feels weird." She shuffled through the junk drawer. "Where are my damn glasses?" she yelled. "Why are all these fucking receipts in here?" She tossed them at Charles, but he said nothing as half of them fluttered to the floor. She took a deep breath and sighed, making no effort to collect them. "I mean, I look at these women in the neighborhood who walk their kids to school with two babies in tow. I think to myself, that was me fifteen years ago, and what have I done since then? What is my life about?" She was picking up steam. Her voice was getting louder. "Look at you! You have set yourself up nicely," she said, her voice quivering. "You go to business lunches and golf outings. You have calls to return, and you're an expert in putting together complex real estate transactions. People pay you huge amounts of money, and you support an entire family."

He tried to inject a thought. "But Charlotte—"

"I'm not through!" she shouted. "I want to make a difference in our community. I don't need the money, but I need something, Charles. Something that is just mine that makes people say, *Wow! Look at that.* And I'm tired of being the supportive wife and having no reciprocity."

"Charlotte! How can you say that? I am tough and focused, but there isn't any doubt that I wouldn't have enjoyed this kind of success without you. I pay tribute to you at every corner. At every step of the way, I tell anyone who'll listen how I need you behind the scenes doing all that you do, so that I could be this successful."

"Well, I don't want to be behind the scenes! I want to be the scene. Do you hear yourself? How about if you go behind the scenes for a while and give me the at-home support?"

Charles sighed as he folded his arms across his chest, resting them on his paunch. He glanced at his watch. "I'm expecting a call, Charlotte. What's really going on? Did you hear from the doctor's office yet about your follow-up test? Is that it? Is everything okay?"

"No, I haven't heard yet," she barked. "And stop asking me about my boob, okay? I'll tell you if anything changes, like if I have to have it lopped off or anything else that might disrupt your precious routine!"

"That's quite enough, Charlotte. Don't lower yourself to this. It's unbecoming," he said disgustedly.

"I can't take this much more, Charles. I just want to be front and center myself!"

"And what is it that you'll be doing front and center, Charlotte? Will it be art consulting or painting or teaching—"

"Don't mock me! I'm serious. And I do have some ideas of what I want to do."

"Pick one of them and carry through on it. Just one idea; do that. I am so tired of hearing how the kids and I have held you back. *You've* held you back, Charlotte. You're afraid of yourself. I'm convinced of it. You have that poor-girl syndrome. That woe-is-me attitude."

"Poor-girl syndrome? Woe is me? How dare you! I actually haven't been poor in a very long time, having nothing to do with you, Charles

Wentworth. What would you know about being self-made, anyway? You just picked up the pieces of your father's business and used his name over and over again."

"Yeah, that's just what I did," he said cynically. "I picked up the pieces that were scattered and shattered and threw them up in the air and, like magic, they came tumbling down into a beautiful mosaic called Wentworth Enterprises." He unfolded his arms and moved closer to her, pointing and yelling. "Don't demean my work. I am not a lot of things, but I *am* diligent and smart and focused. I made this happen because I created it. This is *not* my father's business."

The mailman knocked on the door. Charles marched out of the kitchen, shaking his head. There was a letter that required a signature. While Charles filled out the paperwork, Charlotte sifted through the catalogs and mail. There was a brochure from a high-school boyfriend that she and Charles had met on a shopping trip to the mall several months ago. The experience was awkward, despite Mike's attempts at conversation. He was the lead singer and guitar player in a local band that had reached a notoriety of sorts. He played the nightclub circuit in Vegas and Atlantic City as the warm-up act for some big names. Charles was impressed. Charlotte was uncomfortable in her stiffly pressed Faconnable shirt and Zegna pants, not to mention her jewelry and coiffed hair. Their lives were markedly different, hers and Mike's. Charlotte had a comfortable life; Mike was comfortable in his skin. Now this brochure arrived. *What is this about*? she thought. She showed it to Charles.

"He seemed like a nice guy. Maybe you should have married him. I'm sure you'd have just as nice a life, you know, since you're self-made. I have to go to work," Charles said abruptly. Before he went into his office, he turned to Charlotte, who was holding the mail in the center hall, looking at him. "It's not me or the kids or your friends or your breast scare. It's you. You can have it all, Charlotte. It's just impossible to have it all at once. Pick a horse and run with it."

He shut his office door and Charlotte continued crying. These were tears of anger. *Not all at once, my ass,* she thought. *Who told him he couldn't have a family and career all at once?*

She looked through the mail again. A political flyer for her friend Senator Jennifer Holmes Bartlett from Pennsylvania caught her attention. The brochure came just short of saying she had thrown her hat in the ring for a run at the presidency. Her name had been bandied about by Democrats for a while. Her efforts to restore work in the Rust Belt and her family's roots in the western part of the state made her a superstar and a go-to person for many other states experiencing economic backslides. Outsourcing of jobs for cheaper labor markets had caused huge economic problems across the country, especially in manufacturing and farming areas.

Charlotte remembered how excited she was to vote for her old college roommate and how hard she had worked on her first campaign for local office. Now Jennifer was a potential contender for the presidency, and Charlotte felt like she couldn't even run for dog catcher at the moment. How had this happened? Charlotte read through the brochure three times. Yeah, this was her girl Jen, all right. She was still a champion of the folks who didn't know how to fight for themselves. She was still the voice of the people. Charlotte thought about how she and Jen had talked in the beauty salon and the subsequent calls from her office.

Maybe it was time; maybe this was a cause she could champion. She missed that energy and excitement for something that was all hers. Their boys were out of the nest, and Betsy was well on her way. She was a great, independent kid. It was Charlotte's time for something, or else she'd lose herself forever. The worst thing that could happen was that she'd catch up with an old friend. Yeah! She would return the calls to Jen's office.

She ran upstairs to change into her walking gear. The brochure from Mike fell on the steps, but she held on to the newspaper with classifieds. Holmes Bartlett would hire her in a heartbeat! How fortuitous that of all days, today she'd read the junk mail!

Chapter Twelve

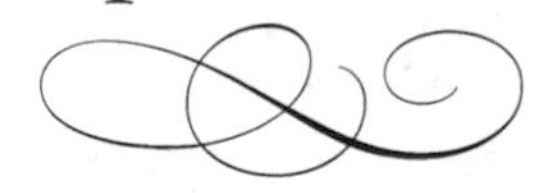

Kate wasn't herself during the walks. She became competitive with her strides, trying to lead the pack. She and Mimmi usually kept company in the rear of the group, but now, since Mimmi wasn't walking, it was too embarrassing to be the lone slacker. Ginny was the unspoken leader of the group and noticed Kate's aggression.

"What's going on, Katie girlfriend?" There was no answer. Ginny glanced at Charlotte, who motioned to be quiet. Charlotte mouthed *Let it go.* Ginny let it go but not happily.

The walkers needed a new energy. There was a discernable change in the group's dynamic since Mimmi's marital break-up. Perhaps it was the uneasiness of being around an unexplained misfortune. The women wanted to understand what had gone so terribly wrong. After all, if it could happen to Mimmi and Graham Biddle, a break-up could happen to any couple.

Their impending divorce shattered the illusion of certainty around marriage precisely because they *were* so predictable. And its occurrence came as such a shock to everyone who knew them. Perhaps Graham and Mimmi shocked themselves the most. But the possibility of marital disaster lingered in all the walkers' minds.

Kate was outwardly the most worried for herself. She was the only one who couldn't hide her concern. They were all in midlife marriages with aging parents, children leaving the nest, and menopause looming in the background. Kate answered Ginny minutes after she had asked the question.

"You want to know what's wrong? Here's what's wrong: we're getting old! I just had my damn gallbladder out! Come on and tell me that you don't think of that as an old person's operation. Look at us! We're walking and walking, and we still look the same. I'm turning fifty in three months and my husband has no idea what I'm going through. He doesn't understand why I'm upset that he hasn't started planning a party or asked me if I want a motherfucker diamond yet." She took a breath and continued. "And yesterday afternoon, I asked my damn dermatologist what I could do about the stray dark hairs on my chin and upper lip, and you know what she told me? She told me I should consider shaving! *Shaving.* She actually said shave. I wasn't sure if she uttered the word at first because I don't hear well, so I said, 'I'm sorry. Is that a technical term?' She looked at me and spelled it out for me: S-H-A-V-E. Shave." Kate stopped because she was out of breath, then whined, "See, I'm out of breath, too!"

"That's because you have us racing down the street," Ginny piped in. "We've been power-walking here."

"Well maybe we *should* be power-walking, Ginny. Look at me. You're skinny. Charlotte's skinny." She glanced at Marianna who was recovering her breath but didn't say anything. "But I'm fat, and I need to walk fast! And, I now know, I need to shave!" Kate screamed as she started racing down the street again.

The walkers chased after her—all, of course, except Mimmi, who was still home enduring physical therapy for her broken knee and contemplating big life changes for her fractured heart.

Marianna shouted, "Kate! Wait! I have a question."

Kate wheeled around and glared at her. "What? Let me guess—you heard something amazing about shaving!" Kate snapped back.

"No, no, no, forget the shaving thing. Your dermatologist clearly isn't middle-aged. What middle-aged woman would shave her face?"

"Middle-aged?" Ginny piped in. "What woman, period, would want to shave her face?"

"Your dermatologist is a sadist," Marianna said, rubbing her head, making her gray hair stand on end. Her bifocals, dangling from a beaded chain around her neck, bounced on top of her matronly, oversized chest.

Ginny responded by rolling her eyes. The walkers continued their power walk. Ginny wouldn't give up. "What happened to you? What is wrong, Kate? Is this a post-surgical reaction?"

Kate turned about-face and, in the loudest voice she could summon, yelled, "Which part didn't you understand? That I have to shave in the morning with my husband who, by the way, still thinks I'm somewhat hot, or the part that I'm fat, or the part that I'm turning fifty?" She huffed and puffed. "If I start shaving with my husband, it's all over!" she yelled. "He actually likes me and thinks my face is beautiful. What the hell do you think he'll do when I say, 'Are you done with the shaving cream, honey?' and then apply it to my fucking face?"

Charlotte burst out laughing. "Oh, forget that nut doctor! Do you actually think middle-aged women are all sneaking around shaving their faces? There's nothing wrong with turning fifty, Kate. God, you're making such a big deal of it. I'm not a shriveled-up nothing-of-a-person now that I'm in my fifties. Life really does go on. I'm sorry you're having trouble with all of this." Then, as if to convince herself she was okay, Charlotte repeated herself. "Really. You're going to be okay too."

The walkers slowed their pace and walked in silence for a bit. Marianna broke the tension by asking for the definition of a "motherfucker diamond."

Kate smirked. "Guess."

"Wait. Before I guess what a motherfucker diamond is, I want to say this. In shrink-speak, I'd ask my patient, *Why now*?" Then she looked directly at Kate. "So, *why now,* Kate? Why the worry now? You are the same Kate that you were two weeks ago, five months ago. Why now?"

Ginny cut the tension. "Thank you, Dr. Silver. Ladies, there we have it. Dr. Silver asks the most pertinent questions of our time. *Why now*?" Then with added sarcasm, she said, "*Why now*? Because she's upset right fuckin' now! That's why now! Do people actually pay you to ask them these asinine questions, Marianna?"

Marianna was a little hurt but answered Ginny. "I'm serious. The now versus later or never or before is an important question because context is important. Triggers ..." She stopped herself.

Kate answered. "There isn't a path anymore. I want to start a business, and I can't get enough traction to stick with anything, because everyone else's something, in my entire family, seems to trump what I'm doing. I feel like I run everyone everywhere, but none of it makes *me* feel better. Lately, the only thing that I feel like I'm really accomplishing is the laundry, and wow—immediate gratification!" Then she hit on it. "And I think we all look like Mimmi and Graham in a way, and I'm scared we, *any one of us*, could be in Mimmi's shoes." She welled up. "I'm really scared, and I'm too busy to change anything. I wouldn't even know where to begin." A few tears escaped.

"Maybe you don't need to change anything, Kate," Charlotte offered. "Maybe you're just going through a rough time. It doesn't mean you're going to wind up like Mimmi." She paused, then said, "How do I say this without sounding horrible? None of us is like Mimmi, God bless her. She is just starting to see life like the rest of us always have." Then she looked at the rest of the walkers. "Come on, girls. A little help here."

Ginny started the walking again, at a walker's pace and at the head of the group. "Watch that car," she said, as they walked around a parked car and avoided an oncoming Mercedes with blacked-out windows. "What's with these cars with blacked-out windows? It makes me feel like bad stuff is going on inside."

"You watch too many episodes of *CSI*, Ginny," said Marianna.

"And how would you know about *CSI*, Dr. Silver?" Ginny sniped.

"Jeremy is addicted to that show."

"Oh, and you just watch it so you know what he's watching, right?"

"I think they're weird," said Kate. "Why does anyone need darkened windows? And Marianna, those boobs of yours have gotten enormous. What's with that?"

Marianna puffed out her chest. "Ladies, I just discovered—"

"Oh, Jesus, don't say silicone, please. Please do not tell me you got a boob job, and that's why you missed a bunch of our walks. Please, I could not handle that," said Ginny. Charlotte was laughing. "What, Charlotte? Like you could handle that, Madam Uptight?"

"You just fracture me, Ginny. Marianna, do tell. What is your magic, dahling?" asked Charlotte. "I could use some magic." She puffed out her small and worrisome bosoms.

"Victoria's Secret has these gals who actually measure you. I've been wearing the same size bra since I don't know when, and as it turns out, I'm a band width and cup size bigger. Isn't it spectacular?" Marianna twirled around for effect. "And the bonus is, no Viagra!"

"Oh, now *I* might get sick! TMI, Marianna! Too much information," said Charlotte. She took off her lightweight jacket and tied it around her waist.

"Oh, my goodness, we don't need Viagra! It's just a joke. If he needed it, do you think I'd tell you ladies? That'd be like taking out an ad in the *Jewish Exponent* for goodness sake!" cried Marianna "But these boobs"—she stuck out her chest—"something, huh? Okay, so I gave you a sexy tip for the day. Let me give you a shrink tip as well. Returning to the subject of Mimmi—or really, Mimmi's failing marriage—here it is: I think Mimmi took her marriage for granted.

"Mimmi just assumed life would happen for her the way it happened for her mother and the generations before her. She'd get married, wait on her family hand and foot, and the reward would be predictability, family, and the kind of love that familiarity and predictability offer." Marianna reached inside her shirt to adjust the new bra. One of the straps had begun to slip off her shoulder. "Mimmi got married right after college and dedicated herself to being a wife and mother. She never talked of wanting a career or personal prestige. Until recently, she wasn't even concerned with how she looked. She's all about family—new school shoes, backpacks, and volunteering at the kids' spring book fair, birthdays, anniversaries, baby showers, weddings, Thanksgiving, Christmas, Easter, and summers at the Jersey Shore. Mimmi and Graham were, if anything, predictable."

"Well, isn't that what we all wanted? Want?" asked Kate. "Don't we all want some predictability and security? I know I do."

The conversation heated up and the pace of the walking picked up again. Charlotte made herself vulnerable. "I get where you're at, to some degree, Kate. These last five years or so, I have felt awkward in my skin, sort of like I don't recognize my life anymore. The kids are almost all out of the house. Charles's business is going really well, but I got lost in the shuffle of his work and the kids' activities. I'm sick of trying things that I can't really sink my teeth into because family stuff keeps getting in the way. But for me, the uneasiness is more about not knowing what I want anymore. I feel as if I missed the opportunity to get what I wanted when I wanted it, and now that I can have almost anything materially, and I have what seems to be unending time, I'm not sure of anything. I'm not sure I like the way my life looks, going forward. That scares the S-H-I-T out of me. Is that what you're experiencing?" She sighed and continued, "So thanks to you, Kate, maybe I'm not okay either. Maybe I'm really a mess too!" Charlotte laughed uneasily.

"I just don't want to think my marriage is so vulnerable," said Kate, somewhat out of breath.

"I'm not where you guys are," Marianna joined in." I do want more challenges in my work, but you know I see Aaron struggle with age issues too. And perhaps it's more glaring for us in our marriage because of our age differences and the roles that each of us has taken on. In part, it's because of that, but aging sucks, period. Whether you're a guy or a girl, it sucks. Aaron—"

"No way, Marianna," Charlotte cut her off. "I don't buy it. It isn't the same for guys. They don't have to juggle parenthood with the job thing. Or the aging parents with the career and kids. And for sure they aren't dealing with the discrimination against aging women in our society. Come on. Aaron could probably still get a nineteen-year-old coed to give him a blow job any time! But try to imagine me getting a twenty-year-old guy to turn around for a second look. Not even naked! Okay, maybe to laugh. But that's it. And that's just awful. It's downright awful."

Charlotte had so much pent-up anger over this aging issue. She couldn't believe life was so unfair and that each of her new friends suffered in this way. Usually, they suffered silently. Each suffered through the first time she thought she looked pretty and no one said anything or gave her a second look. Or the first time a sales clerk said ma'am instead of miss. Each one suffered silently as she applauded her husband's career advancement, while she wore a beautiful dress and sipped champagne at a promotion party. And each woman suffered as she either thought of re-entering the workplace after raising children, or tried, like Marianna, to juggle both.

None of it was horrible. So each woman wrongly assumed silence was the answer. But what they found in their shared discontent was magical: Healing begins to occur in the moment of connecting with like-minded sojourners. They shared their stories and ploughed through anecdotes about their physical selves, which they could more easily laugh off than the evidence of discrimination against women, which still existed in the workplace. They wondered aloud where feminism fit into their full range of issues.

"Yeah, but do you give a hoot about feminism," Marianna asked, "when you walk down the street with your daughter, and some guy blows a cat call at her, and you're thinking, *What about me?*, because you think you're pretty damn hot yourself?"

"I don't know where you ladies come from," Ginny said. "I don't care if some guy I don't know whistles at me. I only care if Joe thinks

I'm hot. And sometimes I even wish he'd not think that, because I'm too damn tired, if you get my drift here!"

"Yeah, but maybe if you weren't getting ... if you weren't having sex with your husband regularly, you'd wonder if you still had your old sexual mojo," Charlotte added.

Marianna was bursting. "Why is it always about sexual stuff? When I look at women patients of mine suffering through discrimination on the job, it makes me insanely filled with rage. Don't you care about that stuff more?"

"We're not as wrapped up in that yet because it's been years since we've been in the workforce, and we've put it behind us. I care more about age discrimination now, because that's where I'm at—where we're at," said Charlotte.

"Well, what about our kids? Don't you want your sons to treat their wives with equal respect regarding work? And don't you want your daughters to have the same opportunities as your sons?"

Although the discussion had shifted topics, it was still too heavy for Ginny. "Damn, you ladies are on my last nerve today. Really. We need a referee here. Can't we talk about something lighter than marriage difficulties or feminism? All the views on sexism, feminism, and women's looks doesn't butter the biscuit when a middle-aged woman just wants to be acknowledged for being pretty and sexy. We know we're accomplished and smart. Some of us have figured out how to be happy staying at home and still feel smart and competent, and some of us have figured out how to successfully manage work and family. And just when our generation figured all this out, pretty and sexy looked like faded flowers in a June bride's bouquet. That's it in a nutshell. We're fucked, if all that matters is how we look. So, who in our group thinks we are our looks? Nobody! So why are we all wrapped up in this today?" Ginny turned to Kate and jokingly hit her with a zinger. "So, girlie, get a grip! You're ruining our fun out here!"

Marianna asked Kate again what a motherfucker diamond was.

"It's one of those huge diamonds that takes up the entire space between a woman's knuckle and the back of her hand. You know, and it looks like it needs wheels to move because it's so damn big. Douglas and I joke that a woman with a ring that big must be married to a real motherfucker!"

The girls all laughed while Charlotte rotated her ring into the palm of her hand. Ginny was still leading the group in their walk.

"You know," Ginny said, "I just want to finish on the Mimmi-not-being-like-us conversation. She really *isn't* like the rest of us. I mean, she's a sweetheart, but she really believes in Santa Claus and the Tooth Fairy. Her husband was like a midlife crisis waiting to happen! We all noticed—I think before you joined the group, Charlotte. We talked to Mimmi on one of our slower-paced jaunts about Graham's sudden late hours at the office. He went on a diet. She was complaining that he was spending so much money having his car detailed."

"You know, sometimes we don't want to see things," Marianna added. "We purposely don't raise issues, either because we know it's already too late, or we're scared we might rock the boat, or that we'll have to take responsibility for some part of what we know is a mess."

Ginny nodded. "Right. But Mimmi actually got mad at us, like we were talking badly about Graham behind his back. Meanwhile, look at what the prick has done to her!"

As Charlotte listened to Marianna speak her therapist lingo, despite every effort to simply be a friend, Charlotte felt like Marianna could have been speaking to her. Was she afraid of confronting Charles? Was she afraid she might have to change her relatively comfy life by taking on more financial responsibility? She couldn't think about it because she was beginning to feel like she couldn't breathe. She turned her thoughts back to poor Mimmi and joined the conversation again.

"Maybe Mimmi isn't all that unhappy anymore. There is a guy calling her and paying attention. The kids are coming around to the idea of living in two different households. Will is already living at college, so maybe it really isn't all that bad. Apparently, Graham was a cheap ass anyway, so the money part is actually better, I think."

Ginny perked everyone up. "Look, I'm going to go home and kill myself or Joe if we don't stop talking about all this gloom-and-doom stuff. Let's talk about Marianna's big boobs again, okay?"

"You really don't have any filters, do you?" asked Charlotte.

"Okay. What's for dinner tonight?" Kate added.

"Oh, crap. I dread dinnertime," said Marianna. "I am so tired of ordering out, but the idea of cooking is too much. Poor Jeremy; he's probably going to marry someone who is a chef or something in rebellion."

"Joe's cooking tonight," said Ginny.

"Oh, shut up. You are so lucky! That man is perfect," said Kate.

"He's impotent, right?" Marianna joked.

"Oh, my goodness, I need to cover my ears," said Charlotte.

"He's a stud, and that is all I'm saying," bragged Ginny.

"Please shut up; I'm begging," Kate said, putting her hand over Ginny's mouth.

The girls all laughed, and Ginny walked with *her* chest a bit puffed out.

Mimmi was the ultimate decision-maker as to just how bad things were for her, and her reality was pretty grim. She had taken her life for granted and now, at forty-five, she had to reinvent herself. The trust with Graham was broken, as far as she was concerned. It was over. No more conversations were necessary. The only thing left was her future. She hobbled around her house, pushing herself to strengthen her bum leg, removing pictures of the "happy family."

She smashed her wedding portrait against the wall unit in the family room. She couldn't bend easily to pick up the shattered pieces. She used her cane to continue mangling what was left of their smiling image. She didn't realize she was crying. She retrieved a vacuum cleaner from the hall closet to finish cleaning up the mess. She watched as the broken images were sucked into the canister. Five minutes later there wasn't a sign of the glass, the mirrored frame, or the image of a young newlywed couple with a bright future ahead of them.

She thought how much easier her life would be if she could change her attitude. She not only needed to suck up the images of her youth in a vacuum cleaner but to vanquish the hopes attached to them. Mimmi needed an emotional vacuum cleaner of sorts. She wanted to turn herself around but she just didn't know how.

She was sick of feeling hopeless. She was tired of eating alone. She was through with anger being the only feeling she could conjure up on a good day. She was, after all, days away from finishing her physical therapy, and before long she would be ready to dance—at least, that's what her doctor promised. She could stand strong again very soon. For now, she was thrilled to move without a cast or crutches.

Forget Graham. That needed to be part of the mantra. Will was away at school, and Meg lived with Graham half the week. But something was missing. She wanted to feel positive about something, anything. Excitement was a long-lost sentiment.

The door bell rang. It was Graham.

"We need to talk." He sounded serious, an unusual demeanor for him. "Can I come in?"

"You should have called. I wasn't expecting you, and I have plans. But if you can make it quick, sure." She didn't want him to think she sat all day and cried, even though that was the activity that filled most of her waking hours lately. "What's going on?" she asked.

"Not much. But we need to talk," he said as he opened the screen door and entered his house as a guest. Graham looked at her disheveled appearance. The cane didn't help her image with him. It was clear this experience had taken its toll on her; she looked especially tired. He was feeling guilty about his culpability. He had caused her so much grief; the accident was just the icing on the cake. And Mimmi didn't realize that it was his fault; she believed that he had swerved to avoid an animal. If she knew the truth, she'd really hate him.

"So, Graham"—she plopped in an overstuffed arm chair—"you look serious. That scares me. Is everything okay?"

"Well, not really, Mimmi." He sat across the room on a tailored sofa. "I mean, I'm okay, the kids are okay. It's just that I've been spending too much money on keeping two households and everything. You know I rented this short-term, furnished rental, because I really thought we'd work it out, so I have that. Plus, we both spoil the kids with extra stuff, and it's all adding up to my not being able to make ends meet for the first time ever."

"Graham, how you can come in here and tell me this is beyond my comprehension! How about getting another job? Or how about working two jobs? Do what you have to do, Graham. Just send my money. Take care of your kids. And get the hell out of my house!"

Graham didn't give up. "I was hoping that you would consider taking a part-time job to help out, Mimmi. I mean, I know it's hard with your leg and all, but really, it's not right that I have to support two households."

Mimmi wriggled her way out of the chair and got up, leaning on the cane for balance. She really didn't need it. She moved to his side of the room, flailing her cane at him, just missing his head but knocking a lamp to the floor. He stood too.

"You lousy son of a bitch! It's not right, for sure, but *you* caused this mess! I was in it for life. I was happy cooking and cleaning and raising our kids. I wasn't planning on your running off with a park-bench bimbo!" She swung the cane again, missing him.

"Mimmi! Stop!" He grabbed the cane pulling her toward him, so she fell forward onto the couch. "You look pathetic, hitting me with that thing. Get a hold of yourself, Mimmi. Just get a grip!" He shook his head.

She righted herself on the couch. "Get a grip? I look pathetic? Are you kidding me? You're asking a woman who dedicated her life to building a family with you, who is recovering from a serious injury, to go get a job and support the half of the life she's left with after you take an axe to the family that was once her dream. I'll get a grip—on your neck! That's what I'll get a grip on. You screwed me over, Graham! You ruined our lives!"

"What if I come back here to live again? Like when you had your accident. It wasn't bad. I can't get that night we had together out of my head. Remember when you took me to your friend's dinner party? We had so much fun, Mimmi. We had that great time afterward, too; really great. I can't stop thinking about how our marriage might have turned out if we'd been like that all along, you know what I mean? More social. More fun. More intimate." He cocked his head hoping to inspire sympathy from her.

"Graham," she muttered through sobs, "I wanted it to work more than you'll ever know. If you think it's easy for a woman to start over at forty-five, dream on. I'm an overweight, unattractive, middle-aged woman with no skills. I never worked outside of my home." Her voice rose as she continued. "I thought we were an item forever! I did *my* forever part. I have the routine down pat. Now what? What do I do now? I can't trust you. You want to come back here to live? Why? Because you can't hold her interest anymore? She found out you don't have any money and that I'm probably going to get everything you do have? Why? *Why*?" She was sobbing and screaming, and her chest felt tight. She gasped for breath. "I want to forget that night too, along with the other twenty-some years. I can't believe I slept with you again! What was I thinking?"

"That you love me?" he suggested confidently. "Maybe you were letting your real feelings show. I know it was special. And I know you do too."

"Shut up, Graham. Just stop with all this and get out!" She looked pale as she curled up into a ball on the sofa, crying and trying to breathe. Graham ran to get a glass of water. By the time he returned, she had recovered her breath and was ready to continue letting him know how deeply injured she was.

Graham realized that his plan to return to his family was not going to happen tonight. He wished she had unleashed the passion he had just witnessed when they were together. He had never seen her so upset. He waited in silence until she calmed herself. "I'll just leave. Don't get up." He turned to walk toward the door but stopped. "I really screwed up, Mimmi. But for what it's worth, it was the first time. If I had the chance to do things over, I never would have made this mess. I get that you can't go forward with our relationship, but I wish you'd reconsider for the sake of our family." He waited, hoping she'd respond, but nothing was forthcoming. "Well, you know where to find me."

"I'm changing the locks again," she said. "I want the house. And I want all your stuff out soon. If your sisters want any of the china and crap that your mother has given me over the years, be sure that's out of here too. Once we're over, Graham, I never want to see you again. Our kids are grown. I do not need to do the child visitation thing or pretend that I'm okay with things at family weddings or whatever. You made this mess, and it is a forever mess. No sharing the joy of our kids' engagements or weddings or grandchildren. I'm not going to be there to hold you when your parents go, and you won't be there for me when it's my turn." Tears rolled down Graham's face, but she ignored them. "It's too little too late, Graham. Where were you when I was crying myself to sleep these last months? Oh yeah—you were screwing some girl half your age. I hope it was worth it. Your kids will hate you for this too someday, and not because I want them to. Believe me, I don't. But they will figure it out. Just get out. I can't even look at you! And the nerve—do I look that hard up? Did you think I could actually forgive you—twice?" He was about to close the door, and she yelled after him, "And you're not the only fish in the sea, you ass!"

He looked back. "Really? Is there someone?"

"Yes! Now get out!" she screamed.

And that was it. Graham left. Mimmi took a deep breath and sighed, shaking her head from side to side, as if she could shake off the feelings of hurt and betrayal.

Chapter Thirteen

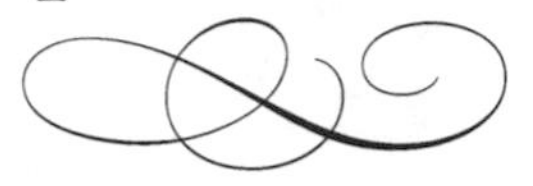

The next day's activities went as well as could be expected for the walkers, especially Mimmi. Her heart was heavy with the knowledge that her family life was permanently altered. She didn't take her decision lightly and felt that almost a year was long enough. In fact, she had mourned her loss through most all of the changing seasons. It was time. She had learned to use the cane, which the girls thought gave her a certain dignity that she otherwise lacked. She looked mature, rather than injured.

The walkers went to Manayunk for lunch and chose an outdoor venue. It was a beautiful, sunny spring day. The sidewalks were crowded with diners at café tables on almost every block. Bella Trattoria was Charlotte's favorite outdoor venue in Manayunk. The food was great, and it was a favorite of the mayor too, so it made for great people-watching.

Charlotte drove because she had the only car that would accommodate all the walkers. The bright-eyed waiter with his stiffly starched apron, a college classmate of James Wentworth, recognized Charlotte as he approached the table. His lean frame cut a dashing figure across the otherwise middle-aged landscape.

"Mrs. Wentworth, how are you?" he said blushing. "I'm James's friend, Jordan, from lacrosse. Jordan Ashton. We met a few months ago when I came home with James and Jonathan Rhoads. I think you were running out to a meeting or something. We only met for a second." He dropped his tablet and fumbled around under the table, looking for it among a sea of middle-aged legs and a few designer pocketbooks. He blushed a shade of red that almost matched his curly red locks. "I'm sorry," he said when he stood up.

"Don't worry about it," Charlotte giggled. "And yes, of course I remember you. These are my friends from the neighborhood, and we're celebrating the end of my friend's physical therapy." She nodded at Mimmi, indicating she was the physical therapy graduate. "See what you have to look forward to, Jordan? Aging is wonderful!"

"Well, good for you, ma'am," he said, turning toward Mimmi. "Ladies … what can I get you all?"

They ordered lunch, and Charlotte sprung for a bottle of champagne.

Kate spoke first. "What exactly are we celebrating?"

"For God's sake, Kate," said Ginny. "The end of Mimmi's physical therapy!"

"No, no, no, ladies," Mimmi said. "Ginny was right to ask. It's not the physical therapy. We're celebrating my ending it with Graham." They all looked at her. "*Really* ending it. I've been so depressed about our family breaking up, so focused on the kids and my parents and all the chatter, that I really thought maybe it would be best to try to make a go of it—to give him a second chance. But it isn't going to work." She swallowed hard and looked for the champagne.

A man walking his bulldog served as a welcomed distraction when the dog smelled biscuits in Kate's handbag and pulled the man toward the table, almost knocking over a bicycle chained to a nearby parking meter.

"I'm sorry, ladies," the owner said and then scolded his dog. "Matilda, mind your manners."

"Oh, she must smell the rosemary biscuits in my pocketbook." Kate reached for her bag as the dog walker tried to calm his otherwise adorable bulldog. "Here," she said, handing a biscuit to the handsome thirtysomething. "For Matilda."

"Thank you. Clearly, you have a dog."

"Dog-za," said Kate. "Two Labs."

"Do you live around here? I'm always looking for friends for Matilda." Matilda was drooling, as her owner hadn't given up the biscuit yet. She barked.

"No, no, I don't live around here. Just visiting my friends," answered Kate, rather nervously. Her friends giggled.

Jordan arrived with a bottle of Veuve Clicquot and five champagne flutes. The dog walker smiled and left. Jordan poured the bubbly celebratory beverage. The women were all aghast with the guy who had blatantly flirted with Kate.

"He liked you," said Ginny. "God, nobody's done that to me in ages, not even my husband. Okay, well, maybe Chas, the newspaper vendor. But he doesn't have front teeth."

"Oh, stop," Kate said.

"Yup, Kate, he was all over you. Believe me, it wasn't the dog biscuits," said Marianna. "As a professional, I can officially say, sexual attraction was at play."

"Gosh, maybe I should start carrying dog biscuits," said Mimmi. Jordan laughed a bit as he poured the last glass of champagne for Mimmi.

"We'll have another bottle, Jordan," Charlotte whispered.

Kate took a large sip of her champagne. "I'm going to be sick," she blurted out.

"What now?" asked Ginny.

"Are you really done with Graham?" Kate asked Mimmi.

"Why does that make you sick?" pressed Ginny. "We're all happy here, girlfriend, even Mimmi. Drink more champagne, Kate."

"No," said Kate, taking a big gulp. "This is really nice, by the way. Anyway, it isn't that you're not getting back with him, Mimmi. It's that it's happening at all. It's been almost a year of your being sad and crying and limping and not part of the group. Because some bimbo on a park bench has daddy hang-ups and needs an older man, your life gets screwed up, your kids, our lives—"

"Kate!" Marianna couldn't be quiet any longer. "This isn't about you or a bimbo. It isn't as serendipitous as you make it sound. Marriages aren't irretrievable because of an affair. They're irretrievable because of the years of damage before the affair."

Charlotte wanted to scream but instead said, "Have some more champagne, Mimmi. Let's celebrate your being over Graham, the end of your physical therapy, and the beginning of Kate's midlife crisis." She raised her glass. They all clinked. Mimmi and Ginny laughed nervously.

Charlotte turned, looking for the waiter. "What's that kid's name? Is it Jordan?" She waved, motioning for him to come to the table.

"Yes, ma'am. The food'll be right out," said Jordan.

"We need that second bottle of Veuve Clicquot, Jordan," said Charlotte.

"Yes, ma'am. Right away.

Kate excused herself and headed for the ladies' room. By the time she returned, the next round of champagne had been poured, and the entrees had been served. Charlotte picked up on Kate's timely exit and cut the tension upon her return.

"Kate, I'm hoping that you will take note that each of us is in a midlife crisis." She turned to the rest of the group. "No offense meant to anyone. We are *all* in a midlife crisis, aren't we?" She turned again to Kate. "Well, anyway. You just have waited too damn long to join our ranks. Turning fifty is going to be fun. And Mimmi, darling, just think. You've had your crisis, and you'll have it out of the way before turning fifty. Fifty will seem like a walk in the woods."

Marianna couldn't contain herself any longer. "Charlotte?"

"Yes."

"When you're in a hole, stop digging!" They all laughed as they ate their pasta entrees and drank bubbly.

Mimmi chimed in, "Well, as timing would have it, I think I'm starting menopause." Continuing in a whisper so the other women needed to lean in, she said, "I've skipped a period. My doctor says it's probably stress, but I don't think so. I am, after all, almost forty-six. My mom was my age when she started. Might as well go through all this stuff at once, right?"

Kate started to cry. The other women didn't know what to do. Ginny jumped in, "Kate, you too? Did you stop too? Joe had a vasectomy years ago, so I don't have that whole issue of worrying about getting pregnant. But I'm telling you, we keep the lubrication companies in business. That's the worst part—the dry factor. Are you dry when you have sex?"

"*Ginny!*" Marianna was appalled. "There's sharing, and there is sharing too much! We don't care what the level of moisture is in your vagina—or anyone else's, for that matter!"

"Okay. I'm sorry. Okay, I'll just say you need to talk to someone about this stuff. It's different for everyone, and you'll need to talk about these things to someone."

Kate went on to say how her periods were so irregular that, after her gallbladder surgery, when she got a period, she thought she'd ruptured something, not that she got a period.

"Oh, my God, you got your period after your surgery? That must have been awful," said Ginny.

"The only awful part was thinking I could be pregnant," said Kate. "I'm not even sure it's possible, and I worry constantly, not unlike the days before we practiced birth control, and we were fertile and thought, shit, why did we take a chance?" She looked at everyone. "Remember those days? And then you'd get your period and promise yourself you'd never take any chances again."

"Oh, my God, we all did that! Thank God that ship has sailed," said Mimmi. "I don't miss the sex part. Maybe that's why my marriage ended."

The topic was uncomfortable for everyone. But Marianna, ever the diplomat, helped out. "No, no, no, Mimmi. Your marriage didn't end over sex. And of course you don't miss sex yet. But believe me, I've counseled enough patients through divorce successfully, and the good news is, there is life with healthy sex again!"

"Yeah, well, why did it end then? You tell me?"

The women gathered their belongings to leave. Mimmi picked up her cane, which more and more she used as a pointer when she spoke. Wielding it around the table, pointing at her friends, she said, "And just for the record, my marriage *did* end over sex. My husband screwed another woman. Put that in your menopausal pipes and smoke it. It's not tasty!" She started off at a fast clip toward the car, tears streaming down her cheeks, with Marianna following.

Marianna needed to explain her way out of this one. She caught up with Mimmi at the parking lot near the canal, off Main Street. The others fell back. "I'm sorry, Mimmi. That was really insensitive of me. I just want you to stop blaming yourself."

"Well, Marianna, here's a news flash: marriage takes two people, and it's rarely all one-sided. So if you really want to help me, stop treating me like some broken-winged bird. I am at fault too. I wasn't very interesting or sexy or passionate. I was stuck, and I took Graham and our marriage for granted." She took a deep breath. "And now I'm starting menopause. That's just great. So I probably won't have any libido by the time I find another guy, if that's even possible, and if I do, we'll need an entire jar of greasy something to get my fucking parts to work. Yeah, life is very hopeful for a midlife, fat loser like me."

"Stop it right now. You are really being too hard on yourself, and this isn't going to be helpful for your healing, either physically or emotionally!" Marianna shouted back.

The others caught up with Mimmi and Marianna. In her most diplomatic voice, Charlotte urged everyone to be grateful for the present moment—one of friendship, caring, and celebration of freedom for Mimmi. "Mimmi, remember that book about mindfulness. It offers such hope. If we string together one good moment after another, soon we have a good day. One good day after another, and we have a good week. And so on. That gives me real hope for a good life."

Kate agreed that hopefulness and happiness were a choice. That life seemed to be divided into two groups: people who got over bad things and people who seemed to just replay them over and over again throughout their lives. She was convinced the severity of the offense wasn't as important to recovery as the attitude.

Kate's emotions were settling down. She was, she realized, an emotional, philosophical drunk—or, at least in this case, a buzzed individual.

During the car ride home, Mimmi and Kate asked Charlotte and Ginny many questions about their respective experiences around menopause. Marianna wasn't sure where she was in the process and admitted she had difficulty thinking she was at this stage of life.

Charlotte described some of her doctor's recommendations, such as more exercise, more soy in her diet, and eliminating caffeine. She shared her other friends' experiences around all the changes, and she offered up a great reading list. Kate and Mimmi begrudgingly made mental notes.

Mimmi seemed to lighten up on the return ride. Ginny was giddy from the champagne. Kate shared her latest idea about building a business that sold handmade, artistic products. She shared her fantasy of selling the goods all over the country while traveling, perhaps in a recreational vehicle. After what she felt was a positive response from her friends, she fell asleep, thinking about her life. As Charlotte pulled into Kate's driveway, the loud roar of a lawn mower made Kate stir. "Wow. I fell asleep," she said, somewhat embarrassed.

"Yeah. That's what happens when you get out of practice with drinking champagne in the middle of the day!" Charlotte turned and slapped her on her knee. "I took everyone else home first. Of course, we all made fun of your slobbering."

"Oh, God, you are a motley crew!" Kate undid her seat belt. "Do you think Mimmi's going to be okay?"

"You know, she's evolving, as we all are, and for her sake, I hope the Mimmi we saw today is the one that'll show up in the lonely, trying months ahead. If that's the case, my answer is yes. And I really hope she will be okay, because I can barely focus on my own crazy stuff right now, let alone help her to this extent on a regular basis."

Kate looked a little shocked that Charlotte would verbalize what everyone else was feeling. But it really was questionable as to how much each of them had to put into coddling Mimmi.

Chapter Fourteen

Kate was singing her favorite gospel song in the shower, and Doug was humming along as he shaved. She opened the shower door and stepped out onto a soft towel.

"I love when you sing in the shower," Doug said. "It reminds me of the girl I married." He turned toward her awkwardly as she wrapped herself in another soft towel. "I'd kiss you, sweetie, but I don't want to cover you in shaving cream. I love you so much, Kit-Kat, girl."

She smiled and kissed his back. "Doug, I'm really freaking out about turning fifty. It's just so weird. I can't even figure out why I'm upset. I just am." She started to laugh, watching him shave. She was thinking of her recent visit to the dermatologist.

"Well, at least you're laughing. That's a good sign."

She decided not to tell him about the shaving story.

"Everyone I know says it's tough, Katie. But just so you know, you look like you're thirty-five."

"It's not about how young I look. It's about not having something that's just about me. I feel like all I do is wait—wait to pick up the kids after school, wait to drive the kids to music lessons, wait until you come home from work to serve dinner, wait for the dryer cycle to finish, wait for the contractor to show up, and lately, I'm waiting for the perfect business to sink my teeth into. Why can't I find something? I've been looking our whole married life and something always seems to take priority over my pushing ahead with a business." She dried her back, holding one end of the towel over her left shoulder the other end at her right hip and rubbing back and forth, back and forth.

"You need to stop that naked wiggle, or I'm going to have to jump your sexy body."

"I'm talking about something serious here," she barked.

"Okay," he said, eyeing her as she wrapped the towel around her body. "You seemed happy when we got married, and then slowly, you turned into a girl who only sings in the shower once in a while."

She wondered if that's how he measured his own happiness. "Yup! You noticed. I only sing in the shower once in a while," she snapped. She leaned into the mirror to be sure no new whiskers were cropping up. "You know, Doug, you talk to me like your dad talks to your mom. Don't you want more from a mate? Don't you want a dynamic woman? Don't you want a woman like the women you work with—someone who can think, do, create, excite? When you are having your reviews with Janey Whatever-Her-Name-Is, do you measure *her* success by how happy she is? Do you ask her if she sings in the shower?" She realized how stupid she sounded.

"Shit!" Doug had cut himself shaving. Kate walked out of the room into her dressing area. She rifled through the racks and reached for her favorite jeans and white cotton shirt. Doug followed her, patting the shaving cut with a tissue.

"You know, I woke up happy today, which is how I wake up every day. You put me in a lousy mood because you're so negative. I'm convinced you don't want to be happy. Turning fifty isn't a death sentence. It's a get-out-of-jail free card, Kate! I do think it's tough for women. You guys do it all. You—"

"Oh, save it, Doug. What the hell do you know about women or working moms? All you know is—"

"I know a lot, Kate. I work with lots of women. And I guess they make it happen because something else gives. Some have no choice, like the single moms, but most work because they chose a career. Imagine that—a career, a marriage, and motherhood."

Cynicism doesn't become him, Kate thought. She felt the rage building. Maybe she had been hiding behind motherhood too long. Maybe it wasn't so much about waiting as it was about hiding. She was scared. Maybe turning fifty wasn't the worst of it. Maybe Douglas was right. Maybe she was afraid that he admired those women as much as she envied them. *Why can't I do both?* she wondered. How was it that life had unfolded so quickly and here she was, in what seemed like the blink of an eye, turning fifty?

She never told the girls that she had missed a few periods. She too was probably in menopause. That was really upsetting to her. She felt like she was single-handedly keeping the drug companies that made early pregnancy tests in business. She started buying them five at a time.

Doug tried to bring her back into a conversation about the issue of work. He believed it was the missing link to her happiness. She was always happy when she worked. She identified herself, like most people, through her work.

"My sister isn't a bad mom," he called to her from behind his closet door. "She works, and look at her success! She feels so good about herself. And Brian is a sweet kid. He doesn't seem any the worse for wear." He finished getting dressed, and she noticed he had on two different socks.

"Your socks don't match. And keep your voice down. I don't want the kids to get up yet. I like having an hour after you leave for work to organize my day." One of the dogs barked behind their bedroom door. She ran quickly, and there the two labs stood, waiting to be fed. "Get in here, guys. It isn't time to eat yet." She ushered them quickly into the room. "Anyway, back to this work thing—yeah, Brian is okay. And your sister and Steve seem good. And yeah, everybody is proud of Dana." She rifled through a messy drawer for underwear. "It's just not how I wanted to do things, and now I'm scared I'm out of time to get it together to start a small business, Doug."

He adjusted his tie in the full-length mirror that hung on the inside of Kate's closet door.

She walked toward the bathroom, saying, "I think I was due for my period last week. I would shoot myself if I got pregnant. Can you imagine that situation?" she asked, and he laughed at her comment. In the bathroom, she tore open the little magic wand's package and peed on it. Doug came into the bathroom and saw her looking at the pregnancy test.

"For real, you're worried? Can you even get pregnant anymore?" he asked, squeezing a tiny dab of hair gel through his graying locks. "Java, stop drooling. It isn't time to eat," he said to the dog who had wandered into the bathroom to make his needs known. He dried his hands on a towel and turned to Kate, who was still sitting on the toilet, holding the pee stick. "Can you still get pregnant?"

"I get my period occasionally but not for the last two months. I felt like I was getting it last week and now, no symptoms. And I've been really tired." She was done sitting on the toilet and wriggled by Doug and Java to the sink to wash her hands. She placed the pregnancy test on the vanity.

"Oh, great, Kate, that's just what we need," he said, moving out of the crowded bathroom. "You're always tired, Kate. Don't mess with me." She picked up the pregnancy stick and threw it at him. "What was that for?" he asked, bending to pick it up. She was crying. "Oh, stop, Kate, no crying." He checked his watch and caught a glimpse of the negative indicator on the wand. "You're not pregnant, anyway."

They brushed against each other as he went into the bathroom to throw away the pregnancy wand and wash his hands. She moved to the bedroom to finish dressing.

"I'm sad that you're so insensitive. *Can you still get pregnant?* That hurt," she whimpered.

"Yeah, that's really something to cry over. You know, there's a woman in our marketing department, Kate, who had a mastectomy last year. She went through hell with chemo and reconstructive surgery, the whole shitty experience, and she's back at work, smiling and running around like nothing ever happened. She's got two young kids, and her husband is our assistant comptroller." He waited but she didn't respond. "Maybe you need to start looking around you, Kate. Need I say more? If you want a business," he went on, "just do it. What's happening with that doll thing you looked at? I thought you'd be great at that. You could use your creative talents and your business skills. The kids are all set, Kate. It's always been part of the plan." He checked his watch. "Crap, I'm going to be late. Can you feed the dogs?"

From across the hall, Kate could here Jake practicing his guitar. "Are you going to his concert this afternoon?" Kate asked Doug. "It's at three in their auditorium."

"I can't, Kate."

She cocked her head and gave him a "you're kidding" look.

"Don't make me feel guilty. I can't make it."

"Just remember this when you ask me why I can't get any traction with businesses, okay? Someone has to show up. And you know what, Douglas? *That's* my job."

"I get it. Soon it'll be your turn to fly, Kit-Kat. Soon. Kiss me; I really have to run." He kissed her on the cheek, grabbed his briefcase, which was sitting in the corner near the door, and yelled *Good luck* to Jake on his way downstairs.

Kate took another look for stray hairs. "Here I come, Java. Stop whining!" She pulled the bedroom door shut, not wanting to look at the unmade bed. "Good morning, my loves. Is everybody awake? Bess, are you out of bed? Rachel, I don't hear any music in there. I made banana muffins last night, girls," she yelled through their doors. Through the window on the second-floor landing, she saw Douglas pull out of the driveway and zip down the street. He was already on his cell phone. She turned her thoughts back to her kids. "Jake, enough guitar," she said as she pushed open his door. "Come on, bud, get a move on, or you'll be late for the bus."

"Mom, I really need to practice more. Will you drive me today? Pleeeease," he begged.

"Sure. No problem, Jakey. By the way, Daddy can't make your concert today, but I'll be there." Jake pouted. "Come on, Jacob, you know Daddy can't always come to these things." She pulled his door shut, went downstairs, and put banana muffins and berries on the table with three glasses of low-fat milk. She flipped on the coffeemaker and picked up a craft magazine with the article about the doll business she wanted to buy.

Java barked to be let out.

Chapter Fifteen

The walkers had a newfound energy. Longer daylight hours could have been the source, but Charlotte thought it was that they were all reaching new places in their respective lives. Ginny was getting used to the idea of her baby's leaving the nest for college. Marianna was doing the same, by adding patients to her schedule. Charlotte was evaluating re-entering the art world or working for Jennifer Holmes Bartlett, but in either case, work was on the horizon. Kate was overwhelmed with managing her kids and thinking about turning fifty, but work was never far from her creative agenda. She was zeroing in on an idea to make dolls. Her idea was a compilation of several concepts she'd seen but with a charity and profit angle.

Mimmi wasn't far behind her friends in her desire to find new meaning in an ever-changing life vista. Now that her kids were grown and her husband had flown the nest, she too was envisioning life outside the home, albeit reluctantly.

Perhaps the women's energy was based on their shared experience. They shared stories, validated each other's experiences, and served as cheerleaders when necessary. None was walking alone, literally.

Charlotte was adjusting her tissue-weight cotton turtleneck when her doorbell rang. "Oh, I'm sorry. I didn't see you coming up the walkway," she said, opening the door for her friends, then taking one last look in the hall mirror to confirm that her neck was sufficiently covered.

Mimmi stepped inside while Kate and Ginny finished a conversation just outside the door.

"Mimmi, I'm so glad you're walking with us again!" exclaimed Charlotte.

"Yeah, well, we'll see how the old leg does today. I've been walking on that treadmill at the PT facility like it's my job," Mimmi answered. "How can you wear those turtlenecks all the time? I'm itchy just looking at you. And aren't you hot? I'm so hot all the time lately."

"Maybe you really are going through menopause. I never got hot flashes, but I did get warm often. You know, like comfortably warmer." She motioned for Mimmi to step outside, and she pulled the heavy mahogany door behind her. "Hello, ladies. Beautiful day, huh?" said Charlotte. "I am feeling summertime."

"Let's not lose our heads," joked Ginny.

"Hey, let's walk by my house so you can check out my landscaping project," suggested Kate.

"I don't know if I can make it that far," said Mimmi.

"Okay, then, let's skip it today. We'll do it another day. But, man, all that running around looking at other people's houses and gardens for ideas last summer really paid off. It's going to be gorgeous!" Kate said excitedly.

"What's with the doll thing?' asked Ginny. "Are you actually going to do this business?"

"I'm working it. I'm working it," she said unconvincingly. They were walking slowly, so Mimmi could keep up.

"None of those workout outfits I bought over the holidays fits me," said Mimmi.

"Well, aren't they for the winter anyway?" asked Charlotte. "Not that I care about seasons, here in my turtleneck. I just can't stand my neck anymore. I look like a turkey, you know, with that wrinkly, hanging thing they have under their chins."

"Do turkeys have chins?" asked Mimmi.

"Okay, sweetie, that's not the point here," said Charlotte. "It's this," and she pulled her turtleneck down with one hand and grabbed the loose skin under her chin with the other and wiggled it. Mimmi grimaced. "See?" said Charlotte. "Gross, right?"

"Well, it's the way you pulled it that makes it gross," answered Mimmi.

Ginny commented, "Well, you are the only person I know who can find short-sleeved turtlenecks. You always look so good, Charlotte. You have such a keen sense of style. You probably look good in your pajamas. If I looked like you, I'd sit up all night looking at myself in the mirror."

Kate piped in, "She does!" They all laughed, including Charlotte, even though she was a bit awkward talking about her good looks. Then she inquired as to Marianna's whereabouts.

"She's working a lot again. She had two patients this morning," said Ginny.

"She's so lucky to have a profession," said Mimmi. "I have no idea what I'm going to do, but I have to think of getting a job. Wouldn't it be great to sit and listen to other people's problems all day? It'd certainly make you feel like your own life wasn't so bad. Or you, Ginny—you're lucky too, that you already know what to do with yourself at this stage of life."

"Yeah, I'm lucky all right. I get to work weekends, get calls all hours of the day and night, and I get to do paperwork until three in the morning for agreements of sale, most of which don't ever happen." She pointed to a growling dog. "Watch out; he looks mean. Where's Sam, Mimmi? I miss that cute beagle."

"I thought I had enough to do to manage myself on this walk. He's getting old anyway," she said. "But back to the career thing, I do think you and Marianna are lucky. Look at Charlotte, Kate, and me. We have no idea what to do at this stage of our lives. As for me, I never wanted to work outside of the home. This is hell for me, you know—the having-to-work thing."

Charlotte felt sick to her stomach. Did Mimmi actually think she was like her or Kate? She let the comment slide because she was so glad to see Mimmi out and joining the group after her long break. *But how does Mimmi think that she is like Kate or me?* thought Charlotte. And how could she think Ginny and Marianna were lucky? Luck was finding a ten-dollar bill next to your car door, not the hard work that went into Marianna's career path. Marianna had worked her entire adult life, including guest lecturing and publishing papers on various topics related to retirement and aging. She chose to work part-time when Jeremy was born and had since worked thirty to thirty-five hours weekly, maintaining a relatively stable patient base.

Charlotte waited for someone else to fill what seemed to her like an awkward silence. Ginny had already defended her position. No one else spoke on the matter. It was just quiet.

"So let me tell you about my business idea," Kate put in. "Remember the doll business I told you I saw advertised for sale in one of my craft magazines? Well, I checked into it, and I really want to buy it. I want to make dolls. Now, before you all make fun of me, let me describe what I have in mind."

"Do you have a plan, or is this another get-rich-quick scheme of yours?" asked Ginny.

"You can be so mean!" said Kate. "I actually have a plan this time."

"I can't believe you have a plan," quipped Charlotte. "Four kids, three still at home, Madam Creative 'I paint and decoupage and cook and design my kids' clothes and, by the way, I have a career plan'! I think I'll go home and swallow a fifth of bourbon!"

"Stop! You have options. We all do," Ginny reprimanded.

"Like I said, I think I'll raid the liquor cabinet tonight. My plan is to stay alive and not die of breast cancer," said Charlotte, feeling sorry for herself.

"How's all that going?" asked Mimmi.

"I don't want to talk about it, but I think it's okay. Who ever really knows?" answered Charlotte. "So, Kate, tell us about dolls."

"Okay," she said taking a deep breath and adjusting her big sunglasses, which always seemed to slide down her turned-up nose. "I remember seeing those sock dolls somewhere for a charity that was trying to raise money. You know the ones I'm talking about. Maybe women from third-world countries made them or something. I don't really remember. But I do remember thinking, okay, I could have done this and at least made them cute—and that's *cute*, as in people will buy them, not because they feel sorry for me and throw them in the trash later, but because they could actually give them to someone to play with and not feel like they were made from some disease-ridden rag or something."

"Yeah, I hate feeling that if you don't buy some ugly charity piece of crap or donate to every cause, you're an insensitive witch," commented Ginny.

"Yeah, me too," piped up Mimmi. "I hate that, especially in the supermarket. You know, you've just gone through the whole shopping-and-unloading-the-cart thing, you're looking at your watch, and then some checker who has not even made eye contact or had any conversation with you asks if you want to donate money to feed starving kids in a country you've never heard of!"

Ginny agreed the supermarket conversation was worth having.

"Ladies, I have a business idea here. Can we please be quiet! Where are your manners today?" asked Kate impatiently. She proceeded to describe the dolls, which would be crafted by moms looking for work. The dolls, each a unique collectible, would tell a story. She wasn't sure about this part yet—how the story would be told—but she wanted there to be a proud-to-be-an-American aspect to each doll: made in America, by Americans, with pride in our shared history.

Charlotte was conspicuously quiet, trying to understand why Kate would choose creating dolls instead of returning to the more sophisticated businesses she was involved with prior to becoming a mom. She also wondered why women were held to such a different standard from men, including by women like her. Mimmi's comment about Marianna's being lucky was still stuck in her head.

Her mind wandered as they picked up speed. *Both women and men could be lucky, after all, but why was "lucky" an attribute often applied to women who had achieved great success?* she thought. She had just finished a conversation with Jennifer Holmes Bartlett the evening before about this very topic. Jennifer was carefully positioning herself as a potential candidate for the Democratic nomination for president in two years. And even though she had prepared for the position her whole life, there were many considerations. She couldn't be too aggressive with her campaign run, and she certainly couldn't appear too lucky—not in marriage, in her work, or in anything else. Women didn't like other women to be too *anything*. Most men didn't like women who seemed too powerful or too lucky.

Charlotte was thrilled to be back in touch with Jennifer; she was positive Jennifer could go all the way to the White House if she put her mind to it.

"You're very quiet this morning, Charlotte," said Ginny. "And you're walking too fast. So, no comment on Kate's idea?"

"Well, I have a lot on my mind." She offered a lame excuse: "My mother's not feeling well, and I'm trying to figure out how best to help her."

Mimmi chimed in, "Doesn't your brother live closer to your parents than you?"

"I'm sure your brother will step it up," added Kate. "If not, you'll have to do what you did last time and just go spend an overnight and make lots of lists. She probably just wants attention." Kate hoped it was just Charlotte's mother that was on her mind and nothing as serious as another health issue.

"I wish my mom's situation was simply an attention-getting ploy, but I think she's really backsliding. She's a lot for my dad to manage lately. Anyway, about you, Kate: I am really excited for you, that you're thinking of work again. I wish I had begun planning a bit sooner for this time in my life. Actually, I wished I'd always kept my hands in something professional. I could have, I guess. But you know the drill. With three kids and a husband with a demanding career, I just felt like I was never at the right place at the right time. So, Kate, yeah, you're smart. You'll figure it out. Are you serious about this one? You've had so many great, creative ideas. Are you going to do the important planning stuff with this one?"

"Like I said, I've already started planning," said Kate. "But I don't want to jinx it, so let's just leave it at that. But yeah, I'm serious, because if I don't get out of the house and do something that's all about me, I'm afraid I'll just wither away. Mentally, I mean. And I'm driving my husband nuts in the meantime. I was thinking, you know, I spend so much time on projects anyway, like the school fund-raisers, or volunteering in the classrooms, and now this landscaping project. I certainly could give up that stuff and still have time for my family and work. I really am excited. I really am."

Charlotte smiled, and Ginny agreed it was a super idea. They all marveled at Kate's ability to think of creative outlets that could translate into revenue.

"I really wish I had kept my hand in the art business," Charlotte said. "I had so many great contacts, and now it just feels overwhelming to even consider returning to that business. I just think so much time has gone by and people have moved on. I mean, I know art. For sure, I know art. And I've kept current by being a docent at the art museum and volunteering over the years at various fund-raisers and so on. But the contacts are the whole game. I think of my dear friend, Jennifer—you know, Holmes Bartlett."

Mimmi stopped walking and crouched over with her hands on her thighs, taking deep breaths. The rest of the group paused too.

"Gosh, I can't keep up with you guys," Mimmi panted. "Maybe I should wait to start walking with you guys again. I'm a real drag."

"You aren't a drag at all. It's just that Speedy over here is off to the races today." Ginny nodded toward Charlotte. "What the hell is happening in that head of yours?" she asked. "This isn't about your mother. Is it about Holmes Bartlett?" Ginny was still trying to catch her breath but added more. "It's not about your mom, because she's like all our moms with the complaining thing. She's always complained." She turned to Mimmi, "You okay?" When Mimmi nodded, Ginny said, "Okay, then, let's take it at a slower pace."

Kate tried to help ease the slight tension. "It's our mothers' jobs to complain! That's what we'll be doing someday." Then, mimicking her mother, she said, "Oh, Kate, my knees are so bad. I almost fell climbing on the kitchen chair today to dust the shelf over the sink." Then in a mocking voice, she added, "Well, geez, Mom, maybe you shouldn't be climbing on chairs if your knees aren't so great." She turned to her walking buddies. "Come on, aren't all of our moms whiners? Please say yes."

Mimmi said she felt bad for her mom. Most of her mom's friends and siblings had died years before. She said her mom felt as if the few friends remaining were at death's door, and she was truly scared of the loneliness. So Mimmi listened dutifully, not minding so much. Helping Mimmi had given her mom new purpose. At least, that's how Mimmi saw it.

Charlotte, meanwhile, was tiring of the conversations among the walkers. She drifted into thinking about Jennifer's campaign and how she could help. She was so ready to work. She was done with chatter about kids, aging parents, volunteering, incompetent husbands, overzealous teachers, and health problems. Charlotte Gibbons Wentworth was done with this chapter. And she wasn't wearing her discontent well.

"Charlotte! I've asked you two times, what's going on?" barked Ginny. "You're walking so damn fast, you've made Mimmi feel incompetent, gotten me out of breath, and made Kate talk too much because you're so shut down! It's obvious something is wrong. What's up?"

Charlotte thought a bit. *Hmm, I've made Mimmi feel incompetent. Well, that's because she is*, she thought. But she held her tongue. "I'm sorry. Really, I am not myself today. It's just that … well, I should just come out with it. I was upset with the whole notion that Marianna is lucky regarding her work life." No one spoke. Everyone walked more slowly, including Charlotte. Realizing she was in the minority, she continued. "I mean, Marianna has a PhD, and she's board-certified. She's worked really hard to build a patient following. She writes. She teaches. She's not lucky. She's smart and hardworking. Why are men considered to be *successful* and women are simply *lucky*?" Again, no one spoke. Usually, it would be Marianna who broke this difficult silence, but she wasn't there. She was working.

Ginny didn't give in. "Well who said *lucky*, anyway? Did anyone say *lucky*? Maybe we just meant a good-for-her kind of thing, Charlotte. I really think it's something else with you. Can you really be this upset over *Marianna's lucky*?" She shook her head, and said disgustedly, "Really, come on."

"This is why I hesitated joining the walking group," said Charlotte. "I mean, women are so sensitive, and they have this group-think thing going on. You all pretend you're comfortable sharing the truth, but you're really not."

"We were walking together long before you joined the group, Charlotte, and we have not always agreed on everything. I think you're the one who's too sensitive," Ginny said, defending the group.

Charlotte felt that she wasn't like other women, and they weren't like her. She was a hybrid of sorts. She could defend an argument, craft a dinner party, design an investment art portfolio, and make love with profound passion. She could raise three fine children, all good citizens—smart, loving, contributing members of society. But what she couldn't do was swap recipes, talk about her husband ad nauseam, or share cute stories of her children, like many of the women she'd met during her stay-at-home mom years. As a result, she felt she was never really accepted by other women, either by those who chose to stay at home or those who chose to work. She was somewhere in the middle of those two worlds.

"Girls, let's just listen to Charlotte," said Kate. "Charlotte, do you feel we don't listen to what you have to say? Or that we don't think you're a super-talented woman? You know, I think, since we're being really honest here, you can come off as a snob of sorts until people get to know you. You can be aloof. I mean, we tried for years to get you to come out with us. And I am so glad you did."

"Yeah, me too," said Mimmi. "And you know what, Charlotte? We never got together socially until you joined the group. You've been a wonderful addition to Team Fairview." The women, except for Charlotte, giggled.

"A snob about what, Kate?" asked Charlotte. "It's interesting, because I feel like my old work friends think I'm a quitter. So I guess I'm just a perfect, all-around loser; a combination of a quitter and a snob." What hurt Charlotte most was that she desperately wanted to fit in with the other women; specifically, these women—the walkers.

Kate pushed her sunglasses up on her nose again and stopped walking. "Charlotte, how about a hug? I think you need a hug today. You know, this menopause thing is a bitch."

Charlotte was a bit weepy when Kate hugged her. "Menopause *is* a bitch!" Charlotte said. "Maybe it's just the whole breast cancer thing looming in the background that has me freaked out too."

"Yeah, you think? Girlfriend, that is big-time stuff you've dealt with in the last year," said Ginny, hoping Charlotte would let her in again.

"Well, maybe we ought to just keep it light here and be happy we have each other," said Mimmi. "And yeah, this menopause thing is hard."

"Hard, it's miserable! Say it, Mimmi. Menopause is a bitch," said Kate. "I have no idea how I'm going to get through this! I have every middle-age symptom that I used to find intolerable in my mom's generation. And I think the gallbladder thing just pushed me over the edge!" She started to laugh. "I mean, really, weren't the whiskers bad enough? Or how about the smile lines?" She pointed to little lines around her mouth. "Or saggy boobs or gray hair? I had to have an organ removed too. I'm convinced God is a man." Everyone laughed. "No, really, what sadistic bitch would do this to another woman? God just doesn't know. You know, it's not like he's punishing us or anything. He simply doesn't know. Like childbirth. He didn't get that either. Like every other man, he just looks at us and thinks we can handle everything."

Charlotte was laughing. Kate's humor had worked.

"Or maybe, like all men, he just isn't in tune with the details," Ginny said. "You know, think about it. Like some of those really ugly plants, or trees, or dogs he designed. Like those Corgis. They're so ugly, they're cute! Anna calls them God's mistakes. She says it looks like God took all the dog leftover parts and made one animal out of them! I get it now—no attention to detail!"

Kate replied, "Yeah, well what the hell does that make a menopausal woman? God's tune-out mechanism gone bad? I am ready to go crazy. Like today, I must have something really bad-ass going on. My boobs feel like they could detonate at any given moment. Really, if it wouldn't look so weird, I'd tell you to feel them. They are like rocks. I feel like, in the middle of the night, someone planted explosives in my boobs, and they are going to just fire at something or someone at any moment." Then she added, "Look out, ladies. You might be the target of a CIA operative!" She cupped her breasts and aimed them like weapons at the women, who were laughing hysterically.

"Stop, stop!" said Charlotte. "I'm going to wet my pants." They all looked at her. "I mean it. I have a weak bladder too." Then Charlotte asked Mimmi how she was doing with the whole menopause thing.

"I don't know for sure. I'm not getting my period, but I'm not as uncomfortable as Kate. I mean, I feel a little bit like Kate, I guess. It's hard, you know. I'm not sure how much of it is just that everything is so new: Graham is gone, Will is at school, Meg is out a lot. It's hard to figure out how much is menopause and how much is just that I'm sad." She forced a smile. "But, hey, I'm eating again and gaining weight. That's a good sign."

"Only you would see that as a good sign, Mimmi," said Ginny. "You are one of a kind."

"Well, there are a lot of benefits to that. My boobs are bigger, not that anyone is looking at my boobs. Well, maybe somebody is. But I mean … maybe I ought to be quiet!"

Ginny piped in again. "No, please tell us. You are our only single friend. We're counting on details, Mimmi, details. Salacious details are in order. Are you getting any?"

Mimmi's face turned bright red.

Charlotte came to her rescue. "Any what? What is it about you? Are *you* getting any? There—how does that feel?" She turned to Mimmi and rolled her eyes, mumbling, "Are you getting any?" Ginny pouted.

Mimmi surprised everyone. "I don't want to talk about it. It's private. But I'm not the prude you all think I am. I know you all think I don't get stuff, but I do. I have adult kids, you know."

"Okay, Mimmi. Will and Meg should not be your in-the-know sources, unless you're talking about social networks," said Kate.

"What's a social network?" Mimmi asked innocently. They all laughed. "Gotcha!" she howled. "I know what a damn social network is! Maybe I'm a Facebook maven, for goodness sake!"

Ginny linked her arm through Mimmi's, and the group chattered about nonsense while they turned the corner and headed toward home.

Chapter Sixteen

Charlotte withdrew from the walking group after the remarks about Marianna, Kate's rambling about a doll business, and Mimmi's inability to power walk. It was adding up to a bad time for Charlotte. She made excuses, but the women sensed something was bothering her, and they thought, like Charlotte, that time would heal matters.

Summer in the neighborhood meant gardens were full of buds and blooms, except for Kate's property. Kate and Douglas had imagined a property fit for *Architectural Digest* when they moved from their Victorian house in Chestnut Hill to their traditional, center-hall colonial in Penn Valley. They both loved a project, as if four children, a beach house, and Kate's constant scheming of new business concepts weren't enough to keep them both occupied. They were finally implementing the garden of their dreams.

Kate hired a landscaper who promised a turnkey approach, working to implement her designs, from planning through installation. The existing amateur gardens were replaced with piles of dirt, a backhoe, and crushed stone throughout the acre lot. The old diseased trees that lined the street were cut down, soon to be replaced with several Italian cypresses being trucked in from a California grower. Behind the trees would be a formal, European-style walled courtyard, the focal point of which would be a small fountain with a spurting fish, settled among a mosaic of brickwork and stonework. There were to be four walkways leading off a circular pattern around the fountain, three leading to a special spot in the yard, and one leading to the front door. The rear yard was designed around several informal gathering areas—outdoor rooms, like a traditional Victorian garden. The property was to be a reflection of the owners: a bit traditional yet comfortable.

Kate had spent the last two years planning the project with the landscape designer. Douglas had helped with budgeting and interfacing with the township on zoning matters. And now the time was here. The ground was ready, the financing was set, the permits were taped in the garage window and, much to Douglas's dismay, Kate was overwhelmed with the amount of work the property project required, given her new interest in buying the doll business.

She was busy with plans for the kids' summer activities and coordinating the first line of dolls to be produced in a makeshift factory in her basement. Her friends thought she was simply talking about another dream. But she was making this one happen. The prototypes were crude, but she had assembled a group of three young seamstresses to help smooth out the rough areas of the designs.

Once the business sale was final, she planned on selling off the equipment and supplies she wouldn't need for her vision of the new company, using the proceeds as seed money. Most of the existing employees were unessential, so she'd taken care of that detail already. Her primary interest in the business was name recognition, supply, and distribution networks and licensing agreements.

To add to Kate's busy life, her father had just decided that the time had come for his hip replacement, which meant that her mother would have to move in with them while her dad was going through surgery, treatment, and physical therapy.

"Maybe your mother could help with the kids and household chores, Kate" said Douglas. "Of course, I've been helping more anyway, but this could be good timing, Kit-Kat."

She rolled her eyes, remembering Jake's recent guitar concert. *Yeah, big help you are,* she thought. "Maybe you're right," Kate conceded. "My dad won't be in the way or anything. And my mom is great with the kids. You will have to make sure there's enough food in the house and that kind of thing. And it's not like I won't be here at all. For goodness sake, I'll be working in the basement."

She was on her way to the basement with another bagful of ornamental trims for the dolls when the doorbell rang. It was the third time in an hour that the workmen had questions. The dogs did their job, running to the door and barking.

"Java, down! Taurus, move away!" she yelled. Then peering out behind the dining room curtain, she saw it was the backhoe driver again. Kate opened the door.

"Miss Kate, I ran into your neighbor's fence, and I think she's upset. Could you come out and talk to her?" The operator looked hassled and a bit nervous.

"Okay, yeah, I'll be out in a minute," she said, quickly shutting the door.

Kate could see from the dining room window that a huge portion of the fence was down. She looked through her pocketbook, which was hanging on the banister in the center hall, for her sunglasses. She touched up her lipstick when a tube of gloss fell out of her purse onto the floor.

"Taurus, leave it!" she reprimanded.

"Arf, arf," complained the housebound Lab.

"Don't you bark at me! I have enough on my plate right now and walking you isn't even close to the top of my list," Kate said to the dog, who sat with its head cocked, as if he understood his master's dilemma. She shoved the lip gloss back in the pocketbook, opened the red front door, and quickly shut it behind her, to be sure Java and Taurus didn't escape.

She walked up a small embankment that divided her property from the neighbor's. She extended her hand, saying, "Hi, looks like we have a real problem here. We met when you first moved in this spring. I'm

Kate Hahn. Your babies are so cute. Oooo, watch your step," Kate said as the neighbor stumbled over a downed piece of fencing.

"Meredith Baldwin. This is Reese, and this is Lily," she said, pointing to her toddler who was hanging on to her oversized T-shirt and the baby she had balanced on a hip. "Ouch! You can't pull mommy's ponytail, Lily. That hurts." The baby puckered up, and Meredith adjusted her blonde ponytail with her free hand. The toddler giggled and remained wide-eyed behind her mom.

"Well," said Kate. "I'm really sorry about the mess. And this fence—"

"And the wall," interrupted Meredith. "I am really concerned the whole thing is going to fall over."

"Well, it is probably as old as the original house, and that'd be about a hundred years or so. It's probably had better days," Kate joked.

Meredith didn't laugh. "Look," the young, cocky neighbor said, "I'll just cut to the chase. This project has been a huge inconvenience, and, frankly, my husband looked at your permits when you were out—the ones you've posted in your garage window. He's an attorney with one of the downtown firms, and he's not sure you have the right to be doing all that you're doing."

"Meredith, I can understand that you're upset, but I don't appreciate feeling threatened. Trust me. My husband procured all the proper permits for this project. So let's just focus on the rickety fence and the hundred-year-old wall, okay? Not my damn landscape project." Just as Kate was feeling like she had the upper hand in the conversation, Java took off across the dirt piles and ran past the workmen, who were laughing, as one of the part-time seamstresses from the basement factory was yelling for the dog.

"I've got to go, Meredith. Look, I'm really sorry, and let's not have any bad blood over this stupid project. I remember what it was like at your stage of the mommy thing and trust me, it doesn't ease up. And when it does, you'll have this kind of crap to deal with." She turned nervously to see Java running full speed toward her. "Stop! Sit!" she yelled at him. And just like that, the dog slid into her, almost knocking her over. "If only my kids listened as well as my dogs," Kate said, trying to ease the tension. She grabbed the dog's collar.

"Doggy," said Reese, the toddler who had now let go of her mother's shirt and was reaching for Java.

"Do you want to pet the dog?" asked Kate in a sing-song voice. The toddler nodded her head, her tiny curls bouncing with each bob. "Java is very friendly, and he loves giving kisses. Watch." She leaned into Java's face, and he slurped her cheek. Reese produced a belly laugh. "Okay, Java," said Kate. "You be nice. Easy … easy." She held the dog's collar firmly with one hand and guided the tiny toddler's little hand across Java's head. The baby wanted to pet the dog too. Kate obliged the frustrated Meredith by holding Java in place for more pets.

"Meredith, again, I am really sorry. I promise we will take care of this whole fence/wall situation. Why don't you talk it over with your husband and let me know if you want to put up trees, or another fence, or if you want something else. I'm sure we can work something out."

"Thanks," said Meredith. "I'm sorry for using my business demeanor. I'm working on changing that."

Kate wasn't sure she understood what Meredith was saying. "Hey, would you be interested in walking with me someday?" Kate asked. "There are a group of us in the neighborhood who get together as often as we can, and we'd love to have you join us. We could use some younger energy. It might get us moving a bit faster."

"I can't walk during the day because I work. I'm a consultant for a firm specializing in M and A—you know, mergers and acquisitions," said Meredith. "But thanks for asking. I see you walking sometimes in the morning as I'm leaving for work."

Now Kate understood the comment about Meredith's work voice. It was her way of telling Kate she had a *real* job. Kate stood up and continued holding on to Java's collar. The seamstress was standing on the other side of the driveway, patiently waiting to ask Kate a question.

"Could you please come and get him, Maria?" she asked the worker. She released Java and told the seamstress she'd be inside in a minute.

"I work too. I have a start-up business," Kate boasted. "Anyway, think about the walking invitation. I'll tell Douglas what happened and that we're waiting to hear back from you on how you'd like us to remedy the situation." She gave Meredith a big smile. "Bye, now." And she started back to her house.

"Wait, Kate!" yelled Meredith. Kate stopped and turned toward her. "I'm actually in between jobs. I'm not even sure what I'm doing right now. Maybe I will come with you, walking. I'd like to walk with you and your friends. But I don't really want to use my sitter then. Do you mind if I bring the kids? I have one of those super-duper strollers that I can jog with."

"That's fine, Meredith," said Kate. "Believe me when I tell you, you don't need a super-duper stroller to walk with us, but we'd love to have you come with us. No set time but usually in the mornings." She smiled and continued heading across her driveway. The backhoe driver was waiting for her. He jumped down from the big machine. She just waved at him, yelling as she walked to her front door, "Call Rich. Isn't he running this damn project?" Then she abruptly turned on one heel, arms folded across her chest, and asked, "And are you telling him about the wall and the fence, or am I?" He indicated he would take care of it. "Today, Jose, today. I want to hear from Rich today." She left him standing in the dust and slammed her front door to emphasize the point.

The phone was ringing. She took a call from Emma, who whined about her roommate or someone in the dorm. Kate wasn't really engaged, because the seamstress had come up from the basement and was standing in her kitchen, waiting for Kate to get off the phone.

"Just a minute, Emma," she said. "What do you want, Maria? Can't this wait? I'm on a call, for godssake." Maria threw her hands up in the air, mumbling as she went back downstairs.

"God, these people drive me crazy. I can't get anything done today because of all the interruptions. What were you saying, Emma?" she asked, looking up at the clock above the oven door.

"I don't remember. I'm a little homesick, though, and I'm really overwhelmed, Mommy. How am I ever going to figure out what to do with my life? You and Daddy have got it all going on. I mean, Daddy went to Wharton and, I mean, look at him and you, well, you are a real Renaissance woman." Kate remembered calling Charlotte a Renaissance woman. Maybe they were friends because they really were reborn women. Kate like to think of the go-getters of her generation as improvisational women, because they created themselves as they went along, incorporating the values of family and work, with virtually no role models who successfully combined the two.

"Emma, you don't need to know what it is now. You'll know when you become passionate enough about something enough to picture yourself doing it every day and for a very long time. Or some opportunity will present itself and, bingo, you'll say, here it is! This is what I want!"

"Mommy, what if it doesn't happen for me? What if all I can do is be a boring, ordinary whatever?" She started to cry.

Although she hadn't been fully engaged in the conversation prior to this, Kate was now fully in the moment. She felt as if her entire life was there in the conversation with Emma, serving as a guide for both of them. She felt fortunate that she had so much life experience to share with Emma. And she felt so full of care and love for this beautiful young woman, who was so much a part of her.

"Emma, if you were here, I would hold you and hug you so tight! Then I would tell you to look at me with those soulful eyes of yours, and I would remind you that you are an amazing human being; that you are filled with life's goodness and light and beauty. I would turn you around to look at the beautiful sky and the trees and the world and encourage you to just be in the moment of enjoying where you are. Your answer will come, because you're asking the question. Just be sure you are listening to life. I promise, you will find peace about this."

The call ended a few minutes later with Emma a bit calmer and Kate remembering that she hadn't missed anything grand, and this was her choice. She had listened to life, and her answer had come in the form of being a stay-at-home mom. She just hadn't bargained for many of the consequences of her decision.

She ran down to the basement with the dogs to answer Maria's question and return to plans for the dolls.

Each doll had a name and a history of sorts. The accessories served as the inspiration for the doll. A miniature watering can and wheelbarrow served as the inspiration for Katie Gardener. *Big leap there!* An art easel and beret were the inspiration for Charlotte Lutrec, and Mimmi Rabbit was a doll with little bunnies in Easter baskets and a huge sunbonnet. A scaled ruler, package of chalk, and a miniature report card were the inspiration for creating the Teacher Ginny doll. Each was special and unique in its own right. Kate was working on using her kids' names and personas as inspiration.

She was thrilled to be working again, although it wasn't the job she'd imagined. But each day she spent crafting the dolls, her entrepreneurial spirit filled her, and as she sewed a button eye here and tacked a crooked hat on a soft cloth head there, she began to envision the business she would grow.

Kate chose to stay at home because, like many women of her generation, corporate life—wages, benefits, legal issues, and the greater national climate—hadn't caught up with the tremendous influx of women into the workplace. These women were like the pig in a python—they had reached a certain level of proficiency in their careers by the time childbearing years were upon them but not enough to make them indispensable. Very few of them were in a position to negotiate. Many women, like Kate, had reached middle management and could easily be replaced. Legally, they had no protection. There was no precedent to point to and say, hey, look how she did it. Men didn't need to juggle much when parenthood was upon them. They simply handed out cigars and hung pictures for coworkers to ooh and ahh over.

So Kate, like her friend Charlotte, had left the corporate world. They spent the first years out of corporate America running their homes as if they were still in the business world. They conducted family business and household chores like the work machines they'd recently abandoned. They would attend parties and talk about what they used to do when they worked and how they were looking for part-time work, just to keep their hands in things. But after several years of not being able to successfully find a little job to keep her hand in things, Kate, like Charlotte, withdrew into family life. Maybe it was more like family life had swallowed her. But there wasn't much time to focus on work when diapers needed changing and preschools needed volunteers, and grandparents wanted a commitment for upcoming holiday schedules, and dinner parties for a husband's career needed to be planned and hosted.

That is, until now.

Unlike Charlotte, who was resentful of her husband's success, Kate felt as if she had made a choice she could live with. She was enjoying the challenges of re-entering the work world and was confident she'd find a balance after the new business got up and running.

Kate picked up the phone and called Charlotte. She knew too much time had gone by, and they needed to reconnect as a group or it would be awkward beyond repair. Charlotte didn't answer, so Kate left a message.

"Hi, Charlotte, it's Kate. I really miss you. The whole group does. Mimmi hasn't been walking much either. I think her leg must be acting up. Whatever, if you're not up for everyone, I'd love to have a cup of coffee one morning and bounce around some ideas for my business. Give me a jingle on my cell, because I'm running around trying to get these doll samples ready, so we can actually have a line of them produced before the holidays. Anyway, really want to see you, Charlotte. Bye. Oh, and Charlotte, my entire property is under construction, so if you'd rather, I can swing by your house for coffee, instead. Let me know what you'd like to do. Okay, for real, bye."

The phone rang a few minutes later. It was Charlotte saying she'd love to see Kate, sooner rather than later.

"How about now?" asked Kate. Charlotte accepted the invitation.

Charlotte arrived with a huge bouquet of purple and blue hydrangeas. They hugged. Kate was so grateful for the fresh flowers. She pulled a vase from under a kitchen cabinet, filled it with lukewarm water, and proceeded to arrange the flowers in the large container, trimming the ends and extra leaves.

"Did these come from your front yard?"

"Yes," said Charlotte. "I have so many, it's insane."

"Do they bloom in this color or do you amend the soil?"

"I buy a few bags of acid fertilizer and put it around them in the early spring. It makes me feel like I've actually contributed to the gardening in some way. Charles does most of it. And we have the gardener." She picked up the trimmings on the counter and put them in the trash. "So what are you guys planning out here? It looks like you're building another house, not redesigning gardens."

Kate pulled out the plans and the two girlfriends laughed and exchanged enthusiastic ideas about the Hahns' garden renovations. They also caught up with each other's lives. In between talking about the landscaping project, Kate talked about all the interferences that seemed to get in her way: the landscape project, her dad's impending hip replacement, and the financial strain of buying a business. She went on about Emma and her confusion over her major and her life's plans, and how Rachel was never around, and when she was, all she could talk about was who was going to apply to the Ivies, as if there were no other colleges.

"Didn't you and Doug go to Penn?" Charlotte asked.

"Doug went undergrad and grad. The little brat. I went to the Pennsylvania Academy of Fine Arts and took courses at Penn. Not exactly slumming it academically."

"Ahh," Charlotte responded. "Well, I know my boys could not have cared less about the whole Ivy League thing. They only cared about the sports teams of the schools they chose. And Betsy has her heart set on Middlebury, because some writer guy she heard speak at an assembly went there, and I think she has a crush on him." They both laughed.

"It could be worse. She could have a crush on some guy named Cheech who went to Podunk U," said Kate.

The requisite giggles and smiles were out of the way, and Kate turned to a more serious topic. "So, is everything okay? I've missed you, and I've been worried about … you know … your health," said Kate.

"No, no, I should have called, I guess. I really didn't know what to say. You know the whole breast cancer scare made me realize how disconnected I was from friends and family," said Charlotte. "And when you guys knocked on my door to go walking last year, I thought it was just perfect for my mental state: we'd walk, keep things light, and get some exercise."

"Yeah, that's pretty much how it works," said Kate.

"Not really. I really don't feel right about it. I'm not like you guys. Actually, you're not like the rest of them either, Kate," said Charlotte.

"We're neighbors who can have some fun while getting exercise, for godssake," snapped Kate.

"Don't take this the wrong way, Kate. You don't fit this profile anyway, but when I walk with the group, I see myself as one of those untoned, flabby, middle-aged women who gets out of bed, sips her coffee in her robe and pajamas, and fills her day with nothingness—jibber-jabber, domestic chores, and marital obligations. You know the type. She wears baggy clothes, a cross between sweats and chic hippie-wear to camouflage her untended body. Or the type that wears age-inappropriate clothes, because she spends her days with a Pilates trainer and starves herself so she can be skinny like her college-aged daughter. Either way, the scene depresses me. It truly depresses me." Kate scrunched her face, looking confused, but she thought it sounded like Charlotte's comment on her son's girlfriend's family being pedestrian. *Maybe*, Kate thought, *Charlotte* was *really a snob who just didn't want to fit in with other women.*

Charlotte was blabbing, an unusual behavior for her. "I used to love my life, Kate. I really did. Charles, the boys, and Betsy were enough for me for a long time. Then something clicked. Like an on/off switch. It just went *snap*! And I started to squirm when introduced as 'Charles's lovely wife' or 'Betsy's mom, the head of the PTA.'"

Kate's phone rang and she was grateful for the break in the conversation. When she returned to the table, Charlotte continued, as if she were reading from a script.

"I miss being happy, Kate. I miss waking up excited about me. I miss those days of little things making a big difference."

Kate was starting to feel depressed herself. No wonder Charlotte had sequestered herself all those years and hadn't joined the walking group before this past year. She wasn't happy. Did she think a new group of people would make this unhappiness go away? How Kate had misread Charlotte!

"What little things made a big difference?" questioned Kate.

"Do you remember when the kids were little, and they'd get excited about mini banana muffins or cut-out valentine's hearts on the kitchen windows? Or better, do you remember the days when it snowed, and you'd feel justified staying in your pajamas and watching cartoons with your kids, even though your husband was going nuts figuring out how to get to a meeting? Those were the little things that made a big difference."

Kate pushed her farther. "I'm not really sure what you're saying. I get the little things being fun. But how did those little things make a big difference? And if they made such a big difference, why did you turn off to them? You could fill your life with that stuff, if it turns you on and makes you happy. Why not? What really matters, Charlotte? Other than happiness and being passionate about something, what matters?" She offered a goofy smile, adding, "Okay, being an axe murderer wouldn't be good. But other than that, what really matters?"

Charlotte laughed and then fumbled over her words for the next few minutes, trying to formulate exactly what she *did* mean by her comment. She really felt as if those times were the happiest in her life. They were the years when she felt the most loved and needed and worth something to someone in a big way. Then she got it.

"It's being needed and feeling loved for those little things that make you really know how much you matter. Of course, the really big efforts, like birthday parties and Caribbean vacations and Christmas, make you feel like you're *it,* but it's those little things like I described that make you really understand what you mean to your kids. And then it vanishes."

Kate was thinking about her conversation earlier in the day with Emma and how meaningful it was to both her and to Emma. She repeated what she thought Charlotte was saying. "So, are you saying you stopped feeling loved when your kids grew older, and they stopped needing you the way they did when they were little? Are you saying when Elliot was a baby, he needed you more than he does now, as he's entering the real world on his own? Or that James doesn't need you, now that he's navigating the dating scene, as he did when he liked Thomas the Train?"

Charlotte just shrugged and wrinkled her nose.

Kate expounded on her relationships within her family. She talked about her importance as a mother to each of her kids and how the relationship had matured as each of them grew up. She loved having young adult children who gave her a glimpse into the amazing adults they were becoming. She took another sip of coffee and made a leap of faith in the conversation. "As each of my kids becomes more grown up and independent, I feel freer and freer to pursue another aspect of myself. I feel like I am growing as much as they are. You know, I think men have very linear developments. Most men go to work and they work at whatever it is they do forever, or until someone tells them they can't do the job anymore. They don't think too much about their lives, other than how they can get better and better at their jobs."

Kate smiled softly and put her hand on Charlotte's forearm. "Don't you feel sorry for Charles? Don't you feel so lucky to have had the chance to explore so many different aspects of life? Like raising kids and knowing your extended family's issues and your community? What about your volunteering and knowing what's happening there? Or politics? You've been involved in politics with your friend. Hasn't that been rewarding? Really, think about how little time Charles has had to explore and grow in different directions. We're so lucky, Charlotte! We are such dynamic beings as contemporary women. And think of our sons' wives and our daughters. Think of how they will live their lives as a result of our influence."

"Are you on drugs?" asked Charlotte jokingly. "You were freaking out this spring about facial hair and now you're ecstatic over your life. What happened?"

"I think my upcoming birthday is firing me up. I want to have some kind of legacy, other than whatever it is I've done so far. I mean, I think a lot of people start to evaluate their lives at the just over halfway mark, Charlotte. Didn't you?"

"I was battling breast cancer," she said without hesitating.

"I'm sorry. I'm sorry I was insensitive. Yeah, that wasn't fair, Charlotte. But then, it never is." Then Kate added, "But look at you! You made it. You're doing great. Now it's time to focus on the other stuff, Charlotte. All that art experience is still in there"—she pointed to her right temple—"and your brain didn't shrivel up. And art doesn't change or go out of style. What about that gallery you've always wanted to open?"

"I've decided to work for Jennifer Holmes Bartlett. I think there's real potential there," said Charlotte.

"That's very exciting," Kate remarked, rather surprised. "What kind of potential?"

Charlotte hesitated. "I'm not sure. I just think she's got great political instincts, and I wouldn't be surprised if she runs for president someday."

"Well, that's great for Jennifer, but I meant you. What kind of potential is there for you in tying yourself to someone else's coattails once again?"

Charlotte was at a loss for words.

Kate couldn't hide her feelings, though. She felt that she had made herself vulnerable in calling Charlotte in the first place and believed it was Charlotte's turn to make herself vulnerable. "I mean, you just sat here telling me how you've lost interest in family life, that you want something that is your very own, and yet here you are, ready to tie yourself to someone else's success or failure."

Charlotte again didn't respond.

"You have so much innate class and style, Charlotte. You have a poise about you that is unmatched. Frankly, it is intimidating at times. Only very confident people can tolerate your style. And you talk about the art world and your consulting business with such a longing. Why not try that again? I mean, it's one thing to tell me you want to re-enter the art world, and working for Jennifer would be a gateway into that world—"

"The two aren't even remotely related," Charlotte interrupted her.

"That wasn't my point," snapped Kate.

Charlotte was short and abrupt. "I'm not an idiot. I get your point. Maybe this was a bad idea." She stood to leave, grabbing her Tod's pocketbook, which was leaning on the table leg.

Kate wasn't about to let their visit end this way. "Charlotte! You have got to be kidding me! I thought you were tougher than that. How can you manage working for a politician if you can't even listen to this criticism?"

"Because it's different when it's someone else that's being criticized. It's markedly easier to defend someone else, especially if you think that person is doing good, which I think Jennifer is. And Kate, as long as we're being honest here, I think that you are selling yourself short, making dolls. You are so smart. And here you are, sewing buttons for eyes on silly dolls that people will give to their daughters, so they can become confused about what their real roles in life are. That's what I think about your big swing back into the work world!"

"I feel sorry for you, Charlotte," Kate shot back. "I do. In the same way I feel sorry for men who don't take more time with their families and with life—yes, with life. Work is part of life, Charlotte. It isn't the whole of life. And just like the women who hide behind motherhood and family life, there are men who hide behind work and careers; men who never take the time to let their newborn baby fall asleep on their chest. Or who don't take the time to hold their father's hand when he's sick and scared; men who never volunteer at their kids' schools or in their communities." She came up for air just long enough for Charlotte to swing her bag over her shoulder and shoot back at Kate.

"Really, Kate, that's what you think? That men are as miserable as we are? You really think men have that same missing and longing that we do, to have our other life back?"

"Charlotte! Not all women feel one way, just like all men don't feel any one way in particular. As we approach midlife, both men and women long for parts of the past we can't have anymore. We all miss periods!"

"I don't think so, Kate. Charles still doesn't get his period, let alone miss it! Maybe that's what's wrong with my marriage: Charles doesn't get a period!" She started to laugh. Then she repeated Kate's comment. "*We all miss periods*? I don't think so!"

They both broke out in hysterical laughter. Maybe it was to break the tension of the conversation. Maybe it was the play on words. But they both needed the comic relief.

"Oh, my God. That is the funniest thing I've heard in a while," sighed Charlotte.

Kate wiped her tears of laughter with her rough, eco-friendly paper towels.

Charlotte thanked Kate for reaching out to her and agreed she would have to tune things out better. She promised Kate she'd reconsider joining the walkers again. "Kate, you are handling the menopause thing so much better than I did. I'm basically in the mess I'm in—not having anything going on professionally or otherwise—because I shut down and stayed inside my own head. I wish I had been more like you—out there with my anger, my frustration, and my confusion." She swallowed the lump in her throat and continued, "Well, maybe I'm out there with my anger. I am so mad at everyone and everything over this breast cancer situation."

"Maybe it's really done, Charlotte. You are one of the most fortunate women who's had to deal with hearing she has breast cancer. It's all in how you frame it. Really. I don't know what it's like to have that kind of scare. And I don't know what it's like to fear each day and search around your body like it's a mine field. But I do know there are examples of strong women who make a choice to be happy and go on. You can be that living example, Charlotte." She looked at Charlotte, expecting a response, but no words were forthcoming. "Did you tell Homes Bartlett about your breast cancer? Does she know?"

"Yes. But I told her no one else can know," said Charlotte, "and that had to be part of the deal. I told her I'm in the midst of three-month checkups right now. She was okay with that. I wish I could be. It's so scary."

"Well, you know what?" said Kate. "It's scary whether you share it with others or you don't. It's scary whether you work or you stay home and wait for the horrible diagnosis you fear the most. You might as well do right by yourself as long as you have the ability to, Charlotte. The only control you have is to work hard, trying to live out your goals and dreams. That's it. Life happens, no matter how you choose, so you might as well have some say in it, huh?"

Charlotte, still with her handbag on her shoulder, leaned against the doorjamb in Kate's kitchen. She conceded that her anger got in the way but still felt she was somewhat justified. "Kate, do you think younger women get how much harder it was for us because we had conflicting signals from society about work and family? Do you think anyone gets the false promise of how college was supposed to free us from the bondage of marriage and family bullshit?"

Kate scrunched up her face and shrugged her shoulders. She pushed the chairs in place under the paint-chipped shabby-chic-style table.

"I don't think women who came of age during the seventies are really understood at all," said Charlotte. "We're like white elephants already. Unless we became professionals, like doctors or lawyers, who absolutely couldn't stop working or risk losing every professional stride; unless we made that choice, we got screwed. The younger generation of women is so much gutsier and ballsier about what they want. They are so much more risk-oriented. What was wrong with us? Why weren't we valued more? Why *aren't* we more valued?"

Kate shook her head slowly while the women made their way to the front door. "Look, Charlotte, maybe we all justify our lot in life, men and women, so we can create value for ourselves. But I really think, as women who came of age in the seventies, we paved a way for girls to have choices. Not so every girl and woman would choose the same thing. That there are choices at all is due to the change we made by going to college and then into the workforce in such large numbers. And I think the residual effects of that transition are still being worked through, even among us. God knows, we haven't figured out the next move yet. Listen to us. Now that we're menopausal and looking back twenty years, we see some of the mistakes we made, both individually and as a group. But for goodness sake, Charlotte, we're hardly in a place of misery. We have choices that we never dreamed of. And therein lies the rub. Because we have the choices, we feel like we should be doing something really big and important, at least by someone else's standards! Yet some of us seem paralyzed. Our husbands appear to have it all, but really, what fucking choices did they have?"

Charlotte muttered a few "yeah, buts," although she let Kate continue.

"You know, we laughed about the missed-period thing, but I know Douglas misses our earlier years in marriage and family life. He was just reminiscing about each time I told him I was pregnant and when the kids were babies. He was really sentimental. I had the feeling he was thinking of how he could have done his life a bit differently. He was never around. He missed so much."

Charlotte moved closer to the door, and she laughed, grabbing the door knob. "I'm not sure what I came here for earlier. I don't mean that in an unkind way. But I have been so disappointed by the group lately, and yet, I miss them. But I think what I miss the most is feeling okay about myself when I'm with all of you. Somehow, in the group, when we talk about all our stuff, I feel so together. I've gone through this whole family-experience thing, doing it differently than my mom and dad and their generation, and yet not like any other family I know. As a result, I've always had a foot in each world. I've sort of helped Jennifer Holmes Bartlett over the years but not enough to declare a real work life. I volunteered at the museums but not enough to even earn a line on a program anywhere. I moved a bunch of times, and created great homes for our family, and stood back and supported Charles through all his ups and downs of owning his own business, yet it's still his business. I don't know, Kate. I'd like to believe it was all worth something, but I feel invisible and dispensable. And then, just as I was getting the whole gallery concept together a few years ago, boom! Breast cancer."

Java barked, and Kate put the leash on him to walk him. "I'll walk you to your car. I have to take him out," Kate said. She opened the door and added, "Look at this! What was I thinking when I signed on to do this?"

"That you'd have a beautiful landscape. And that you love flowers," said Charlotte.

"Yeah, well, I could have just clipped some at your house and saved a lot of money. You'd never even miss any," said Kate. They laughed, as Java pulled her toward the only standing tree on the property.

Charlotte hurried along with Kate, still rambling. "When I saw my mom last week, I thought she looked beautiful, but then I thought, maybe that's all that ever really mattered to her. I mean, she's in a nursing home, and the woman still gets her hair done two times a week."

"Well, Charlotte. Look at you! The pot calling the kettle black! You are the vainest woman I know!"

Charlotte laughed nervously, with a crooked smile—she got her hair done weekly. "You use so many old-fashioned expressions, Kate. You should write a book with all of them. *The pot calling the kettle black*: I love it." She suddenly recaptured her anger, saying, "I was mad at her. Imagine that. I'm sitting there with her and my dad in this little solarium, where my mom loves to look out over their gardens, and she's going on and on about the ladies who are not well, and my father's weight, and bullshit stuff. It's just how she's lived so much of her life, on the surface. Why couldn't she just for once say, *Charlotte, you are the greatest*? She fell short in so many ways, and I was sitting there, still waiting for her approval! I so want her to be proud of me and my huge life decisions—my marriage to Charles, staying home with the kids, my work with Jennifer, and everything that went into those decisions!"

"Charlotte, our mothers didn't come from that mold."

"Well, why not? All my mother ever did right by me was to say that she loved me."

"Jesus, God Almighty. How much more do you want? Are you telling your sons and Betsy that you're proud of their journeys? No! You're not. Because the journey continues until you go into the ground or wherever you plan on going after you suck your last breath. But no, your mom isn't sure yet about how she feels about her own journey, let alone yours. Every generation is an experiment. And the wake of our generation of women was more like a tidal wave in the face of our mothers, Charlotte. How could our mothers *not* resent the choices we had, even if just a little? Really, we have it all. We can make choices our mothers couldn't imagine, like birth control, which led to sexual experimentation; or going to college, which led to esteemed work; or work versus staying at home. And that's just to name a few! And don't you look at Betsy or your sons and their future wives with envy? Just a little? Of course you do. Every generation does. But that's the glory for us as moms. We get to witness our kids as the benefactors of our tough choices." She reached down to pet Java's head. The dog was sitting as if he was listening to Kate too. "Really, Charlotte, you have it wrong with the situation with your mom. I think she's waiting for *your* approval. When we choose something so very different from our parents—in this case, our moms—it's somewhat of a slap in the face. Like, hey, look, you didn't do it right. I think you have it backwards. Maybe your mom keeps it on the surface with you because she doesn't want to rock the boat. Your choices are so different from hers that at this point, she doesn't want to know that maybe she went wrong in her own life. After all, aren't our kids' lives a source of reflection for our own?"

Kate leaned in and gave Charlotte a peck on the cheek. "Go tell your mom you love her," Kate advised, "and that you have this *splendiferous* friend who's awakened you to the error of your ways, and that you are, on bended knee, worshipping her dedication to mothering you to the best of her ability. And tell her you're grateful for her generation's ability to love this quirky group of women who were loved and honored by their moms, despite our blatant sexuality, our frittering away of work opportunities because we were confused, and our goddamn anger over it all. Go tell her and all her little old cronies!"

Charlotte was still processing all of Kate's advice, nodding her head, so Kate continued.

"Just lighten up, Charlotte. Life is too short. Follow your heart and all will be right in the end. And really, let it go with your mom. That's my best advice, despite my sarcasm."

By now they were at Charlotte's car, her sparkling Suburban. Java was sniffing the tires. "Do not let him pee on my car, Kate."

"Oh, he's not going to pee on your car," said Kate. "Go home. Work on a plan. Remember how you all pestered me to come up with a business plan? You need a life plan. If this Holmes Bartlett thing is really it, you better know what you will and won't do. I mean, this is big. Really big."

Charlotte ran her fingers across her lips, like her mouth was a zipper.

"I got it. My lips are sealed, girlfriend. I promise," said Kate.

Charlotte hopped in and started the engine, and Kate went for a short walk with Java.

Chapter Seventeen

Charlotte received a call from Jennifer Holmes Bartlett's chief-of-staff, requesting a meeting with the senator and several of her senior aides. Charlotte agreed to the meeting, which was to be held in a hotel room in Philadelphia the following week. The senior advisor to the senator asked that their meeting be held in strict confidence. Charlotte consented. She took note of her rapid heartbeat when she finished the call and told herself how silly it was to behave like a schoolgirl. After all, this was her college roommate, and they had just talked a few weeks ago. Charlotte dismissed the nervousness as jitters from not having been in the business world for a long time. She decided she needed to brush up on her skills. The walking group certainly hadn't helped hone her social competency.

Over dinner that evening, Charlotte was preoccupied wondering whether she should mention the call to Charles. She wasn't paying attention to the conversation he had been having with Betsy about her driving or the college preparatory class she was taking at her high school. She was caught off guard when her daughter asked her opinion regarding which SAT IIs Charlotte thought Betsy should take.

"My counselor thought I should take bio and Math One, but I am *so* not ready for either one of them. What do you think, Mom?"

Charlotte heard *Mom* and tuned in but not enough to salvage the awkwardness of the moment. "I'm sorry, sweetie. What did you say?"

She picked up her fork and took a bite of the salmon. "Isn't this so good?"

"God, you never pay attention anymore. I bet when Elliot and James went to upper school, you knew everything about the college process. I bet you don't even know my counselor's name, do you?"

"I simply didn't hear you, Betsy. Stop being dramatic, and I know Mr. Johnson is your college counselor. Now what did you say?" She took a mouthful of the roasted potatoes. "Charles, I made these especially for you."

"Thank you, Charlotte. Now I think Betsy has something to tell you," he answered.

Betsy raised her voice. "I said, I've been screwing off in school this year and so I'm not eligible to take the SAT IIs until next year. And Mr. Johnson told me I could potentially be on probation if I don't shape up in the next few weeks. Whatever, I don't give a crap." She slammed down her fork for effect. "Who cares where I go to school anyway, right? Isn't that what you've always said, that it's about being happy, not where I go to school? Maybe I won't even go to college. I hate school anyway." She glanced at her father, who was almost choking on his potatoes as he tried to hold back the laughter. He turned away and took a sip of water.

"*What?* Are you kidding me?" yelled Charlotte. "Why didn't the school notify us?" She looked at Charles, who still couldn't make eye contact with either one of them. "Betsy! What the hell have you been doing in your room until one o'clock in the morning every night?" she continued yelling. "And of course you're going to college. What's with this change of attitude? You know, who you hang out with really influences you. Maybe I need to get more involved with your friends, not your school! Maybe you should be grounded! How's that sound? And you think you're going to drive *my* car and use *my* gas? Dream on!" She turned to her husband, who was seemingly unconcerned. "Charles, don't just sit there. Help me out here," reprimanded Charlotte.

"Why should I? You're having an easy time of it, making a fool of yourself!" he laughed.

Charlotte looked really confused. "What is going on here? Betsy, is this a prank or something?" Then looking around the room, she asked, "Oh, my God, is this one of those *Candid Camera* moments for some stupid, school busywork project?" She scanned the room again. "Betsy! Answer me!" Charlotte yelled as she stood and leaned across the table and got into her daughter's face.

"Relax, Mom. I'm in good hands with Mr. Johnson, who, by the way, is my principal, not my counselor. My counselor is on maternity leave, so Mr. Johnson is filling in for her this year with our class. I guess they figure it's nothing important yet"—then, raising her voice—"except SAT IIs!"

Charlotte didn't know whether she was relieved or angry or both, but she asked again, "What did you ask me then?"

But Betsy simply got up and left the room, shaking her head in disgust. Charlotte looked at Charles, with no idea how to proceed.

He responded, "Charlotte. She's mad. And I don't blame her. When our kids make mistakes, we ask for an apology. Why are you above that? You have such a difficult time saying I'm sorry."

She was defensive and shouted at Charles, "That's the first thing I said. I said, *I'm sorry, sweetie.*"

"Yeah, but it was perfunctory. It all could have vanished if, A—she thought you had any sincerity in your apology; and B—if you had said why you were sorry. You should have been sorry for not tuning in. Period. That's it, Charlotte. That's the beginning and the end of it." Charles had pretty much exhausted his patience with Charlotte's midlife crisis. He wanted someone to tune in to his needs and wants. He felt Betsy's pain.

Charlotte started clearing the table, and Charles got up to help.

"Why isn't she helping? Why did we let her leave the room? God, I have no control anywhere!" she shouted. Betsy was already blaring music. The pounding bass could be felt downstairs in the kitchen, even though her suite was on the other side of the house on the second floor.

"I'll clear tonight," said Charles. "Here's a glass of Pinot Grigio. It's nice. I've already started." Charlotte tapped his glass with hers and thanked him. Then she retreated to the family room, just off the kitchen. She could see him standing at the sink, cleaning the pots and pans.

She plopped herself in her favorite family-room chair, where she had a clear view of her property. She was enjoying the view and thinking about her conversation with Holmes Bartlett's office and didn't hear the ringing telephone. She thought, *Kate has no idea what she's talking about with me riding on Jennifer's coattails.* Her legs were dangling over the side of the arm of the chair when Charles entered the room, about fifteen minutes after the episode at the dinner table. She could see the dinner table behind him as he stood in the archway with that serious Charles grimace. He had already finished clearing it. *Shit,* she thought. *I certainly don't need any more criticism tonight.*

"What?" she barked. "What else did I screw up in this family? Did I breathe wrong?" He just stood in the entrance way. Charlotte realized he looked ashen. She straightened up in the chair. "What is it, Charles? Are the boys okay?"

"I'm sure the boys are okay, Charlotte. It's your mother. She's had a bad stroke, and it doesn't look good. It doesn't appear that she's going to make it." He moved in closer to her. Charlotte had covered her mouth and tears were streaming down her face. She stood, knocking the wine glass onto the Oriental rug, and Charles embraced her. He held her for what seemed like an eternity, and she sobbed uncontrollably.

"No, no, no! I'm not ready! I'm not ready for her to let go yet! We have unfinished business!" Charlotte yelled through her sobs. Charles remained silent. Betsy came into the room, and Charles put his finger to his lips, indicating to Betsy to be quiet.

Charlotte pushed away from him, continuing to cry and sob. "I never told her how proud I was of her. She worked so hard to make me an equal in our family. She would always stand up to my father and tell him how I could do everything Steven could do. She wouldn't back down, either." She wiped her face.

Betsy couldn't keep silent. "Mommy, I'm so sorry. I love you so much. Don't ever die." Betsy stepped forward, ignoring Charles's unspoken advice to be quiet. She hugged her mother and cried over the impending loss of her grandmother.

Charles called their sons and made arrangements for them to fly home that evening. Charlotte wanted the boys to be there if the life support was stopped. Steven's family was already in transit. Charles asked Charlotte who she wanted to make the necessary calls and arrangements. She thought Ginny would be amenable and capable.

"How is my dad holding up, Charles?" she asked. "Who called you anyway? Why didn't you call me to the phone?"

"Your brother and dad were with her when it happened. They'd really like you to get there soon, sweetie. I think your dad wants to turn the machines off. I don't think we can wait for the boys."

Charlotte grabbed a Diet Coke and her Bible. She asked Charles to promise to help Ginny, if required. He agreed immediately.

"I'm ready to go," whimpered Charlotte. He handed her a box of tissues. They got in the car.

Betsy was in the back seat, crying. "Mommy, it's so sad. One minute you're here and then you're not. You have this whole life of waking up and brushing your teeth and trying to make sense of everything, and then it's over. And some people die alone. Some people never find a special someone to hold their hand or hug them. What if I don't ever find someone?"

Charlotte passed Betsy the tissue box. "It's Nana's time, Betsy. It's that circle of life thing. And you know what?" she asked as she blew her nose. "Brushing your teeth for eighty-six years is a pretty good ride. Betsy, you are definitely going to find someone special to share your life with. You are talented and loving and smart, and you know what else? I'll bet that even more than having someone to share your life with, like Nana, when the time comes to say good-bye, you'll be ready, because you will have lived a full and happy life. I'm sure you will, Betsy." She reached her hand over the back of her seat to touch her daughter's hand. "I'm really sorry I blew it tonight, Betsy. I really love you, and I have been so preoccupied that I really screwed up. I hope you'll forgive me."

"Mommy, stop. Let's just think about Nana," said Betsy.

Charlotte seemed surprised that her words soothed not only Betsy but herself. Maybe, despite her earlier protestations, she really didn't have any unfinished business with her mother. Maybe she was ready to take personal responsibility for her own happiness, instead of pointing the finger outward to explain her unease with her life. Perhaps she was overly self-involved, like many of the women she labeled as narcissistic, because they were workout junkies or shopaholics. Maybe Charlotte's narcissism manifested itself in thinking she deserved special treatment, as she was now ready to enter the workforce after the noble job of raising children. Charlotte thought, *More grist for the mill,* as they drove up to the hospital. She felt a huge knot in the pit of her stomach and hoped she wouldn't vomit.

When they arrived at the hospital, Charles jumped out of the car and ran around to open her door. He hugged her as she was getting out of the car. "Great job with Betsy, sweetie," he said. Then he pushed her back by the shoulders, holding on to her. He looked directly into her eyes. "Your mom was ready for this day, Charlotte; are you?"

She just shook her head.

"I wasn't ready when either of my parents went. It's just part of the horrible stuff of life we have to get through. I'm here, Charlotte. I am 100 percent here."

They found their way to the intensive care unit, where Charlotte's family had gathered. Her dad was sniffling, and her brother, Steven, was an emotional mess. They all cried when they saw each other. Charles held Betsy back at the door for a minute.

"Let's let Mommy do this alone for a few minutes. I'm sure she wants you there, but for now, just let her be someone's baby instead of a mommy herself, okay?"

Charlotte was horrified when she saw her mother. She had looked so vibrant and filled with life last week. Tonight, she looked gray and lifeless. Charlotte hugged her as best she could with all the tubes and wires. She told her what a good mother she had been and how she would be so missed. Her brother recounted a few funny stories with her, as if their mom could hear the jokes. It made them feel better.

Then Charlotte said, "Mom, I'm going to read from your Bible. The one you gave me. Then we'll pray, okay?" She started reading a passage that her mother had underlined. The pages of the Bible were dog-eared and the leather cover was worn thin.

Charlotte had always loved the smell of her parents' Bibles and was grateful for the opportunity to grow up in household where there were standards—a code for living, along with expectations. Charlotte never felt she measured up to her parents' expectations in the religion and faith department but grew confident with age that it was more important for her to find meaning in her own path, rather than follow that of her parents. Charlotte loved the old hymns she was raised on and gained comfort from their familiar sounds and words. She was feeling calmed by the words she was reading and hoped that, in some way, her mother was as well.

Her brother was crying again. "Char, I don't think she knows," he interrupted. "Let's get this over with."

"Steven, just hold on." She glared at him and continued reading quietly. "And for everything there is a season …"

Steven held his mother's hand and was now sobbing. His wife and kids walked in, along with Charles and Betsy. Charlotte's dad put his hand on Charlotte's shoulder. The doctor walked in the room and shook hands with the family. Her dad asked the doctor for a minute. He bowed his head, and his children held their mother's hands. Betsy and her cousins were holding onto each other, crying quietly.

"Dear God, we ask you to take our beloved Celia into your arms and welcome her into your kingdom. Have mercy on her, Lord, for she served you first and always." He was crying and his words became so muffled that only Charlotte and her brother could hear. "We struggle to let her go, because she was our strength. She loved us all so devotedly. We thank you for the blessing of the many years you gave her to us. And Lord, most of all, we thank you for the hope and the gift of eternal life. And now, as we give her to you, we ask for you to send your healing angels into our lives to uplift us and hold us, as we grieve for our loss of such a love." He couldn't finish.

Steven helped his father. "We ask this in Jesus's holy name. Amen."

The doctor stepped in. "Are we ready?"

"No! I want to say a few things first!" yelled Charlotte. She turned to her dad, seeking his approval, which he gave. "Mom, I hope you can hear this. I really do. I'm so sorry it's taken me all this time to tell you that I not only love you, but I am so grateful for all the work you did to make our world a better place. For me, I mean." She was sobbing. "You made the world so easy for me. I never realized until recently, and I've been struggling with all kinds of choices, but it's because you made me a can-do girl! You made me believe the sky was the limit, and I only hope I can do half the job that you did as a mom. I know we said I love you a lot, and that is so important to me now."

Her dad put his hand on her shoulder.

"Okay, Mom. It's time for us to let go. Go peacefully and know we all love you so much." Charlotte leaned over her mother's contorted face. "Oh, Mom, I love you. I love you."

Charles pulled her back, holding her hand. Her dad motioned to the doctor, then he broke down and leaned in, holding his wife, saying, "I love you, Ceil. I love you, angel," through his sobs.

They watched as the machine was turned off, and her chest stopped heaving. The heart monitor showed a flatline. The alarms had been turned off earlier.

Steven leaned in and kissed his mother, as did his wife and children. Charlotte took Betsy's hand and guided her to do the same.

"Oh, Nana! I'm going to miss you so much! I loved Christmas and snuggling and all the wonderful things you did for us."

Charles took both of them into the hallway. They waited for Steven and his family and Charlotte's dad.

"Dad, do you want to come home with us tonight?" asked Charlotte. "The boys will be coming in later, and I know they'll want to see you."

"Steven is going to stay with me. I really want to go home, Char. How about if the boys come tomorrow, and they'll see Nana with me?"

Charlotte hadn't really thought about that part, a viewing and a funeral. "Sure, Dad. I know you and Mom had everything in place. Are you okay with the arrangements?" She turned to her brother. "Are we okay with everything? Does somebody need to make calls or anything?"

Steven indicated that there really wasn't anyone left of their parents' friends, neighbors, or relatives. They were really the last of their generation. Charlotte asked about logistics: funeral director, the body, what her mother would wear. Steven asked if she would take care of the outfit and jewelry this evening, because the funeral director would probably want it in the morning, as the private family viewing would be tomorrow evening. The public viewing would be in two days, followed by a Christian burial. Charlotte asked if they could forgo the public viewing, but her father insisted people would come. So she offered a photo of her mother from her wallet for her father to approve, before they gave it to the funeral director.

"Do you want me to wait with you, Dad?" He indicated he was leaving, that he had said his good-byes. So Charlotte kissed her dad and brother, who left with the rest of Steven's family. She turned to Charles, who was talking with Betsy.

"I can't just leave her. What do I do?"

"We'll wait for the undertaker, except I think she leaves from the morgue."

Charlotte winced. Charles agreed to ask the nurses, who indicated Charlotte could take as much time as she needed. Charlotte looked in the room, which now looked eerily sterile, cold, and empty, despite her mother's body lying there looking so dreadful. Her face was still contorted from the stroke, and her coloring was gray. Her mother's hair had just been styled, obviously. *Oh, how vain you are, Celia Gibbons! Celia Elspeth Gibbons. What an elegant name for an elegant lady*, she thought. She moved into the room and stood next to her mother.

How awkwardly life ends. Here she was with the woman who had given her life, watching as its last remnants and warmth slipped from her. It didn't happen as quickly as Charlotte had thought it would. Sure, she was officially dead, but she was still warm, and there were occasional twitches. Death was ugly but then again, so was birth, with all its blood and guts.

Charlotte moved to the chair in the corner and fell into a slumber, dreaming of Elliot's birth. When Charles returned with news that the nurses would release Celia to the undertaker later in the evening, he found Charlotte slouched in the chair, looking less than comfortable but sleeping.

He looked at his watch, reminding him that the boys' planes from Boston and Chicago had probably just taken off.

Chapter Eighteen

Ginny did a fine job organizing Celia Gibbons's funeral luncheon. The reception was held at Charlotte and Charles's home in Penn Valley. There, friends of Charlotte and her brother, Steve, were easily accommodated in the grand old house. Most all the extended family was gone or relationships had fizzled out. An older aunt and a few cousins made the four-hour trip from the central Pennsylvania town of Lewisburg, Celia's hometown, to pay their respects. Charlotte's dad was very grateful for their presence, as were Steve and Charlotte.

A busload arrived from the retirement community, where Charlotte's parents had spent the last few years. As the older women and one man shuffled along the front walkway, an unfamiliar, old-model car pulled down the long, meandering driveway.

"Good day, ladies," said Charles, opening the door for the retirement community friends. "Sir," he said to the lone old man. "Good to see you. Watch your step, now. This can be slick sometimes," he said, trying to cover for his nervousness over their fragile appearance. Charles gave a curious look to the hippie-looking character walking toward him. Unlike the other guests, who had parked along the street where the police had posted reserved-parking signs, this person had parked in the driveway.

"Can I help you?" Charles asked politely.

"Yeah, I'm here to pay my respects to Mr. Gibbons. I'm Mike McManus. You're Charlotte's husband, right? We met at the mall a few years ago. The musician, remember?" The man laughed nervously.

"Oh, yes, do come in. I'm sorry I didn't recognize you. Did you have"—Charles cleared his throat—"such …"

"No, I didn't have all these," Mike replied, yanking on his dreadlocks. "Part of my new image. It's a tough business for an old guy like me." Charles motioned for Charlotte as he stood behind the crowded center hall, where all the old people had congregated. Charlotte left her cousins and the others who had gathered in the living room, admiring Charlotte's art collection.

"Mike? Oh, my goodness, I can't believe you came. My dad will be so glad to see you. Your hair might give him a heart attack, though," Charlotte joked. Charles turned to the old folks and asked if he could get seats for them in the family room.

"Dad, you remember Mike McManus, the musician. He came to say hello," said Charlotte, sure her father had no idea who Mike was.

"Well, hello there," Mr. Gibbons said. "It's so nice of you to come today, Mike." Mike hugged him, as he somewhat welled up, remembering Mr. Gibbons in his more active years, cutting his lawn and gardening. "Mike, are you still playing piano?" asked Charlotte's dad, dispelling Charlotte's concern that he didn't remember Mike.

"Yeah, that's why I have this crazy hair. I need a look to attract the young kids. I write and play. Yup, still at it," answered Mike. Ginny asked if anyone wanted a tea sandwich. She was helping the small catering company she'd hired on Charlotte's behalf.

"Well, why don't you play that song Celia used to love, you know? You'd play it when you'd come over to see Charlotte," said Mr. Gibbons.

Mike looked at a loss. "Give me a hint, Mr. Gibbons," said Mike. Then looking at Charlotte, he asked, "Char? Remember when I was into show tunes, and you'd play the piano and I'd sing? I think he's talking about that."

Charlotte turned to her father. "Daddy, you really want Mike to play the piano? Like songs from the *Sound of Music* or something like that?"

The other guests were busy eating and wandering around the house.

"I know—I bet it's *Man of La Mancha*, Charlotte," exclaimed Mike. "Remember when we went on the class trip to see it at the Valley Forge Music Fair, and then all you wanted to do was sing those songs? Your mom loved 'The Impossible Dream,'" Mike said as he sat down and played a few chords. "Man, it needs tuning. I can do that for you sometime."

Charles entered the room with his arm bracing an elderly woman. "Oh, my," the woman exclaimed quite loudly. "Who's that hippie?" Mike and Charlotte laughed, and Charles turned red. The other guests had begun to focus on Mike's performance. They got up as they heard a soulful rendition of Celia Gibbons's favorite song. Charlotte had positioned herself next to her husband and was now crying.

"Mom would have loved this," she said through her tears. "Aww, look at my dad, Charles."

"Well, I'd be doing the same thing if I'd just lost you, Charlotte," said Charles. He held her closely, with his arm around her shoulder. She was leaning on him, listening to her old friend's music. "This guy is really quite talented. We should go see him sometime. His voice is as good as his playing. Really, I like his stuff."

Charlotte excused herself and was about to open the door to her bedroom, which was at the top of the grand staircase off the center hall, when she heard the doorbell ring.

The caterer opened the door and someone yelled, "Isn't that Senator Holmes Bartlett?" She wasn't prepared for a visit from Jennifer, who had apparently attended the funeral and decided to return to Charlotte's house to make a personal condolence call.

Charlotte had accepted a position working for Holmes Bartlett as part of her support team. Although she had talked with Kate about the possibility of working for the senator, the only people who knew that she had accepted a position were Charles and her dad. Of course, the senator's chief of staff knew too. Jennifer trusted many of her old friends, who were joining her office in numbers. It would soon be obvious to the public that big things were on the horizon. There was much to accomplish in a short time. Charlotte was hired as the events coordinator. She would have the final responsibility in coordinating the details of parlor-room conversations with constituents and fund-raisers. Jennifer was preparing for a national audience.

Charles was already at the door, greeting Jennifer and her assistant with his usual charm and aplomb.

"Charles, so good to see you," she said, hugging him. "Gosh, you look wonderful! I haven't seen you in several years." Charlotte came bounding down the steps. Jennifer stepped forward to embrace her. "Well, hello, Charlotte. Oh, I am so sorry. Your mom was such a great woman! How are you holding up?"

Charlotte wiped more tears away and said she was doing okay. Jennifer had already scanned the crowd to see how hard a job she had ahead of her. "Jennifer, after you say hi to my dad, I want you to come see the kids. You won't believe how grown up they are," said Charlotte. Then, from behind them in the center hall, came Elliot and James.

"Senator Holmes Bartlett," Elliot said, placing his hand on her shoulder. "Hi, I'm Elliot. We haven't seen each other since I was in high school. How's Kimmy?"

"Hello, Senator," said James.

"Oh, my goodness. Well, first, I am so sorry for your loss, boys. Your Nana Celia was amazing. You know she used to put up with our college shenanigans much better than any of the other moms. We were always borrowing her scissors and glue and craft supplies for one campaign or another. She'd get so excited. And, boy, could she cook. Ahh, what a dear. I'm sure you will miss her."

"Oh, yes, ma'am. Nana was one of a kind," said James. Charlotte stood and watched proudly.

As Charlotte walked Jennifer to the living room, she noticed how the crowd tried to observe Jennifer subtly. It occurred then to Charlotte that this is what her life would be like when working for a high-profile senator—watching her be received and making notes of details for adjustments later. How could Jennifer like this part of her job? Who, after all, liked so much scrutiny? Maybe she'd just grown accustomed to living in the public eye. Certainly, she must have felt a great calling to public service to put up with it all. Charlotte realized, however, this wasn't a typical Holmes Bartlett gathering. After all, many of the people gathered to pay their respects to the family already knew and loved Jennifer. She leaned in for a hug from a mutual college friend who'd come to pay her respects too.

"Who's the guy on the ivories?" Jennifer asked.

"An old high school friend, Mike McManus," Charlotte said as she rolled her eyes. "My dad asked him to play a few songs. Now I feel like it's a bit much. Mom probably would have loved it, though."

"Your mother was a special lady, Charlotte. I'm so glad I knew her." She was holding Charlotte's hands cupped in hers. "I'll never forget that first college campaign, when she cooked for all of us while we decimated your parents' garage with paints and dyes for those T-shirts." She looked around the room. "Where's your dad?"

Her father had just approached. "Dad, you remember Jennifer Holmes?"

Jennifer didn't miss a beat. "Mr. Gibbons, I'm so sorry. Your wife was a spectacular woman, and I was glad to have known her."

He nodded, his eyes welling up a bit. "She was that. We'd have been married sixty years in just a few months." He turned to Charlotte, as if he wasn't sure. "Is that right, Charlotte? Sixty?"

She nodded.

Jennifer always had just the right response. "Well, Mr. Gibbons, I always respected you and Mrs. Gibbons so very much for your hard work and love of family. Almost sixty years of a good marriage is virtually unheard of today. Again, I am so sorry for your loss but so happy that you have so many wonderful memories to hold on to. And your children are just sensational. You know I love your Charlotte, and Steve is such a gentleman. Is Steve around?" Charlotte called to him. Jennifer continued talking to Charlotte's dad. "Your Charlotte is one of the sharpest, most intuitive people I know. I guess she's told you she'll be helping me out a bit."

He nodded his head and told Jennifer how proud he was of Charlotte. He recalled his wife's excitement when Charlotte told her she had become reacquainted with the senator. Charlotte realized the din of the conversations had quieted. People were moving closer to hear any tidbit of Jennifer's conversation that they could. This was a good sign—at least that was Charlotte's interpretation; people were interested in Jennifer. Mr. Gibbons went on and Jennifer nodded, with what seemed like a permanent smile on her face. Jennifer worked the room, not missing one person. She hugged, shook hands, and listened, perhaps to everyone's story in the room, even Mike's.

Elliot brought his girlfriend, Zoe, to the funeral and wake. This was the same Zoe who'd attended Charlotte's dinner party as Elliot's guest.

Elliot had recently applied to graduate school at Wharton, where he'd hoped to follow in his father's footsteps and secure an MBA. He was eagerly awaiting Penn's response. His steady girlfriend announced that she had recently been accepted to Penn's graduate program in landscape architecture.

Charlotte felt her heart thump when she heard the news. Zoe was as lovely a girl as she could have desired for her son. She was smart, beautiful, an involved citizen and, most important, she cared deeply for Elliot. Her affection was palpable and, it seemed, was reciprocated by Elliot. Charlotte just wasn't prepared for what she thought could be coming next, an announcement of living together.

Charles broke the tension during their bedtime routine that evening. "It was a lovely day today, Charlotte," he said as he opened the media armoire to turn on the evening news. "It must have made you feel so good about your mom that the funeral and wake were so well attended." She didn't respond but continued undressing in her large walk-in closet. Charles continued loudly enough for her to hear. "I thought it was a great, positive boost to our family that Elliot brought Zoe to share an important day with us. It seems they are more serious than we may have thought." They were both in the bathroom. Charles turned on the water to brush his teeth. He waited for a reaction to his comment about Zoe. Charlotte had already brushed her teeth and hair. She was applying face cream. She rubbed her cheekbones vigorously, massaging the excess into her upper chest. She admired her skin.

"I am so lucky to have inherited my mother's skin. She didn't have very many wrinkles for a woman her age. When I was looking at her after they disconnected everything, I touched her face. It was still warm and so soft." She turned to Charles, and he saw the tears glistening as they ran down her moisturizer-streaked face. She hugged him fiercely, talking through her tears. "Zoe is sweet. It's just that everything is happening all at once. Mother died, Elliot is clearly getting ready to announce something big about his relationship with Zoe, and I'm going to work for Jennifer, who has decided she wants to be president. I didn't think it would happen like this."

"What? You didn't think what would happen like this?" He walked to his closet and quickly undressed. He slipped his trousers onto a hanger. He lifted his sports shirt over his head, gathering a sniff of Charlotte's perfume as he removed it. Charlotte was standing just outside his closet, massaging vitamin E oil into her breast incision. "I love your perfume. I love it!" He turned around to see her fully exposed breast. "God, you really do it for me, Charlotte. I know it's it seems inappropriate on a day like today, but is it perverse too, that I'm feeling horny?" He grabbed his wife and swung her around for a passionate kiss.

"Stop. I'm serious here," Charlotte reprimanded, pulling the sleeve of her nightgown up again, covering her breast.

"So am I." He asked her to continue her thoughts, but he clearly had other intentions. He caressed her neck with light kisses and put his hands up her nightie.

"Stop means stop, Charles. For godssake, I buried my mother today. And the kids are in the other room. They might hear us." Now at their bed, he reached for the television control and turned up the volume. He looked up at the double doors to be sure the lock was on.

"Aha! So you've considered it, huh? I know you feel sexy. I can tell by the way you carry yourself. That nightgown doesn't help me to maintain my dignity at all. Come on, Charlotte."

She giggled as he continued his attempts. "God, you're impossible. Now I'm fucking aroused," she said.

They made passionate, quiet love. She was feeling sexy and yet weird that on this momentous day of mourning, she could possibly want Charles in that way. But she was glad afterward, as they held each other, that they had consummated their desires.

He revisited the conversation about Elliot and Zoe. "I think Elliot wants to marry Zoe," said Charles. "He's asked me how we'd feel about his getting engaged. I told him we'd prefer if they live together for a while and that we thought he was still too young. He's sure she's the one, Charlotte."

"When did all this happen?" she asked, somewhat concerned.

"A few weeks ago, when Zoe got accepted to Penn's graduate program. He called. You weren't in a good way with Betsy or the work thing, and I thought it could wait."

"Oh, I feel bad that he didn't want to talk to me. Should I bring it up tomorrow?" Charlotte asked sadly.

"If you're up for it, I think it'd be fine to broach the subject. But only if you can really handle where it could go should you even *think* of entering into this conversation. This is a big deal for them, and we need to be totally available for this discussion. You know, not bring any residual, unfinished stuff about your mom into it," said Charles firmly.

"That's really good advice." She cuddled closer to him. "This is one of the reasons I love you. You are a really good dad. I really trust you so much with the kids' stuff. I know you love them every bit as much as I do, even though we show our love differently. I really trust your instincts with them." She kissed him.

"Thanks for saying that. Let's just hope the kids feel that way, huh?" he said.

They lay there in silence, holding each other. The streetlight shone through the shutters, casting light on Charlotte's naked body. She looked like a sculpture, her body long and lean and her skin like alabaster. Her breast was shiny from the vitamin E oil. "She's the one—Zoe," Charlotte said. "I can just tell. Well, well. My beautiful baby boy is a man in love. I better get used to it. I really hoped he would date more and work for a while, maybe travel some. But I guess this is how he's going do it. Different from us, for sure." She turned over onto a heap of pillows on their overly decorated bed. Charles validated Charlotte's feelings and agreed that he wanted the same thing for Elliot, but he added that he believed they had raised their children to be experts on themselves and that he trusted their kids' self-understanding.

"You know, Charlotte, I agree with you that Zoe is a great young woman. So I think we need to fall back and support these kids. It's rough out there and, thankfully, they found each other." He kissed her good-night.

The next morning at breakfast, Betsy told Zoe she thought she fit right into their family. Elliot said something to the effect that it was a good thing, because he wasn't going to let Zoe get away! Later that morning, as Zoe and Elliot were on their way out, Elliot checked the mail. The Wharton acceptance letter arrived. He ran into the house, where his family was reading the local newspaper in the family room. Beethoven's Triple Concerto was playing softly in the background.

"That's super!" yelled Charlotte, jumping out of her chair. Her stylish green-lacquer bifocals fell off her nose. She bent to pick them up before hugging her son. "Nana would have been so proud!"

Charles gave him a bear hug.

"Way to go," said Betsy. "Now I have two ridiculous mountains to climb: James at Northwestern Law and you at Wharton. Great." Then, smiling, she said, "I love you Ell." She hugged him. "I'm *really* proud!"

Charles offered to take the family to lunch at the Rittenhouse Club to celebrate.

"Perfect," said Charlotte. "We can look for an apartment for you, Elliot, while we're downtown."

"Thanks, Mom, but Zoe and I were planning on living together if I got into Wharton. So I guess we'll look by ourselves."

Charlotte felt as if she had been stabbed through the heart.

Zoe came to her rescue. "Elliot! What a way to tell your parents that we're in love and making a commitment to each other." She turned to Charlotte. "I'd love your input, Mrs. Wentworth. I really would."

"Thank you, Zoe." Then to Elliot, she sarcastically barked, "Thanks for the sensitivity, sir!" She turned to Zoe again. "Great then," said Charlotte. "We'll do this right and get the two of you off to a good start for graduate school." Then she added, "Call me 'Charlotte,' Zoe. And thanks for including me. I hope this is just the beginning of many wonderful shared times, sweetie."

Charles didn't say anything but felt like his conversation the night before with Charlotte had been timely and actually was processed. It didn't hurt that they had just had great sex, so she was receptive.

Charlotte wound up spending the next few days apartment-hunting with Zoe, while Elliot spent time with James and Charles. Betsy was happily winding down her junior year of high school and looking forward to her senior year. Charlotte was scrupulously observing Zoe, believing she was to become her daughter-in-law. They talked about politics, art, economics, values, and religion. Zoe was opinionated yet polite. She felt strongly that aesthetics were part of a healthy society and that there should be a better understanding of the arts available to children. She was hoping to design parks someday. She had grown up in Washington DC, where parks and museums had made a huge impact on her. As they continued to talk, Charlotte became more certain of Zoe's commitment to Elliot and understood she had missed his cues in previous visits. After all, Zoe wasn't new on Elliot's scene.

By the third day of apartment-hunting, Charlotte suggested they ask Elliot to join them and finalize the plan so the two of them could return to Boston with this agenda item crossed off their calendar. Zoe thought it was a great idea.

"Do your parents know that you and Elliot are moving in together?" Charlotte asked.

"My dad does. My mom died when I was in my freshman year of upper school. My dad never remarried. He loves Elliot. I think it's hard for him, though, thinking of letting go of me altogether. I'm it. I'm an only child."

"Well, why don't you call your dad and have him come see the apartment too. He'd probably like to be a part of things, Zoe. Don't you think?"

"Yeah, well, I just called him to tell him about Elliot's grandmother and to share the news about Elliot's getting into Wharton. But I'm sure he'd like that."

Charlotte planned a dinner and organized Zoe's dad's train trip in and out of Thirtieth Street Station, including a quick look at the apartment the two would share. She chose Parc, a casual French bistro on Rittenhouse Square, to celebrate Elliot and Zoe's new life together, and she preordered a bottle of champagne. Charles was thrilled to witness Charlotte taking charge and multitasking, creating a whirl of activity in her wake. The activity was a welcome relief from the grief she had been carrying around—grief over the loss of her mother; grief over the loss of her youth; grief over time lost being angry.

Charlotte was quickly learning that being positive, being active in her loved ones' lives, and simultaneously pursuing her own agenda was the key to her personal happiness.

Chapter Nineteen

The walkers took a long walk with their newest member, the young MBA mother, Meredith, who was Kate's neighbor. Meredith had become a regular and her joining the group added a youthful dynamic and great energy. They walked faster, added to their distance, and turned their usual chatter into intense conversation. Meredith usually pushed one or both of her children in a jogging stroller and made juggling her attention between the baby, the toddler, and four middle-aged women appear seamless. There was an element of intrigue, woven with envy, on Kate's part.

Mimmi joined them less frequently since her accident, and when she did walk with them, she slowed down the group. She had regressed since the accident—no more physical therapy, working out at the club, or talk of dating.

Marianna raised her concern. "Is anyone else upset that Mimmi isn't showing up much anymore?" She waited, thinking they were all simply focusing on crossing a busy intersection. But no one said anything once they reached the other side of the street, so she added, "I think her regressing is normal, given all that she's been through. I mean, the divorce is almost final, isn't it? But I think it's worrisome that she isn't getting out much. Is anybody on the scene besides us?"

There was another long pause. Then Charlotte broke the silence. "I'm worried but not surprised. I mean, we are all talking about things

Mimmi can't relate to—our futures, our personal goals, and the awful 'W' word—work."

"I don't buy that," said Ginny, quickly coming to her longtime friend's defense. "You guys just started with all your job excitement, Charlotte. Marianna and I have been talking about our work forever. It's just part of who we are. That's never bothered Mimmi before. I think you are being too hard on her."

Kate chimed in, "Yeah, I haven't been working until recently." She hesitated before adding, "Although Charlotte would have you believe that sewing button eyes on my dolls is not work!"

"Okay," said Charlotte defensively. "I really screwed up. The world needs buttoned-eyed dolls just like they need—"

"It's not about making the dolls," Kate broke in, not giving Charlotte a chance to finish the sentence. "It's about finding a skill set and capitalizing on it to re-enter the work force. I develop marketing plans, review competition, and find investors. There's a lot more to it than button-eyed dolls. I hope to employ stay-at-home moms who want to do something that isn't just changing diapers and toilet training." The tension was palpable, and the women were out of breath because Meredith walked quickly, and their egos couldn't handle slowing down the pace.

Meredith's blonde ponytail bounced with each perky step, as did her chest, which she seemed to stick out even more when she carried Lily on her back. She had unusually good posture, which only emphasized her great figure. Her short shorts, crew socks, and rolled down Uggs, along with her two babies, made her look like a poster child for the modern woman.

"Wow, I had such a different impression of you guys," she said excitedly. "I was admittedly a little reluctant to get involved with women who wore so much spandex." Then she added with a nervous laugh, "But then, I thought, what the hell—these women are all ahead of the curve. They've raised their kids, maybe they work or volunteer, and they've survived many years in marriage. Well, the marriage thing didn't work for Mimmi, it seems. I look forward to meeting her." Again, she uttered a nervous guttural sound. "I thought you could teach me some survival techniques for this work/family stuff." No one responded. She was still feeling badly about the spandex comment. She cleared her throat again. "I know you guys are all younger than my mom, but you're older than me. And I look at my mom, and I think, yeah, she raised me. She is so supportive of my success. But how does she manage every day, with nothing on the agenda for herself? Nothing for almost forty years that's just hers. You guys are all doing so much more than my mom."

"Did she go to college?" asked Charlotte.

"No. She lived in the town where my dad went to college, and she worked somewhere near the campus. They met at a diner where my mom used to have lunch, and they dated until my dad finished school. Then they got married. She stayed at home and raised my sister and me. She reads a lot. She keeps a lovely home. But I'd blow my fucking brains out if I thought that was all there was going to be for me for the rest of my life." They crossed an intersection, after looking both ways many times. They were more vigilant when the babies were with them.

"I feel so bad too," Meredith continued. "I feel like my mom gets that I'm disappointed in her. She's so sweet and loving, and she made a lot of sacrifices so I could have a really nice childhood. Really, I am who I am because of my mother. Yet I still wished she'd shown me how to do this"—she pointed to her toddler in the stroller—"and work too."

Kate felt slightly defensive, yet couldn't bring a sensible defense into the conversation. The other women talked about how they wished their mothers had been role models in areas of sexual liberation, education, and the workplace. It seemed as if feminist values were on the line. They realized as they talked that no one generation could create a social movement and fully reap its benefits.

Charlotte asked Meredith, "Why do you feel disappointed in her? You know, each generation paves the way for the next. And there is a huge generational difference between the women of the fifties and the sixties. Think about it. How different is your mom from her mom? And how different are you from your mom? You are probably light-years away from your mom's thinking, and yet your mom is probably not all that different from her mother, right?"

"My mom didn't learn to drive until she was married," added Marianna. "My mom came of age in the fifties, and the sixties were such a freaky time to her. She had no desire to participate in the rebellion around her, yet she was frustrated at home." She turned to Meredith. "My mom could probably be your mom's older sister. The generational stuff between women is so interesting. I see it play out in my practice all the time; very different from the issues between fathers and sons of the varying generations."

The women walked farther than they had ever walked, and they talked more than they had ever talked. The discussion took a turn to the workplace and the impact that Marianna's generation of women had made. She spoke about how birth control kept women available for the job market long after college ended and that they were the first generation in history to compete for white-collar jobs along with their male counterparts. She talked about the historic backdrop of the industrial age's transition to the information age and how that leveled the playing field for women. Women no longer needed to be strong to compete; they needed to be smart, including with their bodies.

Meredith couldn't see a direct connection between her mother's generation and contributions to women's causes in the workplace.

"I had a very good friend in college who got pregnant before graduation," Kate said after a conspicuous silence. "She was engaged already but had no intention of having kids before her career in design got off the ground. I think it really ruined her. She was a mess after that. But I can tell you, she got pregnant because she was stupid, not because she didn't have a choice. And she had options even after she found out she was pregnant. But you know what? Our mothers' generation didn't have options. Imagine the women who wanted to work, or who needed to work, who were held back by the betrayal of their bodies."

Meredith played devil's advocate before realizing she was with a tough group of women. They didn't see themselves as feminists, necessarily. Like many women of their generation, they sometimes felt victimized by societal standards, but they couldn't identify with the radical feminists of their era. They were proud, though, of themselves and their respective peer group of women, who helped pave the way for the next generation of women to have choices. Their pride was becoming obvious, even if they hadn't been aware of it before.

"So what about my mom's figuring out how not to get pregnant, or when we kids were out of school? Why didn't she go out to work then?" Meredith asked. "Really, it isn't just my mom. It's her whole generation. They didn't work; they weren't activists; they didn't run for office; they didn't work out or value staying healthy. I just feel like they didn't stick with anything! And yeah, you can always point to a handful in any generation who did remarkable things, but I think generations and groups of people are judged by the majority. What did these fucking women do with their lives?"

Ginny was ready to burst. She couldn't hold back anymore. "They raised a generation of women who have gone to college, some on to graduate school, taught them about controlling their own bodies, and raised them to be go-getters. Your mom's generation planted the seeds of change that my generation grew! If not for your mom's friends and peer group being unhappy, we would be depressed that the having-babies stage was over! We'd probably be popping painkillers with our five-o'clock cocktails!"

Meredith contemplated what they said and responded, "I guess, then, that the women of your generation, like our senator, Jennifer Holmes Bartlett, are a result of women who said, 'Enough.' Or was it the confluence of a lot of things?" She adjusted her toddler's foot, which had gotten stuck in the seatbelt harness. "I guess it's like a lot of things with timing—like, Reese and Lily, here, won't be thinking about this stuff, because they'll have many role models of women working and having families. What do your daughters all say about this stuff? How do the twentysomethings feel?"

They all laughed together. They told Meredith how their daughters didn't notice or believe in "glass ceilings." Ginny talked about her daughter's goal to be a doctor. She explained how Anna pictured her imaginary husband being a partner in raising her kids. Charlotte said her daughter wasn't sure she even wanted marriage, but she definitely talked about being a scientist who studied environmental impact on health—at least for now.

"But the important element now is that our kids' generation of women doesn't believe there are obstacles to their success in the workplace," said Marianna. "And maybe there aren't—only they will know. But they have our generation behind them saying, 'You can do it. We'll fight for you. Here's what we did. Here are the results of what we did. You have rights.'"

"I want to underscore an important point here, ladies," said Kate firmly. "Our mothers' generation did something very important. As they were getting antsy for something more, they talked about it—with each other, to us, to their doctors, to our dads. We witnessed some of those conversations, ugly as they could be. We heard them argue with our dads about not wanting more kids, or sex, or wanting to work. The ordinary, everyday women were antsy for something more. Birth control didn't just happen. There was a need, and our moms and the women before us brought their unease front and center. And by unease, I mean all of the stuff—you know, the workload at home, their husbands' business travel, raising kids, money inequity, sex, et cetera. I mean, I'm going crazy now, through menopause, with thinking I could be pregnant all the time. I'm too old to be on the pill anymore but terrified I'm not too old to get pregnant. I'm sure before the pill, women went through this feeling all the time." She hesitated as they stopped for another baby adjustment. This time Lily had slipped too far down in the back carrier. Ginny adjusted her.

"There you go, blondie. Who has such an angel face?" Ginny asked the smiling baby. "Oh no, don't smile too much, or you will drop your—" Ginny sighed. "She dropped the damn pacifier, Meredith." Ginny retrieved it and handed it to Meredith, who wiped it on her shorts and then stuck it in her mouth first.

"Here you go, Lily Bo Billi," said Meredith, reaching behind her, as the baby grabbed the pacifier and stuck it in her own mouth. Ginny stepped back to make sure all was well with Lily. "Don't talk to her," said Meredith. "She's too happy, and she'll drop the thing from smiling. We can play this game all day with her."

Ginny stepped up to the front of the group. Lily leaned over her mother's shoulder to keep an eye on Ginny, to whom she'd taken a liking.

"Anyway," Kate continued, "I'd have been frigid, I'm telling you. I swear, I'm always telling Douglas I'm too tired." They laughed. "No, really, it's true. Listen, we have our moms to thank for pushing the envelope on birth control, or we'd all be ice princesses!"

Ginny couldn't deal with the heaviness of the conversation and asked, "What was the et cetera part, Kate?" Then in a voice that mimicked Yul Brynner, she said, "Et cetera, et cetera, et cetera."

Marianna cut the tension by breaking into "Getting to Know You" from the *King and I.*

"Oh, my God! That was that such a great musical. They don't make them like that anymore," Ginny said. "Remember when Deborah Kerr got right up into Yul Brynner's face, in that big hoop skirt, and yelled at him?"

Charlotte continued, with her hand over her heart. "Oh, and that amazing dance scene?"

"Okay, now you all sound old. I'm more of a 'Gimme a head with hair; long, beautiful hair' kind girl," said Meredith.

"We're not *that* old," Marianna snorted, and she broke into a rendition of "Age of Aquarius."

"Speaking of being old," Meredith laughed, "I just found out a few days ago I'm pregnant with our third!" There was a chorus of "awws." The women seemed genuinely happy for her, and the conversation quickly changed from women's rights and parity in the workplace to pregnancy, breast-feeding, childcare, and preschool.

Charlotte had a tinge of "I remember those days" in her crooked smile. Kate was excited to have another baby to whom she could give one of her SoleMate dolls.

"Hey, Meredith, by the way," Charlotte said, "Jennifer Holmes Bartlett was my roommate in college, and she's a good friend of mine. I hope you're on her side of the fence!"

The conversation stayed light and fun, with Meredith being enthralled with the almost celebrity connection to Holmes Bartlett.

"Of course I am, but let's not talk about fences!" she said jokingly.

Kate explained the whole ordeal with the landscaping project and how Meredith was a tad uptight. Meredith laughed at herself.

"Yeah, I have that overachiever thing going on, but I'm beginning to understand how it could turn to mush after the next kid. I barely have my head above water as it is, being the mom of two kids, trying to keep up with my husband, who I rarely see when we both work, and trying not to fall asleep at my desk when I am working. I really am about to say 'fuck it' and give up looking for work." She waited for their reaction.

"Well, maybe you can find some consulting work or something project-driven, so you can keep your contacts and a little piece of your dignity while you're doing the time-off thing," said Marianna.

Charlotte winced at the dignity comment but didn't want to get into anything with Marianna. Instead, she offered advice, assuring Meredith that like the women before her who were trying to figure out the balance of work and life stuff, she'd find her own way.

"It's really hard, and each person's decision should be unique, because, just like families aren't cookie cutters, neither are the solutions that work for each family situation. The good news for you, Meredith, is that you have a choice. And that's a great beginning."

Marianna added that Meredith also had the support of a bunch of women who had already gone through the decision-making that she was dealing with, so she had the benefit of seeing potential outcomes of her choices. Of course, Meredith recognized her outcomes would be measured by her level of happiness with her choices along the way.

Chapter Twenty

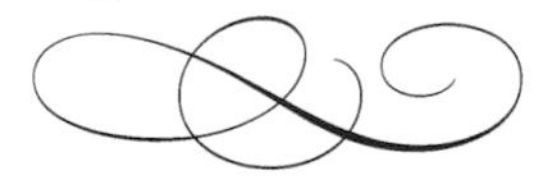

Mimmi missed her friends and invited the women for coffee, since she hadn't been walking much lately. Marianna was the first to arrive and agreed to stay until shortly before her first patient was due at her office. Charlotte and Kate had walked to Mimmi's and were pondering which pastry to eat when Ginny rang the doorbell. Unbeknownst to the group, or to Mimmi, Ginny had invited Meredith for this morning's change of venue. Meredith was eager to meet Mimmi, the only regular with whom she'd had no contact.

The regulars had gathered in Mimmi's living room with their coffees, croissants, and pastries. An oversized chair swallowed Kate, and she suggested Charlotte switch seats with her because her legs were longer. They were rearranging themselves, sharing their respective heights and concerns about shrinking because of osteoporosis, while Marianna looked at photos covering a nearby wall.

"Gosh, Mimmi, you look just like your mom. She's so pretty."

"Thanks. Yeah, everybody says that." Then she pointed out another photo, which included a generational shot of her, with her mom on one side and Meg on the other.

"Now, look at the three of us. Can you believe the family resemblance? And yet, as much as Meg looks like me, that's how much Will looks like his dad. And look at these. Aren't they so cute?" She had pointed to her kids' baby portraits. They looked exactly alike, which made no sense. The kids each looked like one parent, but they also looked like each other. She went to get more food, as the others gathered to check out the photo wall and try to make sense of genetics.

The doorbell rang just as Mimmi came out of the kitchen with more snacks, so Charlotte volunteered to get the door. As Charlotte pulled the door open, she was surprised. "Oh, I wasn't expecting you, Meredith. I should have thought to invite you myself. I'm sorry."

Ginny and Meredith came in, first wiping their feet on the welcome mat in front of Mimmi's door.

"No problem, Charlotte. I've been having such a good time walking with you ladies, so when Ginny invited me for coffee this morning, I didn't hesitate to say yes! And I thought, if Mimmi is anything like the rest of you, it'll be a hoot!"

Mimmi looked up. Kate made introductions. Meredith extended her hand. "You look so familiar," Meredith remarked, as she cocked her head, taking a closer look at Mimmi. "How do I know you?"

But Mimmi looked like she had seen a ghost.

"Are you okay, Mimmi?" asked Kate.

Mimmi ignored Kate and answered Meredith. "We met at Dr. Gehr's office on Monday."

"Oh, my God! Yes! When are you due?" blurted Meredith.

And there it was. Mimmi's secret was out in the open. Mimmi had thought so carefully about how to tell the group and when to tell the group. She had played it over and over in her head but never like this! She had carefully planned a lead-in about how she and Graham were getting along better and how they were thinking of getting back together. She realized the women were in such shock that no one was moving. It was as if someone had hit the pause button. Her friends' eyes were all upon her.

"Yup, it's true. I'm pregnant," said Mimmi. Meredith turned bright red, realizing her blunder. "I'm friggin' pregnant at forty-five. Don't look like I just told you I was going to jail, for goodness sakes. I'm having a baby. It's for real and for sure!"

Marianna was the first to speak. "How far along are you? Are you having it?" The group was still reeling from the news and too shocked to respond to Marianna's overstepping her boundaries. "I'm sorry," Marianna continued. "It's just that I thought ... I thought ... you know, because ... it's just that, I thought since you're separated and at this stage ... I'm sorry."

Ginny was blunt as usual. "Shut up, Marianna. What the hell?" She turned to Mimmi and asked, "Are you excited? I'm excited! Think of all the grandmothers your baby will have! And you'll have fairy princess over here to walk babies with." She motioned toward Meredith and then added. "No disrespect, hon." She hugged Mimmi but rolled her eyes to the other women.

Charlotte wondered how Mimmi had gotten pregnant and by whom. She couldn't imagine that it was the guy from Thanksgiving, and as far as the girls knew, he was the only other guy she'd dated, although Charlotte recalled her being coy a few weeks ago when Ginny had asked her if she was "getting any."

Marianna thought about the cost of raising a baby alone, and Mimmi didn't even have a job. Well, maybe her mom would help, and her friends could be occasional sitters.

None of them could digest the fact that Mimmi had gotten herself pregnant at this stage of life.

"Mimmi, I'm sorry. I didn't realize it was a secret," cried Meredith. "I feel terrible. I just assumed you were far enough along that you'd probably told your friends."

"I'm almost divorced, forty-five, and I have two grown kids. And I got pregnant by my not-quite-yet ex-husband, whom I really love." She waited to see the reaction from her friends, but Meredith didn't allow room for any more bad form.

"Well, Mimmi!" said Meredith. "You have certainly added to my sense of this group of spandex walking women! Good for you, girlfriend! Isn't feminism all about getting what you want, making it happen for yourself? So what if your kids are grown and you're almost divorced?"

When there was no reaction, she continued, "I have an MBA from Wharton and a third bun in the oven! My mother has things to say about that, believe me! Well, the way I look at it, Mimmi, is that you and I are poster children for women's rights. We're doing it our way. What kind of choices do you think I'd have in the workplace with three kids? After the baby starts school, sure, but not right now."

Kate chimed in. "Exactly! That's the way I did it. And okay, so I'm making dolls and manufacturing them by building a cottage industry. But I'm having fun, and I'm still around for family issues. I know I'm smart enough to compete again in the corporate world, but why should I? I've already proven that. I hold a copyright on a piece of software and okay, it's outdated now, but I did it. And I've managed other people's companies and then consulted with others to make them more successful. I just don't want the 'agg' factor anymore."

Mimmi was holding back tears. She rubbed her belly, feeling like her news had fizzled out.

Charlotte walked toward Mimmi. "It's a tough situation, Mimmi Biddle. And maybe all the gibberish is just because we don't know what else to say. But I know this much. We will help you through this. You know that, right? Whatever you decide about living arrangements, child care, breast-feeding …"

Mimmi winced at the thought of breast-feeding.

"We will be there in force. We are our own army," Charlotte went on. "And feminism-schmeninism. A baby is a baby is a baby, and we are happy for you, Mimmi. Really, I know I speak for all of us. We are truly … shocked yet happy." Charlotte hugged her, and her warmth opened a fountain of tears in Mimmi.

"This is what I want. I really do," Mimmi muttered, as if she was convincing herself. "I have always loved Graham, and we are moving in together again. He's actually happy. It's like the old days again, only this time we have arthritis!" She wiped the remaining tears with the boldly striped napkin. "And you know what? I'm glad I know what I'll be doing for the next eighteen years. I know how to be a good mom.

Diapers and late-night feedings will give way to play groups and toilet training, which will lead to ABCs and reading and sports and driving and SATs. The rhythm will all happen again, and my house will be held together with joyful sounds and kids' laughter. I'll cook and run errands and prepare birthday parties and feel like I'm actually making a difference in someone's life again. This is all I've ever wanted."

The women laughed nervously and promised to help their friend through whatever lay ahead. Mimmi served up more food and laughter. The women kept the conversation light, even though their hearts were heavy.

Chapter Twenty-One

Kate and Charlotte took to walking alone for several weeks following the eventful coffee at Mimmi's house. Ginny found other neighbors as walking companions, and she helped Mimmi by walking Sam, the fat beagle. Meredith was having a few pregnancy issues and couldn't walk for a bit. Marianna took a family vacation. Afterward, she had to travel for work. Everyone welcomed the change.

On this particular morning, Charlotte was talking to Kate about her foray into politics and how surprised she was that it suited her. Charlotte enjoyed the energy and commitment that people were demonstrating for Jen's as yet unannounced campaign. The market tests were coming back positive for Holmes Bartlett's chances to hold the highest office in the land. Jennifer had confidence, grounded in her vision of a better world and her place in it as a transformative leader. Charlotte was thrilled for her college roommate's success thus far.

She explained to Kate that she saw this job with Holmes Bartlett as temporary. Ultimately, she wanted to open a gallery that would represent female artists and that this current exposure with the senator was great for her contact list. Charlotte's enthusiasm was building as she spoke. "And if this isn't the feminism that we all fought for and desired, then it ought to be. Maybe Jen isn't the most hands-on mother, but there are many ways to live a life. And I think *that* is a key tenet of the brand of feminism that the next generation is developing. I really think we missed it, Kate."

Kate seemed confused. "What are you talking about? What brand of feminism? My girls don't even believe in feminism. They think of radicals when they hear that word. They don't think of women like us, Charlotte." She stuck out her tongue and wrinkled her nose. "Sometimes even *I* associate radicals with feminism—you know, the bra-burning, man-hating, sexually permissive type. I don't really think of myself as having made a difference. I'm barely figuring out a solution for myself."

Charlotte felt discouraged. She was quiet for the next few paces. She had trouble verbalizing her feelings. Charlotte's newfound vigor for each day was grounded in the discovery that her career sacrifice for family *was* a brand of feminism; it mattered, and it impacted an entire movement. Kate's confrontation of Charlotte's anger a few weeks ago helped solidify this concept in Charlotte's mind. *Why is Kate questioning it now?* she wondered.

Charlotte's frustration and anger over what felt like lost years probably wasn't that different from the feelings of her mother, yet her mother's generation seemed to have few options for acceptable ways out of the home/life quagmire. The bookend generations to Charlotte's peers, her mom's generation on one side and her kids' generation on the other, held the women in a vice grip of competing ideals. Her mom's generation put everyone else's goals ahead of their own, especially their husbands. Her kids' generation questioned why Charlotte's generation didn't have the balancing act of work and life figured out yet. After all, hadn't they marched on Washington for equal rights? Hadn't they burned their bras to prove they could be just like men? Hadn't they fought for parity in the workplace? What, then, did they want? Why couldn't they stay focused on their own goals, above that of the family? According to many of their daughters, they were simply fearful of success, and they were hiding behind motherhood.

The impetus of women who came of age in the seventies to break that generational squeeze was born out of a desire to find value in a unique set of choices. There wasn't a textbook guide or model for how to have it all. The predominant feminist ideal that evolved from the work of these very women was one of personal choice.

Jennifer Holmes Bartlett had her own idea of what worked; Kate, with her button-eyed dolls, a different one. Marianna and Mimmi struggled through their own work/life balance issues, just like millions of other women. Each woman made her choices, some with great difficulty, so women like Meredith and the generations of girls and women who followed would not be burdened with a ridiculous notion of equality, based on the broad brushstroke application that all women aspired to the same ideals.

Modern equality for the following generation was developing as personal choice. Women of Charlotte's age had suffered through a great deal of judgment regarding their choices: no children, too many children, leaving children with au pairs, staying at home, not working, working too much, giving up careers to raise kids, or presenting as too professional. Charlotte's peers muddled through these indignities, forcing a personal, values-based model of equality. This new model of equal rights and parity differed not only from their male counterparts, but, in many cases, from each other. Their impact would forever change the landscape of home and work.

Charlotte was certain Kate had helped her solidify her own idea of happiness and put this feminism stuff to rest. "You're not confused, Kate. You just aren't a bra-burner. That's cool. That was the sixties' generation anyway. Think about all the women you know and tell me one woman who is really okay with her choices. Then think of all the men you know and tell me how many of them even think about their choices for one second." She got up close and in Kate's face. "I am finally not confused, because I've figured it out for myself. You helped me figure this out, Kate. And if only I'd known that equality wasn't based on making the same choices as my husband and male coworkers, maybe

I could have been happy while I stayed at home, instead of looking at job classifieds, as if some part-time career path would be outlined there, or listening to the tick-tock of my biological clock. If only—"

"If only the queen had balls, she'd be king!" Kate chimed in. She looked at Charlotte as they picked up their speed. "Have you lost your mind? What's with all the powerful women stuff? Is Jennifer Holmes Bartlett getting to you somehow? I was happy; I *am* happy. I have bad days, but I am okay with my choices. Women like you give stay-at-home moms a bad rep! My sister-in-law is the same way. She's a lawyer and hates it. She waited to have kids and now is feeling like she's never where she's supposed to be, yet she looks down on me, like all I do is decorate and run carpools."

They went back and forth with the concept of women who work versus women who chose to stay at home, until Ginny Arena ran up from behind them, waving her hands and yelling.

"Hey, I've been calling you chatterboxes!" They were happy to see her.

"Hey, Ginny, are you walking with us?" Kate asked as they hugged. Ginny indicated that was her intention by leading with the local gossip: Mrs. Genova had had a hip replacement and her husband said they might have to put the place on the market. Ginny was thinking of who she knew for that house, because it had been beautifully restored, and she didn't think it should go to just anybody. Anna had gotten into Duke, and Joe was beside himself that she was going to be so far away. She saw Graham unloading a bunch of stuff into Mimmi's house. The walking pace picked up, and she asked Charlotte what was going on with Holmes Bartlett, because she read that her husband was being investigated for tax fraud, and there was a statement from the senator's office, indicating that she stood by her husband and was sure he would be exonerated.

Charlotte hadn't heard about anything but was sure it was some kind of a setup, because she knew John Bartlett to be a fine, morally upright citizen who totally adored his wife and daughter. "He would never do anything to hurt Jennifer or Kimmy. I just *know* this is some kind of crap dealt by the Republicans to undo her. I know it! He is so excited about Jen's political position. He helped her to craft a national platform. He is totally behind her, 100 percent."

"Don't you think this is why a lot of people don't get involved?" asked Kate. "I mean, who would want these animals digging around in their lives like it was a trash heap? Really, I'm serious. It really makes me furious that politics is so contentious."

"I think this is what we were talking about, Kate," said Charlotte. "Women have to work so much harder at earning a position of power." Kate filled Ginny in on Charlotte's newfound passion for feminism and its implications and imprints on the generations.

But then, Ginny piped up with her own opinions regarding Holmes Bartlett's situation. "But ladies, while I think you make good points about our journey as women, I think politics is harsh for men as well as women."

"Oh, come on!" Charlotte couldn't remain level-headed. "Forget politics! Women have to compete smarter, harder, every *t* crossed and *i* dotted—no mistakes or else you're out! That bias exists across industries!"

Kate said she thought Ginny's point was a good one and argued that, at some point, every group of discriminated people had to let go of the past, no matter the pain and injustices, in order to progress. "So, as long as you treat yourself and other women like victims, Charlotte," said Kate, "equality cannot become a reality, at least not for you. Each woman who grasps her personal goals and dreams, plans, plods through, and jumps the hurdles between her reality and her future helps whittle away the discrimination. The proof is in her realized successes. Success by success, one by one, and that's how it works. I'm sure of it." She puffed out her chest, trying to exude confidence.

"Whoa!" Ginny yelled. "Man, this is all too much for me. All I know is this: I get up and I go to work because I like it. I go to my kid's school plays and sports, because that's what you do. And I make myself crazy at the holidays, because I can't do both jobs well at that crazy time of the year. So, big deal, my holidays aren't as cool or as pretty as either of yours. But I'm happy, goddamn it, and I don't want anyone telling me to change or fix anything or mix it up. I'm happy with my life just the way it is. But I have a very important question on a different subject—Holmes Bartlett. Did you know the husband too, Charlotte? I mean, you know her well, obviously. Was he one of your friends in college too, or did he come on the scene later?"

"Before I tell you about Holmes Bartlett, tell me how much nicer my decorations are than Kate's," Charlotte joked.

"Oh, my, aren't we insecure!" Kate playfully punched Charlotte in her upper arm.

Charlotte explained that Holmes Bartlett met her husband during college, but he went to another school, and they didn't really start dating until after graduation. She didn't know him as well as she knew Jennifer, but she defended his honor just the same.

"We are bookin' here, ladies!" Charlotte said, abruptly changing the subject. She checked her oversized watch. "A mile in a little over thirteen minutes is great! We're not bad for a bunch of middle-aged broads, huh?" Ginny continued with her excitement about Anna's getting into Duke. She told Kate and Charlotte of the staggering statistics Anna had to overcome to become part of the elite group of kids in the freshman class. She was hoping her best friend from sleepaway camp would get in, and then they could room together.

Charlotte told her that Elliot's first roommate was his best friend from upper school, and they roomed together throughout college. Charlotte was sure they'd be in each other's weddings someday and, at the rate things were going, she thought Elliot would be the first.

"Really?" asked Kate and Ginny simultaneously. They were both surprised.

"Yeah, really, I can't believe it myself, but he's serious with this girl, and I think she's really good people. I like her dad."

"What about the mom?" asked Kate.

"It's so sad. She lost her mom when she was young, I think to breast cancer. She and her dad are it and, as you can imagine, she adores him. And the dad is amazingly on top of Zoe's life. Elliot has very big shoes to fill, but I really think he's up for the task. Elliot is so sensitive about the dad's being involved, too. I am so happy to have raised such a sensitive man." She smiled. "I can't believe I just called him a man." Charlotte said she thought Zoe was a great fit for their family and, most important, a great fit for Elliot. She proudly spoke of Elliot's consideration of Zoe's career, as they planned their future together.

Kate remarked she hoped there would be a day when that consideration was routine and nothing out of the ordinary. Charlotte and Ginny agreed.

The women finished their walk, talking about their respective kids and how fast time went by. Charlotte's phone rang, and she looked at it.

"I have to take this call, girls. It's Jennifer's office. I'll see you tomorrow, okay?" They hugged, and she answered, "Good morning. Charlotte Gibbons speaking."

Ginny and Kate looked at each other and continued walking.

"Boy, Charlotte's really taking this feminist thing to heart. Since when is she Charlotte *Gibbons*?" asked Ginny.

Kate answered Ginny with a shrug and added, "Who knows how anyone pulls herself out of a midlife slump? If Charlotte needs to change her name as well as her attitude, and it works for her, then all the power to her. I'm just glad she seems happy." She grinned. "Let's think of names to call ourselves to get out of our slump."

"Hey, I'm not in a slump, girlie, but I'm going to be if I continue hanging out with you downers. Geez," said Ginny, shaking her head.

"I think I'll call myself Katherine. Don't I look like a Katherine, Ginny?"

"You look like a damn fool with that sweatband on, like you're some athlete. What? Did you just step out of the seventies? Next thing you'll be doing is wearing a ripped T-shirt off one shoulder." She pulled the sweatband off Kate's head. "You're much too *Katherine* to be wearing this," she said as she stuffed the headband into her pocket. They laughed as Kate struggled to get the headband out of Ginny's pocket.

Ginny and Kate agreed to walk again the next day, if the weather cooperated. Kate thought she'd call Meredith and invite her to join them again. Perhaps her morning sickness was over by now. Meredith challenged them to walk faster and take longer strides. Having a younger person definitely gave them a better workout, even when that younger person was pregnant.

Chapter Twenty-Two

Charlotte was standing at the workbench island in her huge kitchen, watering and pruning her orchids, when Charles yelled from the center hall, "Oh, my! I think an errant trailer from Virginia somehow wound up on the Main Line. Talk about lost in America! Come see, Charlotte. Really, darling, they are in our driveway for some reason." Then he muttered to himself, "Are they getting out? What are they doing here?"

Charlotte had a sinking feeling the trailer could have something to do with Kate and her talk of traveling cross-country in a recreational vehicle. She had recently talked about a designer model. She described how it was outfitted with designer fabrics, name-brand dishes and kitchen utensils, and interior finishes fit for a McMansion. And just as she was hoping her idea was wrong, Charles yelled again, "Charlotte? Is that one of your friends getting out of that thing?" She winced. She put down the small orchid mister, wiping her hands on her apron and went for a look-see.

"Yup, that'd be one of my friends, all right," said Charlotte, untying the denim apron and pulling it over her head. She tossed it on the back of a chair in the center hall. "I sure have unpredictable friends, Charles. You've got to hand it to me for that!" she exclaimed. Charles was staring out the right sidelight as Charlotte peered out of the left side of the windows that framed the oversized mahogany front door.

Kate had made her recreational vehicle fantasy a reality after much planning, negotiating, and scheming. And here she was in Charlotte's driveway, with an Airstream custom model attached to her Volvo SUV. And on the side of the van, in huge red letters, was the word SoleMate—with a little red c with a circle around it, indicating she'd copyrighted the name.

"Oh, dear, she's spelled the business name incorrectly," said Charles, seemingly amused.

"Don't be so sure. The dolls wear really big shoes, you know, in proportion to their size. I think it's a play on words and besides, Kate's really smart. She'd never make a mistake that big," Charlotte said, laughing at her own play on words. After all, the word on the side of the Airstream was really big, as were the doll shoes. Charles opened the door for Charlotte, who walked quickly toward the big rig in her driveway. Kate, who had gotten out earlier, was still fiddling with a sideview mirror on her Volvo.

"Well, look at you, Kate Hahn! You made it happen, girlfriend!" Charlotte exclaimed. Kate turned around from her mirror-adjusting and screeched with joy.

"I wanted to surprise you guys! This was the hardest secret to keep. I swear, I couldn't keep any of my pregnancies a secret but this, well, I just didn't want to jinx it," said Kate. "Check it out! Fully equipped with everything I'll need for my six weeks traveling cross-country. I even had the Airstream people design a little craft area where I can work while I'm on the road."

"Oh, my goodness, you have pictures of the dolls here," Charlotte said, pointing to large blown-up photos of the SoleMates on the opposite end of the trailer as the logo. She explained to Kate that Charles thought she'd made a huge error on the side of her rig with the spelling of the name. The girls laughed so hard, Kate had to brace herself on the car door's handle.

"It's a guy thing," said Kate. "Doug was like, what, S-O-L-E, not S-O-U-L? Please, and he's my husband and partner, and he's seen every prototype. Whatever! I think the name's catchy."

"Men are so dense," said Charlotte. They laughed some more and Charlotte put her arm around Kate's shoulders. "I am so proud of you. I am so, so proud that you actually did this."

"Well, the other little business attempts were all part of this business's success. I realize that now. I had to try a little bit of this and a little bit of that until I hit on just the right venture. And the timing was right with this. You know, my dad's surgery went well. My folks basically moved in with us, so they've been really helpful with the kids. It's been great for all of us. My dad's recovery, I swear, is going so well because he's been helping Jake out with homework, and it's a real distraction from his health stuff." Kate spit on her fingers and wiped a smudge off the trailer.

"That was very hillbilly-ish! Gross," reprimanded Charlotte.

"As if having a trailer, in general, isn't," said a familiar voice.

Both women stepped from behind the Airstream to see Ginny. "Hi, Ginny," they both said, excited to see their friend. "Isn't this unbelievable?" asked Charlotte.

"Joe said he thought he saw a trailer in your driveway yesterday, Kate, with some painting or billboard on it. I said I had no idea what was going on. I guess I'm more out of the loop than I thought," Ginny said, a bit hurt.

"Nobody but Douglas and my parents knew. And the only reason I told them is because they helped me buy it!" shouted Kate. "Really, I was so afraid it wouldn't happen because there were a lot of obstacles. I just didn't think I could face anyone if I had another failed business attempt," she said, explaining her secrecy.

"Well, I feel better knowing that," said Ginny, still a bit unconvinced that no one else knew. "You are something else, girlfriend! I can't believe you actually did this one. Is this part of the business idea and the doll thing?"

"Yup, it sure is! Wait, let me grab something," Kate said, running toward the door of the Airstream. She opened it and yelled, "Hey, why don't you guys come in here and check it out?" Charlotte and Ginny walked around to the door on the other side of the trailer. Ginny climbed up, while Charlotte peered inside.

"Oh, come on, you damn snob," said Ginny, holding out a hand to help Charlotte up. "Geez, it's like being in a tin can, it's so hot in here."

"Well, I don't have the controls all figured out yet," said Kate defensively.

"Yeah, well you better get the air thing figured out soon, or we'll all wind up like dead bugs," said Ginny, tilting her head back, tongue out to one side, face scrunched up, and her hands, with fingers curled, framing her face.

"God, Ginny," said Charlotte. "Does anything in that pea brain of yours get filtered? Kate's excited here. We're doing excited now, okay?" Charlotte made an exaggerated happy face.

"Here, this should help," Kate said, popping open a side window and creating a small cross-breeze between the door and the window. "Do you mind if I shoot a few while we talk?" asked Kate as she took her Canon Rebel out of its case.

"Please, feel free. I'd love to be photographed in a trailer while I melt," Ginny answered. She struck a comical pose for Kate. "It'll seem like I'm in some exotic place, like on an African safari or something,"

Kate ignored her sarcasm and shot several candid photos. *Click, click, click.* "It's very surreal. I cannot believe I've reached this place in my life," said Kate.

"Here, let me shoot some of you now," said Charlotte, reaching for the camera. Kate pulled the wide strap over her head and slipped it over Charlotte's head, as Charlotte bent over like an athlete receiving an awards medal.

They hadn't noticed Charles standing at the bottom of the short stair into the trailer, just a silhouette in the doorway. His deep voice startled them.

"Well, ladies, what have we here?" asked Charles.

Uggh, thought Charlotte, *he sounds so old.* "Charles, smile!" *Click, click* went the camera. Charlotte had captured her husband's reaction to her bold-minded friend's planned venture. He scowled.

"I think it's like an anachronism sitting here in our driveway," he said, "a real throwback to the sixties. Put that thing down, Charlotte. You know I don't like having my picture taken," he scolded. But Charlotte ignored him. She clicked away frantically. He held up his hand. "No, don't, really. I look a mess."

"Oh, my God, are you one of those metrosexuals I read about in *Vogue* magazine?" teased Ginny. When Kate looked inquisitive, Ginny explained, "You know, not gay but really into fashion and the way everything looks." They laughed. Then she turned to Charles and said, "Stop being vain. Let your wife have her way with you, Charles. Right here in front of all of us! Who knows? You may wind up in a picture book on a famous someone's coffee table."

Still standing awkwardly in the doorway, he shuddered at the thought. "Lord, with a trailer in my driveway? For all of posterity, I will be remembered as the real estate developer with the camper in his driveway?" He waved them off and stomped back to the safety of his at-home office.

The women laughed as Charlotte looked at the digital photos of her husband.

"What a stiff! How did I wind up with a guy with such an old head? He acts like he's ninety, not almost sixty!" exclaimed Charlotte.

"Your job is to keep him young," said Ginny.

"Wait, let me write that down," Charlotte sneered. She took the camera off and placed it on a seat.

Kate reached to unlatch a hook, which released a table. She then pulled banquette seating from under the floor surrounding it. "Welcome to my conference room, ladies," she said, motioning with a sweeping gesture that they should sit down.

"This is so cool. Joe has definitely got to see this!" Ginny exclaimed. They all sat down.

"I love the fabrics and finishes, Kate. Did you pick the combinations?" asked Charlotte.

"No, it comes with a few choices," Kate answered. "I liked the stainless appliances and this wood-tone paneling with the reds and warm colors in the striped fabrics. Look at this." She opened the little kitchen cupboard to reveal coordinated red plastic designer dishes and mugs. "Every detail is coordinated. Don't you love the little curtains and the quilted bed comforter? Check out the pillows," she said, pulling them out of an overhead bin. "All the fabric and finishes are washable, for obvious reasons."

"Wait," said Charlotte. "My housekeeper made fabulous iced tea this morning. Let me go get a pitcher and glasses." Then she picked up her cell phone. "Better," she said and pressed a speed-dial button. "Charles, please tell Veronica to bring out that iced tea she made this morning and three glasses with ice." Charlotte waited for his acknowledgment. "Yes, to the trailer. Where did you think we were?" She rolled her eyes at the women. "If you want, you can join us, Charles." He spoke a bit more. "Yeah, I didn't think it was your kind of thing." He said something else. Kate and Ginny sat listening to Charlotte's side of the conversation. "Yes, of course I remember when I wanted to take the trip when we were younger." She was shaking her head. "No, I'll tell them." He apparently said I love you, as Charlotte responded, "Yeah, me too," ending the uneasy conversation.

"What was that all about?" asked Kate.

"I always wanted to take a cross-country trip in a camper. Years ago, when the kids were really little, we hit upon hard times financially, and I wanted to pack it up and go around the country in one of these." She motioned around the trailer with her arms. "Charles would have no part of it. He was just reminding me, like I needed to be reminded.

Like I'd forgotten that he's always been a stiff!" They all laughed, except Charlotte. She smirked.

Kate went on to explain more about her doll business: the cottage industry aspect, the storybook about regions of the United States she'd include with each doll, and the found objects she'd incorporate with each doll's design, like old buttons, broken pieces of jewelry, old hair clips, ribbons, and lace that Kate found at garage sales.

"Wait. This is for real? You are really doing this?" asked Ginny. "You are traveling across the country and selling dolls by yourself? This isn't for, like, a family thing too? How are your kids dealing with this? What does Douglas have to say?"

"Yeah, what does Douglas say about all of this?" added Charlotte, then with a crooked smile. "Go ahead, make me feel even worse than I already feel about my husband and tell me Doug's driving the damn rig for you or something equally extraordinarily supportive."

Kate and Ginny giggled.

"My family is excited that I'm doing this, and they're all supporting me in some way. Douglas is taking over the general family stuff: money, vet visits, organizing the people working at the house, the kids' general well-being—you know, that kind of stuff. Of course, my kids aren't babies anymore, so they'll help out. My mom and dad have already moved in, as you know. And that's working out great. And really, with housekeepers and groundskeepers and everyone else, it should pretty much run itself."

"And speaking of housekeepers," said Ginny.

Charlotte slid out of the booth seating to meet Veronica at the door of the camper and took the beautiful tray she'd set with the tea, an ice bucket, glasses, and toile-patterned cloth napkins.

"Your husband might be old-headed, but man, Charlotte," said Ginny, "you lead a charmed life!"

Charlotte ignored Ginny, annoyed that she'd made a negative comment about Charles in front of their housekeeper. She thanked

Veronica and set the tray on the banquette table. Kate continued with her plans while Charlotte poured the mint tea.

Kate explained that she was eager to catapult herself into the next stage of life, and that all their talks on the walks just made her feel like this was the right time. It would be great for her kids to join her on short jaunts over the summer. They had flexibility, as did Doug. He was excited that she had such energy for her work, which was translating into a much-improved Kate in their personal life. Her parents were on board with helping with kids' activities and being available for emergencies, so she and Doug felt like it was perfect timing. She also had the backing of Airstream, which was financing the vehicle at a super rate just for the publicity.

Kate propositioned Charlotte. "Charlotte, you'd be a great travel companion. You don't need to commit right now, but I'm thinking of leaving soon. Maybe you could look for artists from around the country. You know, make some connections for your someday gallery! It'd be awesome!"

"Kate, I would love to do this with you. You have no idea how much. And the artist hunting would be great. But I am really pumped up about being involved with Jennifer's campaign. She's going to have to decide very soon where she stands and what her commitment to this presidential effort really is about. I want to know I did everything in my power to support her. The timing just isn't right for me to take a trip with you. And don't think that it's just about Jen's success, and that I'm putting myself aside or anything like that. Really, this is my time too. It's a great way for me to get back into my business persona, get my sea legs all over again." She thought about the metaphor. "You know what I mean, just get into the swing of things again. I guess once you get your sea legs, you're not supposed to lose them! Oh, well."

Ginny raised her iced tea glass, and the other two women followed her lead. "Here's to your success, Kate," said Ginny.

"To SoleMates!" said Charlotte. The girls tapped their glasses and drank the tea.

Chapter Twenty-Three

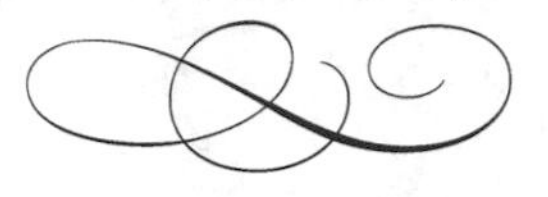

Mimmi was busy reuniting her family and losing herself in the joy of having a second chance at family life. During her separation from Graham, she'd done more than her share of contemplating the failed relationship. She looked through photo albums and read journals from their early years together. She stood in doorways of her kids' rooms, remembering their little faces as they lay dreamily among a collection of stuffed animals, sucking their thumbs and hugging their favorite blankets. There were many nights during that time period when Mimmi buried herself in a heap of her own blankets, trying to extract a leftover scent of Graham, sobbing, knowing that she too had let the marriage down. It wasn't all Graham's fault, but his failing was far less socially acceptable.

She sat on the floor in her family room with a few piles of unevenly stacked photo albums and two shoeboxes of loose photos she'd strewn around her. Mimmi stroked her ever-growing belly and wondered how she could have missed the signals of a declining marriage that seemed to now jump off the yellowed photo pages. She eyed a picture of her carefree self. She sported denim cut-off shorts, argyle knee socks with no shoes, and a cable-knit sweater her mom had knit for her in her freshman year at Bryn Mawr. She was lying across the front seats of Graham's VW Beetle, feet hanging over the steering wheel, and staring up at the blue, blue autumn sky. In another photo, taken a few years later at Mimmi's senior winter formal, Graham was looking down at her like she was the only girl in the room, even though her beautiful roommate was standing just to his left. She contrasted those photos with a snapshot of them lined up at a recent company holiday party—Graham with his arm around his voluptuous secretary, and Mimmi staring off into the camera's eye, hands at her side.

What happened along the way? she asked herself.

"What are you doing down there?" Graham asked. Mimmi hadn't heard him come in from the garage. "More trash?" he asked. "I just put the cans out at the street. It's recycling day tomorrow too."

"No," she said. "Look at these." She held up the Volkswagen photo.

"Look at how gorgeous you were. You look exactly the same to me."

"Don't do that. Be honest," she said, grabbing the photo back.

"I mean it. Okay, you're heavier, but look at your face. And your hair. I love that hair. You really do look the same," he insisted. She let go of his flattery and started to pick up the photos.

"I'll be up in a minute. I have to clean up this mess."

"Let me pick those up," he said. "You shouldn't lift that pile of albums." He looked at some of the photos too, as he helped clean up the images she'd been studying.

"We have a real history, don't we?" he asked.

She cried. "How did I not see the decline in your interest? How did I not notice this?" she asked, holding up the holiday party photo.

"Stop that. We just didn't take the time to communicate very well, did we? Maybe I should have told you I hated that dress and that I was sick of your wearing the same outfit every year for the Christmas party. Maybe I should have told you," he repeated for emphasis.

"Yeah, maybe. Or maybe I shouldn't have weighed forty pounds more than the day you married me," she cried. "Or maybe I should have told you I thought you drank too much at those parties, and I always wanted to have a husband who danced with me and made me feel like he was proud to introduce me to his coworkers." She sniffled. "Did you sleep with anyone else, other than the girl you met in Rittenhouse Square?"

"We've been over this, Mimmi," he said. He sat on the floor next to her. He tried to hold her as she cried.

She pushed him away. "I'm not sure we are going to get over this, ever. I'm not sure I'll ever really trust you or ever forgive myself."

"Forgive yourself? For what?" he asked.

"I gave up. The day I walked down the aisle, I gave up. I felt like all I needed to do was keep a nice house, and pop out a few babies, and take good care of them. I just didn't think about anything else. Like, I didn't think about me, as a woman, as a smart woman with hobbies and interests of my own. What the hell was I doing all these years?" she asked, throwing the pile of pictures she had in her hand. The pictures landed all over the room—pictures of babies sitting in high chairs and strollers and sliding down park equipment. The kids' first days of school photos got mixed up with snaps of puppies, hamsters, and goldfish. There were pictures as well of science fairs and elementary school graduations, but there weren't many photos of Mimmi and Graham.

"I let us down because being a mother was easy, compared to being a wife," Mimmi cried, "and so that's all I did. I never told you how I pictured our future because I never thought about it. I never planned for a time when the kids left, and it would just be us. And now, here we are, and I'm doing it all the wrong way again."

"We," he corrected. "We did some of it wrong then, but we aren't doing this part wrong," he said, touching her stomach ever so gently. "Yeah, you were—are—a damn good mother. And yes, that's what you focused on, often neglecting me, and more importantly, yourself. But listen here, woman. I'd marry you all over again, and I want this baby as much as you do. We are going to do right by this family, because our kids, all three of them, deserve more from us. They deserve an example of getting it right and hanging in." He hugged her, and she reciprocated. Her tears subsided, and they went upstairs to bed, leaving the photo cleanup for another day.

Mimmi stood looking in a full-length mirror in her bedroom, tucking the cotton dress under her blossoming belly. Her new profile brought tears of joy. This baby would bring renewal and healing to an ailing family. She smiled, thinking of the conversation she had just had a few nights ago with Graham. The photos were a springboard for a crucial conversation and one, Mimmi realized, she should have had before she decided to get pregnant. *At least it went well*, she thought, and she was relieved to know Graham felt the same way about their second chance at getting family life right.

The home telephone phone rang.

"You never answer your cell phone, damn it!" yelled Ginny. "We're thinking you should get back to walking. It'll make for an easier delivery, at least that's what I hear. How about if I come by and we'll head over to Marianna's? She's back from Chicago."

"That'd be great. I need to change into pants and pop on walking shoes. Give me about fifteen minutes, okay?" She hung up the phone, excited to tell the girls her latest idea—a renewal ceremony.

Mimmi and Graham's divorce wasn't finalized yet. She didn't really understand what was necessary to reverse any action taken by either of them to restore their original marriage license. But it didn't matter to her right now. All that mattered was her commitment to being whole in the relationship.

She had started walking toward Ginny's house. Within a minute or so, she saw a bob of bouncy, blondish curls and heard her singing. Ginny was so reliable. She was also incredibly upbeat. Waving and yelling, Mimmi picked up her speed. She wouldn't let the girls down again. She'd really missed walking with them, and Ginny was right—it would make for a better delivery if she walked and had some form of exercise.

"Hi, sweetie," Ginny said. "Oh my God, you are so big! There really is a baby in there, isn't there?" She touched her belly. "God, I forgot how hard your stomach gets. Isn't it a miracle? Are you taking any of those classes or anything? I swear, I wouldn't remember anything."

Mimmi laughed. "Really? I wish I could forget. I feel like I remember way too much. I am really scared, to tell you the truth. I mean, I've been tested for everything there is to be tested for. I even had this weird test called a stress test, where they see if the baby can handle the delivery okay."

"I never heard of that. What do they do to test that?'

"Oh, you don't want to know." Mimmi turned red. Very red.

"That good, huh? What, they make you …" Ginny laughed.

Mimmi shook her head.

"Like they make you have an orgasm or something like that?" Ginny couldn't help herself.

"Yup, something like that." Mimmi grinned. "I could have told them that the baby definitely could do okay during an orgasm."

"Oh, my God! Now who's giving out too much information? Stop before I puke. You have sex regularly now? You weren't having sex at all. Your husband cheated on you. You forgave him. You get back together. He gets you pregnant, or you get yourself pregnant, whatever. And now you're having sex regularly? Oh, my God!" Ginny put her finger to her lips. "I won't say anything to anybody!"

"Why? Why not? I want to tell everyone! Everyone thinks I'm a prude, and I'm a loser because my husband cheated on me. You know what? We cheated on each other. He did it one way, and I did it another. I let him down too. I was a stick-in-the-mud. I'm making up for lost time."

"By getting pregnant? How does your mind work?"

"Are you upset that I'm pregnant? Because I'm not. I knew what I was doing when I didn't use birth control. Whether conscious or unconscious."

"Let's just tell people you were unconscious, okay, Mimmi? For me. So people don't think I have a moron for a friend!" snapped Ginny.

"A moron? You think I'm a moron? Look at me." Mimmi stopped walking and grabbed Ginny by the shoulders. "You are one of my oldest friends in this neighborhood. I met you before I had babies. But get this straight," she dropped her hands from Ginny's shoulders. "I am not a moron, and I chose this life, just like everyone chooses her life: by accident, on purpose."

"Huh?"

"By accident, on purpose. If we don't plan for ourselves, we are planned for, and that's a choice. And we could really take it one step further and say that I didn't have the courage to ask Graham if we could do a replay of the best parts of our life together, so I just took the lead on that. He asked me to live with him again, and I just took it one step further with the pregnancy. I really am much more in charge than you think, Ginny. Tell everyone that."

Ginny and Mimmi walked in silence until they turned the corner at Hagys Ford and Fairview Roads and saw Charlotte.

"Shit," said Ginny. "I'm not up for her garbage today. She's so fucking perky about her newfound life with Senator Holmes Bartlett. I think she's a tad over the top."

"Well, she's just the person I want to see. I was going to call her. I want to have a recommitment ceremony, and Charlotte is so good at the entertaining thing. She'll have lots of ideas, I'm sure. Look at her. She's stopping to look at something on Mrs. Edelson's property, probably an antique or something. Isn't her husband the antique dealer?" Mimmi asked. "Mrs. Edelson always has such interesting objects in her garden."

"Her husband is as weird as a three-dollar bill. He's been hanging around in people's attics and garages too long. Did you ever meet him?" Ginny asked.

"No, but Charlotte always buys beautiful things from him," said Mimmi.

"Geez, Mimmi! Charlotte, Charlotte, Charlotte! I get that you think she's a creative genius, but you know I have ideas too," said Ginny, a bit hurt.

"I'm sorry; it's just that I thought maybe you didn't have time with work; that's all," Mimmi said. "You know I think you're great, Ginny." She waved enthusiastically to Charlotte who had stopped looking at Mrs. Edelson's property and was approaching them. As the two got closer, Charlotte ran up to them to hug Mimmi.

"Mimmi, look at you. It's soon, I think! You are getting lower. I wonder what you're having. Do you know?"

"Yup! She's having a baby!" Ginny joked. "She wasn't sure for a while. She was thinking it was a baby elephant, she was getting so big. But yeah, they confirmed it was a baby." It was Ginny's way of saying "I'm sorry" to Mimmi.

Mimmi smiled and laughed. "No, I really don't know," she said. "I thought it would be fun to have it be a surprise. I don't really care, as long as it's healthy. I'm really nervous about all that."

"Oh, honey, I'm sure they've tested you for everything imaginable, including insanity."

Ginny didn't hesitate. "Don't go there, girlfriend. I got my head chewed off a few minutes ago. Mimmi is insane, because she's actually happy about this whole thing. Right, Mimmi?"

"Yup," she said, while rubbing her belly.

Charlotte took a turn rubbing her belly. Mimmi asked Charlotte about ideas for a recommitment ceremony as they continued walking. They had crossed the street and didn't pass by Mrs. Edelson's house, but Mimmi wanted to know what Charlotte had stopped to look at.

"Mrs. Edelson collects antique baby carriages, and she fills them with flowers and plants, sticks, you name it. The woman is so creative," said Charlotte.

"Ooooo! Maybe we could borrow something from her for my recommitment ceremony," exclaimed Mimmi.

"Oh, Marianna called me," said Charlotte. "She couldn't reach you guys to tell you something's come up with work. She'll catch us later this week. Anyway, let's talk recommitment ceremony, Mimmi."

Charlotte had many ideas and offered to help. She explained that she had very little time, though, because of the senator's impending campaign and her commitment to Jennifer's success. But she reiterated her offer to do whatever she could to help Mimmi realize this small part of her dream.

Mimmi was interested in hearing about Charlotte's close ties with Jennifer and her chance at the presidency. But all of it seem to pale by comparison to rebuilding her life with Graham and adding a baby to their family. Mimmi hoped that everyone had moments like this one; where no matter what was happening all around, life just felt perfect, even if just for a split-second.

Later that same day, as Mimmi and Graham were readying for bed, she came out of the bathroom wearing a full-length linen nightgown that was hand-crocheted around the neckline and throughout the bodice.

"You look radiant in that dress," said Graham.

"It's a nightgown, but I can see why you think it looks like a dress. I made it years ago, and the crocheting around here"—she pointed to the bodice and neck area—"was my grandmother's lace. She made this lace. Can you believe that?"

"You have that look, like we need to talk about something," he said.

She sat on the edge of his side of the bed and towel-dried her curly, thick locks. "I was really upset today." She swallowed hard. "Not with you, for a change, but with my walking friends. Ginny called me a moron for getting myself pregnant."

"What?" Graham sat up straight in bed and became red in the face.

"Well, not just like that. She did it using humor, and so did Charlotte. But I set them straight. I told them we really wanted this, and that this was all our life was ever about—family. I told them my feelings. You know, we already talked about all of this. I don't know why I'm telling you this stuff. But, well …"

"What? This is about me. What?"

"Well, I want to be *sure* that I have it right this time," she said.

"What? The baby? Us?" He stood up and paced in front of her, then he crouched down in front of her. "Mimmi, I want this, and you, and all of it." He reiterated what he had said nights earlier. "We have no instructions here, Mimmi. Life doesn't work that way. You know that. There are no guarantees that we'll get it right this time, either. But it won't be for lack of trying on my part; I can tell you that. For sure, it won't be for lack of trying. I was so stupid to squander your trust the first time, and I still can't believe you are having me back. But believe this: I remind myself every day how lucky I am, and if it takes me the rest of my life to earn back your trust and the kids' trust, I am dedicated to that task! Do you hear me?"

"Let's have a wedding, Graham. Not a wedding but a recommitment ceremony. Let's let everyone know how this came down for us, okay? I know you don't think we should care what other people think, but I don't want to wonder if everyone out there thinks I'm an idiot. I really want to do something like that. Okay?" He stood up and got back in bed beside her, as she struggled to make herself comfortable, rearranging pillows.

"Consider it done, Mimmi Biddle. I will make it happen. You can count on it. You should wear something like this for our ceremony." He stroked her belly and the nightgown.

Mimmi laughed. "Surely, you jest! First, as I told you, this is a nightgown, and second, when did you start caring what I wear?"

"Well, maybe that was part of the problem. I should have told you more often what I liked. I like when you flaunt your homespun, girl-next-door wholesome looks, Mimmi. It really turns me on. And I love that you are pregnant. I only wish I was a better, more engaged husband the first two times through this. I promise not to let you down again." He kissed her passionately, and she reciprocated.

They made love that evening like they never had before in their history together. Mimmi cried during the experience. She blamed the tears on hormones, but her response was more likely from feeling appreciated and valued by Graham. She was overwhelmed.

While she fell asleep that night, she dreamed of designing a dress similar to the nightgown for their ceremony. The baby kicked, as if to indicate its approval.

Chapter Twenty-Four

Marianna was thrilled to be back into a routine again. Work was busier, and she would have liked more time to spend with Aaron and Jeremy, assessing potential colleges and narrowing down his options. But something had to give, and Aaron was more than capable at handling this important parenting responsibility. Her girlfriend time was crucial to refreshing herself for the seriousness of life's other tasks, so that remained on Marianna's to-do list.

When the doorbell rang, she ran, yelling, "I'm coming! I'm coming!" and waving to her buddies, who were peering through the sidelight windows. She opened the door, hopped off the step, and pulled the door closed behind her, all in one seamless motion. Lots of hugs and kisses were exchanged, as well as what was now becoming routine for Mimmi, the requisite belly rub.

"Oh, my God, Mimmi! How far along are you? I've been away too long!" exclaimed Marianna.

"Thanks! I'm not that big!"

"Oh, no, sweetie, I didn't mean that at all! I just meant that it goes by so quickly."

"For you, yeah," Mimmi said. "For me, not fast enough. Don't you remember that feeling?" She explained she was somewhere around eight months pregnant. She wasn't exactly sure, because her periods were irregular before she got pregnant. Her doctor said, however, the baby looked great and everything looked good to go. The girls commented that she looked spectacular for that stage.

They started walking from Marianna's driveway, and Mimmi said, "So, ladies. What's been happening since I saw you last? It's been almost six weeks since you were at my house. How's that girl, Meredith? She seems nice. I don't see her at Dr. Gehr's office anymore."

Marianna commented on how serendipitous life was. "Oy, can you believe that whole thing and how it happened?" Marianna asked. "Think about it. We met this girl because Kate's fence fell down. Kate invites her to walk with us. She's pregnant and goes to the same doctor—"

"Okay, Marianna," Mimmi interrupted her. "Do we need to revisit that day again? Not one of our better girlfriend experiences! So, anyway, how is Meredith?"

Ginny told her everything she knew, which she'd heard from Kate—that Meredith was having a little trouble and had decided to take it easy. "I guess with two little ones at home, she doesn't get much chance to relax, and she was spotting, or something like that. Kate's been checking on her but not so much lately, because I think she's doing much better. She may have even been on bed rest for part of the time. I think her mom's staying with her for a bit," added Ginny.

Marianna talked about her work. She talked about doing more training at the University of Chicago. There was a specialized program there in post-traumatic stress disorder, and Marianna talked about the horror of counseling rape victims. She felt so helpless. Of all the patients she'd counseled so far, she had had the most difficulty separating herself from these women and girls.

Mimmi asked why Marianna felt this was the most difficult work for her.

"You really don't want to know, Mimmi. Generally, I think because rape is always nonconsensual and violent in nature. It leaves not only physical scars but horrible emotional traces. And I overly identify, because I'm a woman. Let's change the subject. Let's talk about happy things."

"Okay, I have something happy to talk about," said Mimmi, "but you have to slow down. I am having a hard time keeping up." They looked nervous and slowed down. She continued. "I haven't figured out any details yet, but I want to have a ceremony."

"For the baby?" asked Marianna.

"No, you idiot!" yelled Ginny. "She's talking about for her and Graham. They want to have a recommitment ceremony. Right, Mimmi?"

Mimmi nodded.

"That's awesome, Mimmi! We'll all help get it together," said Marianna. "Geez, we could really use Charlotte right now. She's so good at all this creative stuff. Kate too. But Charlotte can make gold from crap, I swear. But she's so busy lately. I think she's really serious about this Jennifer Holmes Bartlett thing. I haven't had a chance to really catch up with her about what's going on. Do you know what's doing with Kate and Charlotte, Mimmi? I know they've been in touch with you, helping and stuff. Gosh, my life is so out of balance right now. I guess no different from any other working mom."

Mimmi was bursting to tell them about both of the women but reported on Kate's upcoming adventure. She told Marianna about the Airstream and Kate's upcoming trip, which she thought was imminent. She told them how Charlotte and Kate almost induced an early delivery of the baby when they drove up her driveway one afternoon and surprised her with the trailer.

"Kate has this newfound inspiration with her dolls and the great reception she's had wherever she goes to sell them. You know, she's shown the newer models to you, hasn't she? The ones with the little storybook attached. They are affordable, educational, and adorable." She held her stomach, bending over.

Marianna freaked out. "Are you okay?"

Mimmi was taking short, shallow breaths. "Yeah," she said, pulling her torso upright again. "Those Braxton Hicks contractions are murder."

Her friends slowed down the pace, and they continued walking and talking.

Ginny asked if Kate was going alone, or if Doug and the kids were traveling with her. Mimmi thought Kate was going by herself and that maybe the kids and Doug or other friends and family would be joining her at different points on the trip.

Then Mimmi added her opinion. "I really think it's exciting for Kate. You know, I think you guys are really the steady ones in our little group. You have always worked and juggled all the crazy stuff necessary. But Kate and Charlotte and I have really changed a lot over the last two years."

Marianna felt her psychologist self coming forth, and she struggled to remain friend, not counselor or doctor. "What do you mean exactly, Mimmi?"

"Well, I think the three of us—I mean Kate, Charlotte, and me—were in a real slump. And the walking thing really brought us out of it. I really think that. We met by virtue of proximity, not similar interests or anything. Our kids went to school together and Ginny, you, and I worked on a lot of volunteer committees. That's how I got involved with all of you guys. Well, not you, Ginny. You sold me our house. I've known you forever."

"Tell us more, Mimmi," Marianna couldn't help her doctor persona. But Mimmi stopped and took another set of shallow breaths. The practice contractions didn't last as long as the other set, and she assured the girls the walk felt great.

"Anyway," said Mimmi, "I think you two always knew who you were and, in large measure, you are defined by your work. Being a wife and mother isn't the whole deal for either of you. But the fact that you have your work gives you something I never had, which is a sense that if life changes at home, and it inevitably does, you have work. In other words, the whole ship isn't going down if stuff in either part isn't going so great."

Marianna wanted more information. Ginny wanted the conversation to end. All this psycho babble wasn't Ginny's thing. Mimmi continued explaining herself in what felt like a "eureka" moment. "I've always felt like something was missing with my life. Then, when Graham left, I couldn't even face each new day. I thought our marriage was all I ever wanted. I thought I didn't have a choice, and I wanted him back on a no-matter-what basis. But that all changed when we went to the doctor for my leg checkup, and I was humiliated beyond belief when I thought he was cheating again. And you guys were great. You stood by me. You helped me pull the pieces of my life together. You helped me with everything, including picturing myself with other guys. And I dated. You know that. But something was missing. It was passion for something. A dream. Goals. I watched you guys, especially the two of you, talk about your lives, and there were so many more parts than mine had. I wanted that too. Yet the happiest moments of my life were the early years with the kids. And it was because then I had other stuff. Even if it was volunteer stuff, I belonged out in the world, giving of myself and my talents." She stopped again. "I'm out of breath."

They all stopped and Ginny took the opportunity to weigh in. "I think you're thinking too much. I don't know why I do this stuff. I just have to, I guess. We want a lifestyle for ourselves and Anna that requires more than just Joe can bring in, so together, we built the business, and it makes us happy and gives us the ability to send Anna to good schools, to travel, to dress nice—you know what I mean? It's not like Marianna here. You had to think about stuff. You had to say *this is what I want*, because you had to get educated to do what you do."

"Are you ready to walk, Mimmi?" asked Marianna.

"Yup!" exclaimed Mimmi. They took it slowly.

Marianna remained relatively quiet, because her skills repeatedly proved to her patients that none of their lives just happened. Although she agreed that people either plan or are planned for, that in itself was a choice. But instead of going on about her professional findings, she kept it simple. "You're right, Ginny. I had to think a great deal about what

I wanted. I did it earlier than most women. But I did have to make a different kind of commitment. The biggest choice I had to make was when to have Jeremy. Aaron is older, and he had the equivalent of the biological clock ticking. I wanted to establish myself and my practice first. It was a real dilemma." She asked Mimmi to explain more of her feelings.

What Mimmi said surprised Marianna—that she was sure she wanted the baby, and she wanted a chance at her family life again, and that that was enough for her. She didn't desire work outside of her home. She wanted to be available for Will and Meg and the new baby as much as possible. That was how she saw her greatest purpose. She hoped to start volunteering again. Graham was nervous about the money, but she said this time around she wanted to be sure to get what she wanted out of the relationship. "Which brings me to the ceremony thing. Will you guys help me? Kate's too busy right now, and Charlotte is too."

"With what, exactly?" asked Ginny.

"Yeah, Charlotte has more talent in her little finger than all three of us put together," said Marianna. "Are you holding out on us, Mimmi? What's Charlotte up to? Is she going with Kate?"

Mimmi bent over and held her belly again.

"Yeah, yeah, don't fake another Braxton Hicks contraction here! What's Charlotte up to, Mimmi? I know you, and you aren't telling us everything. Is she going cross-country with Kate?" asked Marianna.

She was still bent over—panting, it seemed. "My water just broke! It's time. Jesus God Almighty! It's time! *Ouch!* It's time! Call Graham and the kids." She managed to straighten up. "I'm so embarrassed. Look at me!"

"Stop it! You're having a baby, for goodness sake! Don't be embarrassed," said Marianna.

Then Mimmi surprised them again. "Will you call Kate and Charlotte too?"

Ginny was already on the phone with Graham, who was leaving his office. He told them to get her to the University of Pennsylvania

Hospital. He'd call her doctor and they'd meet up there. He wanted to know how far apart the contractions were. Ginny thought she heard him sniffle. "Are you sick?" When he didn't answer, she realized he was crying.

She took off in a sprint to her house, which was the closest, to get her car.

Chapter Twenty-Five

Charlotte was standing in a crowded stadium on Penn's campus, where hundreds of people lined up to hear Jennifer Holmes Bartlett make a speech, which would include a statement about her husband's alleged tax fraud offense and an informal announcement of her candidacy. Charlotte had organized the aesthetic details, including what Jennifer would wear, her jewelry, and her signature scarf. Charlotte could feel her heart pounding as the time grew closer for Jennifer's appearance. She had a bag filled with extras: top, scarf, deodorant, lipstick, face powder, shoes, and other sundries, should Jen's look need a boost.

She reviewed the podium lineup, had an extra copy of the speech, and confirmed the senator's office was on top of the protocol regarding acknowledgments of supporters from the area, like the new mayor. The mayor's office was in touch to say he was stuck in traffic and was running about ten minutes late. That gave Jen time to hit the bathroom before she went on stage. Charlotte received notice that the show was ready. The crowd was almost all seated, and they were eagerly awaiting the senator. But the mayor was introducing the senator, so everything was delayed until his arrival, which apparently, in the political world, meant when he was actually on site.

Charlotte was rustling through her bag, looking for a permanent marker to make an "occupied" sign for the bathroom door, so no one would enter while the senator was in the house. Her phone rang. She assumed it was a staffer informing her of the mayor's arrival, but the hysterical voice on the other end was Ginny.

"Calm down. I can't understand you!" Charlotte was annoyed. "Say it again." Then she listened closely and could make out *baby* and *water broke.* It all came together for her. "Ginny! Slow down. Mimmi? Did Mimmi go into labor? I didn't think she was due for another month."

Ginny explained through her panic that they were driving her to the University of Pennsylvania Hospital, and that Mimmi wanted her there. Also, Ginny wanted her to get Kate on board.

"Ginny, I'm so excited, and I'll be there just as soon as I can, but I'm running an event for Jennifer Holmes Bartlett. I'm at Penn, though, and I expect it to be over in about forty-five minutes. I promise I'll be there. Got to go. Just got word the senator's here." She hung up abruptly and thought, *Shit! This is it, Charlotte. Compartmentalize. This is your turn. It's not as if Mimmi doesn't have anyone with her. And she isn't giving birth in the next minute.* Then, as if someone threw cold water in her face, she snapped into reality when she saw Jen. And she thought, *This is really your big shot too. Not just Jen's.* A broad smile came over her. She was ready.

"Senator. Mr. Mayor." Extending her hand, she introduced herself to the mayor. "Charlotte Gibbons, sir."

Jen winked at her, then addressed the mayor. "Jim, I'll be ready in about five. Gotta hit the head. Thanks in advance for pepping them up for me." The senator turned to Charlotte. "Gotta miracle in that bag, Charlotte?" Then, acknowledging the sign, she laughed. "You are something else! This is your writing: that classic block printing. You are so good at details. God, I gotta pee like a racehorse! All I've been doing is running around, putting out fires over this damn tax accusation. It's all a lie, Charlotte. Those damn Republicans will say anything to lessen the chance of my candidacy! I am their worst nightmare." She slammed the stall door. Charlotte lined up the cosmetics she'd need to give Jen a fresh-looking face. Holmes Bartlett swung open the stall door and washed her hands. She continued venting.

"Really, it pisses me off. I am so squeaky clean! What the hell! Why don't they look at that—"

"Wash your face," Charlotte said, stopping Jen in her tracks. "Here, use this cleanser. Here's a towel." Charlotte was so high on Jen, she'd forgotten about Mimmi.

"Look at me." Jennifer kept unloading about the tax issue.

"Jen, why don't you focus on going out there in a minute and nailing your speech? Education is such a big issue, and these people are looking for new leadership. You could be it. John's situation will take care of itself, and soon you'll have people to handle that. But you've got to get to that place first. Your speech indicates a brief opening and a clearing the air about John's situation, and then a super fired-up talk about education and personal responsibility. How, as a wife and a mother, you understand the choices people are making on behalf of their families every day. You know it better than I." She hugged her. "You look stunning."

Jennifer looked at herself in the mirror, "Wow, Charlotte, what did you do? I look awesome! I don't want them thinking I had a facelift on my lunch hour." Then she ran out with a big smile. Her assistant indicated she would receive a super welcome.

Charlotte didn't hear her phone ring again over the roar of the crowd when the mayor introduced Jennifer. They went crazy, stomping their feet and chanting her name. This was so powerful. The people were really hungry for leadership. Charlotte was thrilled to be part of a growing trend. Jennifer was becoming a brand, and it was obvious to Charlotte that she was involved in something very big.

She was smiling, watching in a corner of the auditorium as the crowds were hanging on Jen's every word. People were looking to be led. Jen was honorable. She was driven. She wanted the job. Jennifer Holmes Bartlett had prepared for this her whole life. She had been a public servant forever. She wasn't some politically motivated egomaniac. Jennifer's life was a model of living her values. She was hopeful that the world could be better, and she held herself accountable for making a positive difference. The speech was winding down. She was quieter. She leaned into the podium and, as if she were whispering to someone, very quietly asked the crowd a question.

"What will you say to those who ask what can be done? What will you say to those who say there is no better way? What will you say to the next generation, when they ask what you did?" Then in a rousing cheerleader-like voice, she stood back and yelled, "You will tell them of a clarion call to action! You will tell them of this day and this time, when you believed it was your turn to serve your country, and you accepted the challenge! You will be proud when you tell them how each of us marched through the streets of our towns and cities, challenging our fellow citizens to rise up and take personal responsibility for the world we want to create."

Charlotte watched as people were moved to tears. Jen was so inspiring, Charlotte felt as if she could cry herself, and she wondered how she was going to hold herself together. She was as riveted as the crowd.

"I am asking for your support today, ladies and gentlemen, girls and boys, young and old. We, together, can forge ahead and take our place in history along with the great men and women before us, whose undaunted courage changed the face of America for the better. They fought, they struggled, they worked hard."

The speech went on about a new America. Charlotte swallowed hard, fighting back tears as she listened to Jennifer, whose inspirational words, Charlotte knew, were based on her years of experience and service to her country.

Jennifer leaned in again and lowered her voice. Charlotte had goose bumps. She was so moved by her old friend. "I ask you today to make that pledge." Then she roared, "Stand with me and fight with me to take back our America! Thank you! God bless you, and God bless this great nation of ours!"

Boy, was she good! Charlotte had seen Jen give a speech before but never one like this. This was big time, and Jennifer Holmes Bartlett was ready!

Holmes Bartlett started working the crowd, and Charlotte heard her phone ring. She looked at it, and saw there were five missed calls.

Chapter Twenty-Six

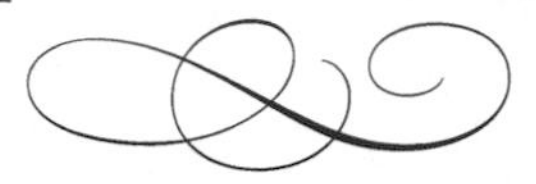

Mimmi's contractions were coming faster and faster, as Ginny drove through midday traffic to Penn. Mimmi sat in the rear with Marianna, who had jumped out of the front seat at a traffic light and saddled up in the rear with Mimmi. It turned out to be the right choice.

"Oh, my God, I'm not going to make it! I need to push!" she kept yelling, crying, and screaming at Ginny.

Marianna was in a full sweat—she'd chosen to earn her PhD rather than go to medical school to avoid this type of scene. "Jesus, Ginny, put your fucking flashers on and start going through the intersections. I am not ready to deliver a baby today," Marianna barked. Mimmi was beside herself in pain. Clearly, she was not in control. She started pulling her pants off, and Marianna almost fainted.

"Okay, sweetie, hang in there." She looked between Mimmi's legs to see what she assumed was the baby's head crowning. "Ginny, we need to get there five minutes ago!"

Ginny responded with, "Roger, chief. Doing my best." Someone's cell phone rang. No one answered it. Then another cell phone played a tune. It was Ginny's. She managed to pick it up and scream at Graham that the baby was about to be delivered in the car and that he should have a doctor and whatever else was needed at the emergency entrance to the hospital. Mimmi was screaming and sweating profusely. Ginny was speeding down Thirty-Fourth Street, through Drexel's campus, about to cross Market Street. The lights were cooperating. She put the phone down but didn't disconnect the call. Graham could hear his wife flipping out in the backseat. Marianna was wiping Mimmi's head with a cloth she'd found in the pocket of the seat in front of her. She had just gotten Mimmi to start taking short breaths and focus on the Duke sticker Anna had put on the side window.

"Five, six, seven … Good, Mimmi … Breathe, breathe, breathe." Marianna was feeling faint from hyperventilating.

Ginny pulled up in front of the hospital's emergency entrance, where Graham, who had held up his end of the bargain, was waiting with an entourage. Two assistants, a nurse, and a doctor were present to take over. Marianna burst into tears, and Ginny just leaned back in the seat and wiped her face with her arm. She had perspired through her shirt.

Charlotte had her nose pressed to the baby nursery window, tears streaming down her cheeks. She felt a hand on her shoulder. Jennifer Holmes Bartlett was standing next to her. When Charlotte had told her that her friend was delivering a baby across the street, Jennifer took the opportunity to shake a few more hands. She gave Charlotte a half hour or so to find her friend, while she pressed the flesh in the lobby of the hospital.

"Aww, which one is your friend's?" Jennifer asked.

"That little chubby one. Biddle," she answered. The two women stared at the seven little miracles in Isolettes.

"Isn't the whole birth thing amazing? I'm always moved to tears when I see a newborn baby. Always," Charlotte said sentimentally.

"Well, it is the great equalizer, isn't it?" commented Jen. "We all come out the same way. No matter our parents' nationalities, social standing, or education, we all come out with one last, final push. Look at them. If not for those name tags—"

"Yeah, I'll have to talk to someone about those ugly things," Charlotte interrupted. They both laughed.

Jennifer continued, "If not for those *ugly* name tags, we'd have no idea of their status. Isn't that wonderful? The playing field is level. They don't even put pink or blue hats on them anymore. So it truly *is* a level playing field. Those little girls in there don't know yet how hard it'll be for them."

Charlotte put her arm around the diminutive Jennifer Holmes Bartlett. "Maybe it won't be as hard for them, Jen. Look at our girls. It's already getting easier."

"Yeah, that's because none of them has gotten married yet and started the big compromise. We'll see. All we can do is move the issues closer to center, where everyone becomes aware that there are still issues surrounding women, work, and family. It'll be up to the ensuing generations to make their changes." She tried to conceal a yawn. "How old is your friend? Can you imagine doing this baby thing again?"

Charlotte's phone rang. She saw it was Kate. She and Jennifer started toward the lobby. A few people recognized Jen and stopped to chat with her. *She is so damn sincere*, Charlotte thought as she continued to the lounge area, where she could hear Kate better.

"Where are you, girlfriend?" She waited for Kate's response. "Vermont? How's it going?" She listened for a few minutes, and responded. "Well, I'm glad. That's terrific. I have some news. You're an aunt!" She went on to explain the harrowing scene Ginny and Marianna had described. She assured her the baby was beautiful and healthy, and that Graham and Mimmi were like two twenty-five-year-olds. Yes, it was a girl.

Kate's excitement was overwhelming. She asked if she should fly home now or wait until Mimmi was settled in.

"Well, I think you should fly in because they're having a recommitment ceremony tomorrow in the hospital's chapel before they bring the baby home."

Kate was confused, so Charlotte explained it was a marriage recommitment ceremony. Mimmi wanted her friends and family to be there. Graham was trying to find the minister who had married them twenty-two years ago and have him perform the ceremony again.

Kate got off the phone and figured it would be easier to drive her rig home, rather than trying to arrange to keep the Airstream in Vermont. She didn't feel secure leaving all her business supplies and equipment there. She could be home by evening, according to her navigation system, so she pulled into the nearest gas station, filled up the Volvo, used the facilities, and then grabbed a few bottles of water and healthy snacks for the road trip.

The next morning was filled with errands, all of which were for Mimmi's recommitment ceremony and the baby's coming-home preparations. Meg and Will were great at helping too. There were diapers, blankets, Onesies, crib sheets, a baby bathtub, bottles, pacifiers, baby washcloths, and all kinds of gels and goops for diaper changing. Will commented that the list seemed to go on forever. That's because Kate had made the list at midnight, after driving for six and three-quarter hours, then drinking wine until three with Marianna, Ginny, and Charlotte, as they prepared to bring Mimmi and the baby home and help glue a family back together.

Kate found a beautiful outfit for the baby to wear for the ceremony and her homecoming. The bunting was among her children's special clothes she had saved. Kate also volunteered to pick flowers from her new gardens for the girls to have, as they intended to volunteer as bridesmaids. Charlotte brought a beautiful dress that was hanging in Mimmi's closet, along with shoes and underwear. She threw in her own jewelry and makeup, because she couldn't find any in Mimmi's room. Graham was at the hospital, where he had stayed throughout the night to bond with the baby. He had a jacket and tie and trousers for the ceremony.

The minister who had married them had moved out of the area, so Graham decided they didn't need an officiant. They'd simply recite their own vows. They also decided to move the ceremony to Haverford College's duck pond, a family favorite spot and a beautiful setting near home. Parking for everyone would be easier there too.

Charles came prepared with a video camera and was filming the school grounds and other surrounding cottages when Graham arrived. He wanted to scope things out while Mimmi and the kids and baby waited in the car nearby. Graham explained that he had proposed to Mimmi at this very spot, twenty-three years ago. Charles was struck with the sentimentality a new baby could conjure up in people.

Guests were arriving, so Graham helped Mimmi and the baby out of the car. Will and Meg were thrilled their parents were back together again.

Mimmi's parents, sister, and brother-in-law stood on either side of them. The kids held the baby, and Graham and Mimmi held each other.

Graham began with a shaky voice.

"Mimmi, sometimes we have to lose something to know how valuable it is. Today I stand before you, our children, our parents, our friends, and our God, declaring my profound love and respect to the sacred bond that is marriage. I ask you to marry me and recommit yourself in marriage, not because I deserve a second chance but because our family does. I promise to cherish the rest of our years together, until the day I die." He took a tissue from his pocket and blew his nose. A few ducks waddled by. Will held the baby very protectively, closer to his body. The girls chuckled, taking notice. Graham continued, more teary-eyed. "Will you join me in matrimony and have our witnesses bless this union, Mimmi? Please say yes."

Mimmi couldn't keep her composure. Through her tears and cracked voice, she said, "You and this family are all I've ever wanted. I have always been committed to showing up, but I promise to devote myself to knowing us, to knowing myself, and to exploring the depths of my own passions. Before all our witnesses here today and God, I declare myself born anew in the virtue of forgiveness. I forgive you, I forgive myself, and I ask my family and friends for forgiveness."

Her parents and Graham's mother stepped closer. The kids stepped in and joined hands. Mimmi was now holding the baby. Graham's father raised his hands above their heads and asked for everyone to pray with him.

"Let us pray. By God's graciousness, we reunite this family in marriage. May the Holy Spirit be yours and the light of love shine around you and through you. May you be a light to all whose path you encounter. God has blessed you. Regard this blessing above all others, and be thankful, in his Holy Name." He bent over and touched his hand to the water and touched each of them, saying a prayer quietly.

The baby cried. Charlotte reached in and took her. Kate, Ginny, and Marianna fussed with her to calm her down. Everyone clapped and cheered as Graham and Mimmi kissed and embraced. Chatter broke out, and Charles took videos, while another guest snapped a camera.

Charlotte kissed the baby's head as she walked away, wondering whether Mimmi would be happy during the long journey ahead.

Kate made sure to invite everyone back to Graham and Mimmi's for a luncheon the women had organized. Then she and Marianna locked arms with Ginny and walked toward Charlotte and the baby. Ginny was already talking about how much fun they'd have babysitting.

Kate commented about her old eyes. "I'll need to get bifocals, because I can't focus on her when she's in my arms. If you hold her across a room, I can see her."

"Yeah, yeah, you just don't want to change diapers," said Ginny.

"Well, you're right about that, but I really can't focus too well without my reading glasses."

Walking the baby to an area away from the family, the women sat on a grassy patch under the shade of a big old oak tree. There, they did what they always did when they were together: they shared stories, laughed, and cried.

About the Author

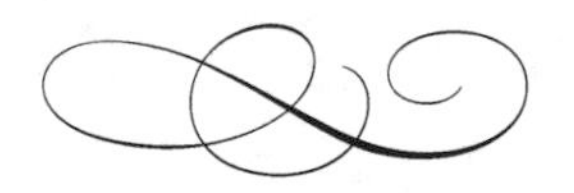

Denise Horner Mitnick is an entrepreneur and management consultant. She earned a Master's degree in Organizational Dynamics from the University of Pennsylvania. There she studied systems thinking and its impact on work/life balance perspectives and earned certificates in leadership and change management. She resides in suburban Philadelphia with her husband and is the mother of two college-aged daughters. This is her first novel.